FOUL TRADE

May Keaps, the Poplar Coroner's Officer, has never failed to provide a jury with sufficient evidence to arrive at a just verdict. The poverty, drunken fights between visiting sailors, drug trafficking, and criminal gangs mean that the courtroom sees more than its share of unnatural deaths. A young man's body in a Limehouse alley plunges her into an underworld of opium dens, the protection rackets of the notorious Kum Tong, and murder. As her investigations draw her into deeper danger it becomes clear that whoever is responsible intends to avoid the hangman's noose by arranging to have May laid out on one of her own mortuary slabs.

FOUL TRADE

FOUL TRADE

by

B K Duncan

Magna Large Print Books
Long Preston, North Yorkshire,
BD23 4ND, England.

British Library Cataloguing in Publication Data.

Duncan, B K
Foul trade.

A catalogue record of this book is
available from the British Library

ISBN 978-0-7505-4082-7

First published in Great Britain in 2014 by Oak Tree Press

Copyright © 2014 B K Duncan

Cover illustration by arrangement with Arcangel Images Ltd.

The right of B K Duncan to be identified as the author of this work has
been asserted by her in accordance with the Copyright, Designs and
Patents Act, 1988

Published in Large Print 2015 by arrangement with
Rupert Crew Limited

Magna Large Print is an imprint of Library Magna Books Ltd.

Printed and bound in Great Britain by
T.J. (International) Ltd., Cornwall, PL28 8RW

Contents

Acknowledgements
Historical Note
Dedication
Quote

Chapter One   19
Chapter Two   27
Chapter Three   37
Chapter Four   41
Chapter Five   51
Chapter Six   63
Chapter Seven   75
Chapter Eight   82
Chapter Nine   96
Chapter Ten   109
Chapter Eleven   115
Chapter Twelve   128
Chapter Thirteen   141
Chapter Fourteen   152
Chapter Fifteen   154
Chapter Sixteen   165
Chapter Seventeen   173
Chapter Eighteen   177
Chapter Nineteen   184
Chapter Twenty   188
Chapter Twenty-One   202

Chapter Twenty-Two   213
Chapter Twenty-Three   226
Chapter Twenty-Four   234
Chapter Twenty-Five   242
Chapter Twenty-Six   254
Chapter Twenty-Seven   260
Chapter Twenty-Eight   272
Chapter Twenty Nine   280
Chapter Thirty   289
Chapter Thirty-One   295
Chapter Thirty-Two   305
Chapter Thirty-Three   314
Chapter Thirty-Four   323
Chapter Thirty-Five   327
Chapter Thirty-Six   338
Chapter Thirty-Seven   346
Chapter Thirty-Eight   352
Chapter Thirty-Nine   360
Chapter Forty   365
Chapter Forty-One   373
Chapter Forty-Two   377
Chapter Forty-Three   382
Chapter Forty-Four   391
Chapter Forty-Five   399
Chapter Forty-Six   406
Chapter Forty-Seven   411
Chapter Forty-Eight   418
Chapter Forty-Nine   421
Chapter Fifty   430
Chapter Fifty-One   433
Chapter Fifty-Two   443
Chapter Fifty-Three   450

Acknowledgements

I owe a huge debt of gratitude to everyone who has held my hand throughout my writing career. I truly wouldn't have got this far without you. Particular thanks go to Paula Bouwer for providing a multitude of ledge lectures over the years and Steve Konya for picking me up and dusting me off when it really mattered. My Arvon cohort has always been there when I've called for help and from day one with this book I've been lucky enough to have Elaine Warden's direction, Sarah Ramsay's research leads, restorative lunches with Lesley Mace, and good advice from Helen Giltrow. Emma Hill was my sounding-board throughout. Andrea Welland, Helen Ringer, Jo Smith and Eric Edwards have all been remarkably forthcoming with practical and emotional support. A loud cheer goes to my agent, Caroline Montgomery of Rupert Crew Ltd. And a sustained shout to Val McDermid for being an invaluable guide and mentor.

Historical Note

The history that happened not so very long ago is often the least cherished. Although, fortunately, relatively easy to research. In the writing of this book I have called on contemporary inquest reports, newspaper articles, and medical journals; the memoirs of celebrated London Coroners, and some excellent on-line resources. The most vibrant and inspiring material has always come from written accounts, and oral history collections: I have done my very best to honour the memories they left for us.

I have deliberately brought forward two events into 1920 that, in reality, didn't occur until later: the introduction into the UK of the stage act set to be the finale of the show, and the documented exploits of BC (which I have also altered for purposes of story). Any other distortions of the truth are genuine mistakes.

If you'd like to follow some of the same research paths you can find route maps on my website: www.bkduncan.wordpress.com. But if you want to immerse yourself in what it might have been like to have lived and worked on those streets then visit the Museum of London Docklands; I would live there if I could.

For Oscar Kirk (1904–1980)

It is a coroner's statutory duty to hold inquests when there is reasonable cause to suspect a violent or unnatural death; but a coroner cannot act unless he is informed.

John Troutbeck, Coroner for Westminster and
South-Western London
(letter to The Times June 10th 1908).

Chapter One

March 1920

May pressed the carriage return. The inquest report was finished but she couldn't let the coroner's concluding remarks be the last words the parents read; the mother had been present at the accident and the implication that she had been careless would haunt her long after she had accepted the loss of her child.

May re-read the previous paragraph and then started typing. After eighteen months of working with him she knew Colonel Tindal's turn of phrase. If she chose her words carefully then he might not realise that he didn't actually say them. *In the absence of any medical evidence to the contrary, it is safe to assume that the amount of noxious smoke present would have rendered the baby dead before the flames reached him.*

She pulled the piece of paper out of the machine and placed it on top of the rest. Now she had to get the coroner to sign it. She pushed her chair back and slid through the gap between the desk and the filing cabinets. Poplar Coroner's Court had been purpose built to the latest designs but the architects certainly hadn't given any thought to the comfort of those who worked there – with the exception of the coroner. He had an ante-chamber behind the courtroom but the caretaker

19

faced a cliff of a staircase to his room in the eaves, and May had to roast in the summer and freeze in the winter in a tiny space beside a window that barely held back the fumes and noise from the High Street.

Her sturdy heels echoed in the short corridor to the coroner's room. She hoped she hadn't over-egged it. She'd often changed some of his stuffy sentences for something an ordinary person like her would understand, but adding something she was sure he wouldn't have wanted to express in the first place was entirely different. If he noticed then he might demote her back to clerk. He'd appointed her temporary coroner's officer when Mr Philby had signed up. Now the poor man would be forever under French soil, the position was hers to lose. It was taxing taking on both roles but she was holding her own; no one could say she didn't work hard and hadn't fully repaid Colonel Tindal's faith in her. Well, faith was probably going a little too far; in truth she didn't think her elevation had occupied his mind for longer than it took to realise he would be spared the effort of finding someone else. This pragmatism also went some way to explaining why he tolerated a woman in the role. So here she was: May Louise Keaps, a twenty-two-year-old, one-time cigarette factory worker, holding down a position of responsibility in the community. She'd never achieved top marks in night school at the commercial college but she had proved to be a natural coroner's officer with a nose for the truth and the tenacity to seek it out.

She rapped on the oak panelled door and waited for permission to enter. Colonel Tindal was a stickler for protocol and liked to remind everyone of his status by letting at least two minutes pass before calling out 'come'. It took slightly longer on this occasion. One look at his flushed face and May was reminded of the time she'd found him asleep at his desk after a Coroner's Society luncheon. Except now it was only mid-morning. She placed the report on the blotter. Colonel Tindal uncapped his fountain pen and signed the end page without even asking whose inquest it had been. He pushed the slim sheaf of papers back at her and stood.

'I'll be in my club if anyone wants me.'

She had got away with it: this time.

He was following her down the corridor when May heard the street door open and close. Colonel Tindal said something under his breath she thought it as well she didn't catch. PC Collier, the constable assigned to the coroner's court, was standing by her desk. Eager and fidgety, in a uniform she assumed had been issued with an assurance that he'd grow into it, he filled the small room with the distinctive odour of the glue factory. That meant he'd come from Poplar Hospital. Having been born and brought up within walking distance of the busiest docks in the world, May could always tell which street someone had just been in by the smells clinging to their clothes and hair.

PC Collier shot her a smile of greeting before adopting what she knew to be his most serious expression. But it couldn't eclipse the puppyish excitement he always exhibited in her company. She might even have felt flattered by his crush if

21

she thought he'd started shaving.

'It has been my sad duty to accompany a deceased person to the mortuary.' He pulled his notebook from his pocket and flipped over the pages. 'One Clarice Gem. I was called to her lodgings last night being Sunday 29th February in...' He cast his eyes down quickly. 'Robinhood Lane. The house of a Mrs...' again a glance sneaked at his notes as if to read them openly might lead to an accusation of cheating. 'Harrison. Dr Swan attended and had the body sent to the hospital first off out of consideration for the lateness of the hour and your caretaker's gout. All the known facts point to a drugs overdose.'

May winced. He'd been doing so well up until then; using the sort of official language they both knew the coroner liked death to be couched in. A wheeze at her shoulder told her Colonel Tindal wasn't going to let it go.

'Whilst in my court I would prefer that flat-footed lesser servants of the Crown kept their ill-informed opinions to themselves and preserved their scant wits for the undoubted demands of keeping louts from stoning cats.' He tugged out his fob watch and tapped the dial. 'This had better not take long.'

May tried to restore PC Collier's spirits with a raise of her eyebrows as she followed Colonel Tindal from the room.

The mortuary was out at the back, down a covered walkway. Tucked away so that the bereaved didn't have to pass it when attending an inquest, it was devoid of the pomp of the mullioned windows, leaded lights and stone dressing of the main building. Totally functional in character it squatted in the bowels of the site behind head-height perimeter walls. Bodies were delivered via an entrance at the end of a passage off Cottage Street, the gruesome business of post-mortems taking place in the adjoining laboratory.

May held the door open for Colonel Tindal and then walked in behind him. The smell was always the first thing she noticed. Even when it was free of occupants, the cleanliness had an edge to it that scratched at the back of her throat. She flicked the light switch and the bulbs in their wide white-glass shades flung out spots of brightness reminiscent of one of the better class of variety theatres. But there was going to be no curtain call for poor Clarice Gem. She was lying on the furthest of the marble plinths used for viewing, her modesty and a modicum of dignity preserved under a mortuary sheet. How May wished it could remain that way but she knew once the inquest process started Clarice would be thoroughly exposed until there were no secrets of her life and death left. May felt as though she should apologise in advance.

They walked down the short flight of steps and along the length of the room. Colonel Tindal made a guttural noise. The moment before the sheet was drawn back was the one time May felt a deep empathy for him. Facing sudden and traumatic death was something you never got used to; it reminded you too much of your own slender grip on mortality. And that of those you loved.

He cleared his throat again. 'Let's get this over with.'

She was young. Ridiculously young. Not much older than Alice.

'Female. White. Seventeen or eighteen. Body fits with description in police report.'

May noted down his comments. The coroner's viewing was nothing more than a formality but it was a legal requirement. Colonel Tindal turned his back and began his ritual of taking a pinch of snuff. It was hardly necessary in this case; there was no smell of blood or disease. May couldn't help remembering the bodies that had been fished from the river or discovered in advanced states of decomposition. Clarice Gem was neat and tidy in death. May wondered if she'd been the sort of person to whom that would have mattered. Her own mother had admonished her from a very early age to not show her up in public; to do nothing unbecoming; never make a mess for others to clear up. Such a pointless waste of energy when it only ever ended up like this. But if Clarice had cared about such things then she wouldn't have liked the fact that her hair – which was thick and curly – had become matted on one side. Presumably from how she'd been lying before her removal to the hospital. May reached out her hand and gently swept the tangles back. There was a bruise on the girl's temple. Or rather a series of small ones that coalesced into a deep stain like that of squashed cherries.

'Colonel Tindal, will you take a look at this?'

He had begun walking towards the door.

'She might have been the victim of violence.'

'When the decline of my faculties requires the intervention of my coroner's officer, that will be

24

the day I resign office.'

May had expected a rebuke but it was her duty to uncover everything she could about the circumstances of a death in order to help the coroner direct the jury. No. That was her job. Her duty was to ensure that no one's death remained as enigmatic as their life. But Colonel Tindal did come back to stand beside her.

'Contusions to the side of the head. You may note that down. This is clearly another in the long line we've had recently. Immoral girls who sell themselves on the streets should expect the manners of foreign sailors.'

May held her breath to stop from responding. Not every woman found dead in Poplar was a prostitute. And even if Clarice Gem had been, there was no excuse for dismissing what may have happened in her final hours so cavalierly. Colonel Tindal held values forged in the crucible of another age which included the unshakable belief that women received no better at the hands of men than they deserved. May felt a fleeting pang of pity for his wife, and thanked the Lord he had no daughters. Then she remembered his son and was sorry; the terrain on top of the moral high ground was always slippery and strewn with half-hidden rocks. She had no right to judge him, as he was in no place to judge Clarice Gem. Not yet anyway. He would in the courtroom, and then heaven help her reputation.

'If there is nothing else to which you wish to draw my attention?'

May shook her head. She pulled the sheet back up.

'Then you are to issue warrants summoning the family, and anyone else the police have already spoken to. Instruct Dr Swan to perform a post-mortem. I will hold the preliminary inquest the day after tomorrow. Make it morning.'

May noted down his instructions as he began to puff up the stairs.

'Jury list three.'

The *suicide list*. When she had first taken on the coroner's officer role, Colonel Tindal had handed her various rotas of names to be summonsed. Although not strictly in the spirit of the law it was perfectly acceptable practice; all inquests needed a jury and panels of local men standing by was the only way they could be held promptly. But list three. May knew it hadn't been a random selection. Colonel Tindal liked to have a verdict reached that coincided with his own views. And he had evidently already made up his mind about what had happened to Clarice Gem. He must've taken more notice of PC Collier's remark than she'd realised: drug taking was always an act of slow self-murder as far as he was concerned.

May watched his shoulders heaving as he held onto the stair rail and fought to catch his breath. She couldn't help wondering if he ever saw his own face staring into the bottom of a brandy glass in the same way.

Chapter Two

The working day finally drew to a close. May slipped her arms into her coat and pulled on her green felt hat. It had been something of an extravagance at the time but had served her well. There was a bit of moth under the grosgrain band but it still looked reasonably smart. She held her gloves in her hand as she went around making sure all the lights were switched off. Alf Dent, the caretaker, was another beneficiary of Colonel Tindal's lax approach to hiring and firing. The only duties the old man could be trusted to perform were to take care of the mortuary, keep it secure, and to receive bodies – although PC Collier had on more than one occasion to fetch him from the public bar of the White Horse in order to do just that. May locked the street door behind her, dropping the ring of keys into her messenger-boy style shoulder bag before heading up Cottage Street. It had been Alice's seventeenth birthday at the weekend and they were going to pick out material for the dress that was to be her present.

Her sister was waiting for her on the corner by the Methodist Chapel, sharing a joke with three girls dressed in school uniform. May felt one of her bands of tension relax a notch. Alice had finished at George Green School in the summer; suitable positions for a bright but restless and

27

spirited girl proving hard to find she'd endured a stint as a temporary shipping clerk before starting in the box office of the Gaiety Theatre two months ago. It wasn't the sort of job May would've chosen for her sister and she'd been concerned Alice's new-found status (in her own eyes at least) would result in her shunning all her old friends to take up with a racier crowd, but it seemed Alice had more sense than she'd given her credit for.

May threw her a wave as she crossed the road. Alice detached herself, her broad grin showing sparkly-white teeth. She arrived at May's side and linked arms.

'You'll never guess what happened today.'

'I'm sure you're going to tell me.'

'Don't be a spoilsport. Come on, guess.'

'A lion escaped from one of the acts and ate the manager.'

Alice chortled. 'That would've been such a scream ... he's such an old woman, coming down every hour and getting me to recite the pro- gramme from beginning to end to check I know what's on. It's a wonder I've any voice left...'

'Now that would be remarkable; ever since you learned to talk I've never known you stop chattering.'

Alice punched her lightly on the arm. 'But you're nearly right ... except it's about elephants... Stinky Sid came in at lunchtime–'

'Don't be unkind.'

'Well he does smell.'

'So would you if you had seven brothers and sisters and no running water.'

'We manage to get to the bathhouse and he

28

lives closer than we do.'

'It costs money and his parents don't have any.'

'I haven't got any parents but I'm still clean.'

This was familiar – but dangerous – territory which Alice trod whenever she felt she was being unjustly criticised. May could feel the melancholy of the day returning. She patted Alice's hand.

'So, what's this about elephants?'

'There's a show opening at the Hippodrome that's got them in. Stin... Sid knew all about it. His dad works in the printers where they do the posters and the man who books the acts let it slip. He told him not to tell anyone but that's just a trick because advance publicity is worth at least a hundred tickets.'

May was impressed at how quickly Alice had picked up an appreciation of the theatre business. They had been back under the same roof for nearly two years but she was still discovering new depths to her sister. They had arrived at Chrisp Street. The market took up the entire length, the canvas tilts of the closely packed stalls jutting out to all-but cover the roadway. It was at its most crowded in the evenings – at pub-throwing-out time you were as likely to get your thoughts jostled from your head as drop a penny without the space to bend down to pick it up. May enjoyed Chrisp Street best when it was up to the full-scale riot proportions of a Saturday night. The shriek and babble of languages fresh off the ships; the joy of the conquest as she snatched exactly what she'd been looking for from under the hand of a less determined bargain-hunter;

elbows in ribs, crushed toes, and sometimes a glancing blow to the side of the head; the welcome respite of a plate of whelks and a cup of tea at the stall on the corner of Carmen Street before doubling back and doing it all again on the other side. But even a Tuesday late afternoon was never dull.

As usual, the first hawker they came to was a man selling pots, pans, and white china. He rattled a wooden spoon in a zinc bowl in a half-hearted effort to attract her attention but both of them knew it was merely a rehearsal and he expected nothing to come of it. But May did stop at the fruit stall spanning the frontage of the chemist shop and bought some oranges, refusing to let the stallholder select them in case he sneaked some rotten ones into her bag. Alice was skittish beside her. The girl had so much energy it made May tired to watch so she switched her attention to wondering if she should splash out on some brazil nuts. The smell of vanilla toffee was making her mouth water. She paid for her purchases and drifted on.

They were at the eel stall now and May had to stop. Not only to rest her feet. The tanks of writhing fish had always held a grisly fascination. The stallholder pulled one out by hooking his fingers under the gills.

'Get in 'ere closer, mother, I've got a right tight grip–'

The woman next to May shuddered but stepped forward.

'–or so my old lady says. And if he does slither out it'll be no more worse than that trouser-snake

30

I reckon you know how to 'andle.'

Like a veteran of the boards he waited for his audience's laughter to reach its peak and then lifted his cleaver to shoulder height – twitching his wrist a little so the metal glinted – and brought it down at the same time as releasing the eel. Whack. The blade severed the head, the wriggling body sliding in its slime off the marble slab and into a pail. The fishmonger had never missed in all the years May had been watching, and neither had any corpse.

Alice was no longer by her side. May looked around for her but could only see middle-aged and elderly women clutching shopping bags. She walked on to where the haberdashery stalls were sandwiched between a collection of thrown-together furniture, looking for all the world as if the bailiffs had just completed an eviction and dumped it there. She was fingering a bolt of cotton printed with tiny sprigs of flowers when her sister finally joined her.

'You reckoning on wearing an apron?'

'I thought it'd make a charming dress.'

'What? And have everyone in the theatre wet themselves laughing?'

'You used to like patterns like this.'

Alice rolled her eyes. 'When I was a kid.' She reached across and unfurled a garish concoction of yellow and black. 'How about this?'

'It's silk. You know I can't afford that. And be-sides, why would you want to go around looking as if you're covered in squashed wasps?'

'Reckon I'd rather do that than have people think I work in an undertaker's.'

May found herself pulling the edges of her coat closed to hide the offending white blouse and charcoal skirt. Alice was going through a phase of thoughtlessly sharpening her tongue, turning everything – even what was supposed to be a treat – into a skirmish. But May was tired and really couldn't be bothered to fight.

'This one then?' Bright red poppies on a buttermilk background. Surely Alice couldn't be afraid of blending into the background sheathed in that?

Alice shrugged. That was as much approval for her choice as May was going to get. She attracted the stallholder's attention and ordered three yards.

'Is it all right if I go to Elaine's now? I mean, you don't need me for anything else do you? Her ma'll give me supper.'

'Go on, then. But don't be in late. Remember you'll be working the evening shows for the rest of the week.'

Alice gave her such a *don't fuss* look that May cuffed her lightly on the shoulder before elbowing her way into the gaggle of women surrounding the tripe dresser.

'You should've heard him. Making out like I ought to be grateful that he would even consider a shiddach with a cripple.'

Sally's shears slid through the material without a stutter. May's closest friend, she was a thirty-year-old dressmaker who lived and worked above her father's tailor shop. She had a mass of blue-black wiry hair, brown eyes, and downy olive skin. Born with one leg shorter than the other and a spine that resembled a drooping flower stem, she was destined to be forever making pretty clothes to drape figures more perfect than her own. But pity was the last thing May ever felt in Sal's company; they shared too much for her ever to allow herself to do that.

'You want another cuppa? Help yourself.'

May did so. Sally drank her tea the Russian way, black with a slice of lemon. It had all the restorative qualities of a magic potion.

'You could make a good match if you stretched to the effort. All those professionals you see in court, one of them will make an offer if you'd agree to meet them at least halfway in the game. With time, even a bear can learn how to dance.'

May picked up a spoon. She clattered it against the china as she stirred. 'I'm perfectly happy as I am thanks. You know you asked me if I could do something about that chair of your grand-mother's... I saw a broken one in the market and it'd be easy to swap the legs over; I've got all of my brother's tools in a box under the stairs.'

May caught Sally looking at her from under her frizzy fringe as she hobbled to the end of the worktable.

'It's not good to be alone, even in Paradise.'

'Just as well I've got Alice then.'

'What makes you think she'll be staying around here for any longer than she has to? Got grand notions of herself, that one, and any day now we'll all be coated in the dust she kicks off her heels.'

'Not if I have my way she won't. I'm biding my

33

time until the novelty of being surrounded by stardust wears off then I'm going to persuade her to take an office job with normal hours and go to night school. She needs some professional qualifications if she's ever going to get anywhere in this world. Everything else is too stacked against the working classes for the likes of us to break out of the patterns of poverty.'

As May said it she could see her father thumping his fist on the kitchen table. He'd been a staunch Communist but she hadn't realised how much some of his views had become her own until this moment. But she didn't want to think about him.

'What do you want for all your efforts, thanks? She's just seventeen. At that age we all think our elders and betters know nothing. It takes time for us to realise that the tapping on the door is not a call to arms, but wisdom. And it's unfair of you to expect Alice to be any different. You want a life that is yours to control? Then do as I suggested and get a husband. And don't even bother to tell me you are still mourning over that Henry Farlow because I won't believe you. I happen to know that you weren't really in love with him.'

'We were extremely fond of each other. From what I've seen of many marriages around here, that's more than most can say. And it would have worked; we were suited.'

'Cloth can be cut one way or the other and made to fit. If you persist in refusing to even take the measure of a man, then the few still around will be snapped up and you'll only have a lonely old age to keep you company.'

34

'There's never any guarantee against that; three-quarters of the women down my street expected to have their husbands by their sides forever before the Great War came.'

'That's as may be but you could at least not throw the bolt across the door yourself. Stop treating every man like a brother. Also try acting a little helpless once in a while. With such big sea-blue eyes and thick dark hair for which a wigmaker would gladly pawn his grandchildren, you should have no trouble having the luxury of picking. And that would be true even if you weren't blessed with a figure most of my clients would have to starve themselves to get. Just because you have a man's job doesn't mean you have to hide your feminine charms; it's only throwing it back in God's face to be so wasteful. Not to say rubbing it under the nose of the likes of me.' Sally wasn't smiling.

May refused to let the airing of her faults prick her. Sally meant well, she just had a very different view of life. One based on marriage and babies as being the most natural and noble state for women. It pained May to realise how keenly her friend must feel it was something she would never attain.

Sally had resumed her cutting. 'You could do worse than taking a tip or two from Alice; she knows already how to use what God saw fit to give her.'

'Why do you think I worry about her so much? She thinks she's a woman but in reality she's little more than a child.'

'That has nothing to do with her age. She'll be just the same when she's thirty. Your sister is a flirt who knows the precise extent of her power and

35

how to use it to be granted anything she wants. The sooner you realise that, the easier a time you'll have of it. Stop trying to change her nature and wise up to her instead; if she's bucking against the reins now, she'll be off looking for soft hay to roll in before long. You mark my words.'

May had to stop from asking Sally what she knew about it – with five brothers it was probably a damn sight more than her.

'I happen to think she'll come good. All she needs is a bit of sense drummed into her and a little steering in the right direction. Like getting this dream of hers about being an actress out of her head. Seems it's what she's ... *wanted for ever and ever* ... which is strange as she'd never so much as mentioned it before she'd started at the theatre.'

Sally interrupted her cutting with a sort of hiccup of the shears on the table.

'Why would she choose you to share the secrets of her heart? She is not the uncomplicated girl who waved you off when you boarded the ship to France, and you are not the same sister who came back. Life and circumstances have changed you both. Get to know the person she is now before she surprises you with something that will cause you both more pain than choosing a profession you think not good enough for her.'

That hadn't had the lightness of loving mockery. May took a sip of tea to stop from leaping to her own defence.

'It'll be altogether too rackety a life.'

'And you and I know each day where the next month's rent's going to come from? My aunt played the Yiddish Theatre in Commercial Road for years and she always had food in her mouth and a bed to fall into at night. Even managed to bring up four children who no one could say were any more wanting than the others in the street, despite uncle never lifting a finger over the shock of having to leave the shtetl.'

Sally was trying to turn it into one of her jokes about the hopelessness of all Jewish men but May couldn't raise a smile. She knew Alice would be more susceptible than most to the temptations the theatre world had to offer. After a life touched by so much grief – sixteen of her schoolmates killed in a Zeppelin raid; losing her mother to influenza; her brother now no more than a name on the Roll of Honour; and finally ... finally ... having a suicide for a father – what young girl wouldn't be spurred on to taste every experience on offer out of fear her time on this earth could be cut short at any moment?

No, for as long as they were living under the same roof May was going to make sure her sister set her feet on the right path. And, one day, Alice might even thank her for it.

Chapter Three

The stage door was tucked down at the end of the passage, a boxed light announcing the recess in the soot-etched wall. It was no different from all the others she'd arrived at – a little shabbier, perhaps;

certainly the management hadn't bothered with a lick of paint in some time – but to Vi Tremins, character actress and occasional revue turn, it promised all the excitement of an opening night. The Gaiety Theatre had once numbered amongst the most popular Music Halls in the East End and still played twice daily with an enviable reputation in the business for being packed out on Friday and Saturday nights. Only, on this occasion, it wasn't the prospect of playing to a full house that was making her chest flutter.

Once over the threshold the familiar smells of rabbit-skin size, stale sweat, and insufficiently-dried canvas filled her nostrils. Vi took a moment to savour the sense of coming home. The small space was almost fully-occupied by a figure swaddled in outdoor things against the chill damp of the morning fog. As an expert in discerning character even under the heaviest of disguises, Vi glanced at the only flesh on show – a neat pair of ankles – and decided they belonged to a girl who'd not long packed away her ragdolls. The doorman – the usual type with pasty indoor-skin, and a cigarette hanging from the corner of his mouth – was leaning through the window of his cubbyhole, entertaining his visitor with what sounded like one of the backstage stories Vi herself had been weaned on.

'...so I says to the string of water, I says, you get yourself down there, ghost or not ghost, and you pull that lever when you're told or it won't be no 'eadless 'arry you need be affrighted of because ol' Swinburn'll 'ave your guts for garters before the tabs come down close of second act.'

38

The back of the coat shuddered like a sack of kittens poked with a stick. Vi smiled. The poor thing was probably due to clean under the stage or something and now she'd spend her entire time jumping at every strange shape and shadow.

'What can I be doing for you, love?'

'I'm Violet Tremins, engaged to get the talent show up and running.'

The girl spun around as if the hem of her coat was on fire. 'A talent show. Here? Really? Are you all booked up, I mean, are there any spaces on the bill? I can sing ... a little.'

Despite a dreadful woollen hat pulled down over her ears and a scarf wrapped over that to obscure her hair, Vi was treated to a glimpse of bright doe eyes, clear skin, and cheekbones that would defy the flattening effect of greasepaint. Even if the girl was no Marie Lloyd she would be pleasing enough to look at and, provided she could hold a tune long enough to get through a verse and two choruses, would probably escape the indignity of having things thrown at her. She was certainly worth the trouble of an audition.

'Try-outs are Saturday week, immediately following the afternoon performance. Why don't you come along? But I warn you that if we offer you a slot it'll be nothing but hard work – the show's to be at the end of April and we only have stage time for five rehearsals.'

'I work here in the box office and can ask the manager to get my shifts so as I can be on stage whenever I get the call. And in the dead times I'll lend a hand with anything you want doing – you know, putting posters up and stuff.'

Had she ever been so starry-eyed herself? It was rather sweet. 'Don't go getting carried away ... you've got to get through the audition first. And, if you do, even then it will only be a mid-week afternoon performance; the management isn't going to risk losing a drop in Saturday night takings.'

'I don't care, really I don't ... to be in a proper show, in a real theatre ... it's all I've ever dreamed about.'

The doorman grunted. 'Put a sock in it, will yer? All this dog-with-two-tails palaver so early of a morning's giving me 'eartburn. The guvnor's already in, love. Take yourself through; you don't look like you need a map.'

Vi walked up to the swing door which separated the civilians of the street from the theatre professionals. She sensed the girl looking at her enviously; not even front of house employees were allowed through this hallowed entrance. Vi reached into her handbag.

'Here. A gift. It's an old tradition for a board-hardened actress to give a newcomer a little something before her first audition. Wear it to bring you luck.'

It was only a half-used tube of lipstick but you'd have thought she'd just handed over the key to His Majesty's Theatre's star dressing room. Vi left the girl caressing the case in her gloved fingers as she plunged through into the dimly-lit and dusty world of make-believe.

40

Chapter Four

May shepherded the three women across the road. The only members of the public she'd called to attend Clarice Gem's inquest, she'd suggested they wait in the coffee house until the appointed time. She hadn't wanted Mrs Gem to be in the vestibule and encounter the jury coming back from the mortuary; their faces would've made it only too clear that they had just visited her cold and silent daughter.

Once everyone was seated in the courtroom, May waited for Colonel Tindal to indicate he was ready for her to read the proclamation necessary for opening the inquest. She wiped her sweaty palms on her skirt. This moment always made her feel heavy with the knowledge that she was about to start something that could end in much worse than the death of only one person. Poplar Coroner's Court saw more than its fair share of murder verdicts. The coroner finished his conversation with the jury foreman and nodded down at her. She stood, her chair scraping back the silence. Even after all these months she still had to read the words from a card; they were too important to fumble and she knew her self-consciousness would confuse them in her head. It didn't help that everyone was undoubtedly waiting for the real coroner's officer to come and take his seat. She cleared her throat.

'You good men of the London Borough of Poplar, summoned to appear this day to inquire for our Sovereign Lord the King, when, how, and by what means Clarice Gem came to her death, answer to your names as you shall be called. Every man at the first call, upon the pain and peril that shall fall thereon.'

The worst bit was over. She heard Mrs Gem stifle a sob: for her it had just begun. There was nothing for May to do now but to read out the jury names, swear everyone in, and take verbatim notes.

PC Collier was the first the coroner called. Colonel Tindal liked to have everyone in the courtroom throughout the proceedings so it was a simple matter for the policeman to walk from his chair and sit behind the low rail opposite the jury. May had typed up numerous requests from Colonel Tindal to the London County Council to have a raised witness box built but they always declined on the grounds of cost. She secretly thought they suspected an element of self-aggrandisement. The setting was formal enough already with its light oak panelling, vaulted and beamed ceiling, and slim minstrels' gallery for press and spectators. She sat in the body of the room at a table long enough to accommodate any legal representatives, the coroner behind a bastioned dais on a high oak chair beneath a matching canopy. And he surely looked to be minor royalty to the ordinary people of Poplar in his tailcoat buttoned over his waistcoat, white stiff-collared shirt, silk pocket-handkerchief and matching tie, and striped trousers. Witnesses

42

would probably think he was dressed so formally in order to intimidate them. But they'd be wrong. This was his ordinary attire, and it was something he did to everyone.

After being sworn in, under the coroner's questioning PC Collier repeated the facts of how Clarice Gem's death had been brought to the attention of the authorities. Colonel Tindal asked if anything had been found at the scene to indicate that it might not have been suicide. The policeman answered in the negative, and was dismissed.

Now it was the turn of Mrs Harrison. May waited for her to settle her ample frame in the chair before walking across to administer the oath.

'The evidence which you shall give to this inquest on behalf of our Sovereign Lord the King, touching the death of Clarice Gem, shall be the truth, the whole truth, and nothing but the truth. So help you God.'

Mrs Harrison responded with the assurance of one not averse to attention.

'Under what circumstances were you acquainted with the deceased?'

Back at her table, May watched the woman's face contort at the coroner's words. Was it from distress or trying to grasp the meaning of the question? Colonel Tindal certainly didn't have the common touch; in her preliminary conversations with witnesses May always gleaned more background information than his questioning ever did but he wouldn't allow her to give him her notes so he could ask witnesses merely to corroborate the undisputable facts. Her fingers tingled with frustration, her pencil poised.

'Reckon she'd been in the attic about three months.'

'So you were her landlady?'

Mrs Harrison looked at May. 'Ain't that what I told him?'

May nodded. Mrs Harrison tightened her grip on the handbag in her lap.

'Came to me, she did, saying as she had to leave her last place all of a sudden. But she had the air of being well-to-do so I took her in. No cause to be asking questions when the rent looks set to be paid. She was never no trouble. Quiet as a mouse you might say. Hardly saw her much in fact. Always out, having a good time like as not, of an evening. Most times, any road. 'Cept she sometimes had these headaches, see, and she had a blinder last Monday. I was all for popping to the herbalist to get a little something but she said she had powders she took that did the trick.'

Colonel Tindal coughed. May was already aware that Mrs Harrison had committed the cardinal sin of giving information not directed by his questions; he was in control of this inquiry and was not going to let anyone appear to dilute his authority. No matter how well it served the cause of getting to the truth.

'Tell the jury when, where, and how you discovered the deceased. Be brief and stick to the facts.'

'She were in my arms, weren't she? Can't exactly say as I had to go doing much discovering.'

A jury member tittered.

'I told you how she had this blinder…'

44

Mrs Harrison was in full flow now, leaning forward with her bosom pressed up against the rail.

'...I was setting about getting ready for my bed when I heard this sort of screaming – first off, I though it was them cats in the yard again – but it was coming from up top so I went to see what was what. I didn't want her causing no upsetment to the other lodgers – the families all got dockers in and they have to be up at sparrow's fart. I reckoned it was no time to be standing on politeness so I opened her door without being asked. There she was, bold as brass, thumping her head – real hard like – on the wall. I knew the blinder was the cause of it so I did a bit of soothing like you would to a sickening child and told her that a little lie down would do her head more good than all that banging. Asked her if she'd taken a powder and she said she'd had two in a glass of water. Meek as a lamb she let me tuck her up. I said as I would come and look in after I'd got me rags in. It can't have been more than half an hour before I was up there again. She was all tangled in her sheets and when she turned her head my way she had...' Mrs Harrison looked across at Mrs Gem, 'begging your pardon, missus ... she had this foam – like pink soap bubbles – around her mouth. I reckon it was the powders what did it–'

'That will be enough!' Colonel Tindal glared. 'Only if and when you become qualified in medical practice can you offer such an unsubstantiated opinion.'

He slid a glance at the jury: his views on expert testimony were well known. Behind her, May

45

heard Dr Swan crack his knuckles.

'Do you have in your possession the packets that these powders were in?'

'Lord above, no. I chucked 'em right quick on the fire. Won't have nothing like that in my house ever again. Terrible it was what they did to her. Terrible.'

'The jury and I have heard more than enough. You may take yourself back to your place, but remember you are still bound should I be forced to recall you. I will now hear what the other person who saw the deceased in her last hours has to say.'

This was Mrs Harrison's unmarried daughter, Anne. About thirty, she was as unlike her mother as it was possible to be. Thin and stooped, she resembled a drab caged songbird that never saw the light of day. Her voice was just as reedy as she responded to the oath. She looked at Colonel Tindal who waved his hand in an impatient manner.

'I heard her come in. I didn't think to as she'd told me she'd be out all night. So I took myself to pay a call.'

'On Clarice Gem?'

'That's right, your Lordship.'

May hid a smile as she watched Colonel Tindal preen a little.

'What time was this?'

'I can't rightly say but we'd had our supper and the range was cold so I reckon it must've been nigh on eleven o'clock.'

'Go on. How did you find her?'

'She weren't like herself at all. I reckoned she'd been crying some; her eyes was all red. She said

46

she was fed up. I asked her if she wanted to talk – you know, like sisters – but she said she knew a better way to lift things. She all but pushed me out the door. Next thing I knew, ma was calling me to fetch the doctor.'

Colonel Tindal thanked her with a perfunctory nod and called Dr Swan to give evidence.

'At midnight I attended the girl in question. Despite the previous witness' testimony, she was not dead at that time but unconscious. I was with her for about thirty minutes, during which time she slipped in and out of lucidity. I was able to ascertain she had been suffering convulsions, motor spasms, tingling and numbness in the limbs, mental confusion, and an incapacitating headache. From my own observations, I would add possible delirium. I asked her what she had taken and she replied it had been cocaine. But to be certain, a number of toxicological tests would have to be undertaken by an expert in the field.'

'I'm sure the jury will agree that the expense for engaging such services can be spared. It seems to me only the pathologically foolhardy would say they had taken a drug they knew to be banned under the Defence of the Realm Act if it were not true. You may return to your seat, Dr Swan.'

The inquest had now reached the stage May hated most of all: the inquisition of the relatives. The truly dreadful ordeal of sitting in front of a room full of strangers, struggling to bury the grief long enough to speak the unthinkable.

Mrs Gem's feet hardly made a sound as she walked across the courtroom. She took the oath with her head almost buried in her chest. The coroner then asked her to tell the court something of her daughter's state of mind immediately prior to the night in question.

'She was always cheery. Wanted to spread her happiness around, too. She was at mine playing with her nephews not two days before. Reading them stories and saying as she hoped we'd all be able to go visiting her other sister in Margate again come the summer.'

'Can you tell the jury why she would want to take her own life?'

'She didn't. She wouldn't. She had no reason to. She was talking of starting a new job. She was a dancer, an artiste, been given her big break in the West End.'

Colonel Tindal grunted. May could have predicted that given how he thought Clarice had earned her living. Mrs Gem began to sob. She made no effort to cover her face as she stared at the jury, snot dripping from her reddening nose. May couldn't pretend to be unmoved by such pain. She slid open the table drawer and took out the pressed handkerchief she kept there and, with a glass of water in the other hand, she went across and stood in front of Mrs Gem, shielding her distress as much as she could. The woman's thoughts couldn't have been clearer if she'd shouted them from the courtroom roof: There must've been some signs she'd missed; a look in her daughter's eye or a silence stretched long enough to be filled with brooding; she should have asked more questions, or asked less and listened more, or stopped nagging her over some irritating habit, or given her the snack supper she'd asked for and not

48

kept it for tomorrow's dinner, or not worn those filthy old slippers, or stopped shouting at her grandchildren to shut up, or suggested a Sunday trip to the country to blow the cobwebs away...

Colonel Tindal's voice made May jump. She flushed as she realised how unprofessional she was being by allowing herself to become involved. A death was a death was a death, no matter how it happened.

Dr Swan was being recalled to give the results of the postmortem.

'The pupils were abnormally dilated. The fingers uniformly blue. The brain, lungs, liver, spleen and kidneys intensely congested. The heart was enlarged and engorged, and it was the failure of this organ that killed her. Prior to that, the pressure in the constricted blood vessels forced fluid into the spaces in her lungs. There was evidence of a pinprick rupture of a blood vessel in the brain which would have resulted in a massive haemorrhage had the heart continued beating. Although there is no toxicology to confirm it, all the pathological evidence points to cocaine poisoning.'

He paused as a member of the jury put up his hand; a weasel-faced man who May knew to be a catmeat shop proprietor. The coroner acknowledged him with a nod.

'If she was one of these dope girls we read about in the papers, could she have taken extra in the way someone accustomed to drink might put a shot of something stronger in his beer? You know, to get the feeling of it back again.'

Dr Swan regarded him. 'A very intelligent question, if I may say so. She might have done, yes, but

49

I consider it unlikely. The quantity isn't really the issue here. It was the dissolving of the substance in water that was her fatal error because it meant the drug was absorbed more quickly into her system.'

'D'you reckon she could've known that?'

'It's possible.'

The juror sat back with his hands clasped across his stomach. He received a pat on the back and a few wise nods from his fellow jurors: Colonel Tindal's *suicide list* was conforming to expectations. May noted the intervention down. Was anyone here going to stick up for Clarice?

'In general terms the young woman was strong and healthy – evidence of the usual childhood diseases of course; a touch of rheumatic fever affecting the joints, and a few chickenpox scars...'

Mrs Gem let out a low quivering moan and May smoothed out the handkerchief on her lap.

'...but there was one other thing.'

Dr Swan gathered himself like a stage acrobat about to turn a somersault.

'I found internal scarring indicating she had undergone an abortion. I can't say exactly when but probably between eight to twelve months ago. Not very expertly done, I'm afraid. It would have caused a lot of pain and haemorrhaging.'

May could almost taste the shock in the room seconds before Mrs Harrison gasped, Clarice's mother wailed, and the wooden benches creaked as the jury leaned forward as one man. Her shorthand deserted her as the picture she'd wanted to hold on to – a temporarily down young woman who became a victim of misadventure – began to slip away. She was aware of Mrs Gem struggling to catch her breath. Dr Swan left the witness stand to go to her side. Colonel Tindal drummed his fingers.

'If there is nothing for you to add, Dr Swan, I suggest you escort the deceased's mother from the courtroom and attend to her in my chambers where she may remain in privacy for as long as necessary.'

May was surprised at his sensitivity. But then remembered that he had been a father once.

'It is clear to me that the truth of the circumstances leading up to Clarice Gem's wilful action was not known by the witnesses present. On behalf of the jury I instruct my officer to identify and subpoena anyone with pertinent evidence to come forward.' Colonel Tindal stood up, his gaze sweeping the room 'All manner of persons who have anything more to do at this court for the London Borough of Poplar, may depart home at this time, and give their attendance here again thirteen days hence, being Tuesday the sixteenth day of March, at two of the clock in the afternoon precisely. God save the King.'

Chapter Five

Friday morning was grey and cold enough to be a reminder that spring often began with a whimper. May trudged past the high wall of East India Import Dock on her way to Mrs Harrison's. She had arranged with the landlady to have a look around Clarice's room in case there was anything – letters perhaps, or an address book – that could furnish clues to other possible witnesses. She was going to place an announcement in the newspaper asking for any friends to come forward but found a personal request on official notepaper usually prompted a quicker response.

She turned past Naval Row and into Robinhood Lane. The houses looked like those in her own street – only taller and thinner – all shunted into two long lines of soot-encrusted brick. The front doors were black or red: ship painting colours. Five grimy windows cracked each façade. The air smelled of Kitson's disinfectant factory, and the goods stored in the warehouses on the other side of Tunnel Gardens; nostril-tingling pepper, wood, coffee, the sweetness of saltpetre, and the sunshine richness of sheds of ripening bananas. Woven within these, and overwhelming them with every gust of wind off the water, was the stench of the tannery. With such a pervasive reminder that Poplar was the dumping ground for industries nobody else wanted on their doorstep, it was no wonder so many hopeless souls passed through the mortuary.

Number sixty-nine cheered May up a little. Mrs Harrison had strung up a net curtain with a butterfly pattern in the ground floor window. Either she'd been charging Clarice more than the going rent, or the woman had ideas well above her station. May's knock was answered almost immediately. The landlady and her daughter were standing in the hallway with their coats on.

'Thought you was coming earlier, dearie. We're

off shopping. You can do what you have to do and let yourself out. Don't bang the door, Mr what's-his-name's on night shift.'

The two women edged past her, Anne Harrison looking as though she was attached to her mother's waist by a string. May checked the narrow hall table for letters addressed to Clarice but found only a catalogue from Gamages and a subscription periodical on dancing. She left them for Anne Harrison; someone might as well get some pleasure from thumbing through their pages, as Clarice no longer would.

May had to rely on the illumination from the grubby fanlight above the door to help her up the first flight of stairs. The fumes of cooked cabbage thickened with the gloom. On the second floor there was some light creeping out from under two of the three doors. Behind one of them, a baby was squalling. If Mrs Harrison was a typical landlady then she would be sub-letting each room to a different family, she and her daughter making do with the front room and kitchen. The stairway was beginning to smell of un-emptied chamber pots and mould. The jauntiness of the butterfly net curtain now felt like a forgotten promise. May wondered if Clarice had thought the same when she'd first been shown the room. But maybe this was a palace compared with where she'd lived before. It was only now she was here that May could appreciate how loud the young woman's screams must've been to have reached Mrs Harrison's ears. What about the families living in the middle? Had they heard? PC Collier hadn't said so. In all probability none of them ever opened their doors to any goings on. Living cheek by jowl with strangers could be dangerous if you poked your nose in with someone brought up to keep things private with their fists.

May was puffing slightly by the time she'd groped her way up the last flight to the top of the house. She hoped that after such a climb her search wouldn't prove as fruitless as PC Collier's. He hadn't even turned up the glass Clarice drunk her powders from. Although that was hardly surprising, it had probably been washed and put away before she took her last breath; people close to the docks were too used to having the police demand to search for stolen goods to leave anything around that might come under the heading of evidence of wrongdoing. Would such an act mean Mrs Harrison knew Clarice had been taking illegal drugs? May remembered the look on Anne Harrison's face when she'd recounted Clarice's impatience to be alone and thought she'd known – or guessed. Had lodger and landlady's daughter indulged in the habit together? Stranger alliances had been formed. Why hadn't Colonel Tindal asked if either of the women had taken any of the powders themselves – headache or no?

She twisted the handle and pushed open the door. A strong smell of carbolic hit her, and underneath it, the reek of vomit ... and worse. She walked across to the small sash window and threw it up. Clarice had rented one large room with no water or cooking facilities. There was a battered and threadbare chair, lopsided wardrobe, mirrored dressing table, and washstand. The bed had been stripped and the mattress rolled up. May wondered how long it would be before Mrs Harrison moved someone else in. She remembered her latest read from the library, a gothic tale of a house where a priest had been walled up only for his spirit to make its presence felt in the brick and plasterwork. Would the new incumbent of this room be able to sense that Clarice's short life had ended in terrible pain and indignity?

May pulled open the wardrobe door. If it wasn't for the surroundings she'd have thought she'd wandered into a flapper's boudoir. There wasn't a dress that could be worn anywhere but to a nightclub. The sequins on a red shift winked at her as if in mockery. She had the uncharitable thought that maybe Anne Harrison had sorted through and taken what might fit her. In fact, she must've done, because there weren't any shoes and, as a dancer, Clarice would have had a number of pairs.

May flicked through the hangers and stopped at a low-backed green dress. There were the ragged edges of a large stain on the skirt. It could have been coffee. Or a spilt cocktail. Or blood. Did cocaine give you nosebleeds? The dress was unwearable so had Clarice kept it for sentimental reasons? Perhaps it had been her lover's favourite; she would've looked striking in it with her dark hair and slim figure. A deceased's effects always hid more of the small secrets of life than they revealed.

Her head was beginning to reel a little in the foetid atmosphere. May perched on the edge of the lumpy easy chair. What was the truth of what had gone on in here after Clarice had closed the door on Anne Harrison? Had the young girl merely been *fed up* and reached for her usual pick-me-up only to absentmindedly tip two of the packets into her glass instead of one? Or had her mood been more one of despair and she'd intentionally taken the overdose? May looked over at the washstand. She could almost see Clarice standing there, picking up the jug she'd filled that morning from the tap in the yard and wrinkling her nose at the scum of dirt that settled on everything left to stand too long in Poplar. She'd have poured the water into the glass anyway and what...? Walked over to the window for one last glimpse of the ships in the docks that, had she had the money, could've taken her away from all this? Or did she sit in this chair, the glass on her floor by her side, and weep a little more over whatever injustice she felt had been dealt her?

But very shortly it wouldn't have mattered whether the two packets had been by accident or design. Clarice's body would have begun its death dance just the same. Dr Swan had said her arms and legs would've flailed around, she'd have had fits, and her heart would be trying to burst from her chest. Which would she have felt first? How long was it before the explosions in her head had started? Worse than anything she'd ever felt before, the only relief she'd be able to think to give herself was to try to get the pain on the outside. May remembered when she'd been in the mortuary and first discovered the bruises. She almost wished now that Colonel Tindal had been right and Clarice had been turning tricks and been beaten by a sailor; at least then she'd have known it couldn't have gone on forever. Just when had her stomach tried to expel the poison, and her bowels loosen? Mrs Harrison hadn't mentioned Clarice soiling herself – and she was undoubtedly the sort of woman who would – so maybe it hadn't happened until Clarice got into bed. May hoped that humiliation wouldn't have been the last emotion she'd felt on this earth. Not that it mattered to Clarice any longer; but it did to her.

May stood up and began to pace, keeping her gaze turned away from the bed. Why? In cases like these it was the question always left to haunt the living. One for which there would never be a satisfactory answer. She used to think that suicides always wrote a note but now knew that not everyone took the time or trouble. She'd searched the house high and low after her father had been fished out of the dock basin. Why had he done it? Why that night? He'd had over a year to reconcile himself to the shock of Albert's death, terrible as it was, smashed to pieces in the troop train on his way home on leave. Cruel deaths always hit hardest. Her immediate response had been to join the Voluntary Aid Detachment who sent her to France to do what she could for other women's brothers; his had been to bury his grief in fighting even more fervently for the Trade Union cause. Alice had been sent for the summer to Aunt Bella in Southend and was said to have barely reacted at all. And just when she was back at school in Poplar being cared for by the local mothers who rallied around in May's absence was when her father had chosen to make a mockery of every hardship and sacrifice demanded by the Great War. The most pointless of the lot.

May swiped away a tear. She should be thinking about Clarice, not him. She brought her pacing to a halt in front of the dressing table. There was a set of green glass pots with lids, and a matching curved tray like the letter C for trinkets. In it was a matchbook, the cover printed with a brown and cream stylised picture of a couple dancing. Her heart squeezed at the thought that was how Clarice probably once saw herself. Amongst the jars of cold cream and emery boards was a cheap brush snarled with hair. May opened the slim drawer to slip it in and spare Mrs Gem the pathetic sight when she came to collect Clarice's belongings. Lying on top of the stockings, scarves, and pink silk camiknickers was a pocket diary – the sort that could be picked up in Chrisp Street market for a couple of pennies. May flicked to the date of Clarice's death. *Billy* was written in pencil with a childish hand. The person she had gone out that night to meet? She would mention the name in the newspaper announcement.

May took one last sad look around the room and left, the unwholesome streets of Poplar beckoning with every stair she descended as if they were a rose garden.

The offices of the *East End News* were in the High Street opposite Wade's Place. The twice-daily newspaper was put together in a maze of offices, corridors, and cubicles but May arrived at the sub-editor's desk with only having to backtrack once. Andy Taylor wasn't in yet. A notoriously late riser he sailed as close to the deadline as he dared, somehow always managing to smooth out glitches

58

and chaos to get the newspaper out on time. And he was a very good journalist who wasn't afraid to risk making powerful enemies. He'd once filled the front page for a week with his coverage of landlords profiteering from the peace with their sky-high rents, criminal overcrowding, and heartless evictions. May liked him. He and her brother had been members of the same motorbike club. He'd been devastated when told – belatedly on his own return from France – what had happened to his friend. She'd gone for a drink with him once; Sally had meant well in engineering it but the memories they'd shared had only made her miss Albert even more. Not to mention Henry. To avoid Andy had been one of the reasons she had come in so early.

May took the announcement she'd typed from her bag and read it through again for errors. The newspaper room was beginning to come alive around her; the clack of a typewriter or two, a few coarse shouts. The unmistakable smell of a bacon sandwich made her mouth water. She found a red pencil, inserted a line that the coroner's office was particularly anxious for Billy – or anyone who knew of his whereabouts – to come forward, and then wrote a note at the bottom of the page to Andy requesting it should go into tonight's newspaper and every subsequent edition until further notice. She popped it into the wire in-tray and hoped that he looked there first.

May was threading her way back to the glass panelled doors at the end of the room when her way was blocked by a pile of boxes with a pair of legs. She tried to skirt around this moving obstacle but whichever way she went, the man mirrored.

'Hold on there. If you'd wanted to dance you only had to say so.'

The voice was Irish. But educated, not like the ones spilling out of the Resolute Tavern every Friday night.

'I'm sorry. If you stand still then I'll slip past.'

But he stood in her way again. This time on purpose. She couldn't see his face behind the boxes but could feel him smiling. 'I'm in a hurry, even if you're not.'

'No call to be snippy with me, now.'

He set his burden down on a trestle table to his right and May was confronted with a tweed jacket in the most livid check imaginable, and the broad features of a man close to her age with too long hair and the skin around his eyes so deeply crinkled he appeared to be squinting.

'Jack Cahill's the name. Junior reporter – for now anyway – on this fine organ.' He held his hand out. 'Pleased to make your acquaintance. And you are...'

'Busy.'

May made to continue walking but he side-stepped again.

'Let's just start again, shall we? I apologise for getting in your way, and I further apologise for detaining you on your urgent business. But I'm not sorry we've met. Yours is the friendliest face I've seen since I arrived from Dublin.'

'You must have made a lot of enemies then.' She noticed the telltale bulge of a spectacles case in his top pocket. Not only could he not see her properly, he was vain as well.

'Come on, do me a favour. Be nice. It won't

cost you.'

May had to smile at that; however short a time he'd been off the boat, he'd picked up what mattered most to East Enders.

'I really do have to be going...'

'Live round here do you?'

Now he was being fresh. 'I'm the Poplar Coroner's Officer.'

He didn't raise an eyebrow, not one. Or give her the shifty up and down look that was usually followed by expressing surprise at her sex.

'Well done you, I say. Can't be many as young able to hold down a responsible position like that.'

He was either genuinely impressed, or a very quick thinker. May suspected a little of both. She started for the door again. Jack fell in step beside her.

'The reason I ask is that I'm on the look-out for somewhere to stay. So I can sleep closer to the job you might say. Bunking in Hampstead with an elderly relative at the moment.' He hunched his shoulders and hobbled as if using a walking stick.

She wouldn't laugh ... she wouldn't ... but she did. He held the door open then jumped to her side again before putting his glasses on. They were horn-rimmed and made him look a little silly, like a boy playing dressing up. So she'd been wrong about the vanity; she really was having a hard time judging him. They were out on the street now. Was he going to accompany her all the way back if she didn't answer? She'd soon see if he wasn't just trying a line; Kitty Loader was an

61

old friend of her mother's and was looking for lodgers who weren't going to up sticks without paying the rent whenever a ship docked wanting a crew.

'I trust you're unusual for a newspaperman and can be relied on?'

'Cross my heart.' And he did. 'I give you my word which, after all, is sacred to any journalist who wants to be trusted on his own patch.'

'On my own head be it, but I believe you. There's a room going in Brabazon Street. It's nothing fancy and it's a bus ride or a good walk from here. Oh, and it's in the same road as the Belvedere Fish Guano Company.'

He didn't even flinch.

'And the oakum works is nearby. Their smell is quite localised of course but when the wind's in the right direction you're also treated to the varnish and paint factories on Limehouse Cut.'

'What's good enough for the fine working man – and woman – of Poplar, is good enough for me. I can see you're itching to rush off but perhaps we could meet after work for a drink and you could introduce me to the landlady and vouch that I'm not any old Irishman: I'm an Irishman with a job with prospects.'

'That won't be necessary. One look at that jacket and she'll know you're not about to run off to sea. Mrs Loader, 41 Brabazon Street. Fork right at the top of Chrisp Street into Morris Street, go by St Gabriel's church, and it's the second turning on the left. You can't miss it. Follow your nose.'

'I'll say you sent me, shall I?'

'You do that. Goodbye, Mr Cahill, it was certainly a different experience meeting you.' And May nipped across the road in front of a slowing tram.

Chapter Six

Throughout the next week, whenever the street door banged May expected it to be Jack come to renew that offer a drink. But it wasn't. She probably wouldn't have gone anyway. She'd been working late. Clarice Gem's death wasn't the only one requiring investigation; there'd been four others since she'd first been admitted to the mortuary. Not that she was there any longer. Colonel Tindal had signed the warrants for the death certificate to be issued, and the body released for burial.

The rain was pattering on the window, adding to May's mood of despondency. It was only eleven thirty and already she was wishing the day over. Not because it was Friday and she couldn't wait for the weekend to start, but because of what she could no longer put off doing. Typing bored her at the best of times and her concentration levels weren't helped when she had to reproduce words she'd rather not have in her head for even the shortest period of time. However often she was called upon to do it, her fingers still hovered over the keys before she typed in the age of a child under five.

The telephone rang. May welcomed the interruption and lunged across the desk to pick up the receiver. As she heard the voice on the other end, she wished she hadn't. It was the secretary to the Home Office Pathologist with the news that he was off with influenza and the post-mortem on an ex-soldier found with a bullet in his stomach would not be performed by the date specified. May ended the call and wondered how irritated Colonel Tindal would be; he only requested the intervention of Bernard Spilsbury when he had no other choice and this delay would strengthen his opinion that medical men made unreliable witnesses. May suspected it was simply that the coroner hadn't caught up with the recent improvements in forensic science but it could equally be that he disliked his theories being challenged in public by someone with greater knowledge. Well, there was nothing for it, she'd have to go through and tell him.

She knocked on the door to the coroner's chambers but forgot to wait for permission before entering. Colonel Tindal was in the act of slamming his desk drawer shut. May heard something clunk as it hit the back with the violence of the movement.

'I will not tolerate insubordination, Miss Keaps. It is no longer 1918 and there are now plenty of young men out there well versed in obeying the simplest orders.'

May took a small step across the threshold. She could smell best brandy.

'I'm very sorry, Colonel Tindal, I didn't mean to be discourteous. I was simply anxious to get this sorted as quickly as possible.'

64

'And you think five seconds of your time too precious to be spent standing waiting?'

'Of course not. It is your time I am concerned with. I am having to reschedule an inquest,' she elected not to tell him the reason why, 'and wondered if you could see your way to making yourself available for another day and allowing me to book one then.'

'I resent the implication that I am not engaged on the Lord Chancellor's business every day of the week.'

'No, I didn't mean that, I know you are, it's just that with all the commitments that keep you away from the courtroom it's difficult for me to fit everything in when I only know for certain I can expect you on Tuesdays.'

'Is it or is it not part of your duties to maintain the courtroom diary, Miss Keaps?' He glared at her. 'I will take your silence as affirmative and therefore suggest you occupy yourself in re-juggling my existing engagements instead of coming in here to criticise the fact I am not in permanent residence.'

May had to stare at the lines on the shorthand pad in her hand to stop from retorting that he was barely in four hours a week.

'Or do you expect me to do that for you? Perhaps I should remind you that the London County Council does not pay the coroner to do the job of his officer. I preside over inquests. I decide what is, or is not, pertinent evidence. I direct juries. I attend official luncheons. Am called upon to give speeches. My name appears on the list to present prizes at all the Inns of Court. Are any of those things within your capabilities, Miss Keaps?'

Colonel Tindal heaved himself up by pressing on the arms of his chair.

'Unless, and until, you inform me that the commensurate knowledge and experience have been visited upon you whilst you slept, I will continue to pay you the compliment of assuming you capable of managing the courtroom calendar. Within its existing limitations.'

He walked around the desk and out of the door. May didn't feel inclined to warn him that it was raining.

When she returned to her desk she found a bunch of violets accompanying a politely formal note. They were from Jack Cahill. He was now happily settled in his new lodgings; could he take her out this evening by way of thanks? It was a sweet gesture and in such contrast to the way Colonel Tindal had just treated her that it made her want to cry. But the timing was lousy. She was going with Alice tonight to see Stinky Sid's famed elephants; Sally had refused to take any payment for making the dress so May had been able to stretch to a couple of tickets. She was surprised at how disappointed she was at having to turn Jack down. And it wasn't just because she'd have had something to shut Sally up with when she next delivered the lecture about her lack of a social life. Despite his fresh manners – and that deplorable jacket – she really did want to see Jack again.

May picked up the telephone and put in a call to the newspaper office. After the switchboard girl dithered a little about whether they had a Mr Cahill on the staff (which made May chuckle about the big splash his arrival must've made) she was put through.

'Miss Keaps, and I thought this afternoon was destined to be unremittingly dull.'

His voice was deeper than she remembered, the Dublin accent more pronounced; or perhaps the wires were distorting it.

'I had wanted to deliver the flowers in person – I trust you liked them? I somehow had you down as a natural posy sort of a woman – but you appeared to be engaged in ... a...'

May felt the heat of a blush; she hoped he hadn't overheard the worst of Colonel Tindal's tirade.

'...conference when I popped in so I decided discretion was the better part of valour and all that. So, am I to have the pleasure of your company?'

May sighed. 'I'm afraid not. If it were any other time I'd be delighted to accept but I promised my sister a birthday treat this evening.'

'I might've known you'd have a better offer, it being at such short notice and all. But my engagement won't be until late so perhaps you could get the celebratory tea or whatever out of the way, and fit us both in.'

The image of jelly and cream made the last of her tension drop away. 'Alice would kill you if she'd heard that. She was seventeen a couple of weeks back and we're going to see the elephant show at the Hippodrome.' What was it about him that made her not want to confine herself to a simple refusal? It couldn't simply be that she was trying to match him word for word.

'Well, if you change your mind – or the beasts all

run amok and the thing finishes early – I'll be at the Palm Court Nightclub in Gerrard Street from about ten thirty. I sincerely hope to see you then ... so it's adieu, May Keaps ... and please pass on a well-wisher's felicitations to your not-so-baby sister.'

With the line dead, the office was extraordinarily quiet.

By late afternoon the sky was so dark it seemed to be a continuation of the roofs opposite. By focusing on the system of doing her least favourite jobs first, May only had the accounts and a further warrant for a witness at the inquest on a stevedore left. Her typewriter ribbon needed changing and she was so engrossed in making sure the clip didn't spring back and trap her finger that she didn't notice Dr Swan's arrival. He was leaning against the doorframe with his arms folded across his chest, his sodden mackintosh bundled up alongside the black bag at his feet. With his florid face, habitual baggy-kneed herringbone tweed suit (now decidedly wet on the shins) and paisley bowtie, he looked as if he should be organising a team of beaters on a shoot instead of eking a living amongst the East End poor.

'I could watch other people working all day.'

May smiled. Dr Swan only had a handful of conversation gambits and this was his favourite; she assumed he had a different set for use around a sickbed. He bent down, opened his medical bag and pulled out something wrapped in greaseproof paper.

'A meat pie. From Mr Levine. Just delivered his

68

wife of twins. Good job he is a butcher or his brood would eat him out of house and home. Why can't any of the jewellers ever pay me in kind? Anyway, for you. Doctor's orders; you could do with fattening up.'

May took the gift in the spirit in which it was intended, she wasn't the sort to put pride before saving herself the trouble of cooking supper. She put it in her string shopping bag on top of the apples she'd bought from the greengrocers on her way in.

'It's a sweetener of course. Because I've really come to give you an invoice for my fees. If you could see your way to getting it paid before the end of the month, I would appreciate it.' He laid an envelope on the desk. 'Forgive the intrusion, but are you feeling quite all right? You're looking a little tired. Been to your own quack recently to check you're not anaemic? Eating your greens like a good girl?'

May let out a bigger sigh than she'd intended. Speaking with Jack had helped, but the events of the morning still disturbed her. And there was no one else she could talk to about it. 'Do you have a moment?'

'Lots. For the next ten minutes you are officially my patient. Wait while I see if I can cram one of the chairs from the vestibule into this rat hole of yours; swollen ankles are the curse of doctors past the first spring of youth and who have to spend half the day climbing up and down tenement stairs.'

May focused on the business of spooling the typewriter ribbon until he returned.

'All right, fire away.' He nodded towards the corridor leading to Colonel Tindal's chambers. 'He's not about to come barging through is he? I do believe in keeping my consultations – even impromptu ones such as this – private.'

'No. He went out earlier. But it is about the coroner.'

'I thought so. Is he working you too hard?'

'It's not that. But I'm worried about him; he seems out of sorts a lot of the time and gets very snappy.'

'Drinking more...?'

It felt like betrayal to agree but Dr Swan had mentioned it first. May nodded.

'You know why, don't you?'

'His son. In the War.'

'Exactly. So that means it is unlikely to get any better. I deal with imbalances of the body, not of the mind, but from my experience if he hasn't learned to accommodate the grief by now then he probably never will.'

Dr Swan sat back and May felt herself flush under his scrutiny.

'This is a hard question and I am loath to place the responsibility on the shoulders of one so young but you are the only person in the position to judge: would you say he was losing his grip?'

'On the job you mean?'

'Yes. A coroner has a vital role and must be relied on to carry out his onerous tasks despite distressing personal circumstances.'

May put her hand to her mouth and nibbled at one of her nails; it was a childhood habit she resorted to in times of stress. 'He is sometimes a little distracted after lunch, but he has never failed to hold an inquest or follow the correct procedures as laid down in *Jervis*. He occasionally forgets or overlooks a few things, but it's my job as coroner's officer to see to those.' She switched her gaze away from the filing cabinet and to the window, being careful not to catch Dr Swan's eye. 'I suppose I can't tell any more when he's just being Colonel Tindal, and when he's a little under the influence.'

'My dear, May, that is not something for you to decide. Your duty is to consider carefully whether you think his behaviour is interfering with his ability to do the job. And if you suspect it is then you must report him to the Lord Chancellor for ... what's the official term? Inability or misbehaviour, if I recall correctly. In the meantime, I prescribe for you more sleep, a glass of port wine on occasion, and a healthy dose of liver salts every Friday night. And if I see no visible results by the end of the month, I'll be ordering you to pack yourself off for a weekend of seaside fun and frivolity.' He stood up. 'I must be off to look in on Fred Ash; do you remember him? Used to accept the Temperance League shilling and spend it in Spotted Dog. He'll be eighty soon. You could do worse than take a leaf out of his book and try to think of yourself more, and worry about others less. The world will still turn without you to guide it – and when you get as long in the tooth as Fred and I are, you'll be grateful for that fact. But for now just ease up on the tiller a little, will you?'

'I'll try, Dr Swan, really I will. And thank you, it helps having someone listen.'

'*Better out than in,* as we say in the medical profession. And if you could see your way to getting that invoice sorted...' He started to scrape the chair across the floor. 'I'll return this from whence it came and you'll be able to get back to seeing if you can swing that cat. Tootle pip.'

It was no longer raining by the time May left for the day. She was a little later than she'd liked to have been. A series of telephone calls from the magistrate's court over a missing piece of paper led to having to pull out every file to look for it. Such a stupid omission made her feel unprofessional and inefficient. But Colonel Tindal was right and the office was entirely her domain. If the committal sheet hadn't been attached then she had no one to blame but herself. She'd take the carbon copy around to them first thing Monday.

The tram was pulling away from the stop as she got to East India Dock Road. The apples and meat pie were making the shopping bag cut into her fingers, but she suspected the walk would do her good. She was surprised Dr Swan hadn't added a bout of vigorous early-morning calisthenics to his prescription. Thinking of him brought back her dilemma of what to do about Colonel Tindal. Could his recent conduct really be regarded as *inability or misbehaviour?* It seemed such a brutal definition – and final. If the Lord Chancellor removed him from office then for a man as proud as Colonel Tindal such a disgrace would be tantamount to a living death.

As May crossed Kerbey Street there were three issues crowding her head. The first was whether or not the coroner was doing his job properly, the

72

second was that she didn't know if she could bring herself to institute formal proceedings even if his behaviour warranted it, and the third was that she had no concrete proof. She'd heard what she thought was a brandy bottle clunking in the back of a drawer; he was sometimes unfocused after lunch; could be short and even rude to witnesses; he spoke to her at times as if she were a wilfully inattentive child; he distrusted expert medical testimony and thought all policemen either corrupt or useless; he made up his mind about the correct verdict for an inquest and ensured the jury knew when he disagreed with them. All character traits that marked him out as opinionated and individualistic ... but not necessarily negligent – certainly no more than she had been to lose a committal sheet.

She swapped the string shopping bag into her left hand. Not too much further now. But she wanted this problem sorted before she got home or she would never be able to relax. It was her duty to do what she could to ensure the people of Poplar had a competent coroner, but she also had a duty to Alice. To keep earning a salary from which she could just about make good her promise to fund her through night school. If Colonel Tindal were to be replaced then a new coroner might want to bring in someone of their own. Even if this didn't happen straight away he'd be bound to discover the ways in which she had been overstepping her authority and covering up for Colonel Tindal. So either way she would lose her job.

May had reached the end of Ellerthorp Street.

They lived a third of the way down. As was customary in all the long rows of terraces in the area the house had been divided to maximise rent – she and Alice occupying the ground and first floors, a coal-whipper and his wife in the basement. In an uncharacteristic fit of generosity the landlord had agreed to let her continue to pay dockers' tariff on account of what happened to her father. May knew she'd never be able to afford the luxury of four rooms (small though they were) anywhere else. The place was damp and the privy in the yard had to be shared with the neighbouring families, but it was home and she didn't want to lose it.

She was at her front door before she could say she'd made up her mind once and for all. She wouldn't report Colonel Tindal. If nothing else he came under the heading of *better the devil you know* and so she would do anything she could to keep him occupying the position of coroner for as long as possible. The relief of making the decision wasn't enough to lift her mood however. She was tired of doing things for other people's benefit and wanted to do something for herself for a change. She wanted to go out with Jack. The elephants were Alice's treat anyway and she'd probably enjoy them more without her big sister in tow. She'd propose an arrangement that should make them all happy.

Chapter Seven

But Alice didn't let her get further than explaining that she'd rather not go to the Hippodrome, before flying off the handle. She flounced around the kitchen for a good ten minutes before May could get her to listen to anything other than her own moaning about how nothing was fair. She sat at the kitchen table and waited until even Alice appeared to grow bored with her histrionics.

'What I was going to suggest was that you take the bus over to Elaine's and ask if she'd like to have my ticket. You've plenty of time to fetch her back here to get ready.'

Alice threw her arms around May's neck. 'Is it all right if I stay the night?'

'If Mrs Gibson says it's okay, then it's fine with me. Are you working tomorrow?'

'Manager's doing the box office. Says he wants to check I've been doing everything right. Except I'll be going there in the afternoon – not going to tell you why yet, it's a surprise.'

'Well, whatever it is you're doing, mind you find the time to take the laundry to the wash-house. Make it before midday or the water in the tubs will be dirtier than the sheets.'

Her sister planted a wet-lipped kiss on her cheek then snatched her outdoor coat from the back of the kitchen chair. 'Be back in a jiffy. Will

I be telling them we'll have supper out?'

Now she was pushing it; Alice's pittance from the theatre barely covered her daily fares and a hot meal when she was working into the evenings, and everything had gone up so much recently the monthly food budget would be hard enough to reconcile without adding in unplanned extravagances. May belatedly remembered that Mrs Gibson had three small mouths to feed, no husband, and only Elaine's wages from the match factory to depend on. It was inconsiderate to expect her to stretch to catering for Alice as well.

'Take that meat pie with you now and you'll be able to have some of that. Tell Mrs Gibson it's by way of thanks for putting up with you.'

Alice stuck out her tongue before dashing out of the room. May hadn't turned the tap on to fill the kettle before the front door slammed and the house was left to readjust to the silence. She fixed herself a slice of bread and marg. She'd much rather have a slice of meat pie – particularly as she'd lugged it all the way home and had the string burns across her palms to prove it – but it had gone to a better cause. Besides, she didn't know if Jack was proposing dinner and she wasn't used to eating twice in an evening. Sally had clients who dieted to keep their figures, but here in the docks most people never got the chance to get fat. The rich turned food away to stay thin: the poor just never had quite enough to eat. A political reality never destined to feature in one of Andy Taylor's exposés of inequality because every East Ender already knew it to be true.

May's thoughts turned to the realities of tonight.

She'd never been to a nightclub before. The prospect was exciting but nerve-wracking, too. What would she wear? Would there be dancing involved? That made her almost reconsider going; she couldn't bear it if she made a fool of herself in front of Jack. Not because she cared all that much what he thought of her – not yet, anyway – but because he would have such a field day teasing her about it. She could imagine his eyes twinkling as he tried to keep a straight face. All the Irish were excellent dancers, weren't they? Didn't they have shindigs or whatever they called them at every crossroads? She'd read that in a periodical article about the Emerald Isle in the library. May slapped her palms hard on the tabletop as she stood as a reminder that even if she felt as unworldly as Alice at this moment, it didn't follow that she had to make every situation equally melodramatic.

She'd filled a further hour with pointless and unsatisfactory housework before her sister was back with her pasty-faced friend in her shadow. May hadn't seen Elaine for a while and burgeoning womanhood wasn't treating her well; her hair was lank, her chin dotted with white-headed spots, and her arms seemingly welded across her chest to hide her emerging bosoms. May secretly hoped that the dream of becoming an actress wasn't a shared one or Elaine would be very disappointed. Alice was striking with dark hair and blue-grey eyes but she also made the air in a room shiver with energy whenever she entered. Elaine sort of plopped into a vacant space. May suspected it was an awareness of this contrast that made Alice like to go around with her.

77

The girls were only in the house long enough to use the water in the kettle May had been heating for her hair wash, raid the washing basket for the least dirty stockings they could find, and for Alice to tuck May's money for the tickets into the top of her bodice.

'Don't lose it.'

May felt she was waving off a couple of over-excited ten year olds. She stood at the door and watched them prance down the street chatting away as if they could only hold a thought in their head for as long as it took a fresh one to dislodge it. What had she been like when she'd been ten? A tomboy almost certainly, always running around after Albert, wanting to join in climbing trees and dangling fishing-lines into the cut. Her sister had been too young to be a companion then, and anyway their mother always kept her youngest tied by her apron strings. Perhaps Alice's current rebellions against responsibility were nothing more than an expression of freedom and not a sign – as May often thought – that she was doing a lousy job as substitute parent. Sally had been right when she'd pointed out how little she knew her sister. They shared biology, a tendency to judge others by their own wavering standards, a prickly defensiveness that was at its worst when tired, and a sense of humour that wasn't always kind. But she was also aware that they both abhorred injustice, could be generous with what little they had, were blessed with quick minds, weren't afraid to stand their ground, and had been schooled in enough Communist philosophy to know that the good of the whole outweighed the needs of the few. Alice just needed to grow up a little more before that last attribute would become second nature. May supposed if she were scrupulously honest then on the side of her own debits she'd have to add impatience because, much as she loved her sister, she did find living with her exasperating.

May stood a little longer on the doorstep to watch the pink trails of an early March sunset spread across the sky, and listen to boys down the street organise themselves into a game of firewood and rag-ball cricket. She could check if any of the clothes she might choose to wear needed pressing; the flat iron was only small and took a long time to heat up. Closing the door behind her, she picked her way up the stairs although somehow still managing to trip over a split in the central strip of lino. She turned right at the top into what had been her parents' bedroom; the other had been Albert's, then Albert's and hers, then hers and Alice's, now Alice's. She pulled open the wardrobe door. The hanging portion held sensible skirts and blouses, a black Sunday-best frock, and an old cotton print dress for when she needed a compromise between her working clothes and the overalls she wore around the house. Not one of the garments was either new enough, chic enough, or – she had to admit – daring enough, to wear to a nightclub.

May opened the door to her sister's room. The bed was still unmade but Alice had remembered to close the window against the bone-chilling damp of night mists drifting in off the river. Her wardrobe was more promising. May hadn't realized how many new clothes Sally had made for her until she saw them hanging together. It was true that Alice had suddenly started filling out in all the right places, and that she needed frocks when she had once worn school uniform, but now it was obvious that what Sally had taken to hinting was true: she was guilty of blatant bribery. The message was clear: *make something of yourself, Alice, and you'll be indulged to be as pretty as a picture.* It came to May that some of the wives she folded her sheets with in the washhouse complained about the same sort of approach from their husbands. Only it obviously wasn't getting a job with prospects but *stay out of the pub; behave yourself; get my dinner on the table; don't say nothing about the fists; give me what I want of a Saturday night.* She really did have to change her approach with the girl before Alice began to believe what those women now took as gospel: that love was just another word for coercion and control.

But for now she had to find something that would both flatter her and, now she'd lost the fresh bloom of youth, not make her feel like mutton-dressed-as-lamb. There was a dress in a soft-green crêpe that looked to be less fitted than the rest. It was a little low in the front for her liking but she could button up her navy cardigan over the top. Shoes were less of a problem. Paul Hill, the cobbler, sold uncollected shoes cheaply. It didn't happen often but sometimes someone would be staying with a church minister or dock official and would have her shoes dropped off, the maid forgetting when they packed to leave. May had acquired two pairs of sandals and some lilac dance shoes that way. She'd let her heart rule her head over that last purchase. It had been love at first stroke of the soft leather. With their thin ankle straps, slender heels, and high instep, they whispered of a glamorous life away from the streets of Poplar where women were whirled around in the arms of handsome beaux – that would never be her, of course, but in her dreams she could dance. Tonight, at long last, she had a chance to wear them. Gloves were catered for, too. Secretly ashamed of her large housework-roughed hands – *dockers' mitts* she called them – she had a dozen pairs in different weights and colours she'd picked up for pennies in tat shops.

She took the dress to her room and laid it on the bed. She would wash her hair and then come back upstairs for a nap. It would be terrible to be too tired to enjoy every second of the only proper date she'd had in over two years.

The tram joggled over the Ludgate Circus points. May felt a fluttering in her stomach at going out when most of the people she knew had drunk their cocoa and were tucked up in bed. This was the last night tram from Poplar to Piccadilly and had been packed all the way with the oddest collection of people she could've imagined sitting together. Some had the pallid weariness of those who had just finished work, some had come from the theatre – possibly from seeing the Hippodrome elephants; she thought of Alice and hoped she'd enjoyed them – a few families with small whining children who had probably been visiting, and at least one policeman who must've grown tired pounding his beat.

May stood up when they got to Haymarket. She

knew her way around this area of the West End, having accompanied Sally many times as her friend had eyed up the latest fashions. She moved down to the platform as the tram's motor changed in pitch, and it slowed. A couple in evening dress got off at the same stop. May wondered if they were going to a nightclub as well or possibly to the Trocadero for cocktails and a later supper. She found herself staring after them but a shout from a carman telling her to *throw herself in front of the horses and be done with it* made her turn on her heels and start walking.

Chapter Eight

The Palm Court Nightclub was in the centre of Gerrard Street opposite the telephone exchange. May hesitated for a moment before going down the short flight of concrete steps. After depositing her coat and hat in the cloakroom she walked through into the club proper. It wasn't as dimly lit as she'd imagined. There were sofas, a drinks' bar, a small platform for the band, and tables dotted around a wooden dance floor. A metal spiral staircase carried a stream of thinly-dressed young women, some pausing on the halfway landing to light a cigarette in as theatrical a way as possible.

There was only one lone man sitting at a table, in front and a little to the side of her. She was glad to see Jack had made an effort and was wearing a dark linen jacket instead of that horrendous tweed. A smile pulled at her lips when she imagined his surprise the moment he realised she had changed her plans She threaded her way over to stand at his shoulder. He threw her a quick glance before staring back down at the half-folded newspaper on the table.

'Sorry, but whatever it is you're selling, I'm not in the market.'

May felt her cheeks flame. The stupid idiot wasn't wearing his glasses. She pulled his spectacle case from his top pocket and laid it on the news-paper.

'Try these. You'll find all those marks magically rearrange themselves into words.'

He put them on, and finally looked up at her properly.

'May Keaps. You came. How fabulous. I'd almost given up all hope. I'm so delighted you were able to make it – I've been drowning my sorrows thinking I was going to have to endure the whole night alone.'

His enthusiasm was so spontaneous May thought there was a chance she might forgive him.

'Take a pew. What can I get you to drink?' He waved at a passing waiter. 'I'm sorry I didn't recognise you all dolled up – how is it that I always seem to be owing you an apology? Lovely frock, by the way.'

May smiled with what she hoped was a demure expression and sat. If she'd thought selecting a suitable outfit was bad enough, it was nothing compared to what to order to drink. What would be sophisticated, not so expensive that Jack decided never to repeat the experience, and might actually taste pleasant? Then she remembered an advertisement she'd seen of a beautiful, vivacious, and elegant young woman holding a glass of ruby-red Campari. It was too much to hope it would confer the same attributes on her but she asked for a small one in a long glass with lots of soda. Jack's face was unreadable but the waiter's expression told of a faint distain, probably at her timidity at not selecting from the extensive list of cocktails on the card he'd waved under her nose.

'So, how was your journey over? What happened about your sister's – Alice, isn't it – birthday treat? Are you sorry not to see the elephants? I trust I can in some way make up for them – not in size and trumpeting ability of course but, you never know, I might prove to be just as entertaining. Thanks again for putting me Mrs Loader's way. She's quite a landlady; formidable but straight if you get my drift.'

He was gabbling. Was he nervous? May smiled.

'That's all right, really. One of the things you'll soon learn about the East End is that people look out for their friends.'

'I'm flattered you regard me as one.'

'I was referring to Kitty Loader.'

That hadn't come out the way she'd meant. This considering the effect her words might have before saying them was tricky. And she doubted the Campari would help any.

'Sorry that sounded so snippy. I didn't intend it to. My only excuse is that I've had a horrible day and I guess I'm still a little punchy.'

'Would you like to talk about it?'

'No thanks. I'd rather put it behind me and just

enjoy being here, with you.'

The waiter returned with their drinks. May took a sip of hers to wet her dry lips and tried not to grimace at the bitterness. She looked down at the paper cocktail coaster. The inner circle contained a brown and cream embossed image of a man and woman dancing so intimately you wouldn't have been able to get a cigarette skin between them. Her legs began to tremble at the prospect of Jack asking her to take to the floor. She replaced her glass carefully so that it covered everything but the man's slicked down hair. But she didn't think it was just the thought of making a fool of herself that'd provoked her reaction, she'd been taken unawares by that blithe couple someplace else. She knew better than to force the memory: it would come up from the depths given time. May pointed at the colourless liquid in front of Jack.

'What's that you're drinking?'

He flung glances over his right and left shoulders like a spectacularly bad actor making a show of being discreet. 'Promise not to ruin my image as an Irishman and tell? Lemonade. Your company is more than enough stimulation this late at night.' He grinned. 'I get this feeling you see, May, that I need to keep my wits about me as far as you're concerned. Don't want to ruin my batting average by failing to return a short sharp crack when it's heading my way.'

She deserved that. And it hadn't been said unkindly. It made her relax a little with its inherent permission not to have to be so po-faced she didn't recognise herself.

'Have you registered your ration card yet? Get

85

Mrs Loader to tell you where she gets her butter and sugar and you can do the same. Most grocers in Poplar will slip in a little extra something if they're catering for an entire household.'

'Thanks for the tip. What's yours like? Household, I mean, not grocers. I asked Andy Taylor about you but he didn't tell me if there was a soon-to-be Mr Keaps with a sweet tooth around and about.'

May felt a flush creep up her neck. She wasn't sure whether it was at his direct approach or her consciousness of her spinsterhood.

'There was someone once. An old friend. We grew up together and had ... an understanding... I suppose is the best way of putting it. He was killed in France.'

'Oh, I'm sorry.'

He looked genuinely pained at causing her to have to say that.

'Don't be. And you'll be out of compassion pretty quickly if you keep on reacting like that whenever someone tells you about who they lov ... cared for ... and lost. Everyone around here has something of a list.' She took another sip of her drink.

'So, how long have you been at the coroner's court?'

She was grateful he'd picked up on her need to change the subject.

'Almost eighteen months. Before that I was driving ambulances in France, and before that, I worked in the tobacco factory. You could say I was in the right place at the right time to get this job because, being a mere woman, if it wasn't for the

86

War I wouldn't even have been considered. But the coroner's officer isn't a legally constituted position so Colonel Tindal can have whoever he likes; my predecessor was the undertaker in the High Street.'

'Handy that, I'd have thought. Cut out the middle man – or woman.'

May didn't smile; Jack could tease her about a lot of things, but not the importance of her job. His flippancy deserved a short version of the lecture she'd delivered in the library to the Workers' Education Group.

'We do all the investigations necessary into establishing how, and in what manner, someone dies. If it turns out that it was at the hand of another then it's the testimony we gather that forms much of the evidence at somewhere like the Old Bailey. We're the first port of call so to speak, a sort of sifting process. And the coroner has a lot of power. If Colonel Tindal decides to indict someone for murder then no High Court Judge can reduce it to manslaughter. And I'm the one who sets the ball rolling.'

May expected Jack's eyes to have glazed over by now but he was leaning forward in his chair, seemingly fascinated. And, she was pleased to see, impressed.

'I tip every hat I've ever owned to you, Miss Keaps. I wouldn't do it for all the tea in China. Give me a job with the living any day.'

'I'm only ever in the mortuary for the first viewing, after that it's mainly talking to people to find out what happened.'

She took off her cardigan and folded it across her

lap. The band had begun to play and the number of people dancing had raised the temperature markedly. She kept her gloves on though.

'Are you the only female coroner's officer?'

'I didn't see any others when they last reissued the list but it could've changed by now. I hope it has because it's about time men accepted we can do things equally as well. Women are to be on juries later this year. God, I hate to think how Colonel Tindal will react; oh well, he'll just have to move with the times or go the way of the other dinosaurs.'

Except May knew he'd make her life hell in the process. But she didn't want to think about that, it was too close to re-opening her decision not to report him.

'Doesn't dogging the steps of a killer put the wind up you?'

'Despite the sensationalist headlines, premeditated murder doesn't happen all that often. My first inquest involved two boys playing with knives and one tripped and stabbed his friend.'

'But there are some bona fide slaughterers out there, right?'

Was his unwillingness to let it go down to his newspaperman's instincts to find out what made her tick ... or a prurient interest in the macabre? May trusted Jack didn't think they were one and the same thing or she would definitely have something better to do the next time he asked her out.

'You weren't involved so can't possibly know what it was like but when you've been surrounded by as much death and carnage as I have – imagine falling over a pile of amputated limbs outside the operating tent in a front line field hospital...' It gave her satisfaction to see him grimace. '...then you'll get the idea.' She unconsciously knitted her fingers as if to feel her hands were still there. 'Most of us who survived stuff like that become fatalistic – you know, if the bullet's got your name on it then your time is up; if not, then you live to fight another day. Worrying about which way it will go changes nothing.'

'Interesting. So you're a gambler at heart.'

May raised an eyebrow. 'I suppose you could say that. Not brave, certainly. But not fearful either. More ... resigned.'

'I doubt you'll be so cavalier about your own safety when children come along. I assume you'd like them to, right?'

'What woman doesn't? And you?'

'I don't really see myself as a family man. But I expect I will settle down one day. Everyone does in the end.'

May wondered if that was true. Settling had always seemed such a bleak concept to her: the unspoken words ... *for second best* ... rang too loudly for her to ignore them.

'I seem to have been talking about myself for hours. What about you? How's life at the *East End News?*'

'Oh, fair to middling.' He leaned forward and squinted at her over the top of his glasses. 'Can you keep a secret?'

'Probably much better than you.'

'Touché. It's never a dull moment with you, is it? I'm working on the big break story every newspaperman dreams about.'

'Isn't it a bit early for that? I thought you'd only just started.'

'Contrary to popular opinion, the grass grows just as quickly over here as it does in Ireland. I've been doing my research like a good New Boy and there's been a recent exponential increase in the influence of gambling on ordinary East End life.'

'That old chestnut? There are much worse things going on you could be writing about: over-crowding and disease for example. Why don't you come up with a solution to those if you want to make a name for yourself?'

'I might just do that one day. But the dens where the desperate can end up gambling for their lives come pretty high up my personal list of resident evils. The places where it happens are closed to outsiders and you have to be invited to attend. So I'm here trying to figure out how to get my ticket in; respectable West End clubs like this are often trawled for likely punters by the dens' gatekeepers.'

May began to get the picture. No wonder he'd been so happy she'd turned up: she was his cover story. His means of blending in so he could observe without being observed himself. She drained the last of her vile drink to cool the lump in her chest that was making it difficult to breathe. She was angry with herself for believing it was a date, for getting excited and fussing over her preparations like a schoolgirl, but mostly with Jack for revealing the reason he'd asked her as casually as if it didn't matter.

'I need to pay a visit.' It was the most she could say without exploding.

She was washing her hands when two giggling young women lurched through the swing door. Eying them in the mirror May wondered if they'd had one cocktail too many with their flushed cheeks and wide pupils glittering like polished jet. They huddled over something the thinner of the two had cradled lovingly in her hand.

'Will she never leave?' Her companion's misjudged whisper bounced off the tiles.

'This snow's the best in town; well worth waiting for.'

May dried her hands on the fancy towel and left them to it. She was passing the cloakroom when she stopped. Of course, Clarice Gem. The logo of the passionate dancers had been on the matchbook in her lodgings. Had this been where she'd obtained her powders? Jack obviously thought it perfectly acceptable to be working tonight so May didn't see any reason why she shouldn't do the same. After all, it wasn't as if there was any other point in her being here.

Imagining she was wearing her skirt and blouse instead of a low-cut dress, she re-entered the main room and strode back to the table.

'Is it easy to get cocaine in this place?'

'My, my, May Keaps, you are full of surprises tonight. And there was me thinking you irredeemably wedded to the right side of the law.'

'Don't be stupid.'

'Take it easy – perhaps it was a little rash of me to order another Campari; that last one really seems to have put a fire in your belly. I'll have you know it's not so outrageous to assume that underneath it all you're not so very different to the other women here. That terrible piece of knitwear apart. They all take it. Most recreationally, but some can't get through a day without it making their lives worth living. Neither of which makes them any the less ordinary. Look at that one over there ... the one with the yellow feathery scarf thing...'

'Boa.'

'Where do you think she works?'

May watched the way she danced, letting the man lead whilst still being careful not to get too close to the couples on either side. 'Shop girl. John Lewis I'd say.'

'I will bow to your superior knowledge of department stores. How about her?'

He was now pointing to a straight-up-and-down blonde in a backless sequined dress that would've had Sally drooling.

'I doubt she's ever done a day's work in her life.'

'And her?'

This one singled out for attention was sitting on a chocolate leather sofa and weeping, seemingly alone and unembarrassed. May couldn't help but imagine Clarice in her last hours of misery.

'Okay, I get your point. Now tell me something; if a woman made an appointment to come here, would it be for drugs?'

Jack surprised her by laughing. A convulsive chuckle that ended with him having to take off his glasses and wipe his eyes.

'Seems I've only got to show you a fence and you're over it and galloping across the field before I can point out the open gate. Snow is fashionable and these girls can pick some up anywhere. They come here to dance and flirt, not risk trying to buy in public and getting nabbed by a plain-clothes member of the constabulary. It's the same with gambling, opium, all the vices: the naïve get trapped, the habitual get careful, and the addicted get dead. It's a sure fire way of telling them apart.'

The Campari she didn't want appeared over her shoulder. Jack slid a tip from the table onto the proffered tray. The waiter muttered something she didn't quite catch; then Jack looked up, did a sort of double-take and reached out to shake the man's hand.

'May Keaps, allow me to present Brilliant Chang. He's the proprietor of this place.'

May looked up to see a Chinaman dressed in a dinner jacket of midnight blue with glistening silk lapels, and a silk shirt that was so white it sucked in the light. His black hair was slicked back, adding extra definition – as if it were needed – to the bone structure of a ... there was no other word for it ... beautiful face.

'Delighted to make your acquaintance, Miss Keaps.' His voice was tactile, flowing over her in a liquid caress. 'Although I fear we have not been introduced properly; my birth name is Nan Chan. The other is my English name. I will happily answer to which ever one you choose.'

Jack patted a spare chair. 'Come and join us for a while. I want to know what chance you think *Valentine's Kiss* has in the 3.30 at Lingfield.'

Their guest cocked his head at May for permission to sit. She readily gave it; his presence had transformed her mood – and the entire evening. She noticed his exquisitely manicured hands with their long, thin fingers as he lightly adjusted his trousers at the knees to preserve the creases. She buried hers deeper in her lap. Delicate flutes of champagne magically appeared. May enjoyed the novelty of crisp bubbles bursting on her tongue as the men talked horseracing form, track conditions, and the likelihood of one trainer or another doing the double. It was only when they started discussing betting odds and totes and accumulators that her attention began to stray. Their host picked up on it immediately.

'Please forgive my selfishness in talking about my passion.'

'Horseracing?'

'The philosophy of man's need to seek excitement through the things over which he has no control. I am not a gambler, Miss Keaps, but a student of Confucius.'

She might have guessed he was a philosopher; she'd been watching him with Jack and he'd been engaged in the conversation but holding something back as if he was observing himself as well as his companion. How he could do that whilst making you feel you were the most important person in the world when he looked into your eyes and spoke to you...

'Billy ... there's a telephone call. Says it's urgent...'

The barman was calling across above the music.

'I'll take it upstairs. Another time I hope, Miss Keaps.'

May watched him walk away from their table. And then it registered. Billy. The name Clarice

Gem had written in her diary for the night of her death. She'd found him. But the next thought made her feel as unsettled as if her champagne had been spiked: Jack had introduced him as Brilliant Chang and *chang* was Limehouse slang for cocaine. Had this elegant and charming man been the one who'd supplied the means for Clarice ending her life? May didn't want to believe it. But the only way she'd know for sure was by issuing him with a subpoena to attend the inquest. The warmth she'd felt in his company had turned oppressive. Since she'd long ago abandoned the notion of being here on a date there wasn't any reason for her to stay. She searched in her bag for the cloakroom ticket, found it, and stood up.

'I've noticed he has that effect on women; one moment I'm pleasant enough company and then he comes along and – hey presto – I suddenly turn into dog meat.'

Jack was smiling but she'd been wrong-footed once too often already this evening.

'I've got a headache, that's all.'

'I'd offer to escort you back to Poplar but…' He raised his hands to indicate their surroundings.

She couldn't bear to hear him spell it out for her. 'It's okay; I'll get the doorman to call me a taxicab. You stay. After all, one of us ought to get what they want out of this evening. I'll see you around. And thanks for the drinks.'

Chapter Nine

May heard the clock above East India Dock gateway chime yet another hour. The whirr and clank of the distant winches and cranes were not meshing into their usual lullaby, and the hoot of a steamer on the river was downright sinister. When she realised she'd never go back to sleep, she hauled herself out of bed, splashed her face with water from the nightstand, and began to get dressed. It wasn't hard to pinpoint the source of her restlessness: Brilliant Chang. She'd been so taken in by his charm as if she'd lost all ability to judge character. And if that was the case she could only put it down to becoming too emotionally involved. It had started when she'd seen Clarice on the mortuary slab and compared her young vulnerability to Alice's: such a novice's mistake. Compassion was important in a coroner's officer because it reminded her that a body had once been a real person with family, friends, feelings, hopes and desires. Sentimentality, on the other hand, simply blurred the edges between truth and fiction.

It was Saturday but she'd go into the office to type up Brilliant Chang's subpoena to be sure he'd receive it in time for the resumption of Clarice Gem's inquest on Tuesday. May left a note for Alice on the kitchen table – with a reminder about the laundry – and closed the front door quietly behind her.

The night mist from the river had turned into a wet fog. Through it the gaslight at the end of the street burned like a little dying sun. She thrust her hands deeper into the pockets of her brother's pea-jacket and for a moment thought she could detect his scent – pipe tobacco and hair oil – rising up from the collar. But she knew it was a memory; cooking, coal gas, and mildew were the only smells clinging to the matted wool. Gripped by an overwhelming need to feel close to him again she turned and headed in the opposite direction. The garage was in Pennyfields, under the bridge carrying the London and Blackwall Railway into West India Docks. When her brother had first brought her here she'd been terrified of the trains roaring like dragons over her head. The walls dripped with slime and stank like a shallow pond but it had seemed then – as now – a magical place fashioned out of necessity, built out of dreams.

May hammered on the small door cut into the larger double one filling the arch. Tom's muffled voice reached her, angry with curses. When he let her in she could see why; the front of his overalls was sodden.

'What you want to make me jump like that for? Spilled coffee all down me, didn't I?'

She wanted to laugh but knew he'd be deeply offended. 'Sorry, Tom. I'll make you some more.'

'No you won't, missy; always tastes like shit when you've been near it. I've got me some best beans I'll have you know. Under the counter for a generator I've been fettling with. You coming in or what? Can't stand here all day.'

97

Tom was like an elderly uncle, and just as tetchily set in his ways. Short and stocky with clumps of white hair sticking up as if coated in engine oil, he had a withered arm from where he'd caught it in the flywheel of a threshing machine as a boy in Suffolk. But that made no difference to his dexterity with anything mechanical. If it had nuts and bolts and belts and pistons, Tom coaxed it back to life with all the skill of a surgeon.

'You come for a look, or what?'

He bent over to fiddle with a small Fairbanks stationary engine. The space filled with the smell of paraffin and a throaty rattle; there was a puff of blue smoke and the bulb hanging from the ceiling pulsed with light.

'Was working on it, Sunday. Reckon I could have her good as new. Excepting I ain't got the parts. Can't buy them with coffee beans.'

He wheezed a laugh and May joined in. She'd been visiting often enough to know not to rush him. Tom had ways of doing things and had been known to hurl an oilcan – and on one memorable occasion a heavy spanner – if his patterns were thrown by something unexpected. And then he'd be forced to start from the beginning again. Slow and sure were his mottos: it made him a good engineer but a frustrating companion.

May was going to perch on a wooden crate but changed her mind when she saw the grease. She had her work skirt on after all.

'I've been putting a little by. It's not much but if you tell me what you need then maybe I can find the rest.'

Had it been wise to make what would've

amounted to a cast-iron promise to a man like Tom? But she'd told Albert she'd look after it for him – in that final letter – and she wasn't going to let a lack of money turn her into a liar.

Tom was rubbing at the wet cloth stretching over his belly with a sheet of newspaper. She wondered how much longer she'd have to wait before he'd let her see what he'd been up to. Would he feel the need to boil up some more coffee first? It all depended on whether he felt he had to start that from scratch again, or if he saw the spilling of the pot as the beginning of something else; perhaps changing into another set of overalls. It was impossible to second-guess Tom.

But he managed to surprise her by doing neither, instead sucking air through his teeth as he walked to the back of the workshop. The place was littered with half-finished projects but hers was the only one kept in hiding. He grabbed the corner of the canvas tarpaulin, and with a flurry worthy of a stage magician, pulled it to the floor. The motor-cycle sat on its forks like a roped horse brought to its knees. The wheels lying like an afterthought on one side.

'Oh, Tom, you've mended the handlebars.' May wanted to rush over but didn't want him to cover it again.

'Don't know how you can see nothing from there. Step up here, missy, and get yourself a proper look. No touching, mind. The gear lever's only resting.'

The 1912 Norton Brooklands Special had been Albert's pride and joy. He'd won it in a card game with a Speedway racer. It had been a wreck then but he and Tom had begged, stolen, and improvised what they could to turn it back into something like the record breaker it had once been. And that had been its undoing. Whilst home on leave, Albert had taken it for a spin, opened up full-throttle, lost control on a bend, and ended up in a ditch. He had been thrown clear and limped back, but the Norton had suffered the indignity of travelling for its final journey in the rear of a coal cart. Tom had been tinkering with it ever since. Two and a half years of painstaking stripping and welding and educated guesswork.

'Been all over her. Had to replace some of them leather pieces on the drive belt but foreman of the tannery owed me; came across some bulbs; cleaned the brake pads; given her as much oil as she can take – the caps on the ends of the rocker spindles topped up, push rods, arm ends, cables and controls. Checked tappet clearances, gaps in magneto points, whistled through carburettor jets. Only thing left now is a new spark plug.'

And to put the wheels back on, May wanted to add. She was feeling dizzy from the paraffin fumes and Tom's monotone recital of activities she couldn't begin to visualise. Wood she understood. Wood you could listen to through your fingertips, smell if it needed a fresh coating of linseed or beeswax. Metal was altogether too artificial. But the machine itself was a thing of beauty. One day she would take it out of here. She would learn to ride and return it to the life it had been built for and deserved to reclaim. The life that Albert should have had. Her chest quivered. She was grateful for the train passing overhead and setting everything loose rattling. Although she doubted if Tom would have noticed if she'd burst into tears because he had lifted one of the wheels and was pushing it towards his workbench.

'Handful of spokes wouldn't go amiss. Can't do nothing but have them new.'

What passed for sunlight in Pennyfields was strengthening through the open doorway. May remembered how much she had to do today.

'I'll bring you some money during the week. I can't say exactly when because we're very busy at the moment.'

'There ain't really no rush. They're coming to take me away.'

'Who are?'

'The family. What's left of them.'

May hadn't known he had any.

'My brother's the only other one of our generation not dead. Seems he's now set on giving me that honour. And they want me there to watch his passing. I ask you; ain't as if there's nothing I can do about it.' He slid his hand like a blind man over the top of his workbench. 'Got something for you.'

A chain dangled from his index finger. On the end of it was a key.

'Cut a spare. Let yourself in and out, why don't you? She could do with a good polish. You touch anything else but the chrome, mind, and I'll winch the whole thing up and toss it in the river.'

May took her badge of trust with the solemnity with which it was offered. By the time she had composed a short speech of thanks Tom had his back to her and was attacking something with a pair of pliers. She waved her fingers in a silent farewell and stepped back out to face the demands of the real world.

Once in the office, May discovered two of Clarice's friends had responded to the newspaper announcement. She wrote them letters with the date and time of the inquest, finishing everything she had to do by mid-morning. She gathered up the envelopes to post. Brilliant Chang's subpoena she'd decided to deliver in person and slipped it into her shoulder bag before setting off to see if Sally wanted to make the trip into Town. Her friend had no qualms about breaking the rules of Sabbath – maintaining that God valued industriousness over piety – Saturdays being the only time she could go into the West End shops to look at the new fashions. May would tack on the offer of such a trip now in return for having a witness when she handed over the summons.

They got off the tram at Oxford Circus. The streets were crowded. It was exhausting being surrounded by so much conspicuous consumption and May was grateful when they reached Liberty's. The first of the large window displays was magnificent, as were the shoppers emerging from the revolving doors laden with bags and boxes.

'I wonder what she had to do to get shoes like that.'

Sally laughed. 'Probably something you wouldn't approve of by the quality of that fur.' She hobbled to one side to avoid the woman bumping into her. 'On the dope, too, I'd say; half my clients can't walk up and down the workroom in a straight line either. What do you think that would look like in a soft pink?' She was pointing to a dress in the centre of the display with a dropped waist and handkerchief hem.

May thought it looked shapeless on the boyish mannequin but would probably perk up if draped over a pair of real hips. 'I don't know where I'd wear something like that.'

'No, you wouldn't, because you never go out except to work or to sit in the dark at the Hippodrome or the pictures.'

'You forget you're now talking to a woman who's been to a nightclub.'

'That was for work.'

'But I still had to dress up a bit.'

'The glamorous you didn't last long did it? Why are you wearing that awful jacket? And that skirt looks like you should be scrubbing the step.'

'It was cold and damp first thing this morning.'

'You'll never attract anyone if you look like a tat shop.'

May ignored her; she didn't want to go around that loop again. Sally was tugging at her sleeve.

'Come on. The landlady of the Vine Tavern gave me a little extra for making that awful garment she wanted to wear to the Licenced Victuallers' do. I'll buy you a scarf.'

'That's kind, but really, don't waste your money.'

'I want to. Anyway, I happen to think it's about time you had a lesson in how to receive things gracefully. Men expect that.'

Knowing Sally was formidable when she had a

103

bee in her bonnet May allowed herself to be led into the emporium and up to a glass counter containing trays of folded silk squares. But she drew the line when Sally pointed at one that was so scarlet it almost made her eyes hurt.

'If you insist on doing this then I'd be happier with maybe a mustard yellow or perhaps that peachy colour.'

'So the red will make you stand out a little? It's all very well to see politics and justice in black and white but when it comes to clothes you could do worse than to allow yourself to stray a little from the straight and narrow. Choose to walk a different path from time to time to the one you are used to, May Louise Keaps, before it becomes the only one available.'

May felt as though she was being stripped naked in public. And there was more humiliation to follow as the sales assistant asked if she wanted it wrapped but Sally said May would wear it now. The woman shook it out then rearranged it into a triangle before reaching over the counter and tying it around her neck.

'Suits you, miss,' she said as she admired her handiwork. 'Bright on the outside, bright on the inside, as my old mother always had it.'

May smiled at her. That was a nice thing to say. Even so she wasn't going to risk accepting the proffered hand mirror to look at her reflection. But the silk did feel much better than the prickly collar of the pea-jacket against her skin. She waited for Sally to pay, thanked her for the gift with a peck on the cheek, and told her she'd wait on one of the chairs at the bottom of the stairs while her friend went up to look at what was on offer in the first floor haberdashery department. There was only so much exposure to garish patterns and colours a girl could take.

They arrived at the Palm Court Club at half-past three. A man with an empty crate hanging from his hand was walking up the steps. May waited until he had reached street level then led Sally down, past the cloakrooms, and through the swing door. The room was dimmer that it had been last night; the air heavy with stale perfume, sweat, and a slick of disinfectant swabbed over the floor. The barman was stacking bottles on shelves. A blonde, with her cleavage fighting to stay inside her blouse, was straying through a torch song, sotto voiced, to the accompaniment of a plinky piano. No one seemed to have noticed their entrance.

'Excuse me.'

The barman kept his back to them. 'Wait over there. Hope you've brought your music. Not that I reckon you could be any worse than her without it.'

'I've not come to sing.'

'No novelty acts. Told 'em 'til I'm blue in the face that we don't want no strippers or spoon players.'

Sally sniggered. 'That'll be your sadness because I'm famous for doing both at the same time.'

He turned around now. 'I'm sure you are, darling.' His gaze raked May up and down. 'But not dressed like that, eh?'

She was glad of the low lighting as she flushed. 'Is the owner in?'

'He never sees no-one working the floor. Try-outs is one of the things he pays me for.'

'I'm here on official business.'

'If it's the tax then he ain't here now nor never will be.'

Sally stepped out from behind May.

'Jesus. Didn't know you lot came mob-handed. What are you, the money collector?' He flicked his cloth at the stage for the others to acknowledge his wit.

May placed her hand on her friend's forearm and squeezed.

'The office is this way, isn't it? We'll just take ourselves up.'

She steered Sally towards the spiral staircase.

'Oy. Hang on a mo. You can't come waltzing in here without a by your leave and go where you please unannounced.'

'We're hardly that, are we? I told you, I'm on official business—'

'Who's she then, the Jew cat's mother?'

Sally began twisting away from her grip. May heard a door on the floor above open. She looked up to see Brilliant Chang leaning on the wrought iron rail.

'Miss Keaps. How delightful to see you again so soon. Do come up. Jonnie, bring these ladies some tea. Earl Grey.'

He waited at the top of the stairs, then stepped back to usher them into the room. Sally still had enough breath left to gasp. May clutched her shoulder bag to her chest to stop from doing the same. The high ceiling, bright white walls, and floor-length windows swathed in muslin all gave the impression of being in a cloud. There was a desk, three wicker chairs, and a coat stand in the corner – all painted white. Brilliant Chang was the only accent of colour in charcoal grey. May remembered she had that ridiculous red scarf on and wanted to tug at her jacket collar to hide it.

'Do please sit down.'

'No thank you, we won't be staying long.'

'I will if you don't mind. My leg's gone stiff from all those stairs.' Sally lowered herself with a sigh. 'I'm Sarah Goldman. Sally to her friends.'

'Enchanted to meet you, Miss Goldman.' Brilliant Chang gave her a little bow. 'And I am Nan Chan. Billy to my friends. Do I take it that you are a fellow Alien here under sufferance until they decide we are *undesirable* and decide to deport us? There have been far too many incidences of that happening lately for me to sleep easy at night.'

'Not me. Poplar born and bred. But my grandparents came over from Russia; worked passage on a ship.'

'Then we have that in common at least. I, too, started my adult life as a sailor.'

May was disconcerted to see Sally smiling at him with obvious admiration. He had an unerring knack of being able to connect with everyone. He was still good-looking and charming – she had to give him that – but watching Sally wilt into a little girl made her appreciate that he was also a smooth operator. They were talking about clothes now.

'...with a fine pinstripe in the softest wool you can imagine.'

'Softer than this?'

He held his arm out and Sally actually stroked it. May grappled with the flap of her shoulder bag. Sally's enchantment reminded her too much of her own last night.

'...been a tailor all his life. Was born with a tape measure instead of a cord according to bubba.'

Brilliant Chang laughed. A tinkling sound like the shake of a tambourine. May pulled out the subpoena at last.

'Miss Goldman and I have to leave now.' She caught Sally's glare; she'd be made to pay for that with sulky silence on the journey back. 'But not before I give you this.'

He took the envelope without a change of expression. 'Can I enquire what it is?'

'An instruction for you to attend the inquest on Clarice Gem when it resumes on Tuesday 16th.'

Still his smile didn't droop. He either had nothing to hide or was an accomplished actor.

'Ah, yes, I heard about the unfortunate girl's death.'

'Then why didn't you come forward?'

'I had no way of knowing I would be required. Our paths crossed little.'

May wanted to fling her suspicions at him that it'd been his cocaine that'd killed Clarice to see if he'd flinch but knew she'd have to wait to get her satisfaction. In the same courtroom where he'd get his come-uppance.

'I am sorry that it is only business that brought you here on this occasion. Perhaps you and Miss Goldman–'

'Sally.'

'–Sally will return one night as my honoured

guests.' He placed the subpoena almost reverentially on the gleaming desk. 'And until that time I shall see you again at the inquest, Miss Keaps. I will be asking my solicitor to accompany me; a man in my position can never be too careful of his reputation.'

Perhaps she had him rattled after all.

Chapter Ten

Vi shifted her buttocks in the tight-fitting auditorium seat. The worn plush was scratching at her thighs through the muslin of her costume. The wardrobe mistress had insisted she wear it to 'stretch it a little, dearie' and the humiliation of sitting in full rigout as a Cockney Flower Girl was just as uncomfortable as having to endure the parade of very bad try-outs going through their paces on stage. So far she hadn't deemed any worthy of appearing in the first – and she hoped, only – Barley-Freeman Talent Night.

'Next!' Her voice failed to convey any enthusiasm. She tried again. 'Can we have the next act? As quick as you like. Just come on stage, tell me your name, and launch on in.'

She knew the prickly terror of standing on the apron desperate to perform well enough to land a part in a show: no footlights, no magic, nostrils full of the reek of rabbit-skin size and fresh paint, impossible to concentrate when chippies and sparks were banging around at your back and the

ASM was tearing someone off a strip in the wings. But theatre life was like that and, if they wanted to be a part of it, they'd have to rise to the occasion. It seemed unlikely – Vi glanced down at her list of would-be performers – *Lillie Barton, virtuoso on the penny whistle* could make the grade, but you never knew. The rough diamond was what every impresario hoped to unearth and, as his stand-in, it was her task to see beyond the voices warbling with nerves and the poorly-delivered comic routine to find a half dozen.

She allowed young Lillie the dignity of finishing her first verse before calling a halt. The pianist who had been sitting on stage throughout made a show of removing his fingers from his ears as the girl left the stage, and she burst into tears. That had been unkind, every artiste – no matter how amateur or appalling – deserved respect for having a go. The next up was a vent act. There was a chance it might be so cack-handed that it would at least make the audience laugh; if not he was likely to be pelted with some well-aimed rotten tomatoes. The Gaiety regulars were a tough but knowledgeable crowd. Real skill was rewarded with a place in their hearts forever but attempting to insult them with a badly rehearsed turn was tantamount to a declaration of war. And the mob always won. Vi remembered fondly how the great Walter Aubrey had once left the stage after dying a death to announce to the wings: *I'm off to pee on my props, and sod the profession.* A sentiment she'd echoed many a time.

The ventriloquist wasn't half bad. Not good, but not too terrible either. The dummy was crudely made but Vi thought the audience would appreciate the homespun touch. True, the man's lips moved – more often, in fact, than those of the dummy – but his patter was a refreshing take on the old favourite of two tramps sharing a park bench. The snobbery of not wanting to admit falling on hard times was the sort of truth an East End audience appreciated. At last Vi had a name on her list she could tick.

She'd see one more and tell the rest to come back next Saturday or she'd have no energy left to convince the ASM their rehearsals wouldn't have the stage hands firing off about how they only had the time between shows to prevent everything from falling to pieces and if the whole run was a disaster then on someone else's head be it ... a speech she could recite without a prompt. Plus she had an interview with the manager to secure herself engagements on the current bill; it made no sense to be twiddling her thumbs in a theatre if there was paid work going.

A young woman had appeared on the stage without being called. A good sign of initiative. And, even better, she was handing sheet music to the pianist. She was tall and slim with a mass of dark wavy hair falling around her shoulders – a bonus because the short bob that was all the rage was so limiting and Vi doubted the Gaiety had a stock of wigs that didn't look like rats had nested in them. The girl had presence, too; a sort of confidence mixed with innocence. As she turned and walked forward, Vi shuffled to attention with surprise: it was the girl she'd met when she'd first arrived.

111

'Hello, again. We were never properly introduced, were we; what's your name, sweetheart?'

'Alice Maud Keaps.'

'Well, Alice Maud, whenever you are ready, let's
hear if your singing ability measures up to a
fraction of your keenness.'

The girl took a deep breath – good technique,
right from the diaphragm – and nodded to her
accompanist.

'You called me Baby Doll a year ago.
You told me I was very nice to know.
I soon learned what love was.
I thought I knew,
But all I've learnt has only taught me
how to love you.
You made me think you loved me in return,
Don't tell me you were fooling after all.
For, if you turn away, you'll be sorry some day;
You left behind a broken doll.'

Her voice and attitude were so sweet Vi found
herself actually wiping away a tear. The backstage
bedlam had slackened off, too. The girl was a
natural. She could be the find that turned this
show into a cut above the usual airing of amateur
follies. But Vi suspected young Alice Maud might
harbour a similar thought herself – and it didn't
do to single out favourites so early in the proceedings – so she simply thanked her, asked her
to give her details to the boy in the prompt
corner, and announced the auditions over for the
day. Now all she had to do was find the wardrobe
woman and get out of this ridiculous dress.

112

Free from her constraints, Vi made her way into the foyer. Alice was in the box office counting the tickets for the afternoon show; there was already the beginning of a queue outside the double doors.

'I assume you'll be able to make good your promise to get free to attend rehearsals?'

'Do you mean you're giving me a slot?'

The girl's excitement bounced off the walls of her cubicle.

'I think we'll bill you as *The Gaiety's Very Own.*'

'Was I all right then?'

'Very passable. But you've a lot of work to do. A performer needs to learn to give something of themselves if they're to command the stage – let alone the audience.'

'I ain't afraid of them.'

'Well, you should be. But if you listen to what you're told then you'll be fine.'

'This is what I've wanted to do all my life – not sell tickets but be a proper actress.'

'You're singing a number, Alice; there's a long way to go before you could consider yourself part of the profession.'

'Oh, I know that. Except you've got to start somewhere. My sister's always on at me to get a job in an office or something – I'd rather die than do that.'

Her mobile face screwed up into a look of disgust. Vi found her charmingly dramatic; not unlike herself at that age. Maybe she did have a future on the boards. The door from the stairs to the gallery swished open. Horatio on his way to collar the theatre manager. So he'd been watching the auditions; Vi hoped he concurred with her choices. He blew her a kiss as he strode across the foyer and entered the auditorium.

'Who's that?'

Alice's voice was husky with admiration. Vi felt a proprietary frisson: Horatio was strikingly handsome, particularly in the black silk-lapelled suit he thought befitted an impresario.

'He's the sponsor of the show, or his father is to be precise, but most importantly he's the producer and director, so you make sure you do everything he says. I'm the one selecting the turns, but he's the one who can just as easily fire them.'

'I ain't never seen someone so ... so ... like he's come off a film poster.'

Vi laughed. The girl was so smitten she'd lick the stage clean if he asked; such adoration would make her a breeze to work with.

'See you later, Alice. Make sure you sell a lot of tickets, won't you?'

'I'll tell them all about the talent show as well.'

'You do that.'

Vi walked back into the auditorium smiling. It was nice to know that theatre life could still evoke such radiant enthusiasm. She wondered just how long it would be before the shine rubbed off Alice Maud Keaps.

Chapter Eleven

May had been sitting at her table for ten minutes waiting for the inquest to start. The courtroom gallery was full. There were more reporters than usually turned up for a non-sensational inquest and the rest of the seats were occupied by young women dressed as if for a matinee. May thought it no coincidence that Poplar Coroner's Court should suddenly become the place to be. But how had any of them known Brilliant Chang was due to appear? Had he been bragging about his day in court? She hoped he would prove to be just as self-serving on the witness stand. It would be the one time she'd feel someone deserved the edge of Colonel Tindal's tongue. She could see the coroner was getting close to unleashing it as he was patently ready to begin.

May issued the proclamation for the opening of the proceedings and reminded the jury of their obligations. She sat back down into the silence. Then the street door banged. No hurrying footsteps across the vestibule. He entered the courtroom with all the aplomb of an illustrious actor making his grand entrance. A ripple of female admiration shimmied down from the gallery. The late arrival was a vision in a blue overcoat trimmed with a luxurious fur collar, black trousers with turn-ups and a wide satin stripe down the sides, and pearl-grey spats. His legal adviser looked like his bag-carrier.

One quick glance up over his shoulder to his audience, and he slipped into a vacant seat. He shrugged off his coat to reveal a single-breasted jacket the colour of Indian ink. His solicitor sat beside him. They exchanged a whisper or two and then Brilliant Chang looked up and smiled at May. A flush spread up from her neck at his apparent belief every woman was half in love with him and in that moment she knew nothing would give her greater satisfaction than Colonel Tindal not instructing Jury Three to deliver a verdict of suicide. She wanted Brilliant Chang indicted for manslaughter for supplying cocaine in a negligent and culpable manner. She thought there might be a chance of the coroner complying as he stared at the sweaty bald head of the solicitor.

'Please instruct your client that the epigram *better late than never* has no currency in my courtroom. Should he need to be called again, in this or any other case, any further demonstration of contempt will be rewarded with the longest stint at His Majesty's pleasure it is in my power to confer. Now, Miss Keaps, swear in the first witness and let us get this over with.'

Rose Flood had barely sat after taking the oath before Colonel Tindal fired his salvo.

'Did you, or did you not – at the time or subsequently – know about the deceased undergoing an abortion? We have medical testimony that she committed the gravest of illegal acts and if you know who procured, or even performed, the child-murder you must reveal their names so they can be passed on to the police.'

116

Rose Flood looked terrified. May wondered how loudly the words *there but for the grace of God...* were sounding in her head.

'She didn't confide anything of the sort to me. I wouldn't say we were bosom pals as such. In fact, we weren't really that well acquainted.'

The distancing had begun, death and transgression being viewed by many as contagious. Rose Flood was going to use this opportunity to immunise herself against both.

'We passed the time one evening at a club. We weren't exactly the same type. The only thing I knew was that she'd been disappointed in love. But that could be said about any girl these days.'

'Then why, if you had nothing in common, did you tell my officer you'd been to her lodgings the afternoon following her death?'

'There was this matter of a little money I lent her.'

'For drugs?'

'No, no.' Her silly little hat wobbled with her sincerity. 'I knew she took cocaine, of course, you can always tell one who does. The twitchy jaw for starters. She was always chewing gum to try to disguise it and everyone recognises that a dead giveaway.'

Colonel Tindal shot a glance at May. She knew he had expected her to furnish witnesses who would draw this inquest to a speedy conclusion. But could any other coroner's officer have done any better?

'If I may have your attention, Miss Keaps?'

May flushed.

'I was instructing you to swear in the next

117

witness; I only hope she can enlighten the jury a little more than this last one.'

Rose Flood virtually scuttled back to her seat. May escorted Helen Jennings across the courtroom. 'If you were even a little fond of Clarice,' she whispered, 'tell us everything you know; she didn't deserve to be remembered like this.'

Helen Jennings waited until May was back at her table before taking a deep breath and fixing her gaze on the picture of the King just above the jury's heads.

'I knew she had sadness in her life, but not about the baby. Four months back, a man she was crazy over up and chucked her for another woman. Just like that. Beside herself she was. She got worse as time went on instead of better; stopped eating. Then she lost her job as a dance teacher because the manageress said her sour face was bad for business. It weren't fair; it wasn't like she was unhappy on purpose.'

May prayed the jury had been listening as closely as she had because it was now a real possibility that it had been a carelessness in looking after herself that had caused Clarice to take an overdose. And neglect and negligence did not add up to suicide. She thought Colonel Tindal was arriving at the same conclusion because she could feel the emanation of his displeasure.

'I think that is more than enough prattling of emotion and unsubstantiated opinions from which to draw conclusions as to the deceased's state of mind. The next testimony, Miss Keaps, and I sincerely trust it will prove to be more informative than everything else the court has

118

had to listen to.'

May stood and walked across to the witness stand. Brilliant Chang joined her for the last few yards. He leaned in until she could smell the spicy perfume of his hair oil.

'Please remember I am a student of Confucius. I do not wish to cause you embarrassment by refusing to take the oath so please do administer the affirmation in the Chinese way.'

She clenched her fists in an effort to keep from responding. How dare her patronise her as if it were her first day in the job? She'd already placed a saucer on the floor in front of the stand but now was almost tempted to step on it and making him wait while she went to the kitchenette to fetch a new one. She settled instead for thrusting it at him as if it was red-hot.

Brilliant Chang acknowledged that he would declare to speak the truth the whole truth, and nothing but the truth; and if he said anything contrary to the truth then may it draw down an imprecation upon him. Then he lifted the saucer to shoulder-height and brought it down on the wooden rail. There was a scream or two from the gallery as it exploded into shards.

'That will be enough of that.' Colonel Tindal glared the residual fluttering into silence. 'Those present who are not appearing as witnesses are here on my sufferance and I will have all of you evicted if there are any more interruptions to the proceedings.' He sat back. 'Now you may enlighten the jury as to how you were acquainted with the deceased.'

Brilliant Change looked directly at Mrs Gem. 'I

119

knew your daughter, madam, only fleetingly. I had seen her in my nightclub on occasion and, as a kindness, gave her a trial as a dancer. It was in the week before the tragedy of her death that she came to me and I agreed. It was true to say that I felt sorry for her. She told me that she was desperate for what she called a fresh start. Everyone deserves as many of those as they can get and I was in the fortunate position of being able to grant her one. But she turned up on the appointed evening looking most unsuitable. It is with much heaviness in my heart that I have to tell you that I sent her away with the instruction to get a good night's sleep and to come back when she had reclaimed her pretty looks. For that I am truly sorry.'

He bent his head for a moment then looked again at Mrs Gem. She nodded once. May could feel the sharing of sentiment between them. This was no act on his part.

Colonel Tindal didn't seem to be as impressed. 'Were you the deceased's secret lover?'

'No. On my life, no.'

'That may come to pass. If you were merely acquainted by virtue of being her potential employer then why, as my officer has seen fit to remark in my notes, did she refer to you by an inappropriately informal sobriquet?'

'When I first left life onboard ship to settle here, I found that the English have difficulties distinguishing between one Chinese name and another. So I adopted the name that many had already begun to call me, Brilliant; they said for my smile. This some shortened to Billy. In my world I have dealings with many women – mainly singers and

120

dancers – and most appear to have a fondness for calling me by this name. I regard it as the English do as a sign of affection, not intimacy.'

An outburst of giggling from the gallery which Colonel Tindal silenced with a look. 'So that we do not misunderstand each other over semantics I will ask you directly: did you make it possible for Clarice Gem to undergo an abortion?'

Brilliant Chang appeared to totter slightly. As before, May was sure his reaction was sincere; the man was a curious mixture of emotional honesty and studied artifice. His solicitor leapt to his feet.

'The coroner is well aware that such an accusation must be withdrawn unless any evidence can be produced to substantiate it.'

Colonel Tindal's facial muscles twitched. 'I am at liberty to make any postulations I see fit appertaining to an unnatural death. You however, sir, are permitted to speak only when I request that you do so. I suggest that you serve your client by sitting back down, and preparing yourself for such questions as I may choose to ask being repeated in a higher court. Such as this one for example: it is well-known that your race freely engages in the practice of taking drugs. Did you supply the cocaine that killed Clarice Gem?'

The solicitor was on his feet again. May had to admire his dedication, if not his self-preservation; Colonel Tindal had handed out spells in gaol for what he thought of as professional undermining of his authority.

'My client can only tell the truth as he has sworn to do and cannot defend himself against

121

ill-informed rumour. Needless to say, he is not – and never has been – involved in such a terrible business as trafficking drugs. He is a respectable entertainment entrepreneur.'

May was expecting Colonel Tindal to fire back a withering comment but he unaccountably seemed to have run out of steam. She sat with her pencil poised as he pulled at his side-whiskers and examined something fascinating on the wooden surface in front of him. Someone in the gallery shuffled and coughed. Eventually the coroner turned his head and focused on Brilliant Chang.

'You may return to your seat. I feel sure that the jury has heard enough to make up their minds. I will now sum up the evidence.' He cleared his throat. 'Clarice Gem died of cocaine poisoning in the early hours of the morning of...' He looked at May.

'Monday 1st March.'

'...Administered by her own hand. It seems she was in the habit of taking the substance on a regular basis but on this occasion dissolved it in water which, according to medical opinion, would have led to a prolonged and agonising death.'

May paused in her note taking long enough to shoot a glance at Mrs Gem. The woman must've become hardened to the whole ordeal because she didn't flinch. But just because she hadn't felt the force of the blow now didn't mean that she wouldn't later. In fact she would probably replay it in her dreams forever.

'You have heard witnesses attest on the one hand that she was perfectly happy in the days prior to the incident, and on the other that she was *fed up*.

It is up to you to decide what her mood might have been on the night in question. Further, you have heard she was involved in an unsatisfactory love affair with a man who may, or may not, be present in this courtroom. Lastly, she was a young woman with such a flagrant disregard for the sanctity of life that she, at some time undetermined, murdered her unborn child. However not content with committing one grievous sin, she ended her life with another.'

May moved her forearm across the table. The shorthand pad hit the floor with a dull slap. She'd had to stop him; there were too many reporters present for him to continue making such outrageously prejudicial statements. Whether he took the hint or had finished his summing up anyway, Colonel Tindal motioned for her to rise to accept her oath.

'You shall well and truly keep this jury upon this inquiry without meat, drink or fire; you shall not suffer any persons to speak to them, nor speak to them yourself, unless it be to ask them if they have agreed upon their verdict. So help you God.'

Knowing their cue, the jury stood up and followed May to the coroner's chambers.

It was less than half an hour before they were all back in their places in the courtroom. It felt to May as if everyone was holding their breath as the jury foreman stood, tucking his fingers into his waistcoat pockets.

'We find that the deceased, Clarice Gem, killed herself while unsound of mind.'

Colonel Tindal's jowls turned puce and his face

123

seemed to be melting with sweat. 'This is the verdict of you all?'

'It is.'

'The coroner's officer will enter your decision. But the court will hear why I feel it is an erroneous one. There is no doubt that the deceased was an habitual drug user which is in itself an illegal act. Furthermore, she took her life via a proscribed substance. Therefore on both counts she was guilty of self-murder and the only verdict according to the letter of the law is felo de se. *Jervis* is quite clear on the definition ... *he who deliberately puts an end to his own existence, or commits any unlawful act, the consequences of which is his own death. It is a direct and deliberate purpose of self-destruction...* I do not hold with this modern notion that people who kill themselves are blighted with insanity. Before long it will be said about all murderers too and then the laws of retribution – an eye for an eye and a tooth for a tooth – will be nothing but a hollow mockery.'

His previous lethargy seemed to have left him completely. May could almost believe he'd been helping himself to some of his brandy in the recess if she hadn't been standing outside his door keeping watch over the jury. He pointed at Brilliant Chang.

'As for you, I have seen too many cases pass through this court where a craving for cocaine has led to white women cavorting with foreign devils who, with their wiles, succeed in transforming them from innocent, to tainted, prey.' He looked up at the gallery. 'I hope the men of the press present will take the opportunity to pillory this

124

perjurer in their newspapers; when the law's hands are tied for lack of evidence, then let the voice of public opinion take over. If I had my way, all those connected to the foul trade of selling drugs would be flogged.'

He stood up and left for his chambers to a chorus of booing from the women in the gallery. May was too stunned to leave her seat and watched as some of them leaned over the rail to wave at Brilliant Chang. The reporters were falling over each other to be the first to file their copy. She felt sickened and cheated that Clarice's death had been turned into such a sideshow. Mrs Gem seemed to be the only person in the courtroom – apart, she had to admit, from Brilliant Chang – to be comporting herself with any dignity. May went over to her and, once more, offered her condolences. Mrs Gem stared at her with tight lips, grunted, and walked away.

May finished typing up the report. She was about to take it through for Colonel Tindal to sign when she sat back down and scrolled a sheet of headed notepaper into the typewriter. There hadn't been a whiff of justice in the entire life of the case. She couldn't do anything about the verdict but she could try to do something to make sure Brilliant Chang didn't get off scot-free for his part in Clarice Gem's final misery.

The letter she typed was to Scotland Yard stating that the coroner requested they take action to put a stop to the cocaine trafficking he had reason to believe was operating out of the Palm Court Nightclub in Gerrard Street. She hammered in the last full stop. There, nothing like a bit of police harassment to wipe the self-satisfied smile off Brilliant Chang's face. May pulled the letter out with a flourish. Colonel Tindal would be anxious to get off to his club and if he did bother to read her words he'd probably assume he had asked her to type them; he was forgetting so many things these days.

She had got her signatures and was back at her desk when Jack Cahill popped his head around the door.

'Hello, busy lady. Seems I missed a treat. There's a real buzz in the pressroom; d'you think I could have a copy of the coroner's closing speech?'

'I doubt any of it was much fun for Mrs Gem.' She opened the drawer to find a stamp. 'If you are so interested in courtroom proceedings then you should have been there.'

He pushed his glasses up the bridge of his nose. 'I would've been if I hadn't had other fish to fry.' He took three paces across the room and reached the window. 'So this is where it all happens is it? More of a sweatbox than even my little cubicle. Didn't think conditions could be any worse than for a junior reporter.' He raised his fist. 'Up the workers I say.'

He came back and perched on the edge of her desk. May snatched up the letter to Scotland Yard before he could read it. He didn't seem to notice as he set about straightening a paperclip.

'You might have to start referring to me as your partner in crime from now on for other reasons.'

'It may surprise you to learn that I don't refer to you at all.' His crackling energy was beginning

126

to grate on her frustrations.

'Aren't you even a little bit curious as to why?'

'PC Collier is going to arrest you for being drunk on the evidence of wearing that jacket in public.'

Jack tugged at the lapels. 'What's wrong with it? Fine Donegal tweed I'll have you know.'

'Give it back to the sheep then.'

'I'm to have my first front page story. A piece I've written about winkling out the key witness in Clarice Gem's terrible demise. Just filed it.'

'What? You didn't do anything. Of all the cheating liars...'

'Hey, take it easy. In my honourable profession it's called working together, co-operation.'

'I can't see ever wanting to work with you. All you care about is a good story. My concern is to uncover the truth, yours is only helping yourself.'

'We would be helping each other. Don't you want people to know what a resourceful and efficient coroner's officer you are?'

May looked into his eyes for traces of sarcasm. Could he have guessed about her systematic covering up of Colonel Tindal's mistakes and omissions? He'd only need to have asked Dr Swan a few questions about past inquests to draw his own conclusions. And that was without knowing the origin of the sentiments in the letter she was holding.

'I'll deliver the text of the coroner's closing remarks to your office by the end of the day. Not that I expect you'll bother to read it; I'm sure you'll have made up your own version of events by then.'

He gave her a wink and skipped off the desk and out of the room, leaving her at least with a focus for her anger.

Chapter Twelve

It was Saturday and May should've been humping the basket of dirty bed linen to the washhouse. Except she couldn't face it. Why do something as boring as housework when there was a sticking door that – literally – cried out for attention? She fetched her brother's tools from the cupboard under the stairs; Albert had been apprenticed to a master carpenter and had ambitions to be a cabinetmaker. But of course he would now never get the chance. The soft stroke of wood under her fingertips always brought him back as she imagined him looking over her shoulder and sharing in her pleasure. She rolled up the sleeves of her overalls, selected a screwdriver, and sat cross-legged on the kitchen floor to set about removing the hinges.

May hummed as she coaxed the damp pine into obeying her will. It was only when she was doing things like this that she was grateful for her dockers' mitts – a daintier pair of hands could never span enough to grip the plane at just the right angle. She shaved away the last sliver and checked the edge was now completely smooth. She'd done a good job of it; Albert would be proud. There was just enough time left to re-fit the

128

door, sweep up, and start on the apple, raisin and cinnamon pie that was to be her peace offering.

Sally was due for supper. May hadn't seen her since their frosty ride back on the bus from Gerrard Street. She knew her friend had been offended that she'd treated her like a soft-in-the-head relative in front of Brilliant Chang but it would've been unethical to explain what she suspected him of, and what a danger she thought him to susceptible women. She'd sent Alice to the tailor's in Grundy Street with the invitation on Wednesday, only for her to return with a reply that could hardly have been said to be enthusiastic. But that was moody girls for you; it was impossible to separate the message from the dismissal of everything not of direct interest. She was up in her room now probably ticking off the remaining hours to her first rehearsal – the only thing she seemed to think the sun worth rising for these days.

May had washed her face and changed into her print frock by the time Sally let herself in the back door. She paused beside the range, sniffed the air, and shrugged.

'No one can say I'm hard on the pocket to win around.'

'I'm sorry, Sal.'

And that was all it took. Sally hobbled over to give May a peck on the cheek. Then she sat at the kitchen table, the hessian bag she'd been carrying at her feet.

'I wouldn't say no to a glass of beer if you have one.'

May pulled a pottery flagon from the pail of cold water under the sink. 'I sent Alice out to the Spotted Dog. Supper will be about an hour. Boiled chicken do you?'

'I'd eat the coalman's horse if it was cooked for me.'

'Are things that bad?'

May filled two glasses and set them on the table.

'I'm tired, that's all.'

'Well, drink this. The working week's over now.'

'Not until I've done Alice's fitting.'

'That can wait for another time; I want you to relax.'

'It won't take a minute. Besides, it's a gift from God to see how good my clothes can look for a change.' She pushed her frizzy fringe away from her eyes. 'Is she in?'

'It's her night off. Shall I go and call her?'

'Ask her to slip this on.' She handed over the hessian bag.

When May returned to the kitchen Sally had moved the glasses onto the draining board, her box of pins and a triangle of buff-coloured tailor's chalk in their place on the table.

'Sal, before she comes down, I've a favour to ask.' She tried to keep her voice light.

'When have I not had to sing for my supper?'

'You don't have to do anything. Just hold my hand as it were. I need to have a talk with Alice and I'm scared it'd end in a row without you here.'

'She in trouble?'

'No. One of the recent inquests has been upsetting me, and I realised it's partially because what happened to the young woman made me think of how vulnerable Alice is. I know I can't stop her working in the theatre if that's what she wants but I don't want her prey to those racy types who think picking up a local girl comes with the price of the ticket.'

'Like you're suddenly an expert?'

May bit back her reply as Alice made her entrance. She'd taken it upon herself to borrow the dove-grey sandals but the effect was too stunning for May to complain; her sister looked tall and film star slim with just the right amount of curves in just the right places. Alice dropped her pose to give Sally a quick welcoming hug.

'On the table. I want to pin the hem.'

Alice stepped up using the chair. Her head skimmed the ceiling.

'You seen the cobwebs up here? Look, over there in the corner.'

May flicked at her legs with the teacloth she was holding. Sally tutted.

'If you don't keep still I'll be sticking these into you instead of the dress.'

Alice stood with her hands by her side. She exuded a confidence in her beauty possessed by those who were unaware of the effect it caused on others. May hoped that wouldn't change as Alice grew up, and that she wouldn't have her heart broken too often. The water began to spit and she dropped in the potatoes.

Sally finished marking out the darts. 'Go and slip this off without pulling at it. And be careful of the pins, blood will be hard to shift from such a light background.'

'Twenty minutes, mind.' May replaced the lid on the saucepan, 'before supper's on the table. And, guest or no guest, it's your turn to do the clearing up.'

Alice skipped down off the chair, gave May a mock pout, and sashayed away as if she'd been wearing heels all her life.

They finished the flagon of beer over supper. May sent Alice to buy some more. Her sister had been lively and entertaining over the meal – giving a bitingly accurate impression of gossipy Mrs Green – but she'd felt in need of another glass or two if they were to have that talk. She put the kettle on for the washing up before sitting back down and watching Sally sewing running stitches.

'If you won't let me repair that chair for you, what else can I do in payment for making the dress?'

'You can come and read to bubba sometimes. My eyes get sore and she says she's tired of the sound of my voice anyway. Maybe something else as well...'

'What?'

'Let me make you a blouse. There's enough of that material left.'

Alice breezed back into the kitchen.

'I was telling your sister she needs to brighten herself up.'

Alice poured them all some beer. 'I saw Mary Pickford and she had all these frills around her neck like soap bubbles.'

May frowned. 'In case you hadn't noticed we

live in Poplar, not Hollywood.'

Sally bit off the end of the cotton and bundled the dress back in her bag. 'A little softness around your face would be flattering. In all that schmutter you wear you could be from those old photographs in the library – the ones of women chopping fish on the quay.'

'And there I was thinking you see me more as a ship's weathered figurehead.'

Her friend shrugged as if to say that it had crossed her mind only she was too polite to say so. May laughed; it was good to be with someone who enjoyed the challenge of a spirited tease.

Alice, however, was regarding her seriously. 'It's lipstick and powder that'll make the real difference. Let's have a go now; I've some upstairs.'

'If you've money for extravagances then I could do with something towards the housekeeping.'

'I didn't buy nothing. Vi at the theatre gave them to me. They were her old and she said I should use them to practise for when I'm on stage.' She threw herself out of the room.

May wiped away the beer suds from the rim of the glass with her finger. 'Next thing she'll be painting herself to go out on the street. Our mother would never have approved.'

'Times change. She's young and having fun growing up. Drink up and quit with the sour face.'

'I know you think I'm trying to interfere too much in her life but I don't want her trying to look any more sophisticated that she is; it'll only get her into the sort of trouble I'm not sure she's equipped to get out of. And this Vi might not be

133

the best influence as far as that is concerned; I was pleased for her when she got a part in the show, I really was, but I'm scared this might just be the beginning.'

'Make a point of meeting the woman, and then judge if you have to. But remember your sister will choose her glamorous new friend over you, if pushed.'

Alice came back in carrying a lipstick and compact as if they were the crown jewels. She pulled a chair over to where the light from the gas mantle was strongest.

'Let me do you. Please.'

First Sally with the scarf and then this; it felt like a conspiracy. But if she capitulated then Alice might just repay her by listening to what she had to say without flying off the handle.

'I think I need some more beer first.'

May drained her glass and topped them all up again.

'Off you go then, I'm all yours. Do your worst.'

Alice began by stroking her hair off her forehead and pressing it back gently with her palm. Then she dabbed the powder puff here and there. Next she slicked on the sticky lipstick. It was a strange feeling to be ministered to in such an intimate way. May realized that she hadn't been touched so caressingly for a very long time and her eyes filled with tears. She blinked hard.

'The powder is getting up my nose; I'm going to sneeze.'

'Another second. That's all ... there. What do you think, Sally?'

'That you're a pair of bookends in your beauty.

134

Your mother would be proud of you both.'

That did make the tears flow. But May didn't mind because now she had a legitimate reason for crying. Alice blotted her cheeks with the corner of the teacloth.

'Don't spoil it. Look in the mirror.' She held the compact out.

May felt shy in the gaze of the reflection examining her. The cherry redness of the lipstick made her eyes brighter and the powder smoothed out her skin tone without looking plastered on. She looked fresher rather than painted; Alice was certainly talented.

'I'll do it for you whenever you like. Why don't you keep this?' She handed May the lipstick. 'Vi gave me a pink one, too, which looks much better than that.'

May caught Sally looking at her. What was that she'd said about learning to accept gifts graciously? 'Thank you.' She slipped it into her frock pocket. 'Now, set to with that washing up while I make the coffee. Want a cup, Sal?'

'Who am I to turn down what I am not so well placed to come by?'

May felt herself bristle. Yes, it was true she didn't come by her beans in a strictly legitimate way but everyone in the docks did it – a split sack here, a damaged crate there; how else were families supposed to make ends meet? She was, however, acutely aware of this chink in her integrity as coroner's officer.

Alice clattered a plate on the draining board. 'Don't know how you two can drink that stuff. It's revolting. I've more of a sweet tooth myself;

135

shame we never have chocolates for afters. Strawberry creams are my favourites.'

May wondered how many boxes had been slipped under the grille with the money for the tickets. This was the moment to bring the topic up. The coffee could wait.

'Leave the saucepan to soak and come and sit down. I need to talk to you.'

'I thought we'd been doing that all evening.'

'But this is serious.'

Alice dried her hands and joined them at the table. 'What have I done wrong now? Because it's not very nice to tear me off a strip in front of Sally.'

'I've no intention of doing that. I just want to make sure you know to keep your wits about you when it comes to men.'

'This ain't going to be the birds and bees is it? Because you're years too late to tell me about sex.'

May knew her face was registering shock.

'I don't mean that,' Alice leapt in, 'what sort of a girl do you think I am? And I can spot a stage door Johnny a mile off. Blimey, what it is to be thought a tart by your own flesh and blood.'

The beer was making her even more defensive than usual. May looked across at Sally for help.

'Listen to what she has to say and cut the smart remarks that feel good in your mouth but leave a taste like the bitterest of coffee beans. Your sister is concerned for your welfare and you should be grateful she loves you enough to be so. Spurn her efforts now, then when you have grown into enough humility to ask for her wisdom you may find she has decided you are no longer worth the effort.'

May was astonished to see Alice dip her head. Perhaps failing to adopt such a direct approach was the mistake she'd been making all along. Or it could simply be that harsh appraisal was easier to swallow when it came from outside the family. She took a steadying breath.

'You're at the age when it's natural to be interested in boys – and maybe try on a little romance for size. But I need to know you'll be careful who you agree to go out with.'

'Be like you and stay at home all the time, you mean.'

Sally held her finger to her lips and Alice flushed.

'Women my age had everything messed up by the War. I'm glad things will be better for you – truly I am – but the absence of men in our lives recently hasn't exactly been a good preparation.'

'I see plenty of them right enough. Some are always at it bringing different girls to the theatre each night. Hanging on their arms they are, all giggling and twittering, but anyone can see how they're going to be treated by the end of the night. I ain't stupid. I know what goes on.'

The contempt in her voice was the confirmation May needed: like every other young girl Alice would make her mistakes, but throwing her virtue away wasn't going to be one of them.

'You should see the way Vi treats them. Like she's gazing over their heads to the gallery while she tells them she's delighted they enjoyed the entertainment and next time to bring their friends.

She's a real pro, is Vi.'

'Well she certainly sounds like just the person to show you the ropes. Look, I've an idea, why don't you invite her here for tea? I'd really like to meet her.'

'When? Tomorrow?'

Alice's excitement was like stage lights all being turned on at once.

'She's got herself a spot in the regular show come Monday next and I don't reckon she'll have much time then.'

'Hold your horses. Vi isn't the only one with responsibilities and pressing commitments. I'll check the courtroom diary and you let me know when your gruesome manager needs you and we'll work something out.'

'Can I leave the saucepan until the morning and write her a proper invitation?'

'Go on then. But don't promise anything fancy.'

Alice kissed her, then Sally, and left the kitchen humming.

'Not bad, May Keaps, not bad. I'll make something like decent wife and mother material of you yet.' Sally raised herself stiffly from the chair. 'And while we're in the mood for delivering and receiving truths, I will say this one more time and then may my tongue flame in my head if I mention it again. Don't leave it too late or when you are old and lonely you will wonder why you did. Now I'm off to get my beauty sleep. Thank you for a lovely evening. Sleep well.'

She kissed the top of May's head before letting herself out of the back door.

The world was spinning as May slipped on her nightgown and got into bed. She shouldn't have sat up to finish the beer. The sheets felt clammy against her skin. She turned and hugged the pillow as the sounds of a nighttime in the docks cradled her – men's voices returning from the pub; dogs barking; the distant rumble of the trains shunting in the coal-yards; the raising and lowering of cranes and winches. The hoot of a steamer. It was comforting to know that in the morning it would all still be waiting for her to take up her part in it again. She slowed her breathing and relaxed into sleep.

The current is pushing against her arms as she swims. A series of humps in the water – the wake of a ship long gone – buoys her up then drops her. She flips onto her back to look at the moon. It isn't quite full yet – another day or so and then the tide would turn and sweep her out to sea like a message in a bottle. Where would she wash up? On a desert island ... or the shores of Africa where the sun would beat down and the spaces in her head fill with the scents of cinnamon and nutmeg?

But then the water starts rushing in her ears, down her throat, up her nose. The wet is wrapping itself around her lungs and choking her. She wants to cough. She wants to scream. The river bottom is clawing at her. Fingers of weed entwining her ankles. If she cries hard enough maybe she can make herself light enough to float again. She is desperate to be back on the surface feeling the air on her face and gazing at the moon.

May jerked awake. The bedclothes were twisted

around her, trapping her arms. Her nightgown was soaked with sweat, her cheeks wet with tears. She stayed conscious long enough to strip herself naked, throw the blankets off, and pull the sheet up to her chin.

She turns the key and is walking inside. She crosses the space between them; it isn't so very far. Now the feel of the cotton under her finger-tips as she runs her hand along one side of the outline. Taller than she remembers. She clutches at the sheet and pulls it down. His eyes are star-ing back. He is wearing the red scarf Sally bought her. It covers the tidemark of his dockers' tan. A ripple goes through his muscles. He sits up.

'Hello, Dad,' she says.

'You took your time.'

'I came as soon as I could.'

'As soon as you felt like it.'

'As soon as I could.'

'They tell me you're allowed three questions.'

'Who?'

'That's one of them.'

'How?'

'Did I get here? I was swimming over to France; I wanted you home.'

'Why?'

'To look after Alice. I knew I couldn't do it much longer. She needed you. I needed you. And now you know what it's like to be left holding the baby.'

'But why did you have to show me that way?'

He mimes threading a needle. Then, stitch by stitch, sews up his lips.

'You could speak to me again if you wanted –

they can't stop you. Just tell me why...'

He reaches with a bony hand and pulls away the scarf. A bloodless gash grins from ear to ear.

May fought against the hands. They were holding her shoulders. Pressing her down. Trying to suffocate her. To take her with him.

'Wake up. Wake up. Please...'

Alice. The fear in her voice cutting through the last veils of unreality.

'You were screaming. I was so scared. And then you wouldn't wake up. I thought you were dead.' She began to sob. 'I didn't know what to do. I thought you'd left me too...'

May jumped to her knees and hugged her so tight she heard her spine crack. When Alice had stopped shuddering she laid her down and covered them both up. The last thing she saw before she fell asleep again was her little sister sucking her thumb.

Chapter Thirteen

Monday morning found May jittery from emotional exhaustion and lack of sleep. Sunday night had hardly been much better than Saturday. Alice had followed her around all day like a puppy – even lending a hand to clean out the range; this sticking to her side like glue had culminated in her asking if she could share May's bed. She wouldn't talk about it but it was as if she was scared May would disappear the moment she lost sight of her.

Alice's snoring had been disturbing but at least the sleep May did get was nightmare free. She'd had variations on those dreams almost every night for the first few months after she'd come back from France but then it dwindled to just when she'd been overwrought or distressed by something that had happened at work. She assumed it was Clarice Gem's suicide that had triggered it this time. The lack of answers. The absence of anyone asking the right questions.

But groggy though she was, she still had a job to do. There was Dr Swan's invoice to chase up with the London County Council's accounts department, and some papers to append to a report for the Registrar of Deaths. She knew Colonel Tindal wouldn't be coming in today, a dentist's appointment he'd said. Two letters had arrived in the post addressed to him and marked *personal*. May walked through to put them on his desk.

When she came back, she had a visitor. PC Collier. Obviously not here on official business because he was making no effort to rein in his schoolboy excitement at seeing her. His cheeks were the colour of blood-oranges.

'To what do I owe this pleasure?'

He shuffled from one foot to the other. 'I wondered ... if you can spare the time ... if it isn't too much of a palaver ... if you could see your way to...'

'Spit it out, man.'

Her impersonation of the coroner was so accurate – down to the husky catch in the throat – that they dissolved into giggles. This young man's company was just what she needed.

142

'A cuppa and a rest of me feet what's called for. They had me on point duty again. Corner of East India Dock Road. You ain't seen nothing like it. Traffic all backed up. Reckon there must be a passenger steamer due in.'

He was properly relaxed now. Talking as he would do to a mate in the station instead of to the coroner's officer. May realised she didn't know his first name But she wasn't going to ask, she was pleased he had sought her out but it wouldn't be fair to encourage him He'd flicked the chinstrap off and laid his helmet on top of the filing cabinet.

'Bring in a chair from the vestibule while I put a kettle on the gas.'

The amenities in the kitchenette consisted of a tap and a sink, one ring, and a small cupboard for crockery. May was always grateful that grieving relatives invariably came singly or in pairs. Any more and she'd be hard pushed to fulfil her offer of a soothing cup of tea.

'Aching to take my boots off, truth be told, but even removing the helmet's against regulations while on duty.'

She hated to admit it but it was nice to hear a male voice calling through to her, it made her feel secure. Where had that word come from? A hangover from the nightmare probably.

At last the tea was brewed and she carried the tray through. 'The milk's on the turn I'm afraid. I could pop out for some fresh.'

'Don't you be putting yourself out none. I'll take it as it comes.'

May poured them both a cup. There was a slightly awkward moment as she had to brush his knees to get past to her chair. A gentleman would have stood up and stepped away. But he was not much more than a boy really, and one that was hardly going to complain about her being in such close proximity. She squashed a spurt of irritation. This was why she chose to *keep men at arms' length* as Sally put it; they always seemed set on imposing their needs on you: another undigested morsel from the world of her dreams. May watched as he plopped in five sugar lumps then took a sip.

'Shouldn't you be stirring that?'

'I like to have it all standing at the bottom. As if having a toffee for afters.'

May smiled. He reminded her so much of Alice.

'D'you remember the Pryer family used to live at the end of your street? Moved to Seymour Court.'

May vaguely recollected drunken rows, and bundles of men's clothing being thrown from the top window for the milkman's horse and cart to run over.

'Well, we had him in the cells last week – something and nothing really. He'd been caught relieving himself in someone's doorway then threw a punch at the sergeant when he asked him to move along. I went to see his missus to tell her he'd be up in the police court and not to expect him with the wages. But she weren't in and I was checking the nippers had something to eat when I found the larder fall of watches and wallets and other stuff that'd been nicked. Seems she came home with them of a Friday night. On the game she was. Put me in a bit of a pickle, I can tell you. I couldn't see my way to arresting her and leaving

144

four young 'uns with no one to care for them.'

'So what did you do?'

'Took the stuff and left a note saying as she'd be robbed again regular if she weren't there to see that she wasn't.'

The young man would never go far in the police force but his inherent compassion made him a remarkably decent human being. May hoped she brought even a little of the same to her own role.

'Got to do a shift next on the beat down Canning Town. Reckon they'll find me asleep at my post one day. Station's light on bodies – some's gone and got the influenza and some's been called in by Scotland Yard on account of a Sinn Féin plot they've got wind of.' He stood, retrieved his helmet and put it on. 'Those few of us left ain't hardly got the time to wipe our ... shine our boots.'

After he'd gone, the room felt smaller instead of marginally less cramped. May wondered if that was because his visits were always peopled so much by the outside world.

May worked through until three-thirty and then tidied her desk. She was taking the rest of the afternoon off. She sometimes helped serve the refreshments at the tea dances in the Social Club and had been asked if she'd do the same for a benefit at the Town Hall. It had been organised by the National Federation of Discharged and Demobilised Sailors & Soldiers to raise funds for the Fatherless Children's summer outing. She'd approached Colonel Tindal a month ago for permission. There weren't many causes close to his heart but her request had resulted in him giving

145

his assent in a gruff voice and with a pull of his side-whiskers. He'd covered this by adding that, as all the local dignitaries would be there, it was appropriate the Office of the Poplar Coroner should be represented – although that didn't mean she wouldn't be expected to make the time up. She didn't mind about that: a couple of hours free from the tyranny of the typewriter now were worth an evening of paperwork any day.

She walked the short way to the Town Hall. The dance wasn't due to start until seven o'clock but would be preceded by an official reception attended by members of the press. The room would need to be decorated with bunting, the tables and chairs arranged so as to make the space more inviting, the punch made, and the food laid out on trays. She hoped they weren't relying on her to do it all.

May needn't have worried. On the stairs she met Mrs Kessler and Mrs Zinzer on their way down to fetch supplies donated from the local pubs and shops; the Reverend Hislop was pinning up a sign above a wicker basket for donations; and through the swing doors a half a dozen women were dashing around correcting what each other was doing. May spotted Mrs Gibson and waved then went over to help Kitty Woodcroft who was struggling to put up a trestle table whilst keeping an eye on her toddler playing in the corner.

Before long it began to look as if something more exciting than a committee meeting might be taking place tonight. May took charge of the punchbowl and glasses as soon as they arrived. The crates of bottles were already stacked against the wall. Taking care not to splash the white tablecloth she made a weak concoction of red wine and lemonade, flavouring it with slices of orange and a handful of cloves.

She was just debating whether she had enough time to go home and change – the physical work had caused her to sweat more than she would've liked – when Jack Cahill waltzed in. She wondered if he was early for the dance in his drive to get the scoop on everything, or merely strategically too late to lend a hand with the setting up. He was wearing a paraffin-blue suit, the jacket sporting four patch pockets with box pleats and button flaps. To make things worse he had on a red bow tie. He looked as though he had mistaken the event for a fancy-dress party. He made a beeline for the musicians – the only other men in the room – and began talking with them, jotting a few things down on his notepad. A combination of Sally's recent advice and PC Collier's solicitous approach to his fellow man made May swallow the memory of their last social encounter and wave when he looked her way. He took his time in coming over.

'Don't tell me you're wearing that as a favour to the Donegal sheep as well?'

'This is the latest fashion in Dublin, I'll have you know. Okay, I'll admit it took some time getting to us from America. But at least I've made an effort; don't you ever let your hair down just a little? A wisp of lace here and there perhaps? Every time I see you in your skirt and blouse I think you're going to shove a summons in my hand.' He peered over his glasses at her. 'You're not, are you?'

He'd said it all with a smile and May had to admit that she'd deserved the ribbing. *Don't dish out what you can't take* Albert had always told her when she'd run away from him and his friends in tears.

'Not that I'd be surprised if you did; everyone seems to have it in for me these days. I reckon Andy Taylor didn't just pick my name at random when this riveting assignment came up. Good job there's no such thing as garden parties in Poplar or he'd have me covering those as well.'

'We do have an annual allotment competition. The council have turned one of the bombsites from the Zeppelin raids over. Stick around long enough and it could be your lot to judge the carrots.'

Jack pulled a face. It was clear he wasn't exactly local newspaper material.

'He gave me a long list of who to speak to and what angle to take – cheek of it; as if I've never put pencil to pad before – but he didn't tell me it was against the rules to mix a little pleasure with business. So ... Miss Keaps,' he performed a stiffly formal bow, 'will you do me the very great honour of being my partner for the first dance when this all kicks off?'

'Not on your life.'

'Don't sugar-coat it now; tell me what you really think.'

'I come to these things to help out, that's all – do my civic duty you might say – I don't join in.'

'Well maybe you should. Make tonight the first in your letting your hair down campaign.'

She dropped the empty bottle she was holding

148

into the crate and picked up a full one.

'I'm going to tell you something and if your face so much as cracks, so help me, I'll whack you over the head with this... I can't dance.'

'You've got two left feet you mean?'

To give him his due, he didn't even have a glint of amusement in his eyes.

'No. I just don't know how to. I never got around to learning and now I feel a little long in the tooth to be staggering around a dance floor like a child who's just moved up from standing on her father's shoes.

Jack dipped a glass into the punchbowl and took a sip. 'I think even I'd need something a little stronger than this inside me to get going – despite the fact we Irish are ready to dance a jig at the drop of a hat.'

'How's life at Mrs Loader's?'

'Now you're treading on my toes. It doesn't look like I'm going to be there for much longer.'

'I hope you weren't just messing her around by taking the room, she might've lost a better tenant because of it.'

'It won't be by choice, I can assure you, but my career hardly seems to be taking off in the way I expected.'

May harboured the evil thought that it was no more than he deserved after his blatant highjacking of her identification of Brilliant Chang. She'd read the piece in the paper; her name hadn't been mentioned once. Perhaps Andy Taylor had seen through Jack's unsubtle self-promotion and had sent him here to clip his wings a little. But taking pleasure in someone else's disappointments and failures wasn't kind so she forced a look of sympathy.

'Give it a little more time, you've only just started.'

'You don't get many chances to make a big splash in the newspaper game and it looks like the one I was pinning all my hopes on is dead in the water. I've let everything else slip to make it come good and if I can't produce something like a story then I'm going to be accused of not pulling my weight and probably get the sack.'

He looked so despondent May began to feel genuinely sorry for him

'What went wrong with all your grand plans?'

'It began with the police mounting a series of drugs raids on that nightclub. The touts for the gambling dens stopped coming in. Then things got a whole lot worse because the club closed – doors just locked for good with no warning. So there's me, on the street with no contacts and no way of finding them. All those wasted hours drinking overpriced watery spirits and ruining my eardrums with singers whose only talent lies in making it impossible to mistake them for a man.'

May shifted the crate of empty bottles to the floor so she could smile without offending him. Her plan to scupper Brilliant Chang's cocaine sideline was working. Maybe he had even been arrested; she'd ask PC Collier to make some enquiries. She straightened up again.

'Somehow it doesn't sound like you to give up so easily.'

'Funny you should say that because suddenly

150

I'm having second thoughts about that myself. It's seeing you again that's done it; you're quite an inspiration to me, Miss Keaps. I've realised I'm here staring an alternative source of information right in her pretty face.'

'You won't get anything out of me that isn't public knowledge; everything else is the property of the coroner.'

It was as if he couldn't stop from being annoying for long. His willingness to exploit her yet again in the service of his ambition was nothing short of insulting.

'I don't expect any spilling of state secrets, just proposing you keep your ear to the ground and let me know if you hear who's doing the inviting to the gambling dens. After all, you may well need my help one day and, to a reporter, an obligation is almost as sacred as his word.'

She doubted that. On both counts.

'I don't know how the coroners operate in Ireland but over here if I need your assistance in investigations then you are legally compelled to give it. So, as there'll be no back-scratching going on I suggest you go and interview the mayor, who's just arrived, and start worming your way into your editor's good books. But I will give you one piece of insider information...'

She leaned across the table.

'...you'll find a list of forthcoming inquests in the stop press of your own newspaper. Goodbye, Mr Cahill.'

May picked up the empty plate and walked to the kitchen to slice some more oranges. As she pushed open the door she threw a glance over her shoulder. He was standing where she'd left him, cleaning his glasses. From now on maybe things would be clearer for him in more ways than one.

Chapter Fourteen

'Okay, but only on the understanding that you take the kid under your wing; she looks as prey for wolves as if she'd just stepped out of a production of *Red Riding Hood*.'

Horatio was wasted at the beck and call of his father's cough linctus empire, but he was a poor judge of character when it came to young women. Vi had already clocked how often the delectable Miss Keaps batted her eyelids in the box office to flirt her way around the manager's demands; if anything, it was the would-be predators who needed to be on their guard.

They were snatching a quick cup of coffee in the dining rooms down the road from the Gaiety. Vi had been running through the bill positions she'd envisaged for the turns she'd decided on and, when they'd come to her proposal that Alice should open the second half, Horatio had looked doubtful. Vi had acknowledged the girl was inexperienced, but had pointed out that the patrons would've been propping up the theatre bar in the interval and therefore needed a touch of winsome sentimentality to quieten them down.

'Whatever you say, boss.'

'You make it sound like I'm actually paying you.'

Vi returned his smile. 'Not in money, no. How are the arrangements for Glasgow coming along?'

'Full steam ahead. We're both booked for the whole week. You're to do your Shakespeare scene; I'm the headline act of course.'

Vi tried to ignore the stab of professional jealousy. Although Horatio was a competent magician with a good line in patter, this was his first legitimate theatrical engagement. She wondered what inducements he'd had to offer to secure his place as top of the bill. She drank her coffee to allow the resentment to settle.

'So we're to go straight up after the talent show?'

'I'd prefer it if you remained here for a day or two. Travel up separately. We don't want tongues wagging. And, besides, I've a few things I need to finalise. On my own.'

'That'll mean I have to give the landlady another week's rent. Even with the slot in the regular show I'd be hard pushed to manage that with enough left over for my new costume.'

'I'll see you right if it becomes necessary. And, believe me, it'll be worth every extra penny when you see what I've got lined up for us north of the border.'

It wasn't like him to be so secretive. In all the theatrical – and other – dealings they'd had over the past two years, Horatio had always been forthcoming; remarkably so at times. Vi smiled. And then it came to her that maybe whatever he was so intent in keeping from her had nothing to do with business at all. Perhaps it was personal.

153

The most personal thing there could possibly be between two people. Conducted far away from the puritanical gaze of his father. Horatio was a romantic underneath it all and an elopement to Gretna Green would be just the sort of surprise he'd relish pulling out of his hat. She hugged the delicious prospect of spending the rest of her life with the man who had stolen her heart – and her favours – the first night they'd met. But she wouldn't spoil his little boy excitement by letting on she knew.

'Come on, back to the fray. We need to tell the scene painters what we want on the flats.'

He pushed his chair back. 'Good job I've got you to keep me on the straight and narrow. I'd be lost otherwise.'

Vi thought she couldn't have put it better herself.

Chapter Fifteen

May was awoken at sunrise by a loud knocking on the door. It was PC Collier with the news that a body had been found and the coroner wanted her in the office immediately. She dressed, left a note for Alice, and was there in a little over thirty minutes. She deposited her coat, hat, gloves, and bag on her desk, picked up a pad and pencil, and went through to the mortuary to see what couldn't have waited until eight o'clock.

Colonel Tindal was standing over the new

154

arrival. With him was Detective Inspector Beecham, who looked across at May.

'I'd advise you not to come too close.' He mopped his brow with a handkerchief.

'Thank you for your concern but I have seen dead bodies before.' The abrupt start to the day had made May tetchy.

'Don't mean that. It's the influenza; reckon I'm the next one has his name on that particular bullet.'

The detective inspector was a wiry man with a face like a whippet's. In the glare of the electric light his grey pallor made his cheekbones even more pronounced May knew he had three small children and hoped his sensible wife had already quarantined them from the infection

'You can take notes from over there, Miss Keaps,' Colonel Tindal waved a hand in her direction. 'But I don't expect to have to repeat myself so pay close attention. The body was found where and at what time?'

The detective inspector took out his notebook. 'An alleyway in Limehouse. Just off the Causeway. First discovered at approximately five o'clock this morning by dockers returning from the timber wharves. I'll be able to be more precise when they've sobered up.'

May waited as Colonel Tindal went through his ritual of taking a pinch of snuff. DI Beecham watched him over the body with a look of acute longing; no doubt any stimulant on offer was the next best thing to being in bed. She made a mental note to go and get him a strong cup of Java from the coffee house across the road before he set off back to the station. Colonel Tindal let out a sharp sneeze before pulling back the sheet.

'Young man in his twenties, I'd say. Looks to be well nourished. Not a sailor certainly. Torso and face badly beaten. Make that, savagely. Was anything found in the pockets?'

The policeman consulted his notes again. 'A wallet. Empty. And a ration card showing an address in Epping. A constable is on his way there now.' He glanced over at May. 'I'll let you have the details for the warrants when we've gathered all the facts.'

'You will supply the names and addresses of the witnesses who discovered the body and any other relevant information to my officer within the hour. A post-mortem will be conducted before the end of the day, and the inquest convened for tomorrow morning.'

Colonel Tindal held his lapels and leaned back as if he'd already heard the jury's verdict.

'Robbery and murder clear as you like. Rest assured this case will be back in the not-so-capable hands of our esteemed police force in no time at all. Now, Miss Keaps, we might as well make a start on other business; I have some letters I wish to dictate.'

May waited until the two men had left the mortuary then walked over to pull the sheet back up over the body. She flinched when she saw the dead man's battered face. Would his mother or father be able to recognise him? She wished they could be spared having to look but the possession of personal effects was not enough to establish identity. She would ensure that she was on hand to escort

156

them through the ordeal in preference to PC Collier or one of his colleagues; in the absence of any other comfort they would be grateful for a woman's presence.

The turnout for the preliminary inquest was the bare minimum – the jury, the two men who had found the body, and Dr Swan. May arranged her papers on the courtroom table. The victim had been identified as Miles Elliott. His father – a shipping owner in the import/export business – had done so with the air of a man who was doing his duty without engaging any of his emotions; a protective strategy she often saw in the early stages of shock. He hadn't yet arrived in the courtroom but May knew the coroner wouldn't wait for him and, for once, she was grateful for Colonel Tindall's refusal to let anything throw him off course. The preliminaries were always difficult for any parent to sit through.

May had sworn in the jury and formally opened the proceedings. The coroner was now engaged in a heated discussion with the foreman. Every now and then he pulled at his side-whiskers and shot accusatory glances at May. She couldn't work out why: it was the jury he'd specified and the foreman one of his favourites, always able to procure a unanimous decision. Colonel Tindal cleared his throat.

'The jury has requested to hear from the witnesses who discovered the body, and then to go and see the location for themselves. Although I regard such a procedure as unnecessary, the law demands that I accede. The first witness.'

May nodded to the docker sitting nearest her and walked with him to the stand. She administered the oath and sat back down.

Colonel Tindal leaned towards him. 'You found the body, did you not?'

'Yes.'

'In a Limehouse alley, I believe?'

'Yes.'

'If you insist on confining yourself to one-word responses then I suspect we will still be in this courtroom when Hell freezes over. Elaborate, man...'

The witness looked at May who nodded encouragingly.

'We was walking home. Having had a bit of a skin-full, truth be told. Humping planks of wood being thirsty work and all that. There was only the two of us, the others having taken for a hankering after a meat pie–'

'Are we now to be subjected to your life story? Place, time and circumstances will suffice.'

'Well, I reckon it was gone five – we'd heard the clock – and was in the Causeway when Norm said he was aching for a slash and I reckoned that was not a bad idea so we nipped into the alley and there we found him. Dead. No mistaking that. Dead as you like. So we did the business we'd come for then off to find a copper.'

'An edifying tale. Makes me proud to be British. Next witness.'

The second docker's version differed in only minor details – mainly whose idea it had been to go into the alley in the first place. He finished just as Colonel Tindal began to look as if he'd burst a blood vessel.

'Miss Keaps, you will arrange for three taxicabs to be at our disposal in ten minutes' time. We will recess until then. However...'

He raked the jury with such a look that some of them flushed or stared at their laps.

'...I will remind you that inside or outside this courtroom, you are on His Majesty's business and will conduct yourselves in the appropriate manner. I will be in my chambers until required.'

He pushed his chair back with a grunt and walked out, muttering to himself.

At first May was unable to find anyone who could come at such short notice but then inspiration struck and she telephoned the Pickford's Removal depot just down the High Street and asked if they had anything that might be suitable. They provided a charabanc they used for staff outings and now it was at the court entrance, some of the jury already sitting at the back as skittish as if they were embarking on a trip to the seaside. May hoped they would settle down before the coroner stepped onboard. He would be in a bad enough mood as it was.

The journey to Limehouse was short and unmemorable. The trouble started when the driver tried to turn off Wills Street into the Causeway. A costermonger with his barrow occupied the corner and refused to move. May had a humiliating vision of the coroner sending her to remonstrate with him. They were attracting enough attention as it was from women with baskets of washing on their hips who stood and stared while raggedy children sidled up to squat beside the wheels and poke at the tyres with sticks. May knew the area – Tom's garage was a stone's throw away in Pennyfields – but that didn't mean she was immune to the poverty. Poplar had its fair share of destitutes but Limehouse embraced them as its own: after all, they had no further to fall.

The driver exercised his power as the only motor vehicle in the vicinity and switched off the engine, the charabanc blocking both the Causeway and Wills Street. May, the jury, and Colonel Tindal got out and plunged past an Oriental grocer's, a bag and sack shop, and a Chinese herbalist. May was looking for the restaurant she'd been told flanked the alleyway. She smelled it first. A warm aroma of fish being fried with something like aniseed. On the other corner was a ship's chandler. With the shouts of a man hawking catmeat from his cart she found it impossible to imagine the circumstances of the young man's death. It was all too ordinary. Thomas Cook brought their tourists here to thrill at Chinese in full robes chasing each other with cleavers but they were actors; in reality the threat of unfettered violence had no more basis in fact than Sax Rohmer's *The Mystery of Dr Fu-Manchu* which May had once returned to the library in disgust.

The jury was now huddled around the entrance to the alleyway. There seemed to be some debate going on concerning how far down a body would have to be before it would remain hidden from the street. May had the uncomfortable sense that some of the men were enjoying this. A break in their humdrum routine it may be but she won-

160

dered how they'd feel when they returned to the courtroom to find Miles Elliott's father waiting for them. It wouldn't have such an air of colourful detective fiction about it then.

She was aware of someone arriving to stand beside her. With a flip of her stomach she recognised Brilliant Chang. She had thought – hoped – that he was beginning a long stretch in prison prior to deportation.

'Would you be so good as to tell me, Miss Keaps, what all these people are doing outside my restaurant?'

So this is where he'd gone to ground after he was forced to close his club. It must've felt to be quite a comedown. Should she seek out Jack and tell him? No, if he was such an ace reporter as he liked to make believe then he could find out for himself. May stepped away from the smell of the Chinaman's cologne, and the aura of his energy.

As she detached herself, she heard a voice call her name from the other side of the street. A group of dockers – all three friends of her father – were waving at her. She felt assaulted by the collision of the worlds of her past, work, and the suave debonairness of the man-about-town scanning her face so intently.

'Miss Keaps, I will ask you again if it is a collusion of the authorities that brings you here. If so, I would like you to know that my business interests are many and varied, but all of them legitimate.'

Colonel Tindal materialised at his shoulder.

'Have you come to Limehouse to seek the confederacy of your countrymen in the practice of extorting money from young girls and plying them with cocaine?'

'I have never done such a thing. And, despite their best endeavours – some less generous than myself would say *hounding* – the police have found nothing to substantiate such a slanderous accusation.'

'There is no automatic corollary between the absence of evidence and the absence of truth. If I find that you are in some way connected with what went on here then I will make it my personal crusade to ensure that you and your evil ilk–'

Acting instinctively, May had pinched his sleeve and pulled him discreetly to one side. Although she agreed with Colonel Tindal in his assessment of this man, as the coroner he should not be expressing such opinions on the public highway.

'I'm sorry, Colonel Tindal, but it is my duty to remind you that Mr Chan has no legal representative present, and besides, the jury might overhear. On your instructions I'll issue a warrant for him to attend the second inquest and you can question him then.'

She thought he was going to spontaneously combust; his jowls were mottled with purple, his mouth hung open like a fish's, and he'd clenched his fists. He'd make her pay for her insubordination later but she'd had to interfere before he'd compromised himself even further – and removed the possibility of them ever getting to the truth of what'd happened to Miles Elliott. He spun away.

'We have been subjected to the distasteful odours of this place long enough. I order everyone to get back to our transportation immediately.' He

162

turned to Brilliant Chang. 'You, sir, I will deal with in due course. And I am not as easily hoodwinked as stupid star-struck girls. So beware.'

He strode off across the road, causing a minister on a bicycle to swerve and hurl curses. May refused to make eye contact with anyone as she herded the jury over to join him.

'The post-mortem examination revealed a number of interesting facts.' Dr Swan put on his half-moon spectacles and glanced down at the report in his hand. 'There were visible contusions on the face and torso but the resulting eccyhmosis indicates the body was beaten after death. Had this violence occurred prior then the skin would've been generally dark and much discoloured by the infiltration of blood throughout its whole thickness, which, in itself, produces an increase in firmness and tenacity in the skin. Once animal heat has left and the muscles are lax, this cannot happen. The blood, in essence, is no longer available due to cadaveric lividity – blood pooling, if you will – which in this case occurred in the lower limbs which were slate blue. There were several ugly gashes – also rendered post mortem – on the deceased's back that could've been made by a docker's hook.'

'Tell me, did you find such a weapon conveniently lying on the slab beside the body? Perhaps with a note attached?'

May sucked in her breath. She knew how much the coroner disliked speculation from medical witnesses but she wished he would occasionally remember that there were relatives present. She

163

looked across at Mr Elliott to see how he was taking it. A tic in the muscle under one eye, nothing more.

Dr Swan hardly missed a beat. 'I found traces of wood chips in his hair and on his clothes. A certain amount of evidence,' he looked at Colonel Tindal, 'evidence, mind, of rats gnawing the ends of the fingers therefore making it reasonable to conclude that he may have been dead for some time before discovery. There is one other thing: the young man was in the habit of taking opium. The vessels of the head were unusually congested; the sinuses engorged; and there were hardened faeces packing the intestines, bowel, and rectum – the young man would have suffered from chronic constipation as a result of his drug habit.' He laid the report on the rail in front of him. 'I was not able to determine the precise cause of death. Therefore, begging the coroner's leave and given that it was imperative to act before any signs were lost to decay, I took the liberty of sending tissue and fluid samples, and the entire stomach with contents, to the pathology laboratory at St Mary's Hospital where they have the facilities to perform toxicology tests.'

Colonel Tindal grunted as if he wanted to take Dr Swan to task over this as well, but instead settled for dismissing him with a curt wave. May caught a movement out of the corner of her eye. PC Collier, who along with Mr Elliott had been waiting for them on their return from Limehouse, was motioning that he had something to contribute. She signalled that to the coroner by tapping on the court Bible with her pencil. He responded with a nod and May escorted the policeman over to the witness stand and swore him in.

'Detective Inspector Beecham – unhappily now taken to his bed – asked me to conduct further enquiries in the course of which I heard talk of someone who might have seen something. I am hoping to be able to let the court know who that person is shortly.' He returned to his seat.

May wondered if it had been worth the effort of the oath. But PC Collier had been right to raise it formally in front of the jury. Colonel Tindal hated surprises.

The coroner looked at his watch. 'In addition to this mystery witness, on behalf of the jury, I instruct my officer to trace and issue warrants to all the friends and associates of the dead man who may have something relevant to contribute. This inquest is adjourned to be reconvened at a date to be announced.' He stood. 'God save the King.'

Chapter Sixteen

Much of the following day proved to be unremarkable. PC Collier came in with the details of his witness – a Chinaman who he said worked in a laundry in Pennyfields – and the rest of the time was taken up making a first stab at compiling the annual statistical report required by the London County Council. There were no new arrivals in the mortuary, and Colonel Tindal hadn't been around to add to her workload. But she had been too quick to thank her lucky stars because he came in as May was gathering her things to go home.

'I want you to accompany me to Epping. There is a taxicab outside. Mr Elliott has requested an interview which I have granted.'

'My sister is appearing in a stage production and I promised to go through her paces with her this evening.'

'If you're not up to the job of coroner's officer, Miss Keaps, then I will find someone who is.'

May could see that, for once, he wasn't issuing it as an idle threat. Why was it so crucial she be there? In fact, why was he even going at all? It wasn't unheard of for relatives to ask to see the coroner during an inquest – especially if they were rich or influential and wanted certain aspects of their lives to remain private – but he'd always asked her to write a formal letter of refusal. Why not this time? He was flushed and a little agitated but no more so than when he'd come back from one of his Coroners' Society lunches. He was tapping his watch. She had to go. Alice would understand. Or rather she wouldn't, but she'd just have to accept it.

The trip into Essex seemed to take forever. After two stops to ask directions, the cabdriver pulled into a long avenue of imposing houses with neat front gardens. May wondered what it would cost to live somewhere like this. Except Mr Elliott would no doubt trade every perfectly manicured blade of grass to have his son back. The thought

166

jolted her out of her shallow preoccupations; Colonel Tindal was right, she had a job to do and this meeting might well furnish some valuable information about what had happened to Miles Elliott.

A maid showed them into a room furnished with high-backed leather armchairs, and shelves of books running around the walls. May suspected it was Mr Elliott's domain; there was a painting of a three-masted schooner in full sail above the fire. She waited for Colonel Tindal to tell her whether he wanted her to take a deposition but he was pacing on the rug as if regretting his decision to come.

'Sit. Sit. Do sit. Can I get you anything?'

Mr Elliott stood on the threshold for a moment before closing the door behind him. He looked to have shrunk since the inquest, the sleeves of his jacket were hanging over his hands and his stand-up collar floated around his neck. May perched on the edge of the chair closest to her. Colonel Tindal took the one opposite. Mr Elliott walked over to the sideboard then turned around brandishing a decanter.

'Drink? I'm having one.'

May shook her head. Colonel Tindal accepted a large measure of something that looked to be whisky.

'Thank you for journeying out here.' Mr Elliott cradled his glass in his hand as he crumpled into the chair beside the fireplace. 'Since it happened I've not wanted to leave my wife for any longer than strictly necessary. She isn't taking it well – not at all well. Would anyone? After all, it's not

167

what you ever expect to do, is it? A parent's worst nightmare in fact, to have to bury their child. She's under heavy sedation – doctor calls in twice a day. I don't know what will become of her, really I don't. Never been strong on nerves.'

It was as if words were the only thing giving substance to his presence. May wanted to tell him that it was all right, that she understood how he was scared he'd explode if he let any thought stay in his head for too long. Colonel Tindal drained his glass and held it out for a refill. Now she understood. This was why he'd had to come: to plug the gaping hole in his life with someone else's pain. Two bereaved fathers together. She felt she should tiptoe from the room.

Mr Elliott poured the coroner more whisky then walked over to stand in front of May. He reached into his pocket and for one terrible moment she thought he was going to pull out a weapon – a razor or knife – to end his suffering. But it was a piece of paper.

'I made a list. His friends. I told them you'd be contacting them. The only one I couldn't get hold of was his ex-fiancée. They broke up a few months ago. She's abroad visiting the Italian Lakes. But her brother, Richard Weatherby, will be available if you need him.' He handed the neatly annotated sheet to May. 'I thought that if I got things moving then maybe we could get this over as quickly as possible. She won't have to come into court, will she? My wife, I mean. I don't think she'd be up to that.'

May waited for Colonel Tindal to answer but he looked as though he hadn't heard a single word

168

since Mr Elliott had asked him if he'd wanted a drink.

'No, I think that should be fine. Do you know when she last saw your son?'

His moustache quivered. May wanted to reach out and stroke his hand.

'Miles was often away from home. Ships docking in the night, storms at sea, urgent orders to be fulfilled; all that sort of thing meant he had to be on hand and he'd sleep in the office for days on end sometimes. He was due for another long stint over a ship from the East – we import for the Barley-Freeman Company – but he came home just before.'

May recognised the name. They were the people sponsoring the talent show at the Gaiety. The son was impresario and director. She'd make a note to pay a visit when they were next rehearsing. Mr Elliott cleared his throat.

'For a decent meal and a hot bath,' he said. 'The next morning Elsie, our maid, took my wife breakfast in bed. Miles had packed a few clean clothes and left the house by then. The last thing he said was a joke about his mother being like the Lady of Shalott and life passing her by up in her tower...'

He went back and refilled Colonel Tindal's glass for the third time. He hadn't touched a drop of his own.

'You've seen more of this sort of thing than me – obviously you have – but what I don't understand is why he would have taken drugs. The doctor said he used opium, didn't he? I don't recall anything else about what he had to say but I do remember that. It's one of the reasons I'd rather Mrs Elliott

169

wasn't there. I haven't told her. I know she wouldn't be able to bear a stranger saying that about her boy. I found it hard enough, I can tell you. Do you know why he did? Why people do? I just don't see that he'd have a reason to. He was happy. Here with us. So much to live for, you see. I was grooming him to take over the business. "One day all this will be yours, son," I said. And now it never will be.' His voice broke. He coughed. 'You might as well know I'm shutting up shop at Elliott Shipping. There's no point any more, is there?'

'You have so much hope for their future from the moment they are born.'

May had been wrong about Colonel Tindal not listening: he had felt every word. He stood up a little unsteadily.

'The taxicab is waiting. Miss Keaps will set the inquest for Tuesday 30th in the afternoon. I promise we will see an end to this dreadful business by the end of next week. Tell your wife she shall have her son back then.' He laid his hand on Mr Elliott's shoulder. 'Although you will grieve for him as much as you loved him, it will never be enough. If you live to see doomsday, it will never be enough.'

The driver gave her a funny look as May helped Colonel Tindal into the taxicab. As well he might; the coroner had tears rolling down his cheeks. May gave his address in Highgate as their destination but he insisted she be dropped off in Poplar first. She didn't think it wise to argue.

They were on the road skirting Epping Forest

when she decided she could no longer keep quiet about his promise to Mr Elliott.

'It's already Thursday and what with the weekend and the influenza, we might not have the toxicology report by Tuesday.'

'What?'

'You asked me to set the date for the inquest.'

'So I did, my dear girl, so I did. Whatever the good doctors say won't bring him back though, will it?'

He was no longer weeping but his voice held the sad defeat of so many men his age who'd seen too many wars come and go.

'But the death certificate won't be signed by the end of the week.'

'A mother needs her son...'

'Dr Swan wasn't able to determine what killed him; we'll have to call on expert testimony.'

'He did it.'

'Who?'

'The Chink dope peddler with the fancy suits. I'll indict him. I'll say he did it and the boy can be buried.'

May was sure he didn't mean that, he was drunk and upset. His face had turned puffy and was an unhealthy puce.

'Are you feeling all right? Colonel Tindal...' She took his hand in both of hers. 'Would you like me to get the driver to stop somewhere so you can have a drink of water?'

'A drink. Yes. That's what I need, another drink.'

They were driving into the outskirts of Bow; May could see the hulks of the gasometers in the

171

distance. She really didn't feel comfortable leaving him like this.

'Will Mrs Tindall be in when you get back?'

'There is no Mrs Tindal. She died. Not long after.'

May hadn't known that. Why would she? The only things she'd ever gleaned about his life away from court had been from the newspapers. Mrs Tindal's demise hadn't rated a mention. The poor man, no wonder he sought solace in a bottle.

'Let me come back with you.'

He reached up with his free hand and stroked her cheek. 'You'll make a lovely wife and mother one day. Please don't waste any of your concern on me; my housekeeper will make sure I get tucked up safe and sound. You see, I do know when I've had a little too much … it seems I've always had a little too much…'

He rested his head against the window and fell asleep. May leaned forward. 'Can you drop me here? By the tram stop.'

The driver pulled over. May got out and handed him the fare, what she assumed was enough for the onward journey, and a generous tip.

'Take the coroner home. And wait until you see him safely inside, will you? He's not well.'

'Don't worry, ducks, I'll take care of grandad. Reckon I'd be poorly, right enough, with that much inside me.'

May resisted the urge to tear him off a strip for his cheek. Instead she waited until the taxicab drove off and then joined the queue for the southbound tram to Poplar railway station.

Chapter Seventeen

In the morning, May was at her desk by seven-thirty. If she spoke to the woman at St Mary's and reminded her of how understanding they'd been about that late pathology report on the soldier with a bullet in his guts then perhaps she would ask the chemical analyst to make Miles Elliott top priority. The warrants she would type up and get in the post by first collection. She could call around to each of the jury in person and tell them they would be required on Tuesday. Not forgetting PC Collier and his witness. She'd pulled together a non-preliminary inquest in less time than this before. Even though it was unlikely that a verdict could be reached by the end of next week, no one could say she hadn't done what she could to move things along. The coroner had given his word and after last night it mattered to May terribly that he shouldn't be seen to have been deliberately lying.

It was late afternoon and she was in the vestibule pinning up the official notification of the date and time of Miles Elliott's inquest when the street door opened.

'May, my dear.'

Dr Swan.

'I'm glad I caught you. I wanted you to hear it from me.'

'Alice?'

Was her name going to be forever first on her lips?

'No, not Alice. But it isn't good news, I'm sorry to say. Let's go into what's laughingly called your office, I think it best if you were to sit down.'

May felt her legs wobble. She was grateful for Dr Swan's arm as he led her the few yards to her desk.

'Won't be a minute...'

He disappeared down the corridor to the coroner's chambers. When he came back he was carrying a bottle of brandy and a glass.

'Medicinal. Here, drink this.'

May was too confused, and distressed by all the awful things he hadn't said, to refuse. The spirit was so smooth she hardly felt it on the way down.

'I'm sorry to have to tell you that Colonel Tindal died in the night. I was called to attend him late evening but nothing could be done.'

'I ... I didn't know you were his doctor.'

Why was that the only thing she could think of to say?

'The old devil wouldn't have anyone else, said he was overly familiar with the results of practitioners with butcher's hands. It was all too predictable I'm afraid – he was fast approaching his allotted three score years and ten, was overweight, had gout, took no exercise, and drank too much. What we, in the business, with our gallows' humour, call *a death certificate waiting to happen*.'

The taxicab ride together replayed itself slowly. May should have insisted on going back with him. At least tried to stop him accepting so much of Mr Elliott's hospitality. She hadn't realised he was that

174

ill. But perhaps it wasn't anything that would have responded to treatment. She remembered the look of hopeless misery on his face when he'd been referring to his son's lost future. Was it possible not to want to live any more? Not to do anything about it like her father, but to allow yourself to die because the alternative contained nothing but years of unutterable bleakness.

'Go home, my dear. Doctor's orders. If there are any new arrivals, then your caretaker will only be able to slot them into the mortuary anyway until a substitute coroner can be tracked down. So there will be nothing you can do here. Lots of sweet tea – and sleep, if you can manage it. I'll stay while you lock up then walk with you as far as the end of Chrisp Street. Mrs Stibbings has another baby she'll need help delivering. The relentless circle of life, eh? Do try and see it like that if you can; trust me, it makes the whole messy process so much easier to deal with.'

It took a while for her to get the key to turn in the lock. She hadn't gone home. With Alice at work there was nothing there to take her mind off what had happened. The workshop was gloomy and reeked of petroleum. May didn't trust herself not to blow everything up by attempting to start the generator and wondered if she could open the large doors instead. The bolts set into the holes in the concrete floor slipped up easily enough; she should've known Tom would never have allowed anything to succumb to the grip of rust. The doors swung on their pivots as she walked them aside. The Norton was uncovered in the centre of

175

the room. With the wheels on and the footrest down it looked as if the rider had just hopped off for a cup of tea or bite to eat.

May found a pair of Tom's overalls hanging over the end of his workbench and slipped them on. The arms and legs needed rolling over but they were baggy enough in the crotch to accommodate her skirt, and smelled of nothing worse than coal-laden smoke and stale coffee. He'd left a bundle of rags and a tin of metal polish for her. The tears that had been clogging her throat fought for release. It was the little kindnesses that always took her by surprise. She sat cross-legged on the floor beside the slender exhaust pipe and let them fall.

For a while she tried to pretend she was crying for Colonel Tindal. But she knew it was really for herself. For the way everything that had ever come close to fulfilling who she was got snatched away. First it had been the ambulance work in France, now her job as coroner's officer – it was certain she wouldn't be allowed to keep it. It wasn't fair. The cold damp of the concrete set her muscles trembling until she was shaking and sobbing as she hadn't since they'd received the news of Albert and Henry's deaths. And even then she'd had to take herself away like a wounded animal to cry in private. The thought of never seeing her brother again had made her ache with a pain that dragged at the very centre of her being. They had shared so much together, including the affection of his best friend. She and Henry had never actually discussed the fact of marriage but they had both known it would happen in time. And now that future was gone. Everyone had left her. Everyone but Alice, and that would come soon enough.

Her chest heaved convulsively as she wiped her snotty nose on her sleeve. If all the people she had lost were still alive, how different would things be for her now? And how could she possibly know if they'd have been any better? She gripped the top of the metal polish and twisted the tin open. None of it mattered. What might have been never mattered. Especially to the dead. And if life was nothing but existence then she counted herself amongst that faceless army.

Chapter Eighteen

Horatio clapped his hands. 'Right! Let's have a bit of hush.'

It had no effect on the backstage boys scurrying around the apron but the line of amateurs stood to attention and shuffled a few paces downstage. This was the moment Vi had been dreading: the first rehearsal. It would only be a walk-through but she was anxious none of the turns let down her faith in them.

'The ASM will do the blocking for each of you in the order you'll be on the bill. It'll only be chalk marks for now, we'll use tape on the night. Do not, I repeat not, stand anywhere else but with your toes on the line unless you want to be performing in darkness. And if the spot is off, don't walk into it; let it come to you. Okay, first up … you … the male impersonator. What's your name?'

'Ethel, sir.'

Her voice was thin and wavering and Vi hoped the girl would get through the ordeal without having to rush off to be sick; even in the sparse illumination of the auditorium chandelier she looked to be green around the gills.

'You'll open and close in number ones.'

Vi took pity and sidled up to her. 'In front of the tabs – the first row of curtains – it's a real honour to be asked to do that.'

She didn't add that it also gave time for Mr Dansi to clear up after his poodles. Why had she ever thought they'd be a good idea? The girl allowed herself to be pulled down centre by the ASM. And then promptly fainted.

'The first change of the day will be that Miss Tremins will now be first call after the animal act. See to her somebody; don't just stand there like a bunch of lemons.'

Vi left Alice and the Japanese acrobats to do the necessary and walked through the wings to the pass door into the auditorium. She joined Horatio in the first row of stalls.

'That wasn't part of the deal. I agreed to head-line your show but I won't be the opening serio-act. Not following the novelty; you know as well as I do it's the graveyard slot when up against the sort of audience we're sure to attract.'

'All the more reason to give it to a pro, then. Come on, Vi, be reasonable, who else can I get to do it? That drink of water will never be able to muster what it takes and, unless you want every-one sliding around in dog shit, the poodles have to

178

be on first. You put them on the bill, remember?'

That'd been below the belt. She had half a mind to tell him to drop them and she'd do a double slot, when he unleashed one of his eye-crinkling smiles. God she hated the ease with which he could put a flutter in her stomach and the fact that he knew it. He let his hand slide down the small of her back to cradle her buttock as she stood up

'We'll have a little less of that, Mr Barley-Freeman, if you're going to treat me as one of the bill fare on stage, then that goes for off-stage, too.' She threw him a wink before sashaying back to the aisle.

The rest of the blocking went off without a hitch. Ethel returned in due course, visibly relieved to be lost in her new position between the vent and the quick-fire comedy duo. The turns were going through their entrances and exits when the theatre manager called Horatio away for a short conference about a problem that'd cropped up. Vi was left in charge. She gathered the band of, now decidedly less eager, hopefuls around her.

'I know you all thought you'd be doing your routines but that comes later. The way it goes is that we have this walk-through so you can familiarise yourself with the feel of the thing, your first priority is to get used to ignoring the pandemonium from backstage. To the audience it will all look as smooth as clockwork – that's the idea – but up here there's always something about to go wrong. Backstage at any theatre is a dangerous place and this more than most: there's equipment here that was old hat in Henry Irving's day. Watch the ropes and especially the iron dogs – they're the

179

long spikes propping up the flats; you trip over one of those and you'll be going on with a bloody nose: from the flyman, if not your fall.'

That had them focused.

'I'm going to give you the rehearsal schedule as it stands and, unless you die in the night, you are expected to turn up at every one. Now, Mr Barley-Freeman has hired the theatre for Sunday 18th April for the dress rehearsal; other that that we have to fit in stage time between the standard bills. Our performance will be on the afternoon of Wednesday 21 – exactly three weeks and two days from now – which gives us five more sessions after this one: count them, five. You will come to each rehearsal knowing your routine backwards because when we are on stage it is about pulling the whole show together, not drilling you on your business. I'll post the dates backstage – and it'll be your responsibility to check for changes – but they are to be: Wednesday 7th; Sunday 18th; Monday 19th; and Tuesday 20th. The last will be a mop-up the morning of the day itself. Music is to be with the band director by the Saturday and all costumes ready for Sunday. I know it sounds as everything will be left to the last minute, but that's how it works in the theatre. Trust me: it will come together in the end, it always does. Until Mr Barley-Freeman comes back, walk around a little. But don't touch anything. And get out of the way quick when told; the regular show's on in an hour and the boys have a lot to do.'

Vi watched them disperse and hoped at least one of them would remember a word she'd said. She walked down stage to the footlights to wait for them to finish their tour. The cleaners were rolling up the winding sheets of brown holland that protected the front two rows from the dust and filth that came off the stage. The back door swished and someone was coming down the centre aisle; it was impossible to see who in the gloom. She heard a pleasing female voice ask for Mr Barley-Freeman, and receive a *couldn't care less* response. That was no way to speak to a civilian: they were the ones who bought tickets. Vi retreated to the wings with the intention of going front of house when an agitated voice began doing a perfect rendition of a stage whisper on the auditorium side of the pass door. She suspected Alice was the only one who could inject that much anger into *what are you doing here?* and knew the layout well enough to have dragged the visitor to a spot where they would only be seen from the OP wings.

'You come to spy on me, is that it? Just because that's what you do in your job doesn't mean you can do it to family. The theatre's my world and you ain't welcome here 'less you pay for a seat like everybody else. I wish you'd get it into your head that I'm grown up now – anyone would think you hadn't been out working three years at my age. Mrs Gibson don't treat me like a silly kid; she's offered for me to bunk with them so as to cut the bus ride and I reckon it'd just about show you how things are if I took her up on it.'

Presumably this was the disapproving sister. Vi was torn between going through to announce herself and taking a peek at the woman who might well try to prevent her one class turn from appearing. Curiosity won. Vi scurried backstage,

181

crossed behind the safety curtain, and arrived in the right hand flats panting slightly. The woman was facing her way, the small light above the pass door picking her out clearly. She wasn't as striking as Alice but she had a finished quality about her, a professional confidence – the sort Vi knew Horatio found attractive. Except she was dressed in an appalling severe skirt and unflattering blouse, and her shoes ... well, they were the sort a maiden aunt would chose for *comfort*. Vi couldn't eavesdrop from this far away but she watched as they played out what looked to be a well-rehearsed spat.

'What's going on here? Where are they all?' Horatio's voice boomed down from the back of the auditorium. 'Vi, wherever you are, round them up will you?' He was coming down the right aisle. 'We've work to do.'

Alice's sister started walking across towards him. Vi stepped back but didn't leave her spot.

'Mr Barley-Freeman? I'm May Keaps, the Poplar Coroner's Officer; I'd like a quick word if that's convenient.'

'Ah, I can see where Alice gets it from.'

'I beg your pardon?'

'Her poise onstage; I expect it's second-nature to you, having to do all the courtroom dramatics I mean.'

'It isn't the least bit like that.'

Vi sniggered: if there was anything Horatio hated it was an opinionated woman.

'I understand Elliott Shipping imports the spices for your father's business. No doubt you know that Miles Elliott is dead?'

'Yes. A terrible thing to happen. Poor Miles.'

182

'You knew him then? If so, I'll be issuing you with a subpoena to appear at the inquest; the coroner wants to hear from all his friends.'

'I wouldn't say we were that. Played the odd game of cricket when we were boys, but that's as far as it went. Our fathers were as thick as thieves and tried to get us to like each other except we didn't and, besides, we both resented the feeble attempts at matchmaking – I know I did. No, I knew Miles when we were about seven, was packed off to boarding school not long after and he ... did whatever it was he did. That's about all I can tell you about Miles Elliott, Miss Keaps. I'm sorry. However I hope it goes without saying how sad I am he came to such a sticky end; found outside a Chinese restaurant in Limehouse, or so I believe. Now, if that's all I have to get back to it; we've a show to put on in under a month's time. But you know that: Alice. She's very good, by the way...'

Winkled out of her corner by the arrival of three of the acrobats, Vi didn't catch just how wonderful Horatio thought Miss Keaps the younger. She thought it was just as well or she'd only get irritated by his tendency to praise a pretty face out of all proportion to their talent. Making a mental note to make sure no one act would outshine the others, she retreated backstage to gather up the rest of her charges.

Chapter Nineteen

It was the day of Miles Elliott's second inquest and May wasn't having an easy time of it. She'd been reprimanded by Mrs Pringle, the cleaner, for walking over the wet courtroom floor, had dropped a packet of tea in the kitchenette as she attempted to tidy up, and had jammed the typewriter ribbon. Added to which she had a nervous headache. The Lord Chancellor's Office had informed her that the deputy coroner – one Braxton Clarke – would be arriving some time in the morning to take over until elections could be held and the appointment filled permanently. May hadn't known such a person existed; Colonel Tindal had never referred to having a deputy in all the time she had been working for him. The only thing she knew to expect was that the deputy would likely have misgivings about her being his jack-of-all-trades. So here she was, on her hands and knees sweeping up tealeaves with a dustpan and brush.

'Bugger and blast.' She'd managed to get a streak of dirt on the cuff of her best blouse.

'Tut, tut. Language...'

She turned her head to see a pair of chocolate brown suede shoes walking past. She scrabbled upright but they had vanished down the corridor to the coroner's chambers. May wanted to scream. If first impressions were everything then she

184

couldn't have got off to a worse start. The one time she hadn't been listening out for his entrance. She darted through the vestibule and into the lavatory where she splashed water on her flaming cheeks. It was a full five minutes before she could bring herself to stop hiding and walk back to her desk.

One telephone call after another restored some sort of order to her thoughts. She found the expenses chits and logged them, then filled out a stationery requisition form. The post contained replies to the warrants she had issued. She was scrolling a sheet of paper into the typewriter when she heard the door to the coroner's chambers open. His stride down the short corridor was sure and purposeful. May wanted to run back into the lavatory but knew she should stop feeling like a naughty schoolgirl and just pretend it hadn't happened.

Nothing could have prepared her for her first sight of Braxton Clarke. She felt the heat in her cheeks again. Tall, broad shouldered, trim, dark hair which was greying enticingly at the temples, laughter lines emphasising the deep blue of his eyes. The only thing stopping him from having stepped from the pages of *Film Weekly* was that his suit, although obviously expensively tailored, was crumpled. And those inappropriately casual shoes. His loose-limbed walk covered the space between them before May realised she had her mouth open.

'Deputy Coroner for the City of London and Southwark District reporting for duty.' He perched on the edge of the desk. 'You must be the admirable Miss Keaps.'

185

'May.' Her voice had turned croaky.

He held his hand out for her to shake. 'How do you do. Not well, I assume, given the circumstances. I was so sorry to hear about Colonel Tindal; he served the office of coroner for many years, he'll be hard to replace. I met him a few times at official functions – the Lord Mayor's dinner being the last occasion – and he struck me as an authoritative and committed man. Heaven knows why he had my name down as his deputy though. I can only assume that he was being pressurised to get the slot filled and he chose me at random from his Coroners' Society list. So, this is Poplar. Do we have any guests staying?'

'What?' It seemed she couldn't quite manage more than one word at a time.

'In the mortuary.'

'Only Miles Elliott. The undertaker has taken the last of the others. It's his inquest this afternoon. Not the undertaker's, Miles Elliott's.'

Braxton Clarke laughed. A growl that started in his throat and burst out from between his lips as if he could no longer contain it.

'I've a feeling we're going to get along very well. Tell me, do you like it here?'

'It's...'

What could she say that would make her sound capable, enthusiastic, dedicated and, despite her outburst in the kitchenette, professional.

'...interesting.'

'Not dead end, you mean?'

May looked but couldn't see any signs of teasing on his face. Maybe he was just being light-hearted to try and put her at ease. He undid his

186

jacket buttons. His blue silk tie below the gold clip was smeared with something yellow. He noticed her looking and lifted the end away from his shirt.

'I can only echo your well chosen words: bugger and blast. Boiled-egg yolk. One thing you'll have to promise me, May, is that you'll check me over whenever I have to go into court.' He licked his finger and smudged the stain even more. 'You see, you're not the only one with the unfortunate habit of spilling things. Except I always seem to manage to make it on myself.'

At last May relaxed enough to smile. This man had a soothing informality about him.

'I must say that I've never come across a female coroner's officer before.'

She felt herself stiffen again. 'I try hard to ensure being a woman doesn't impair my efficiency. I was born and raised in the docks and consequently don't shirk the more physical aspects of the job. Colonel Tindal never had cause to complain.'

'And I'm sure I won't either. You just carry on running things in the way you always have, it's unlikely I'll be around much to interfere as people have a habit of dying left right and centre on my current patch.' He bent towards her. 'Between you and me, I think it's a fiendish plot by *the powers that be* to ensure I earn every farthing of my King's shilling. Now, do you have the papers for this afternoon's inquest?'

May closed the folder and handed it to him.

'Right, I'll go through and study it.' He stood up. 'But first I'm going to telephone the Town Hall and see if they can't find a spare corner to

187

archive the contents of at least one of these filing cabinets. I would expect a caged animal to have more space to move around in than you do. See you later, May, keep up the good work.'

May sat with hr hands in her lap. Things were certainly going to be different from now on.

Chapter Twenty

May was surprised to see that Mr Elliott wasn't in the courtroom. Perhaps his wife had taken a turn for the worse and he hadn't wanted to leave her alone. Or maybe the thought of finding out any more about his son's hidden life had been too much. Either way, Coroner Clarke had asked May to administer the oath to the witnesses and had said he would act as the family's representative during the proceedings. Brilliant Chang was present – with his solicitor but minus his adoring entourage – as were three of Miles' friends, a small selection of pressmen, and PC Collier's witness. As she'd been warned the latter spoke little English, May had arranged for an interpreter.

They were the first to be called. The witness – Sing Quong – was dressed in the blue slop-shop suit of a laundry worker. May guessed he hadn't been long in Limehouse because he still had a pigtail despite the local joy boys and their liking for trophy hunting with knives. Or maybe they had tried already and failed because he had a long puckered scar scything his cheek and jaw.

The interpreter was a slight young woman who looked as though a river breeze would unsettle her. Braxton Clarke asked that she stand behind the shoulder of the witness so the jury could see him clearly.

'Miss Liu. The court is indebted to you for coming here at such short notice. I'd like to remind you that you are here to report the witness's words faithfully to us but that you are not under any personal scrutiny. Just relax and do your best. Now, if you could ask Mr Quong to begin, we will hear his evidence.'

After she had done as instructed it was as if a dam had burst in the witness's mouth. Streams of words gushed out, accompanied by looks darted in the direction of Brilliant Chang. Someone in the jury giggled. Braxton Clarke raised his hand.

'Miss Liu. If you could request Mr Quong to bear with us and pause for a moment...' He turned to the jury. 'Each and every witness in this court will be respected, as will their testimony. I will have no hesitation in dismissing and imposing a heavy fine on anyone who disregards that.'

May watched as the foreman tried to stare the coroner down but, in the end, was forced to cross his arms in defeat. She, too, hadn't expected such a steely centre inside the expensive suit.

'Now, Miss Liu, if we can start again please? A little slower this time. Don't be afraid of asking Mr Quong to repeat something if necessary; I want my coroner's officer to be able to transcribe every word.'

May felt the tickle of a blush. She supposed that he did own her in a way: her fate was certainly in his hands. If she could impress him by making a really good job of this inquest then maybe he'd decide that Poplar Coroner's Court couldn't function without her. But the interpreter was speaking in her singsong voice and she had to concentrate.

'He said that he saw that man there–'

'Nan Chan?'

'Yes, him, at the entrance to the alley where the boy was found.'

'When?'

'On that night, that very night. He swears to it.'

'That's okay, Miss Liu, he has already taken the oath. Please confine yourself to translating his exact words.'

'I am very sorry, sir. He is so excited that he has got me that way, too. He is scared also, I think.'

'Then tell him from me not to be. He has nothing to worry about.'

She did so but May didn't get the impression the Chinaman was convinced. He was staring at the courtroom door as if he wanted to get back onto the streets as quickly as possible. Or was expecting someone to come in.

'Is he sure, beyond any possible doubt, that it was Nan Chan he saw?'

The question was translated and the witness responded with another torrent. Miss Liu kept tapping his shoulder to encourage him to slow down. He finished. She asked something, got a response, then nodded.

'He says it is well known in Limehouse that this man has rich white people in his restaurant who he tempts into the upstairs room to smoke the

190

pipe. Then, when they leave with their wits still chasing the dragon, he has them beaten and robbed. He said he has seen it happen with his own eyes.' Miss Liu raised her gaze from the floor and faced the coroner. 'He wants you to know that may his eyes be pierced with a hot sail-maker's bodkin if he hasn't.'

Brilliant Chang's solicitor stood. The coroner waved him back down.

'It will be your turn next. After I give time for the jury to ask any questions of this witness.'

None were forthcoming.

'Then I thank you very much for attending this afternoon. You, particularly, Miss Liu...'

May noticed the young woman give him a shy little smile.

'...You may return to your seats.'

Sing Quong grabbed his interpreter's arm and said something.

'He asks that he may be excused.' She seemed to shrink inside her clothes. 'A call of nature.'

Braxton Clarke sat back in his chair. 'Of course, this is not a torture chamber. Please tell him that he is free to avail himself of the facilities, but not to leave the court.'

The interpreter had barely finished relaying this when the witness leapt from the chair and scurried from the room. He slid Brilliant Chang a peculiarly violent hand gesture as he passed. May was surprised to notice the restaurateur's composure crumple in the gap before he realised she was watching. Had that been guilt? She was sure Braxton Clarke would see beyond the smooth guile of his solicitor if it was. The latter now stood up.

'My client has asked me to speak on his behalf for the remainder of these proceedings. Therefore I will issue a statement and answer any supplementary questions.'

'Then please proceed; you have the court's full attention.'

'Mr Chan is not, and never has been, a drug dealer. The Commissioner of the Metropolitan Police can confirm that their investigations – instituted, I believe, at the behest of Colonel Tindal – have resulted in them not being able to find even the smallest trace of any illegal substances. Further, in response to the perjury from the last witness–'

'Can I remind you, and the jury, that there is only one person here possessing the authority to decide what does, and does not, constitute contempt of this court? Please continue.'

'My client was nowhere near Limehouse seven days ago. A well-known society luminary – whose name we will reveal if it becomes strictly necessary – can confirm that he was with her on the evening of 23rd March. When he returned to his premises it was to find the late coroner and this jury crowding his doorway. I'm sure the court clerk can testify to his shock at the time.'

'Miss Keaps, when you are ready, if you will be good enough to go and fetch Mr Quong and bring him back inside. I'd like to hear if he has any amendments to make to his statement. In the meantime, I would be grateful if everyone could just wait patiently.'

May didn't think there was much chance of that. The pressmen present were already beginning to buzz at the revelation that Brilliant Chang had been out all night with a white woman. As she passed underneath the gallery she could hear excited speculation as to his mystery companion's identity – someone's wife perhaps?

It only took her a few minutes to scout around the public areas and ascertain that the witness was no longer in the building. Would Braxton Clarke take the news the same way as Colonel Tindal would've done and unleash a tirade against unreliable and untrustworthy foreigners? She would feel unaccountably let down if he did.

She walked back into the courtroom and approached the coroner's bench. As she could have predicted, Brilliant Chang's solicitor was on his feet before she'd finished explaining the situation.

'Will you now accept the truth that my client had nothing to do with this?'

Coroner Clarke made his hands into a steeple and rested his chin on his fingertips. 'The witness's failure to reappear simply tells me that he feared being cross-examined. Miss Liu, your services will no longer be required here today. If you present your account to my officer then she will ensure you are paid for your time and trouble. Miss Keaps, issue a warrant for the arrest of Sing Quong.'

May began to feel queasy as she realised that the witness had sought PC Collier out and therefore there was no way of knowing if his address, or the laundry he'd said he worked in – or even his name – were genuine. But she wasn't about to tell Braxton Clarke that and prompt him to ask

193

how it was possible she had allowed the police to furnish an uncharacteristically eager-to-volunteer non-English-speaking witness without checking his identity.

'Well, Miss Keaps, who will we hear from next? Someone I trust who will not attempt to bolt from this court before we have had a chance to glean all they have to say.'

He was smiling. She breathed out again; he hadn't picked up any of her tension.

'Miss Fogle.'

'Very good. Let's have her up here then.'

Rose Fogle, the first of Miles' friends Mr Elliott had put forward, was well-groomed in a navy coatdress, the cloth primroses on her hat nodding as she walked confidently to the witness stand.

'Please sit down, Miss Fogle, if it would make you more comfortable. Just make sure you look at me and speak loudly and clearly enough for the jury.'

May didn't think there was a chance of anyone's gaze straying from the coroner. Even the most habitually inattentive jurors had their attention focused on him. The young woman gathered herself as if she was used to explaining herself in public.

'We were companions, Miles and I – not in any romantic way you understand but we'd pair up for country house weekends and such.' She dabbed delicately at the corner of her eyes with a lace handkerchief. 'He was a fabulous dancer. We were going to Highclere together at the end of next month; it was to be a fancy-dress weekend, all very Egyptian and Valley of the Kings – my mother's a

194

distant cousin of the Earl of Carnarvon.'

'Had you seen each other in the last four weeks, say from about the beginning of March?'

'Not that I recall.'

'Take your time, Miss Fogle; this is very important.'

'I'm pretty sure of it. No. I had a cold and thought I'd keep my ugly red nose to myself. And I knew we had a date for April 23rd and that's not too long to wait so I wouldn't have bothered to contact him.'

'What did you do together when you did see each other? I assume it wasn't all rubbing shoulders with nobility.'

'Of course not. We did what everyone does ... everyone of our sort, I mean. Dinner, a visit to a picture palace, or sometimes to the West End for a show; the occasional nightclub.'

'Did you ever indulge in the current fashion amongst young people for drug taking?'

'Never. I'm not that sort of girl. A little harmless sherry or a crème de menthe at Christmas...'

The coroner forestalled a potential eruption of mirth from the jury with a raised finger. 'Were you aware that Miles smoked opium?'

'No.' She appeared to think for a moment. 'His clothes smelled a bit funny sometimes when he came to meet me straight from the shipping office but I thought that was just what the East End was like ... no offence, but never having been here before...'

Now May did expect to hear the blurt of a laugh – from the press gallery if not the jury – but Braxton Clarke's earlier demand for respect seemed to have done the trick.

'And I'm sure some of us in this courtroom wouldn't know what a breath of fresh air smelled like either. Thank you, Miss Fogle. You may return to your seat or leave the courtroom; I won't be needing to call you again.'

So he wasn't above indulging in a little gibing humour. May began to hope there would be a need for him to come to Poplar quite often. Then felt terrible because that was as good as wishing for people to die. He was looking at the last two witnesses.

'Which of you would like to speak next?'

It was the young man who put up his hand. 'I'll go.' He was big and bulky and strode across the room with a faint swagger.

'Could you please restate your name for the record?'

'Richard Weatherby. Miles was once engaged to my sister, Amelia. In fact, I curse myself to this day that it was I who introduced them. We had a mutual friend and that led to us having the occasional drink together. Then one day he called for me and met Amelia. It was love at first sight – for her anyway – leading to what they call a whirlwind courtship. And unfortunately they became engaged.'

'From the way you are speaking about him, I take it you didn't like Miles Elliott?'

'I did at first. He was a pleasant enough chap. Or I thought he was. But then he started messing Amelia around – breaking dates, not getting back in touch for days; sometimes turning up without warning as if nothing had happened.'

'Was there perhaps another woman involved?'

Richard Weatherby let out a high-pitched stutter of a laugh at odds with his bulk. 'I doubt anyone who wasn't as lovesick as my sister would've put up with him. One evening there was a flaming row – I was up in my room and could hear her crying. I ran down the stairs and threw him out of the house. Bodily. I was a boxing blue and he wouldn't have stood a chance. Except he didn't even try to put up a fight. I told him never to come to the house again. And he didn't.'

'When was this, Mr Weatherby?'

'Back in the middle of January.'

'And, to your knowledge, did your sister see him at all after that?'

'No. She was confined to bed with nerves for a long while afterwards. She was becoming so ill that I packed her off to stay with our cousin on Lake Garda.'

'Are you acquainted with drug taking, Mr Weatherby?'

'Not personally, no; I spar at my local gymnasium and a man has to be in peak physical condition to be able to do that.'

'Would you perhaps say that Miles Elliott's behaviour was consistent with someone who frequently took recourse to opium?'

'Don't know enough about it to say. But if acting as if you're the only person in the world who matters, and breaking an innocent girl's heart without a by-your-leave is typical, then I suppose he could have been on the stuff.'

'Now I have one last question and I want you to answer it as honestly as you can, Mr Weatherby:

what would have happened had Miles Elliott come calling on your sister whilst she was lying under your roof in a state of distress?'

'I'd have thumped him black and blue. No question of it.'

'The court is very grateful for your forthrightness. You are free to return to your seat. And now if we can hear the final witness?'

'Elizabeth Newick.'

May had to tap her pencil on the table to get the girl's attention. She was staring at the glove she was twisting around and around in her hand.

'Miss Newick, I'm Braxton Clarke, the coroner. Are you all right? Would you like a drink of water?'

'I don't want to be here.' She sounded like a three-year-old who'd awoken from a bad dream.

'None of us do, Miss Newick, not in these circumstances. I can see you are agitated, would you like a moment to compose yourself?'

'I don't want to be in the same room as a man like that.' She pointed a blood-red fingernail at Brilliant Chang. 'He scares me. He's the yellow peril I've read about in the *Daily Express,* isn't he? All this talk of opium and being drugged and murdered.'

'There's no need to get hysterical, Miss Newick. Just a couple of questions and then you're free to go.'

'It's the white slave trade at the heart of it. I know for a fact that's what dirty foreigners like him get up to. It happened to a friend of mine. She was walking down the road when this Oriental came up and sort of mesmerised her with his slitty eyes and the next thing she knew she was–'

198

'Enough of this nonsense.'

In the still courtroom, May could hear the whisper of pencil lead scraping on paper in the gallery.

The coroner must've also noticed the flurry of activity. 'Impressionable youngsters with empty minds should not believe all they read in the press. Gentlemen,' he looked up as if regarding a pack of salivating dogs, 'this inquest is being conducted in order to get to the truth behind the death of a young man, not to sell your newspapers. It is thanks to your irresponsible reporting that someone like Miss Newick here can even entertain such wild and ridiculous imaginings. I demand you act with such slim codes of ethics as your profession holds and confine your coverage of everything that happens in this court to the indisputable facts or I will exercise my right under the law and have all future inquests held in camera.'

He shifted his glance to May. 'Miss Keaps, I trust you took a preliminary statement from this witness when she answered the summons?'

'Over the telephone, yes.'

'Did it contain anything that in your experience is of any relevance to the circumstances in which Miles Elliott met his death?'

May glanced briefly at her notes, then shook her head.

'In that case please enter that into the record; I feel this court will hear nothing likely to provide any more enlightenment. In addition, please chase up the outstanding toxicology report and subpoena the expert witness to appear.' He pushed his chair back and stood. 'This inquest is adjourned to

199

reconvene after Easter on Tuesday 6th April at twelve o'clock. Can I remind the jury and all witnesses who may be called again to appear that they remain under oath until they are released by this court. God save the King.'

Braxton Clarke left for his chambers. May collected her papers amid a babble of excited conversation from the jury members as they hurried out; by tonight they'd have traded drinks and tales of their first encounter with Braxton Clarke in every pub from here to Canning Town. She was conscious that Brilliant Chang had detached himself from his solicitor to stand by her side.

'You and your new coroner have to believe that this tragic event has nothing to do with me, Miss Keaps. A man in my position cannot fail to attract enemies and I am afraid they have seized the opportunity of that unfortunate young man's death to take their revenge. I saw how you looked at me when you were convinced I was the one who caused Miss Gem to take her life and know that a thirst for justice burns in your soul. I only ask that you do me the honour of allowing that to continue to guide you. But I would be neglectful if I did not warn you to be careful. As is only too evident from my predicament, a carefree future often rests in the hands of those with the means and inclination to destroy it; do not put yourself in the position of having to learn the truth of that firsthand.'

He let his solemn gaze drop to the floor, and left.

May walked around the courtroom collecting water jugs and glasses, her hands shaking at the man's temerity. Had all those silken words just been a cocoon to deliver that final remark of a threat, or had they been the truth? Was the witness who had attempted to frame him working for these enemies he mentioned? If so, it had to be someone who wanted him out of the way – permanently if a murder charge could be made to stick. Was it to do with drugs? His arrival in Limehouse would've upset the local pattern of trade; with the patronage of his society friends he'd easily be able to corner the market. It made sense. In May's experience, money was almost always at the root of any power struggle.

The first thing she needed to do was see if she could find out anything to back up that theory. If this was about a cocaine war then maybe Miles Elliott had been nothing more than in the wrong place at the wrong time but exactly the right sort of target to get the law up in arms against Brilliant Chang. The end of the week would be the best time to catch the Black Cat Café in Pennyfields full. It was Good Friday but that wouldn't make any difference to the clientele – other than perhaps a Bank Holiday providing more opportunities for work. If anyone knew for certain whether Brilliant Chang dealt in drugs, the Limehouse prostitutes would. And they would talk to her. Not because she was the coroner's officer but because she'd worked with a handful of them in the tobacco factory before they'd been forced by circumstances to find more lucrative employment: it wasn't only the poor souls passing through the mortuary who had firsthand experience of what a tough place the East End could be.

201

Chapter Twenty-One

May emerged from the café, the smells of fried eggs and chicory-laced coffee clinging to her clothes. The women had been friendly and chatty – asking about Alice, and wanting to know the gossip from her side of the tracks. If it wasn't for their low-cut dresses and cheap hats they could've been traders resting up and counting their takings after a long night in Dolphin Lane market. None of them believed that the Shanghai Palace restaurant was a front for an opium den. They all knew the place of course. Three Colt Street was one of their best Saturday night haunts, particularly when a new ship was in. Or Thomas Cook had one of their tours on; the men who came down for the thrill of slumming it often regarded a knee-trembler in a dark doorway as the highlight of the experience. When she asked if Brilliant Chang was a cocaine dealer, they explained that the drug was widely available on the streets but that it was impossible to tell the supplier behind the men who loitered on the corners and offered packets of powder from beneath their jackets. It was a cutthroat business and many was the time they had encountered a swift altercation that left one man in a pool of blood and a fresh face standing in his place. May remembered three inquests over the past year which fitted those circumstances; of course the police had drawn nothing but blank silences.

A fog was rolling in off the river. May shivered and did up the buttons on her coat. She retrieved her gloves from deep inside her pockets and pulled them onto her stiffening fingers. The buildings on either side of the tight street seemed to be oozing damp. The smell of rotting wood suited her sense of failure. She now had no choice but to accept there wasn't any evidence connecting Brilliant Chang with cocaine and that she had judged him with a prejudiced harshness worthy of Colonel Tindal. To make matters worse she could no longer avoid drawing the conclusion that if she hadn't taken it upon herself to set the police onto the Palm Court Nightclub then he wouldn't have felt forced to retreat to Limehouse and perhaps Miles Elliott would still be alive.

It was now even more important than ever she find out exactly what had happened to the young man, and why. The truth wouldn't make any difference to poor Miles but it would to Brilliant Chang who could find himself swinging at the end of a rope if she couldn't come up with reasons why the jury should not choose him as their scapegoat. As for her, it wouldn't be a question of waiting for Braxton Clarke's dismissal: she'd have to resign if it turned out it had been her interference that had set the whole train in motion. She'd never be able to do her job with that on her conscience.

She began to walk for home but then turned and plunged into one of the unlit streets leading to the main road. The least she could do whilst she was here was to see if she could unearth any trace of the false witness. His arrest would go some way towards making amends. She'd start with the obvious places and see if she could get any leads. Even a man bumping along in the silt of Limehouse had to lay his head somewhere.

The Strangers' Home for Asiatics, Africans and South-Sea Islanders was an imposing building with stone steps and a fat-columned portico. May had never been inside but knew it to be a clean, well-ordered place. She pushed open the door to find herself in a large room. A fire was burning at the far end, a group of Lascars sitting around it chatting. A Cingalee in a grubby turban was lying on a bench. In the centre was a table scattered with books and periodicals. The blackest African she'd ever seen was playing on the bagatelle board in the corner. The air smelled of mint tea and cigarette smoke. No one gave her a second glance.

She was in luck. The man sitting alone reading a newspaper was a Malay she recognised from the stevedore's inquest. He had stood out because of his egg-smooth head; she was familiar enough with Asiatics to know such baldness was rare. Speaking slowly and pantomiming a long scar on her cheek, May described her quarry. He did her the politeness of pretending to think before shrugging his shoulders. She thanked him and turned to leave. At the door, she felt a tug on her sleeve. The Malay pressed something in her hand before slipping back inside. It was a playing card. The Queen of Hearts. One of the hearts had been coloured over in crayon to resemble a Chinese lantern. The sign of the Red Lamp. Opium. She suspected the queen was random and the entire suit had been adulterated – what better way for sailors with no common language to enquire as to the whereabouts of a little shore leave recreation? Did he know for certain this was where the man would be or was it an educated guess? But she didn't know where they dispensed pipes of the drug. She would have to scour the streets and alleys looking for the dim lamps glowing in the windows. It was surely worth another hour of her time.

In fact it was close to midnight before May stumbled across Sing Quong. Or thought she had. But she needed to see his face to be certain. She'd been outside the third of the dingy places sporting a lantern. A man had emerged moments before and was walking – with all the non-urgency of a Sunday stroll – away from her. He had the blue serge baggy suit, cap, thin frame, and stoop of a dockland Chinaman. It was the pigtail swaying across his shoulders like a rope in a breeze that made him different from all the others she'd seen. He paused at the corner under the gas lamp and fumbled in his pockets. In the flare of a match struck against the brickwork she saw a long puckered scar. He lit his cigarette and turned down to his left.

May felt a flicker of triumph. But she wasn't stupid enough simply to go up and ask him why he'd lied in court. He was heading in the direction of West India Dock Road. She'd follow him up to the intersection; there should be a constable checking in at the police box about now and she could ask him to accompany her. Something scurried in the doorway beside her. A rat probably. Limehouse at night was no different from Limehouse in the daylight hours except for the boldness of concealment.

Keeping at least half a street-length between them, May tracked the Chinaman to the Causeway and right into Mission Road. There were more people here – men mainly, on their own or in small tired groups trudging back from the docks. It was easy to tell the sailors as they still had the gait of expecting to feel the ground move under their feet. But no bobbies on the beat. She remembered that Poplar Police Station was decimated by influenza and wondered if it was the same for Limehouse. The river fog was coalescing into something more dense. It scraped at the back of her throat and made her want to cough. She wasn't sure what to do next, only that the decision to continue would be taken away from her if she kept dithering. In the absence of any arrest tonight she could at least give PC Collier something with which to narrow down his search. It would be even better if she had an address to type on the warrant of course; Braxton Clarke need never know she hadn't had it all along.

The clocks over the gateways of both the West, and East, India Docks chimed the beginning of a new day. The unison of sound from near and far seemed to penetrate the Chinaman's opium daze and he picked up his pace. May set off after him. Two streets on she had to scurry a short way to maintain the same distance between them. Wherever he was going, he looked as though he had a deadline to meet or an assignation that couldn't –

or mustn't – be missed. Into Pennyfields and the thunderous shadows of the docks. He led her down a series of dark streets, deserted by everything but the smell of smoke lingering from the last night-train on the London and Blackwall Railway. They now seemed to be going back on themselves; May would have believed the Chinaman was deliberately misleading her if she wasn't certain he had no idea he was being followed – he hadn't once turned around or cut short a stride, and she was hugging the brickwork. Another corner. Another high wall.

May wasn't exactly lost but she was no longer sure they were heading east. It wasn't south because the smell from the Thames mud at low tide wasn't getting any stronger. Lozenges of light were turning the fog up ahead a sickly yellow. As she got closer she heard the sounds of men with time on their hands, a day's wages in their pockets, and too much beer in their bellies. A clot of brawlers fell out of the pub doorway to span the street. May didn't want to push through them – a fist or a blade unleashed wouldn't be fussy about where it landed – but she couldn't afford to wait for the quarrel to fizzle into drunken incoherence; Sing Quong was on the other side and wouldn't be stopping to watch the melee.

She pulled her arms and neck in like the giant turtle shell on the wall of the Resolute Tavern and walked ahead, one shoulder brushing the wall and the other a brawny back. She felt both contacts as if on her naked skin. She half-expected to feel a swift blow and then the stone sets she was staring at rushing up to meet her. Four more strides, and she was clear. A quick scan of the empty street up ahead confirmed she'd hesitated too long. There were breaks in the buildings on either side. The first one she came to appeared to be a passage threading back towards the warehouses. May continued on then stopped by the alleyway on the left. The tops of the walls leaned as if they longed to touch each other. There were few gas lamps this far off the main thoroughfare and she couldn't see well enough to tell where the passage might be leading. She held her breath and listened. The men in the street were still arguing; a baby was squalling; a cat on heat was screaming her lust into the night. No footfalls echoing along the length of the tunnel-like alley.

May's eyes adjusted to another degree of darkness as she breached the mouth. She reached out her arms and traced the progress of the walls with her fingertips as she took slow steps forward. Damp soaked into her gloves, patches of slime causing her to lose contact every now and then. But there were no doorways so far. No windows at any height to break the blankness either. She counted her paces. Ten ... twenty ... thirty. At fifty, she could smell wet brickwork dead ahead. She was wasting her time. A blind alley with no discernable exit. The Chinaman couldn't have come down here.

May tucked her cold hands into her coat pockets and retraced her steps, allowing herself to imagine the luxury of a cup of cocoa. The evening hadn't been a complete waste of time but it had hardly been an endorsement of her detective powers either. Perhaps she should see if that other passageway had led somewhere more promising. She exhaled a little laugh; it couldn't possibly have less to offer in terms of destinations than this one. But she was too tired to check now. The hoot of a steamer made her jump. Her nerves had needed the release. She peered ahead. The sides of the alley, where they met the street, seemed to be leaning together at the bottom now as well as the top. A trick of perspective as her eyes focused on the river-breeze blown fog sliding by in the background.

She was almost at the exit when she realised that it had been a trick of altogether different proportions. Figures had emanated from the brick walls. Three? Four? She couldn't tell where one ended and another began. For a second she wondered if the brawlers had fought their way up the street. But these were breathing lightly, and in unison. She could feel a shiver of movement in the damp air as they took a collective pace towards her. There was nowhere she could go.

'What do you want?' Her voice sounded like that of a victim. She tried again. 'Let me pass.'

'The question is what a person of the authorities is doing here.'

He sounded foreign. And he knew who she was. Had the follower been followed?

'This is no place for such a pretty young woman.'

A second voice, higher pitched and more Oriental. May's stomach clenched as she remembered Miles Elliott's friend at the inquest with her wild tales of white slave trading. Everything was getting too close to fitting together: Miles had been found dead in an alley; she'd been tracking the witness who'd tried to frame Brilliant Chang; she was in the streets where the drug barons reigned. She could feel a sort of desperate shiver begin to rattle her bones. It was the penetrating dampness of the alley. If she kept telling herself that then she wouldn't let out the scream that was forming in her throat.

'Do you know of the many, many bad things that can happen to someone so cut adrift on the sea of chance as you are?'

The first voice again but from behind her now. Close.

'We have not spent our lives like rats in basement laundries and holds of ships not to be able to move with the soundless swiftness of the wind. Our methods of ensuring co-operation are like that, too. No one knows from which direction they will come, or when they will strike.'

A ripple of laughter passed between them. The fizzing in May's legs wouldn't let her stand still any longer. She screwed her eyes shut and lunged for the safety of the street. Something touched her cheek. She did scream now. A cry that came out like that of a chicken being hung upside down by its feet. She ran into a mass of muscle and bounced to the ground. A hand grabbed her arm and pulled her up.

'What you doing here?'

The same enquiry wrapped in a different voice. May opened her eyes. Two hulking men were standing on either side, a third peering down into her face. Charlie. A lighterman who'd been a drinking pal of her father's and worked the riverside wharves. She gulped down tears.

'There were these Chinese...'

She whirled around. The entrance to the alley-way was empty.

'You all right, love? Look like you've gone and given yourself a bit of a scare. Come on, me and the boys'll walk you back. Can't have you going getting lost in the fog again.'

May breathed deeply to still the tremors that threatened to unhinge her joints. She shoved her hands deep into her pockets, clenching them into finger-numbing fists. Terror was something she'd learned to suppress in the mud and blood of France but she knew no way to stop it from mak-ing its presence felt after the danger had passed. It was a tiger that could be caged but never tamed. Back then she'd take herself off somewhere to vomit in private. That was the other thing she'd learned: what men respected as natural instincts in other men, they regarded as an unstable weakness in women. And that held as true for a coroner's officer on the streets of Poplar as it did for a war-time ambulance driver. Film reels had begun flick-ering behind her eyes, each with an ending where she was butchered more bloodily than the last. She had to think of something else. Focus on why she was here. Use the power of her mind to chase the shadows away rather than bringing them to life.

'Do you know who they were, the Chinamen?'

'We didn't see none, did we, boys? Reckon they'd scarpered by the time we got there. Either that or they were just the bogeys used to scare you as a nipper.'

May forced the required laugh. The pictures

211

grew dimmer. They had almost vanished by the time she could see an ooze of light from the street up ahead.

Charlie was rolling a cigarette in one hand as he walked 'Who's this turf belong to, Smudger? You got a load of Chinks on your ships.'

'Heard them jabbering about the Bow Kum when they've been setting off of a night.'

The voice behind her held a trace of something like awe. Charlie stopped and clutched her arm again. She felt his fingers squeeze her flesh into bruises.

'If that's kosher then you'd best learn to watch where you're going a bit better; your old man–'

'What's so special about them?' She wasn't interested in hearing whatever else he'd been about to say.

Charlie stopped walking long enough to light his cigarette, and then strode on. She almost had to run to keep up with him.

'The Bow Kum Tong is the worst in Limehouse – you don't want to go mixing none with them, fog or no fog. They're a gang of Chinks in the pay of the more bastard of the wharfingers.' He hawked and spat. 'They do his dirty business – roughing up any docker seen as a troublemaker's the least of it – and in return they get to use a storeroom as a yen-shi den. I've heard said there's an arrangement so as the wharfinger sends sailors aching to chase the dragon soon as the ship ties up. It all helps keep the wages out of an honest man's pocket, and the holds emptied for less than you'd pay a monkey in bananas.'

They were outside Poplar Institution now and

212

May waved off her escorts with assurances that she would go straight home. But there was no point in doing that because it would be hours before her tiger stopped pacing and let her sleep. She waited until she saw Charlie's broad shoulders disappear around the corner of King Street and then doubled back a few yards to walk up Lower North Road in the direction of Brabazon Street.

Chapter Twenty-Two

The place was in darkness. May skirted around the back, picked up some stones and threw them at the window of the room she knew Jack would be in – the one overlooking the privy that every landlady gave to her more cash-strapped lodgers.

It took him a while to come down. May was waiting by the low wall at the end of the terrace.

'You keep your ear to the ground, and I need some information.'

'And a good evening to you, too, Miss Keaps.' His voice was fuzzy with sleep. 'My, they do make you work long hours in your job, don't they? But, you're right, I am a newspaperman and, as such, entirely at your disposal day or night; provided there's a story in it for me, of course.'

'What do you know about the operation of the Bow Kum Tong?'

'Only that if you've uncovered any connections with them then I strongly advise you to leave them to dangle. I don't relish the thought of yours being the next inquest your handsome new coroner presides over. I'm not saying this to put the wind up you – really. The gang leader is the owner of the gambling den I've been staking out. Lots of fingers in lots of pies. All of them full to overflowing with rancid meat.'

'Do you think him wanting to frame Brilliant Chang for murder has anything to do with a drugs war?'

'Is that what's going on? Interesting.'

He took off his glasses and polished them with the edge of the pyjama jacket peeking out from under his jumper.

'There could be any number of reasons. Billy's an influential man.'

'When you were going to his club was it for the gang leader to turn up?'

'More likely one of his lackeys. Except, now I come to think of it, I don't know what he looks like so I suppose I could've come across him.'

May chewed at the side of her thumbnail. 'Could that be another of Brilliant Chang's sidelines do you think?'

Jack surprised her by laughing.

'You serious? Billy? The leader of the Bow Kum Tong? I've heard he's been accused of a lot of things in his time, but never that. Okay, he's far too cool a customer for anyone to be able to pin down exactly what keeps him in such good health and expensive clothes; however he fundamentally uses nothing more than charisma to get what he wants. That sound like the approach of the head of a vice gang to you? Sit down and take a lesson on how a real operator gets and keeps his power,

Miss Keaps.'

He put his glasses back on and perched on the wall.

'It all starts with a harmless game of pak-a-poo – a few pennies spent on buying a piece of paper printed with a Chinese character in the hope of matching them in a draw – but money thrown away on a game of chance when there's none to spare leads to vulnerability. And once in that position, it's easy to persuade them they can win it all back by getting involved in the drug game. And they are nearly all women because it's widely held they're easier to control – although in suffering this delusion they obviously haven't come across one like you. It works by getting them hooked and relying on the fact that in their jobs as cloakroom attendants, milliners, pub landladies, waitresses or manicurists, they will come across other women looking to escape the drudgery of their lives. They put them the way of the dealers, and get paid for their referrals in drugs. Thus the net grows and the money flows in hand over fist.'

May sat and listened as the night slipped into early dawn. The rattle of the milk cans being washed in the dairy ready for the first delivery; the Mail Train on the way to Victoria; the rumble of a cart's iron-rimmed wheels; the heavy whoosh of coal being tipped down chutes in Poplar Docks. How many of the men engaged in those activities knew of the things Jack had been talking about? Probably more than she'd realised. Some child of the docks she was; she knew what made the Grand Old Lady's blood flow and kept her stomach full, the grist she needed to keep the winches grinding,

215

the power of her lock-gate jaws that could flood holds with a yawn. But May had never peered inside at what kept her heart beating. Maybe it was about time she did.

'You haven't been listening to a word I've been saying, have you?'

Jack was prodding her in the ribs. She pretended to yawn.

'I was remarking on the fact that this could be one of those helping each other out moments I told you might come some day. While I was musing out loud I got to thinking perhaps the drugs angle is the ticket to busting the gambling rings wide open. Street rumour has it that the Bow Kum Tong run a yen-shi den in Shoulder of Mutton Alley. Maybe I should get myself in there and see what I might find. And if I come across anything I think you might consider useful then I'll fill you in. Can't say fairer than that, can I?'

It was a good idea and the link May had been scrabbling for since the moment she'd spotted the bogus witness coming away from the sign of the Opium Lamp. But she wasn't going to give this self-opinionated know-all the satisfaction.

'It'll have to be tomorrow night ... tonight... Saturday, anyway, if your playing an undercover spy is to be of any use to me; the coroner has scheduled the inquest to reconvene immediately after the Easter break.'

Jack mashed his half-smoked cigarette into the dirt at his feet. 'Better get my beauty sleep then.' He stood up, pushing at the base of his spine with his palms. 'I'll have you know you can wake me any time you like if it's to drop prize plums like

216

this one into my lap.'

He walked away then turned and gave May a pilot's daredevil wave.

'Night, partner.'

May stuck her hands in her coat pockets to stop from making an obscene gesture back. Jack's arrogance was insufferable; fancy him taking it upon himself to decide what was appropriate for her to know. As if she trusted him. He didn't even begin to grasp the meaning of the word *partner*. Then she grinned. Yet.

May managed a scant three hours sleep before Alice's clattering about in the kitchen made more impossible. She threw on Albert's moth-eaten dressing gown and went down to see why, this of all Saturdays, the girl couldn't have indulged in a lie-in.

'You'll never guess what?'

May wasn't up to this game right now. On rising, the queasiness that invariably accompanied the realisation of how lucky she'd been to escape from danger unharmed had asserted itself. And her head was pounding.

'Vi says I'm doing so well she's going to tell Horatio to beef up my bill matter. Call me a ... a chanteuse ... or something.'

'Don't you think you should show a little more respect by calling him Mr Barley-Freeman?'

'Everyone uses first names in the theatre – we're like a family in that way. Anyway, Vi says I'm the only one with any talent; much, much better than all the others put together.'

'I'm sure she wouldn't have been nearly that

rude. And it doesn't do to go around with a swollen head.'

'Confidence is what I've got, and that's a good thing.'

Alice had her shoulders in the cupboard searching for something. And making a teeth-jarring amount of noise in the process.

'So I take it the first rehearsal went well?'

'Horatio says it wasn't too bad seeing as it was only a walk-through.'

'I do hope amongst all this self-congratulation you're finding the time to concentrate on what they're actually paying you for; we can't afford for you to throw this job away over a small slot in a local talent show.' May knew she was being churlish and didn't like herself for it.

'That proves how much you know because the manager's right happy with me. He's agreed I can work double shifts so as I can have the week of the performance off. Kettle's just finished singing; want me to top up the pot for you?'

It wasn't like Alice to sidestep a skirmish over what she'd see as bossy interference; or to be so helpful. Then May remembered. Today was when they'd arranged for Vi to come to tea. The thought made her want to go back to bed and pull the covers over her aching head.

'Where's the bun tin? I'm going to make us rock cakes.'

'You'll have to go easy on the sugar – it's the last of our ration. And I'm not buying any more sultanas; that packet cost me one and sixpence.'

Why was she behaving like this? Was she jealous her sister had found a new friend to bring

218

excitement into her life? The sour taste of what she had hoped Jack might become unsettled her stomach again.

Alice straightened up, the tin in her hand. 'How long do you reckon the rock cakes have to be in the oven for? I'll do the ash and get some more coke in so it's nice and hot.'

May took her cup of tea back up to bed and let Alice get on with it.

She spent most of the day in a haze of sleep and recuperation. By mid-afternoon she was feeling much more like her old self and decided to pop out to scour the tat shops for a few things. Alice was meeting Vi at the Gaiety at four o'clock and walking her back. May thought it kind to give them a little time in the house together before she started sizing their guest up as a suitable influence for a young and star-struck girl.

The sound of Alice's giggling accompanied by a warmer, deeper laughter greeted her as she let herself in the front door. May took the bag of purchases up to her bedroom and then walked through into the kitchen. The comforting smell of baking made her heart clench at the memory of her mother's fruit loaf. She blinked away the threat of a tear and appraised the woman sitting as relaxed and at home as if she'd been sharing jokes with Alice all her life. She looked to be a little older than herself – twenty-four or five perhaps, with her mobile face and make-up it was difficult to tell – well proportioned without being fat, and sporting fashionably short hair. Her green eyes were large

219

and expressive, her mouth a little wide for true beauty but her full painted lips offered enough sensual promises to compensate. Her clothes – a mauve boxy jacket and pink blouse – were immaculately pressed. Vi was a woman who knew the importance of making a good first impression. And she had the confidence to capitalise on it with the sort of easy charm that had Alice seemingly wanting to kiss the ground on which she walked. May felt a little of it lapping her way and smiled. The blaze she received in return made her feel at once both regarded as an equal, and held in high esteem. Vi Tremins was either an unusually open person ... or an extremely good actress. May shook off the suspicion that served her well as a coroner's officer but put up too many barriers in her personal life, and went over to shake her hand. It was warm, the grip self-assured.

'Miss Keaps, I'm delighted to finally meet you. I'm sorry we missed each other when you came to the theatre, but Alice has told me so much about her important sister I feel I know you already. Thank you so much for inviting me into your home. Easter weekend is so dreary for an actress, the theatre is closed much of the time and it's purgatory rattling around digs. After all, there is only so much washing and ironing a girl can face doing.'

May laughed in collusion and was rewarded with another spotlight-bright smile.

'Please call me May; I suspect you've gathered by now there's never any ceremony in this house.' She pulled out the chair at the end of the table and sat. 'Has Alice offered you something?'

'Of course I have. Vi said we should wait for you.'

So May could add politeness to the growing list of Vi's accomplishments; her prejudices about actresses were going to take a hammering this afternoon.

'Tea's in the pot. Be stewed if we don't have it soon.'

'Okay, Alice, I'm sorry I'm a bit late but you can pour now.'

Her sister did so then fetched the rock buns from the draining board, placed one on each of their plates, and sat back down.

'I hope they'll be okay. I've never done any baking before.'

'Well, I'm very impressed; I can hardly boil an egg myself. I'm flattered you've gone to all this trouble on my account. And they look delicious.'

Vi picked up the bun and crammed half of it into her mouth in a distinctly unladylike manner. May was liking her more and more by the second.

'Mmm, just as I thought, scrummy.'

May just caught the wink thrown over Alice's bent head. Taking the hint she broke hers up to get to, what she hoped, would be a more edible centre.

'How long have you been on the stage, Vi?'

'All my life. Almost literally. I was born in digs next door to the White Rock Pavilion in Hastings and a week later was carried on in a production of *Darlings by Twilight*. My parents were in rep. Never the leads, you understand, but always in work. I made up my mind pretty early on to follow them

221

but dad insisted I miss the tours and stay with Granny Tremins so I could go to school. He said I had to prove I could study hard before he'd approach the ASM – sorry, assistant stage manager – to give me a job backstage. Dad wanted me to learn the ropes first, you see, just as he wanted me to have a decent education to fall back on. He and mum had done all right but knew a few had the stage door closed in their face one day only to end up starving on the streets.'

May hoped Alice was listening to this. Perhaps if Vi was sticking around for any length of time she'd back her up in the campaign to get Alice to go to night school.

'All that's made her a proper actress. Not one of those Music Hall turns we normally get at the Gaiety.'

Vi replaced her cup noiselessly in the saucer. 'If you're going to get anywhere on the stage you'll have to drop that attitude, young lady.'

She was smiling but May had picked up the edge of brittleness.

'Never look down on your fellow artistes – holds true if you're an amateur or make your living on the boards – because in this game you can be up one minute and down the next. And when you're down you'll find yourself lower than those you once turned your nose up at. Always show some respect for those with the courage to stand up there and face an audience; love them when the walls are ringing with applause, and dry their tears when they die the thousand deaths of public humiliation. Someone who truly cares for this profession treats every performance they witness as if it were their own.'

May had to lace her fingers together in her lap to stop from clapping. Alice's energy level dropped for a moment but then she brightened.

'Horatio says I'm a natural. Got stage presence. He says that's the most important thing. Although I've been working hard on my song, haven't I, Vi?'

Her guest smiled as she patted Alice's hand. 'He's a good director; knows how to bring the best out in everyone.'

'But you've got to have talent in the first place, right?'

'It helps. Makes the whole thing a lot easier. There's many don't have that to rely on and so they're terrified out of their skin every time they step in front of the floods.'

'That's just stupid to get into such a state when you're doing something you love.'

'Everyone gets scared at the mercy of an audience's approval.'

'Not you though?'

'Of course. Do you know I used to throw up whenever the knock would come telling me I was on next?'

May knew a little of how Vi felt; reading the proclamation at the opening of an inquest always made her stomach lurch.

'But I've found ways over the years to manage the worst – correct breathing, small sips of water, reciting nursery rhymes – and now I just suffer with the feeling my arms and legs belong to somebody else.' Vi took a sip of her tea. 'Nervousness is good, Alice, cultivate it a little. Because, in its absence, a performance has nothing of yourself behind it and has all the depth of an empty façade.'

May was enjoying listening to this woman's wisdom born of pitting herself against her limittions, and seeing her sister blossom under the attention. She found herself wishing the Barley-Freeman Linctus Talent Show was some time in the summer and not at the end of the month.

'Do you know him well? The director, I mean.'

'Oh, they're really good friends. Done lots of shows together, haven't you, Vi?'

'Enough. But that doesn't mean he lets up on me any. Directors have a will of iron, May, and a heart of ice to go with it; I expect you come across men like that in your profession.'

May thought of Colonel Tindal. And then of Braxton Clarke. Would she remain long enough in the job to get to know what he was like? But that thought was depressing and she was having such a nice afternoon.

'And how do you find the tyrant of the theatre, Alice?'

'Wonderful.'

Her sister had two spots of colour high on her cheeks. As she'd hardly spoken about him before, this was the first time May had seen any evidence of her king-size crush. She supposed a certain amount of hero-worship for the man who was making Alice's theatrical dreams come true was inevitable.

'An attentive director often has that effect as well.' Vi gave May another sly wink. 'You'll get over it, Alice. Just you wait until he makes you say a line over again and again, telling you he wants

224

it given a different emphasis but with no clues as to what he means, I promise you won't think him so wonderful then.'

'Bet I shall.'

May had been about to tease her a little as well but Alice's voice had held a trace of enough childish hurt for her to take pity instead. Although she could hardly remember being seventeen – a combination of the Great War and the tragedies in their family life had made her grow up pretty quickly – she knew it to be a time of blistering emotions. She didn't doubt unrequited love must be the most painful of the lot. She scraped back her chair.

'Thank you so much for the tea, Alice.'

Her sister beamed to be given the honour of hostess.

'I've got a few things to be getting on with upstairs.'

Vi made a move to get up.

'No, please stay as long as you like. And I do hope you'll regard yourself as welcome to pop in any time; it's been such a pleasure to have your company. At least come and say goodbye before you leave Poplar, won't you? I'm afraid I won't be able to be at the talent show but, as I've explained to Alice, my work is particularly demanding at the moment and I can't possibly take an afternoon off. However I'm sure I'll hear all about it – probably on a daily basis. Please feel free to take the rest of the rock buns with you.'

She could still hear Vi's full-throated laughter at the top of the stairs.

Chapter Twenty-Three

That night was the warmest of the year so far and May was sweltering in her pea-jacket. A glance in the mirror before she'd left had told her that in her tat shop finds she'd pass as a sailor – albeit a slight one – recently arrived after a long stint at sea. She had on canvas shoes, dirty baggy cotton trousers, and a coarse tunic top. Her hair was tucked under a wide-brimmed bowler hat, the black felt turning green with age. With her face stained with tea and grimed with soot she looked like a Lascar.

She'd been stalking the end of the street for over an hour. Jack couldn't have left already could he? A group of Saturday night revellers on their way to the bus stop competed with each other to throw colourful insults her way. May pretended not to understand them – or to smile at the thoroughness of her disguise. A figure emerged from Mrs Loader's front door. He stood on the step for a moment before taking off his glasses and tucking them into his pocket. For someone new to the docks, Jack hadn't done a bad job at all. He was dressed as if he worked in the boiler-room of one of the large steamers. Not a stoker or fireman – he didn't have the muscles for that – but in his filthy overalls and bandanna tied over his forehead he did a fair imitation of an oily-rag engineer.

May waited until he was halfway down the road

and then caught up with him.

'Going my way, sailor?'

His aghast double-take was worthy of a stage comedian.

'Jesus, Mary and Joseph, May. You had me going there. What the hell do you think you're doing in that get-up?'

'A little undercover spying I think we agreed to call it.'

He stopped. 'No ... no. You're not coming. There's nothing can persuade me. I work better alone.'

'What happened to all that partner nonsense of yours?'

May was enjoying herself. Jack looked as though he wanted to run back indoors and hide. But she hadn't gone to all this trouble to stand here teasing him.

'Jack, let's get this straight: it may have been your brainwave, but it's my investigation. And although you're probably not used to someone being this honest, I don't altogether trust you. Getting a lead for your precious gambling story is the only reason you're doing this and I can't be sure that won't involve you doing or saying something that might prejudice the inquest. I could issue a warrant and make it a court order.' May was only half-joking.

Jack moved his hands towards her shoulders as if he wanted to shake her, but then shrugged.

'Not a word. Not one single bloody word from you when we're in there. Play the dumb foreigner out for a bit of diversion and I suppose we might just get away with it; they discover you're a woman and God knows what they'll do to you.'

'Don't be stupid, that'll be nothing compared with them finding out you're a newspaperman. Come on, hadn't we better get going? We've a long walk ahead.'

She fell in step beside him. They trudged the streets in silence.

Shoulder of Mutton Alley was off the street fronting the riverside wharves. True to its name it started off as a head-height arched tunnel then kicked off left into a tiny square of dilapidated houses. May had seen privies in better condition – but the stench was the same. Thin threads of light seeped from shuttered windows. She stumbled once or twice into Jack's back. He must have got his information from a reliable source because he made straight for a door half hanging off its hinges. He creaked it open. Behind was a thick curtain. When pulled to one side it revealed a narrow staircase. The smell of rotting wood made May not want to trust it. But Jack was going first and she'd attempt to watch where he put his feet so as not to end up with a splintered shinbone.

Someone above must've heard their entrance because an oil lamp's dim light appeared at the top. May began to shiver with the damp; if she didn't know any better she'd think they were at the water's edge. The woman who met them was no more than a girl really. White and Chinese blood had given her face high flat cheekbones but rounded eyes and a square jaw. She led them along a passageway. The house had to be connected to its neighbour in some way because they seemed to walk further than the frontage. The girl opened a door for them then retreated. A smell – a combination like treacle, the glue factory, and singed hair – snatched at the back of May's throat. A wizened man in a Chinese cap and blue robe with long sleeves over his hands was squatting behind a low table. Behind him, the room was furnished with some raised platforms covered in matting and a line of bunks against one wall. A miserly fire burned in a small grate, a jug and battered iron pot beside it.

'I am Ling.' The man's voice was oddly beautiful. 'You are wise to come to me. Here you will find the best yen-shi, straight from China; my cousin brings it on the ships.'

Jack reached into his pocket and placed some money on the table. The old man sucked it up his sleeve.

'Take the place of your choosing. You will not have long to wait.'

May let Jack lead her over to one of the low plinths. He selected the corner bunk. She could see why; it was close to another tight stairway and out of the circle of light from the oil lamp so he'd easily be able to disappear to explore what secrets the house contained. She waited for whatever would happen next. The old man rang a tinkly bell and a trapdoor opened in the floor to the right of the fireplace. A birdlike woman dressed in faded threadbare silk and bowed with age emerged. She was carrying a tray. Her movements were delicate and purposeful as she laid the tray on the floor in order to put some water from the jug into the pot and settle it in the embers. Then

229

she squatted and began shredding a lump of what looked like coal into a small strainer. This she hung in the heating water. May thought the whole process was like making tea – apart from the sickly smell. The woman stirred and prodded at the mixture with a wooden spoon.

Ling had now joined the woman at the fireplace. She handed him the rest of the things on her tray; two pipes, a long needle like a sail maker's bodkin, and a small brass lamp. Each time the old man received an item he walked slowly across the room and placed it on his low table. The woman was poking about in the pot with her spoon as Ling lit the brass lamp. When she pulled the spoon out there was a gob of dark syrup coating the bowl. She shuffled across the room and offered it to Ling. He stuck the needle in and twirled the shaft between his fingers until he had a lump the size of a pea. Somehow May couldn't stop watching the slow movements even though her eyelids were getting heavy. She followed the progress of the needle as Ling slid the end towards the brass lamp. The opium frazzled in the flame. The smell of carnations grew suffocating. May had the sensation of being wrapped in a blanket so tightly that she could no longer feel her limbs. Across the distance of a lifetime she could see Ling offering a pipe to Jack. He would come over and make her take one. She could hear him as his sleeves flapped the air and slapped against his sides like water on a ship's hull.

May didn't think she'd been asleep very long. Everything was the same. But then there was a scream and the thump of feet on the floor over her head. Moments later, Jack came flying down the stairs. He broke stride long enough to grab her hand and wrench her upright, then dragged her out of the room. They burst out into the night. From the doorways on either side streamed a handful of Chinamen. Her arm felt pulled out of its socket as Jack bolted for the alley. She briefly thought that it'd be a miracle if they got to the end without either of them smashing their brains out on the walls then saved her energy for running as fast as she could.

May grasped her side as she got a stitch. Her throat felt as though she had been swallowing molten metal. She had to stop. Doubled over and gasping like a stranded fish, she waited for Jack to notice she was no longer beside him. She had her breath back and had wiped her streaming eyes before she realised he wasn't going to. She limped up to where he was standing – as serene as you like – by the churchyard wall.

'What if I'd have twisted my knee or something?'

'Well you haven't, have you?'

Jack was wide-eyed and smiling. May watched as he traced the outlines of the moss-covered bricks with his fingertips.

'Can we stop now d'you think? We must have left them behind miles ago. Anyway, I don't think I could run any further in these stupid canvas shoes. They're biting at my ankles.'

'Take them off then. Feel the ground beneath your feet: *Here we will moor our lonely ship, and*

231

wander ever with woven hands; murmuring softly lip to lip, along the grass, along the sands; murmuring how far away are the unquiet lands.'

'What are you on about?'

'William Butler Yeats, my lovely girl. The greatest Irishman that ever lived.'

'You smoked some, didn't you? The opium.'

'Don't tell me you didn't have a little puff yourself...'

'Of course not. I'm not that stupid.'

'Well that's where we differ. Not in the denseness of our comprehension – I wouldn't want to have a competition with you on that front – but in our desire to throw ourselves wholeheartedly into the thing that must be done.' He held his hand up, palm out, as if taking an oath. 'To perfect the air of verisimilitude alone is the reason I did it, your honour.'

May wasn't so sure. She was beginning to believe that he was a man wedded to trying new sensations and excitements for their own sakes. He had a satisfaction about him that spoke of enjoying the whole escapade – even the chase.

'So. Did you find anything out?'

'You could be Chinese, you know, with a name like May. A pink may blossom hanging tantalisingly out of reach on a high branch. Or would that be Japanese? Either way, I thought you looked quite at home sitting cross-legged on your little pallet.'

'Jack. I'm being serious; what was upstairs? Who screamed? It frightened the life out of me.'

'Worried they'd stabbed me with one of their hot needles? How sweet.' He grabbed her hand.

232

'All that Yeats has given me a thirst to smell water. Come on, there must be some close by.'

May planted her feet and refused to be dragged along. Jack let her go but continued on.

'When I was a boy, I used to stroll on the banks of the River Liffey with my father. You could taste the salt on the tide. Sometimes, if we were lucky, we'd find a piece of driftwood and he'd spin me a tale about how it had come all the way from America because it wanted more than anything to be thrown on our fire to warm my little Irish heart.'

He turned around and stretched his arm out to her.

'Won't you come with me, Blossom of May, and see what delights your river holds in its watery grip?'

She shuddered. In his state, a slippery quayside and a plunge to the bottom were the only things waiting for him. As they had been for her father.

'You're going the wrong way. Regent's Canal is over there.' She pointed beyond the church. 'If that's water enough for you.'

'I don't mind what shape it comes in, so long as it smells of the dreams of nations.'

May snorted. 'The varnish works, more like. Let's get this over with then we can both go home to our beds.'

But she had to admit that she needed something to calm her racing senses; perhaps his poet's soul knew a thing or two after all.

Chapter Twenty-Four

They sat on the swing-arm of the lock gates, their shoulders touching. The water was still and dark, the sky tinged with the yellow glow of the lights in the streets beyond the bridge. It wasn't a lyrical Dublin night, but they had this little corner of the world to themselves.

'Are you feeling better now?'

'Not feeling anything at all, if truth be told. Interesting stuff, this opium. It sort of takes you inside yourself and holds you there. After a few glasses of the Black Stuff I find myself wanting to be friends with everybody, words and music spilling out of my mouth as if they can hold back time. But now I'm perfectly content to be here with you. Just be.'

May watched the head of a water rat break the surface.

'Tell me, Blossom of May, can you pinpoint the most important moment in your life: the one where everything changed forever?'

Of course she could. Albert and Henry's deaths. Before that she'd been an ordinary girl working in the tobacco factory and going to night school; afterwards she was driving ambulances full of mortally wounded soldiers in France. And now she was someone who needed the close proximity of death to feel anything like alive. However she didn't feel inclined to open herself up to a drug-doped man by saying so.

'I can. Easter Monday 1916. I take it that date means something to you?'

'I'm not totally ignorant of the world outside Poplar. The start of the Irish Rebellion.'

'Easter Rising we prefer to call it. Our bid to throw off the yoke of the British oppressors. My father was one of those involved in the planning. Took an active part, too.'

'He was a Sinn Féiner?'

'And a Freedom Fighter. They held out for six days until they were finally machine-gunned and bombed into submission. Unfair odds, wouldn't you say? He was climbing over a roof in Abbey Street when he was picked off by a British bullet. He is a hero back home. You might not agree with his politics and methods but he lived and died for what he believed in. It's impossible to ask any more of someone, don't you think? And ever since then I've tried to honour his example – not with guns and violence, but with words. Words that may one day change what people think. Provoke action to right wrongs and challenge injustice. It's a weight I barely feel on my shoulders and one I'm happy to carry to my grave. There are those who light the way for others to follow, Blossom of May, and I hope that my name is one day numbered amongst them as my father's is now.'

She was sure she should feel something like shock at his revelation but instead it was envy cloaking her thoughts. Her father had left her a legacy, too, but it was one that dragged her down until sometimes she felt as if she were drowning along with him.

'You can't choose your family, can you?' Each syllable felt heavy enough to plop into the water.

'What is it, Blossom of May? You can tell me. There are no secrets between co-conspirators.'

May picked at a cotton slub on her trousers. She had never said this to anyone but if she didn't release it now then she knew she never would; it would continue to eat at her until there was nothing left inside but bitterness and fear.

'My father was a suicide. I was stationed in Etaples so have no idea what drove him to it; everyone I've spoken to has a different story of his mood at the time. But don't you think losing your only son would be enough to plunge anyone into a black melancholy that would seem impossible to climb out of? Daughters not being nearly enough to live for.' She sniffed and wiped her nose on her sleeve. 'I've attended enough inquests to know that a tendency to despair can run in families and I'm scared for Alice's future. I've noticed how she lives on extremes of excitement and I think it might be because she knows she's walking a tightrope stretched over a yawning chasm. What if, as an actress, she plays one too many tragedies and loses her footing only to find nothing at the bottom but a conviction that life is merely a longer version of the same play?'

Jack took her hand

'She's met a new friend – Vi came to tea and seems very nice. I hope she'll be a steadying influence but she's not going to be around for long whereas Alice's memories of the night our father walked out and never came back will be with her forever. So even if she isn't tainted by melancholy,

236

she still has the burden of feeling second rate. Losing out on love to a dead brother.'

May rested her chin on her chest so Jack wouldn't see the tears. She knew Alice felt this. She knew it because the legacy was shared equally.

'You forget...'

He lifted her fingers and kissed the tips.

'...Alice has your influence, too. You are strong and independent, and the most determined woman I've ever met. And you love her very much or you wouldn't be so distressed. Because I've smoked the black pearl the emotions I've been indulging in this evening are partly illusory but yours are as deep and real as the canal. Start believing that your guidance and wisdom are much more important to your sister than any quirk of fate, and she'll be fine. Come on, I can feel your bones begin to chill. Let's leave our shadow-selves to be sucked away on the tide and go home.'

They stood and, hand in hand like old friends, turned their backs on the brooding water.

Jack's lodgings were closest so they headed there first. The corner of Upper North Road by the guano factory was unusually lively. Groups of people – women with babes in arms and rags in their hair, men with un-tucked shirts and hanging braces – were huddled in cloaks of excitement. There was an unfamiliar taste in the air. Smoke. They crossed the road and turned into his street. Police. A fire engine. An ambulance waiting for the worst.

'You can't come down here.'

PC Collier.

'Miss Keaps, I nearly didn't twig it was you. Been to an Easter fancy dress party at the social? Didn't know one was on myself. Bit of an unexpected do here tonight as well.'

May let go of Jack's hand and took the stupid hat off.

'What happened? Gas?'

'Not likely. Chief Fire Officer reckons it was deliberate. Petrol bomb at first guess. Yard reeks of the stuff. Keep back now.'

'Whose house is it?'

'Number forty-one.'

'That's Kitty Loader's. Is she all right?'

'Reckon so. Neighbours say she came running out and raised the alarm. Ambulance boys are checking her and the others over now. Let's just hope they all got out, eh, because them flames look set to eat their way to the front however much water they spray on them.'

The firemen's brass helmets gleamed in the street lamp; the horses stamped and whinnied as jets of steam escaped from the boiler used to pressurise the water; thick hoses writhed on the ground as they snaked into the passageway leading to the back of the house. Sparks floating up in the air, then snuffed out like tiny red shooting stars. Mini rivers flowed in every direction. The explosive crack of windowpanes.

Something in the activity suddenly brought Jack to life.

'I need to get my notes.' He dodged PC Collier's restraining arm and ran down the street.

'Oy, you can't go in there. It ain't safe!'

But Jack's bid for freedom had set the others off.

238

PC Collier's attempt at crowd control was no contest against the spectacle of a burning building; East Enders loved nothing more than to watch someone else's possessions being turned to ash. May had always thought it was partly gratitude that it wasn't their own. She followed with PC Collier in the wake of the, now almost jubilant, inhabitants of Brabazon Street.

'Ten to one there's not a stick left.'

'Won't be as good as that Chink blaze last June.'

'You there?'

'Not half. Hell of a show it was. They should never have tried to move them families in. Not with one of our brave soldiers needing a roof over his head.'

'Ain't right is it? White women marrying foreigners.'

'I should sodding well think not. Anyways, we showed 'em. House went up like a roman candle. Every scrap burnt to the ground.'

'I reckon this'un had it coming to her as well. What with taking in a bog Irish and everything. Asking for trouble in my book.'

'Read in the paper they dragged a Beak from a tram in Dublin and shot him dead. Who's to say they ain't started to bring their shenanigans over here?'

May watched Jack slump back down the street, his overalls soaked with spray from the hose.

'They won't let me in.'

'You surprised? If the flames hit the gas, the whole place could go up.'

He pulled off his bandana and wiped the grime from his face. May felt sorry for him, he looked so defeated.

'Maybe they'll catch it before it reaches your room. If it started in the yard then it's got three floors to go up.'

'All my work for the story's in there; I didn't think it was safe to leave it in the newspaper office.' He grabbed her arm. 'Of course. That's the whole point. You know who did this, don't you? The Tong. Don't you see? It has to be them. After tonight, they know I'm getting too close. This is a warning that next time it won't only be property that's damaged.'

'Sorry, sir, you're under arrest.' PC Collier was clutching Jack's shoulder. 'One of your neighbours has fingered you as living in the house. There are some questions you need to be answering.'

'What? Don't be so bloody stupid. Why would I firebomb my own place?'

'Insulting the uniform won't be helping your cause none. We're on the alert for any suspect activity involving an Irishman and I reckon this – and you – fit that bill well enough. Now, are you going to co-operate or do I need to use the cuffs?'

May watched as all traces of Jack's previous befuddlement left him. He undid his wet overalls, stepped out of them, found his glasses in the pocket, and put them on. Then he straightened the collar of his crumpled shirt. He turned to her.

'I'd be obliged if you could see your way to doing me a favour. Can you find a telephone and call Sir Ernest Pollock. Tell him to come to...' He looked sideways at PC Collier.

'I reckon we'll be heading straight for Scotland Yard.'

240

'Better make it there, then.'

She must've looked confused because he spelt the name out slowly before giving her the exchange, and telephone number.

'Jack, is this some kind of joke? I've seen his name in the newspapers, he's one of the most famous barristers in London.'

'The very same. And that's why I want him with me.'

'But you'll never be able to afford his fees. Let me go around to Mr Gliksman, he's a solicitor we've had some dealings with in court. Or maybe Andy Taylor knows someone your paper calls on in times like these.'

'Now, May, you seem to be labouring under as many misguided notions about me as my erstwhile friendly neighbours. I've never told you I'm without means – far from it in fact. My uncle owns a number of the prominent local newspapers in the area. Needless to say including the *East End News*. Sir Ernest is a good friend of his. So please, run along and help me out before some inspector or other decides to throw the book at me in retaliation for getting him hauled out of bed at this ungodly hour.'

The bond they'd forged at the waterside fell away and May felt she was staring into the face of a stranger. Nothing about him was as it seemed. Probably all that stuff he'd told her about his father being a hero was just one of his little games. He was simply a silver-tongued liar who got kicks from sucking people into his deceptions. She had no doubt he'd be a famous journalist one day, even if he did have to play everyone for a fool along the way – and rely on his uncle's patronage.

May refused to return his smile and walked away. There was a public kiosk in the all-night chemist on East India Dock Road. She'd ring from there – because he'd asked her to, not because she cared what happened to him.

It was only when she'd turned into the silence of Guildford Road that it came to her that Jack could be right about the perpetrators, but wrong about the reason. What if this was something to do with the inquest on Miles Elliott? What if her presence in the yen-shi den had made the Tong realise she hadn't paid enough attention to the threat she'd received on the streets of Limehouse? Just because Jack had been the only one they'd recognised didn't mean that, with the all-knowing powers Charlie said they possessed, they hadn't established it had to be her with him. This firebombing might've been only half of the warning. Alice. She started to run.

Chapter Twenty-Five

Back at work after the Easter long weekend, May was typing up the notes Braxton Clarke had sent over in preparation for the afternoon's inquest. With her fingers clacking on the typewriter keys, Saturday night began to feel as if it had happened to somebody else When she'd arrived home – feeling sick and out of breath – the house had been just as she'd left it. It had taken her until she'd reached the front door to remember Alice had been over in Cawdor Street helping Elaine with her Easter bonnet for the factory parade. When she'd arrived back for Sunday lunch, May had suggested her sister take up Mrs Gibson's offer to lodge there until the show was over: Alice's gloating at getting her own way was easier to swallow than the thought of her coming to some harm at the hands of the Tong.

Now the problem of the moment was how to head off Braxton Clarke from asking what had happened about the arrest and return to court of the man they knew as Sing Quong. May had issued the warrant but it was sitting in her desk drawer. PC Collier would be hauled over the coals for not verifying the identity of his witness and he was far too good a policeman to receive a black mark because he'd been inexperienced enough to be taken in. So, how to address the fact that the perjurer wasn't going to be turning up, without dropping the constable in it? The solution came as she scrolled a fresh piece of paper into the typewriter. She'd insert something into the coroner's notes to say an unsuccessful investigation had been conducted – she had found and followed Sing Quong after all – which pointed to the likelihood of Brilliant Chang being a victim of a conspiracy to deceive. Worded that way no one would be made to suffer for the pigtailed Chinaman's lies.

She pressed the carriage return lever twice and began to type. The resumed inquest started off in the usual fashion with May administering the oath to any new witnesses – in this case, Dr Wilcox, the chemical analyst from St Mary's Hospital. Those of Miles' friends who had turned up before were all present, as was Brilliant Chang. Elizabeth Newick had obviously not been able to rationalise her prejudice and was casting fearful glances at the Chinaman from her seat on the other side of the room. The Elliotts had sent representation. May wondered if it was Mr Elliott's way of demonstrating his displeasure that the inquest hadn't been concluded as promised. After the coroner had given a brief summary of progress so far, he gave the Elliotts' solicitor leave to ask questions of Brilliant Chang. These consisted of an extended dissection of the fact that Miles Elliott had been known to eat at his restaurant on occasions when a ship was due to dock during the night.

When the solicitor had finally run out of permutations Braxton Clarke thanked him, asked the jury if there was anything they wanted clarified, then glanced down at his notes. There was a long pause before he looked up again and announced that as it was nearly one o'clock, they would break for lunch.

May was sitting in her office when he came in from his chambers.

'What, precisely, do you mean by this, Miss Keaps?'

He had a page of his notes in his hand and was stabbing at it with his index finger.

'Do you think I need you to do my job for me? I've been Deputy Coroner for City of London and Southwark for four years and I've managed very well in all that time to formulate my own opinion

244

as to the veracity of witness testimony. Furthermore, I am entirely at liberty to accept or refuse any evidence as I see fit and instruct the jury accordingly. That is my role, Miss Keaps, not yours. How dare you overstep your authority? You are my officer and it is in the nature of the job that I have to rely heavily on you ... but that does not include telling me what to think. It may interest you to know I had already come to the conclusion that we were unlikely ever to see that particular witness again.'

There was a knock on the door. He stalked across and wrenched it open. 'What?'

It was the postman with the early afternoon delivery.

'I'll take those.'

He snatched the letters and threw them on the desk. May felt her cheeks grow hot to be caught being reprimanded like a naughty schoolgirl. Braxton Clarke slammed the door shut.

'I don't know what else to say ... really I don't... Congratulations, Miss Keaps, you are undoubtedly the first person ever to render me lost for words...'

He had lowered his voice which made his anger all the more intense. May couldn't do anything but stare at the strewn envelopes and wish she was anywhere but here.

'I am too outraged ... yes, outraged ... by your temerity to continue this now. I'll speak to you later.' And he marched off back to his chambers, waving the offending notes like a battle flag.

May laced and unlaced her fingers, cursing her stupidity. How could she have forgotten this man wasn't anything like Colonel Tindal? He took pride in his abilities and she'd insulted his competence. But there was more to it than that, and she knew it. She'd been trying too hard to prove to him how clever she was, what an invaluable coroner's officer she made. Well, she'd blown that now. Gone were the chances of him giving her a glowing reference when the new coroner was appointed. She'd be out of a job for certain then. And he could still sack her straight away. What had Dr Swan called it? *Inability or misbehaviour.* Well, if that applied to a coroner there was no reason why it couldn't also be true of his officer.

But she still had the rest of the inquest to get through. She should eat something. Except her mouth was so dry she didn't know if she'd be able to swallow. She bent under the desk to get her fishpaste sandwich from her bag. She hadn't heard him come back into the room. He was standing in front of her, an uncertain smile ghosting his lips.

'I'm really very sorry, May. I shouldn't have shouted at you like that. It was unprofessional with a colleague, and downright unforgivable behaviour towards you as a young woman.' He ran the fingers of one hand through his hair. 'I have this terrible habit of letting my emotions get the better of me; my wife is always ticking me off for it. I understand that you might have had a different way of operating with Colonel Tindal, but it won't do for me. As I said before – or rather as I remember shouting...' A trace of a blush highlighted his cheekbones. 'I prefer my coroner's officer to be my representative behind the scenes and for me to do the work in the courtroom. Now, do you think

246

we can put it all behind us and start again … please?'

May nodded. She didn't know how else to respond; it was the most gracious apology she'd ever received. Braxton Clarke clasped his hands together like a reprieved miscreant.

'Splendid. A cup of tea to seal the bargain, I think, before we go back into the fray. No, you sit there and eat your sandwich. I'll make it.' And he walked, faintly whistling, into the kitchenette.

The courtroom gallery was now peppered with a few press reporters. May guessed the jury had been gossiping in a pub over lunch and word had got around that something was brewing. Either that or the reporters had only just got up. The coroner asked Dr Willcox to give his evidence and the medical expert immediately showed his experience by addressing himself directly to the jury.

'I will keep my statement brief. If there's anything or any point that you don't understand please interrupt me and I will be happy to go over it again. I concur with the post-mortem results that the deceased had smoked opium just prior to death. I'm afraid it's impossible to say how much but, quite frankly, it wouldn't make any difference to my conclusions. Because there was a completely different drug in his system. That is, one not from the family of narcotics. A tropane alkaloid: namely, cocaine.'

May felt a shift in the air surrounding Brilliant Chang. She sneaked a glance. His placid expression hadn't changed but she noticed he had crossed his legs and his free foot was twitching.

That wasn't what he'd wanted to hear.

'And that – beyond any doubt – would not have been taken by the deceased voluntarily. Either before or after the opiate.'

The whole courtroom was charged with energy now; it was as if the chemical analyst's words had set a bomb ticking.

'Let me explain: opium addicts search for release through narcotic dreams and torpor. Cocaine is a stimulant and would immediately heighten their senses to such an extent they would be consumed with hyperactivity; the two are counterproductive and a seasoned drug taker such as the deceased would've known this.'

A member of the jury held up his hand. 'How can you know that for a fact? Dr Swan only said he'd smoked some opium in that Chinaman's restaurant before he died...'

Brilliant Chang's solicitor stood and opened his mouth to speak but the coroner motioned for him to sit down again.

'It's all right, I had noticed.' He turned to the jury. 'I want you to be quite clear on the fact that no link – none whatsoever – has been established between Mr Chan here and the taking of narcotics. Nor yet is there a direct link with the deceased himself, other than the fact that the body was discovered in close proximity to his establishment.'

May admired Braxton Clarke's technique. He hadn't exactly dismissed Sing Quong's entire testimony – which, of course, he couldn't do without her being able to furnish the proof that he'd been lying – but he had placed it firmly in the realms of speculation. Brilliant Chang wasn't going to have his name put forward for trial at the Old Bailey quite yet.

'Please, Dr Willcox, if you would continue with your explanation...'

'The tissue samples I tested showed abnormalities in the liver and spleen. The fluids – bile, urine and blood – all similarly demonstrated changes associated with the long-term use of opium. However, that is of secondary importance to the evidence I found of acute congestion in the heart and brain tissues and the large volume of cocaine in the stomach contents. I would stake my reputation on the fact that it was an overdose of cocaine that killed Miles Elliott.'

The coroner waited for the buzz in the room to die down and for the jury to focus on him.

'Thank you, Dr Willcox. This court is indebted to you for your thorough work, and the fact that you have stated your opinions in so clear and unequivocal a fashion. Do I take it there are no further questions for this witness?... In that case, you are free to leave.'

The medical expert returned his notes to his briefcase, nodded once to the coroner, and walked to the door. Braxton Clarke waited until nothing could be heard except the ticking of the clock.

'Such testimony leads me to question how it is possible that none of his friends here present, who professed to know Miles Elliott well, could have missed the obvious signs of habitual drug use. I happen to find that most unlikely. As I do that Mr Chan here was anywhere other than where he said he was on the night in question; in fact, I have

249

personally corroborated his alibi with the woman concerned. From now on I will have nothing but the truth told in this court and, believe me, the penalties at my disposal for doing otherwise are severe indeed. So, Mr Weatherby, Miss Fogle, Miss Newick ... do any of you wish to re-take the stand and modify your testimony in any way?'

None made a motion to rise.

'Very good. That was your last chance for leniency. I suggest you go away, think about the implications of what we have heard here this afternoon, and consider that there is such a thing as manslaughter for knowingly allowing a person to endanger their lives with the use of illegal drugs.'

Was May imagining it, or did Braxton Clarke choose to let his gaze rest on Brilliant Chang?

'We will reconvene at a date to be announced. I can promise you that the real story of why and how a young man met his death will come out in this court: this inquest will not be concluded until it has.' He stood. 'God save the King.'

May went up to the caretaker's flat to tell him that the undertaker would be arriving some time in the early evening to take charge of Miles Elliott's body. Then she checked that the lights were switched off in the main building, and locked up. She turned the corner and headed up Cottage Street. Jack was there leaning against a wall, smoking.

'I thought you were never coming out.' He fell in step beside her. 'How are you, Jack? I'm fine thanks...'

'With all your strings, I assumed you would be.'

'That's unnecessarily dismissive of you. I had an uncomfortable time for a while back there. But it was Sinn Féin conspirators they were looking for and the only thing they had on me was my Irish accent. The upshot being that I was able to keep my recent activities to myself and the lid firmly on my gambling story until I'm ready to blow the whole thing wide open. Oops, I suppose a man arrested for being a suspected fire-bomber shouldn't say things like that. In case you're interested, I went back to the house and all my notes were intact.'

'Good, I'm so glad for you.'

'I have one piece of news at least that might make you drop the sarcasm. My uncle has agreed for the paper to carry a series of articles on the East End craftsmen in the building trades. Mrs Loader's house will be better than new in the blink of an eye, with no cost to herself and a bit of cash left over to compensate for her loss of rent. She's very happy and even trying to wangle an indoor toilet as part of the deal.'

May supposed she had to accept that he wasn't being completely self-absorbed.

'Where is she staying?'

'With her sister. And I'm back bunking up with Uncle Paul in Hampstead for the time being. Not that you were going to ask.'

May stopped at the greengrocers for some onions and potatoes. Jack waited, and then offered to carry the bag for her. She thought he might as well be useful as he obviously was intent on accompanying her at least as far as the railway station.

'I got to thinking whilst I was sitting in my lonely cell waiting for Sir Ernest to turn up – thanks for making that telephone call, by the way – where did Miles get the money to smoke opium?'

'He obviously managed it pretty well. We found out in court today he all but lived on the stuff.'

'Even more reason to ask the question then. If the Tong run their drugs operation the way they do their gambling dens, they'd have charged him as a middle-class white man well over the odds. So, I say again, where did he get the cash from?'

'We'll have to wait to find that out at the inquest.'

'Don't tell me, Blossom of May, that you've lost your taste for entrepreneurial adventure already?'

'I wish you wouldn't call me that. And this isn't some sort of boy's comic book story: it's a young man's death. Manslaughter at the very least – probably murder.'

'Which, I'd have thought, makes it all the more vital you keep digging. Whoever did it won't just walk into a police station, wrists at the ready. It's up to you to crack this.'

May winced; he was touching a nerve. But the only way she had any hope of Mr Clarke not writing an adverse report on her to the new coroner was to play everything strictly by the book.

'I'll have you know that I came very close to getting the sack after that business with the yenshi den.'

'And Mrs Loader and the other lodgers could have lost their lives.'

'That was down to you. I'm not responsible for

the Tong knowing who you were. It was a half-baked idea anyway. From now on I'm only going to follow up the leads the coroner stipulates; that way I might stand a chance of him actually thinking I know what I'm doing.'

'What is known amongst fighting men as a coward's way of looking at things: don't stick your head above the parapet and you won't get shot at.'

May stopped in her tracks and stared at Jack's back as he walked away from her. That had been an unbelievably cruel thing to say. He knew how much she had already put herself on the front line, and how much she still felt, as a woman, she had to prove.

He was waiting outside the pawnshop for her. She wasn't going to give him the satisfaction of seeing how much his accusation had stung and pretended to be searching in her shoulder bag for something. But neither was she going to fuel the man's arrogance by letting him believe he was the only one prepared to take risks. She caught up with him, her mind made up.

'I go out to Essex with a rambling club some weekends.'

'My, my, with such an exciting life I wonder you find the time to talk to me at all.'

'You really are an insufferable prig. One of the group is a chap called Roger. He's a bank clerk in Epping. Where the Elliotts live. I think I might just join them this Sunday and see if he can uncover anything untoward in Miles' financial affairs.'

'Glad you're seeing sense and grasping my little tip. But I think I should come with you – as a

253

newspaperman I'm highly trained in knowing the right questions to ask without giving anything away. I'm correct in my assumption you want this little bit of nosing around kept secret?'

Was everyone today hell-bent on telling her that she didn't know how to do her job properly? However much she wanted to point out that he hadn't shown himself to be such an ace investigative journalist, she could see how getting him involved could work to her advantage. If she happened to learn of something whilst in the company of a companion who was researching a story on Miles Elliott's tragic death ... and the information was ultimately instrumental in helping bring a killer to justice... Even Braxton Clarke couldn't find fault with her for that.

Chapter Twenty-Six

'Okay, hold it there.'

Horatio was sitting on a chair at the footlights, the stage empty except for the figure of Alice standing in front of a bucolic backdrop. From the prompt corner, Vi thought the effect would come over nicely. She'd had the turns in one by one during the last week in an effort to add some sophisticated polish to their stage business. With the majority it had been like pulling teeth, but Alice had picked up every nuance. The girl must also have paid some attention to sweet-talking her way into the stagehands' affections; it's a fair bet they wouldn't have offered up the use of such a pristine drop for anybody else. Now all that remained was to decide on costume. The amateurs were expected to provide the bulk of what they needed but Vi thought she might jettison the flower basket and give it to Alice; it would enhance the girl's innocence – and enable her to secure something more befitting her own pro status. Maybe a coster barrow laden with bunches of big daisies.

Horatio had turned to the piano player in the band pit. 'Take a break, mate, but don't go far.' He stood and walked up stage. 'This isn't working, Alice. It's not your singing but the way you're presenting the song. It's all too ... twee.'

Vi felt her jaw muscles clench. She thought that's what they'd decided on... What she'd decided on.

'And you're much too pretty to come across as somebody's maiden aunt.'

Alice's bright laughter bounced around the stage.

'Flyman! You got a pub scene up there? Tables, chairs, bottles in the background; that sort of thing.'

A curse floated down from the gantry followed by a lot of banging about.

'This do you, guv? Stand clear!'

There was a rumble as he unleashed the ropes and a second backdrop scrolled down. The wooden roller weighting the canvas bounced off the stage. A cloud of dust flew up and set everyone in the vicinity coughing.

'Much better. Now come downstage with me

and take a look.'

Alice moved to join him but Vi could see only too well what Horatio was proposing. It was a crudely-painted scene but from the gallery it would look deeply atmospheric: a forlorn tap room after closing time full of spilt dreams, dashed hopes and broken promises. Alice would look radiant in front of it.

Horatio had his arm cradling the girl's waist. 'I know you think you've only been engaged to sing, but I'd like you to have a go at a bit of acting. Do you think you could manage that, Alice?'

'I'll do anything you ask.'

'Spoken like a real trooper. Now, I want you to imagine that... Anyone, fetch me another chair, will you?'

A stagehand brought one on, and Horatio positioned it opposite his.

'Sit down, Alice. No, don't shuffle away; I placed the chairs close for a reason. I expect you played *let's pretend* often as a child, didn't you?'

Vi felt a twinge on Alice's behalf; for someone so quick on the uptake his tone would be insufferably patronising. However, the girl didn't seem to mind, just leant forward a little more as if to breathe in his every word.

'So, the scenario is this... You and I are a courting couple.'

Good God, the girl was actually blushing.

'We haven't been seeing each other for long but you are as keen as mustard – told all your friends about me, planned the wedding in your head; that sort of thing.'

Now he really was stretching his notions of

make-believe.

'And all that has led you to expect that the next time we meet will be a big occasion. Look...'

His hand disappeared momentarily inside his jacket. With a flourish he produced a bunch of yellow paper roses.

'...I even sent you flowers'

He handed them over, and Alice giggled. Vi put down the stocking she'd been darning to pass the time. That had been the self-same trick he'd used on her that first night. Except then it had been slightly stage-soiled carnations. The turns weren't the only ones who'd been learning something about sophistication.

'You were so excited that you couldn't wait, and arrived early. Here you are, sitting at a table in the snug, and you see me come in the door. Your face lights up – yes, just like that. Perfect. But I don't take off my coat to join you. Instead I make a little speech about how you are a special girl, and I will always think of you fondly, but that I have fallen in love with another... Now, Alice, how do you think that would make you feel?'

Vi could hardly wait to hear the answer herself.

'Heartbroken ... sad ... foolish...'

She was biting her lip so hard it looked as though she might draw blood.

'...Angry ... but most of all like I'm not going to allow you to make me feel I'm dirt.'

'Good ... that's the ticket. What else?'

'Sort of used up. Like a squeezed orange.'

'Spot on. Vi, didn't I say she was a natural? All right, with all those emotions in mind, I want you to sing the song again. Focus on what you've lost

257

– what you thought was all there for you bar the taking.'

Vi grudgingly had to admit that as director Horatio had the final say in all the performances but the familiar flame of jealousy was licking at her rationality. The girl was already half in love with him for Christ's sake; did he have to give her any encouragement?

'Okay, from the top, but without the accompaniment. Don't worry about hitting the right notes; it's what's inside I'm more concerned with at the moment.'

Alice walked back to her mark, and sang the song. Her performance was powerful but, when she'd finished, Vi was gratified to see Horatio's face cloud with disappointment. It served him right for expecting too much.

He had his arm around her shoulders now and was steering her into the OP corner. And then ... and then ... the snake kissed her. Not a consoling peck on the cheek from an encouraging director, but a full mouth, breast-to-breast clinch. Vi felt tears spring to her eyes closely followed by a fury that had her picking up the stocking again and ripping it from heel to garter band.

Alice, flushed and flustered, returned to the stage. She faced the backdrop for a moment before turning and delivering the most perfect rendition of the song imaginable, full of every nuance Horatio had asked for and a deep melancholy all of her own. A spattering of applause issued from the wings. Damn him.

'That's my girl. I knew you could do it. Now toddle off and get yourself a cup of tea or something to keep your throat warm.'

Alice chose to exit the stage via the prompt corner. Vi tried to look busy as the girl arrived at her side.

'Was I okay? I was so scared I'd mess it up again. I've watched you do your song and want so much to be a fraction as good.'

Although she wanted to, Vi couldn't resist the pleading in Alice's voice. It was nothing less than the naked insecurity of one performer to another.

'That was lovely, Alice, just right. It was very clever of you to be able to switch your perform- ance like that. Not many pros could do it, believe me.'

The girl left her, beaming.

'Vi, where are you? Come on, let's run through the monologue following your song. For the timing of the thing. The same backdrop wouldn't go amiss, actually; perhaps with a gauze in front to look like you're on the street outside. In fact, that would work quite well: the world-weary flower seller then, at the beginning of the second half, the ingénue experiencing love's dagger thrust for the first time. Remember that for me, will you?'

It was a good touch, but not one Vi wanted to dwell on. She positioned herself down stage centre, Horatio back in his chair in front of the footlights, and delivered to the gallery the comic- ally moving skit on her degradation brought about by a love for gin. It was the first time she'd per- formed it in rehearsal but it didn't raise a titter backstage. Probably because the old cynics were still smitten by Alice.

Horatio slapped his hands on his knees. 'Really,

Vi, is that the best you can do? I suppose you've got that hoary notion in your head about saving the best for the night. But that won't wash with me. I'm relying on you to lead by example; you've more experience in your little finger than the rest of the bill put together – including Mr Dansi's poodles – and I wouldn't mind seeing some of it now.'

The bastard hadn't even had the professional courtesy to take her to one side; he was sitting there with a superior smirk on his face berating her in front of all and sundry. He was right: she was an accomplished artiste and, as such, didn't have to take such a breach of theatrical etiquette from anyone. Refusing to let the tears fall, she walked – straight-backed and with as much dignity as she could – off the stage.

Chapter Twenty-Seven

After she had checked the morning post, May made sure that all her files were locked away then pinned a note in the vestibule saying she would be out for most of the day and any urgent business should be left on her desk. If no one at the inquest was prepared to be forthcoming about where Miles Elliott had got his opium from, then she'd go to where she could watch the Three Colt Street dope-runners at work to see if the patterns of buying and selling gave her any clues.

May sat in the window of the Black Cat Café, a cup of scummy tea in front of her. She'd popped home to change and in her printed frock, a slick of lipstick, and one of Alice's dressing-up hats, she looked every inch the harassed housewife taking a breather on the way back from Dolphin Lane market. She fiddled with her spoon as if deep in thought as she sneaked glances at the two men in shabby suits leaning against the walls of opposite street corners. Business looked to be slow. Only once was an approach made. By a young woman in an unseasonably heavy overcoat. May had watched as money changed hands and the woman slipped something into her handbag; the buying of drugs conducted as casually as the purchase of fruit in a greengrocer's.

A figure walked into her eye line. It was Liza, one of her old friends from the tobacco factory. May banged on the window. A flash of a professional smile before Liza saw who it was, then she grinned properly and walked towards the café door. May called the waitress over as Liza bowled up to her table.

'Fancy seeing you down this way. Here, buy us a tea, there's a dear. I was up all night coughing and I've a right cobweb throat on me now.'

May ordered a pot for them both.

'You're not working at this time of day are you?'

'Lord love you, no. The punters don't like coming down here much when it ain't dark.' She fell heavily onto the chair. 'My Cyril's sick. First I thought it was summat he ate – the little bugger's always putting all sorts in his mouth – but then he went down with this cough too so I took him

261

'round to mum's so she could fetch him to the quacks. He won't see me no more on account I ain't settled my bill. I'm off to see how she got on. Hope he ain't said as Cyril has to have no medicine or I'll have to be turning tricks 'til I'm black and blue to raise the bleeding wherewithal.'

May hoped it wasn't the influenza because no amount of money in the world would be able to buy a cure for that.

'Alice knows the man who manufactures Barley-Freeman Cough Linctus – it's supposed to be very good – I can get you a bottle if you like?'

'Very grateful, I'm sure. Anyway, what you doing here? I like your titfer.'

May involuntarily reached up and patted the silly little hat. 'I'm keeping an eye on the dope-runners as part of an investigation.'

'You don't want to be having anything to do with that lot. Things are nasty with the gangs that run them. Before, it was like they was in the market with their pitches and everything. Oh, there'd be trouble when someone new came on the scene but now...'

'What's changed?'

'See him over there?' Liza gestured in the direction of the man in the battered trilby May had seen cutting a deal. 'He ain't been here five minutes. Word is he was moved in from White-chapel. Most of the old faces, their mothers would be hard pushed to recognise.'

'Beaten up, you mean?'

'Before maybe. But that ain't the half of it. They was all topped.'

'That must be street rumour, Liza, because we

haven't had any inquests recently fitting that description.'

'That's because no one's found what's left of them. Dumped at sea, like as not.'

'Do you know any of the names of those involved?'

'More than my life's worth to tell you if I did. Don't like to ask but could you see your way to standing me a bun or summat? I'm starving.'

May felt her cheeks flush. She should have offered in the first place. She signalled to the waitress who shuffled over with bad grace, and asked for two toasted teacakes and another pot of tea. While they waited Liza smoked and gazed past May's shoulder. Something she saw made her tighten her lips until they were fringed with white. May swivelled in her seat to look. A man with broad shoulders was engaging the second of the dope-runners in conversation. They both laughed at something and then the new arrival turned and stared straight at the café window. Liza jumped back in her chair as if she'd been scalded.

'Bleeding hell. Now I'm for it. Think he saw me? Jesus, I hope he don't know who you are.'

But he did. It was the man from Miles Elliott's inquest. Richard someone-or-other. The brother of the ex-fiancée. May saw the shadow of an expression cross his face before he looked away. What was he doing here? He lived in Epping and as far as she remembered had said he'd never visited Limehouse. But here he was as comfortable as if he knew his companion of old, and the dope-runner was exhibiting a deference which she thought due to more than being in the company of

263

a respectable suit. Could this Richard be in the business himself? To cover his own involvement would be a good reason to deny in court any knowledge about Miles taking drugs. What if it had gone further and he had been the supplier? It would explain his acquaintance with Miles. And his anger when he'd been talking about the broken engagement. He would've been torn between wanting his sister's happiness and the social shame of having a hop-head as a brother-in-law. What if Miles had also felt a twinge of divided loyalty and had taken the decision to start buying his drugs elsewhere? That would all add up to a pretty solid motive for revenge – an inappropriate relationship; a not inconsiderable drop in income given the amount of opium Dr Swan said Miles was smoking; and a heartbroken sister at the end of it all.

May leaned across the table and grabbed Liza's hand. 'What do you know about him? It's very important. I won't say you told me, I promise. You don't have to come to court. I'll say I just found it out on the street... Please, this could be what I need to save my job.'

Liza snatched away from her grasp 'You ain't got the foggiest, have you? Coming down here and getting yourself up to pass as one of us like it's some sort of game?'

She bent her head over the table and lifted her hair from the back of her neck. May was appalled to see a livid scar, thin and clean as if it had been done with a razor.

'That's what I got the last time I got fingered and they thought I was squealing.'

'From him?'

'Him, them, they're all the same. There ain't no one 'round here not in the pay or the know, or on the nod, of the drug gangs – word will be out you was here before your feet hit Pennyfields. And your beefy bloke's down here so regular he has to be in the thick. The geezer who keeps the dope-runners on their toes – putting the willies up them so they don't go snorting all the profits – he did this on account of nothing. He runs some of the girls down Ratcliffe Highway. Acts like that gives him rights to go having any of us he fancies without paying. Well I wasn't having none of that, so I gave him the sharp edge of my tongue. And he gave it right on back, only in steel. But where it won't show of course. Reckon he thought he didn't want to be damaging goods he might one day move in to own himself.'

May didn't know what to say. She had never felt so ashamed. To even consider her need to impress Braxton Clarke worth the trade. Liza had finished her teacake and was on her feet.

'Don't take on so. Weren't you it happened to and I've had worse. Least it didn't hurt none.'

May fumbled in her shoulder bag for her purse. She reached out to take Liza's hand again but this time pressed a florin into her palm. Sunday's leftovers would just have to stretch a little further. 'For your boy's medicine.'

'Ta very much. I ain't too proud to take what's offered. Never get far in my game elsewise. But I'll not see you getting nothing in return. You want to know what goes on down here? Man keeps that dope-runner supplied has snow parties for the posh what like to come to Limehouse to slum it.

What's the date next Friday?'

'The sixteenth, I think.'

'That'll be it then: third of every month. House two down from the Chink herbalist on the Causeway. Top floor. Dress smart. Go early. Before supper's best. Say Sadie sent you; she won't mind.'

May squeezed Liza's fingers then watched her leave. She'd sit here a while longer so no one on the street would put them together. For all the big talk of the slicing not hurting, Liza's animal fear when she'd thought she'd been spotted had been chilling.

'... I don't know what to do, Sal.'

May was perched on a hard chair in her friend's workroom while she fitted a floaty dress on a mannequin.

'If she's on the game then she knows well enough what to expect.'

May had never known her friend to be so intolerant. It came to her that, as she held marriage in such high esteem, Sally might in some way deem prostitutes responsible for so many turning out to be less than happy ever after.

'But if something does happen to her then it will be my fault.'

'If a man is destined to drown, he will drown even in a spoonful of water. Give up on your feeling you are responsible for all life's ills; God does not think you so important.'

Her voice had a hard edge to it and May watched as she stabbed a pin viciously into the material. She realised that Sally was probably angry at her. Because everything she'd said had

266

centred on her guilt and Sally carried so much for being a crippled spinster that she despised the emotion. Or thought she cornered the market in it.

May decided to approach the situation from a different angle. One more suited to the role of coroner's officer. She might be focusing her energies in the wrong direction with the drugs connection but she couldn't be sure until she'd eliminated all the other possibilities.

'I'm no nearer finding the person who murdered Miles Elliott – and it seems pretty clear now that manslaughter's out of the question – but maybe if I concentrated on why someone would kill another then it might give me some clues. You've got such a sharp mind, Sal, I'd value your opinion...'

She only received a grunt in response but thought that was the most she was going to get given the mood Sally was in.

'First up, there's greed. But, as far as I can work out, Miles had nothing anyone could profit from. What little he earned must've been spent on opium. He would've inherited the business of course but his father isn't so old and, anyway, it would surely only be a partner who could gain from the both of them being dead. And I know there wasn't one of those.'

Except there could've been a partner in the drug smuggling business if Miles had been involved in doing such a thing... But she was in danger of climbing back on her hobbyhorse again.

'According to lurid accounts in the newspapers, jealousy's always a strong motive – a love affair gone wrong or a rival on the scene. I don't see that in this case; Miles was engaged but it was broken off ages ago. Besides, his fiancée's sick with nerves and seeking a health cure in Italy. It seems very unlikely she'd fill him full of cocaine in any event. Her brother, on the other hand, might. So maybe I'll keep that one on the list...'

This was really helping. Voicing her thoughts was sorting out the jumble in her head, and distracting her from how she might've compromised Liza. But Richard Weatherby had been the man they'd seen in the street; she needed to move on again fast...

'Getting rid of someone because they are an inconvenience or seen as a danger in some way–'

'Enough!' Sally's eyes were poisonous. 'Death is not some puzzle set out for you to solve so you can feel clever. You want to know why people slaughter? How they can treat another as if they are no more than animals whose blood must be let to purify a world they are deemed too filthy to inhabit?'

May couldn't stop herself from cowering at the venom in Sally's words

'I'll tell you... Because from envy grows hate... Because a powerful man sees what he can do not what he should not do... Because a weapon honed on the whetstone of right itches in the hand... Because God can be made to speak the words most sweet to the ear...'

She had started stabbing pins into the mannequin again.

'Whole villages – blind bubbas, red-cheeked babies, beautiful girls on their wedding night –

can you give me a good reason why they are now dust in the rich Russian earth?'

The pogroms. Sally's pain and anger made May think of Albert and Henry, and the countless other sons, brothers, lovers and husbands who now forever lay beside them. Perhaps, in the end, it came down to something as simple to name – and impossible to understand – as evil.

'So, are you going to that opium orgy of yours or not?'

That Sally wanted to change the subject was clear enough, but May wasn't nearly so practised at turning away from raw emotion and had to close her eyes for a moment to dispel the images in her head.

'I think so. There'll be people there who've never heard of the East End code of keeping your nose clean and other people's secrets to yourself. Except I've nothing suitable to blend in. Liza said to dress smart.'

Sally snorted. 'And how would she know what that was?'

'Don't be so unkind, Sal. She's just a woman fallen on hard times. We all have to find some way to eat – and she's got a little boy.'

'That he should ever learn the things she does to put bread in his mouth. The Poor Law Guardians exist for a reason and it is to them she should be going, not to the sailors in the docks.'

May decided to let it rest. 'Do you think – if I promise to take care of it – I could borrow something?'

'You mean a dress that has made my fingers bleed for a rich client who herself will only wear it once before announcing it not à la mode?'

She shouldn't have asked; Sally was getting more irritated with her by the second.

'I'll leave you to get on. I'm sorry I interrupted your work but I had to tell someone what happened this morning.'

'Go to the cupboard over there and fetch out the purple evening dress with the black beads. She is about the same size. There is a cocktail bag to match; the sort you wear on your wrist. That will be in the box on the shelf above. Underwear you will have to find for yourself. Or go without. The lines will be better that way. You can change behind the screen. I want to see you are doing it justice before I agree to it going out of here.'

May wanted to kiss her but, given her prickly stiffness, didn't dare. She hung the dress on the back of the screen and stripped off. It felt strange to be standing in her camiknickers and stockings about to appropriate another woman's vision of loveliness. The dress fell down over her body under the weight of the beaded skirt as she slipped it over her head, the silk under-bodice caressing her breasts and hips.

'Hurry up. I haven't got all day.'

Standing in the centre of the room, May felt, for the first time in Sally's company, embarrassed. As if she was exposing an inner self she'd much rather remained hidden. Her friend eyed her up and down, gave a little suck of her teeth, then made her turn slowly on the spot.

'You'll do. There's a mirror over there; take a look at yourself.'

Her reflection was beyond what she could've

270

possibly imagined. She was draped in an asymmetric sheath of glistening purple, the low v-shaped neckline revealing a glimpse of the black silk bodice. A swathe of material from one shoulder to the opposite hip was held at the waist by a clip to create a fabric waterfall that fell to below the hemline. The ankle-length straight skirt was covered in thousands and thousands of black glass beads.

'Oh, Sally, it's beautiful.'

'The dress is a dress. It is you who are beautiful in it. I'm only sorry you'll be wasting it on those too busy chasing the dragon to notice the workmanship; every bead placed just right so you appear bathed in frosty moonlight when you walk.' Sally sighed heavily. 'But I know, and you know, and that is all that matters.'

She turned back to the waiting mannequin and picked up her box of pins.

'A reason to silence another can be because they know something they should not. You are like the sister I never had and in my selfishness I beg you to be careful.'

In the spring sunshine flooding through the attic window, May rubbed at the goose-pimples on her arms.

Chapter Twenty-Eight

During the next two days May felt tired and low in spirits. There were no new bodies in the mortuary so she was denied the routine of setting up an inquest to dilute her worry over Liza's safety. Even one of Colonel Tindal's tirades would be preferable to being left alone to wallow in her sense of failure. Braxton Clarke hadn't been in touch and she was beginning not to like shouldering the entire responsibility for the activities of the Poplar Coroner's Office. It was scant consolation to know that Sunday would bring the ramble out at Debden Green and the possibility of following up a lead into what had happened to Miles Elliott.

Her mood was considerably brighter once she was finally under the wide skies of Essex. She had met Jack at the train station as arranged and they had travelled out together. She'd let him do all the talking as she'd looked out of the window and tracked their progress away from London by the increasingly peaceful emptiness of the country-side.

Walking up to the signpost at the start of the footpath she was pleased to see all the rambling group regulars had turned up. May greeted them all in turn, giving Jack an airy introduction in the process: Sybil Overton, a retired schoolteacher but still as sprightly as when she used to catch little boys by the collar to give them a cuff around the ear; Clive Parks who had lost a leg below the knee in the War and came walking as therapy; the Murther twins who were hard to tell apart, impossible to understand when talking together in broad Glaswegian; Mr and Mrs Flower, married last year and still at the stage of gazing into each other's eyes. Plus, of course, Roger Barker – thin, stooped, and plagued by asthma. Laces tied, and knapsacks hoisted, they trooped in formation towards the nearest stile.

May was chatting to Sybil Overton as they skirted a cornfield, the scars in the ancient wood ahead testament to the previous half-decade's insatiable demand for trench props and duckboards. She glanced around for Jack. Lagging at the back, he was looking hot and uncomfortable already. She smirked; he was a city man through and through in that ridiculous heavy tweed jacket, and shoes she'd raised her eyebrows at when they'd met at the railway station – more suited to an evening out than negotiating the ruts of ploughed fields, she fully expected to witness him falling flat on his face before long. She had thick-soled boots she'd got at the pawnshop, a short-sleeved blouse, shorts and long woollen socks. A windcheater jacket was scrunched into her knapsack. She began to lengthen her stride as her lethargy left her and the smells of the hedgerows, sun-warmed grass, and the clean sharp tang of soil pushed the odour of the docks from her lungs. Roger caught up with her.

'There's said to be a lost village beyond that ridge over there. It's not on the OS map though.

Did I tell you I'm thinking of taking my holiday in Lewes this year? I'm planning to walk the South Downs Way.'

'All of it?'

'Well, no...'

Roger was a stickler for the truth.

'But from Alfrison to Ditchling Beacon at least. I won't be able to get the time off to go the whole hog to Seven Sisters.'

'Maybe next year, then.'

'It would be infinitely more pleasurable to journey with a companion. If you, perhaps, one day...' He dissolved into a fit of wheezing.

May thought of a future when Alice would be out in the world on her own. Roger was knowledgeable about history in the landscape as well as native flora and fauna, and he wasn't overfond of the sound of his own voice – unlike some she could name. She took another look back at Jack. He had taken off one shoe and was shaking something out. It would be restful to spend some time with someone like Roger in the undulating chalkland of Sussex; they could camp on farms and stop off in pretty villages for tea.

'Who's that you've brought with you? He seems a bit of a queer fish. Wouldn't have thought he was your type at all.'

May resisted the temptation to snap back. Why was it people always assumed she was desperate to have a man in tow? There was such a thing as ordinary friendship wasn't there? Except she was reluctant to put Jack in that category either. Friends were people you could trust and did right by you, and she'd seen precious little evidence of either of those things with him. But she had to give Roger some reason why she'd brought him with her.

'Let's stop for a moment for him to catch up and you two can meet properly. He lodges with an old friend of the family and fancied getting out of Poplar for a while. I don't know him very well but he seems nice enough – if a little full of himself. He works on the local newspaper.'

Roger nodded as if that told him everything. As they waited and the others overtook them, Roger crouched over a clump of low-growing flowers with a magnifying glass in hand. Jack arrived looking sulky. May took him to one side.

'At least try and pretend you're enjoying yourself.'

'I'd have more fun poking my eyes out. Your mummy's boy had better come up with the goods after all this tramping just to gawp at one big fat load of nothing. What's he looking at anyway?'

'Pansies.'

Jack snorted. 'That figures.'

She'd had just about enough of him putting the dampener on the only free time she'd had for ages. 'Why do you always have to think yourself so superior to everyone else? Just because he's fascinated by something you don't give a damn about.'

'Where's the big attraction in eyeballing leaves? Things grow in the dirt – so what?'

There was a slight tremor in his voice under the cock-sure dismissal. She had found his weakness: the mighty Jack Cahill was afraid of the countryside. She glanced at Roger and, just past him,

275

into the ditch. She'd have a little fun at Jack's expense. He'd asked for it for making her look such an idiot in front of PC Collier over that Sir Ernest Pollock business. May squatted down to examine the remains of the grass snake. It was flat – nothing more than head and skin really – probably trampled by one of the plough horses. Then she squealed as if startled, scooped the corpse up with her hand, and flicked it to land at Jack's feet. He really did scream. May turned and grinned. Jack only looked as if he wanted to murder her for a second and then, to give him his due, he did at least attempt a wobbly smile.

Roger had finished with his botany. May composed herself enough to formally introduce the two men, then stepped away to pretend to be admiring the view – and get the giggles out of her system. Jack didn't get off to the best of starts by offering an asthmatic a cigarette, but it wasn't long before he was back in his stride.

'Miss Keaps tells me you work in a bank, Roger. It must be quite a relief to get away from all that paperwork. Have you come far, or are you lucky enough to have this on your doorstep?'

She had to hand it to him; mustering something like enthusiasm, he sounded genuinely interested.

'Epping. A bus ride away. I could walk it actually – if it wasn't for this weak chest of mine. Traffic fumes, you know.'

'Ah, bring back the days when there was nothing but horse carts. I can't really understand all this need for speed – progress at the expense of being alienated from everything around you.

Not like here, eh? A man can feel he truly belongs in a beautiful place like this.'

May was worried Jack was tipping over into insincerity but a peek at Roger's face told her he was still on track.

'Have you seen this hedge laying, Mr Cahill? I've rarely seen a neater job.'

Jack followed Roger to the side of the field, throwing May a look of despair as he passed. It served him right for masquerading as a son of the soil.

'Actually, Roger, I'll admit that I'm more interested in us having a word; Miss Keaps told me about you and I immediately grasped the opportunity to come out here today so we could meet. You see, I'm a journalist...'

'She said. You must have to be up to your eyes in even more paper than I do.'

Jack gave the smothered chuckle of one man's acknowledgment of another's appreciation.

'Well the stuff that's littering my desk at the moment is all related to a story my editor wants me to write on a young man who was recently found dead in Limehouse. Miles Elliott. As you also come from Epping, I wondered if your paths might've crossed.'

'I never met him but we undertake all the Elliott Shipping financial affairs and accounts at our branch. So I am acquainted with his father somewhat.'

Jack gave May the thumbs up behind his back. 'It's always a point with me to write about the deceased as real people, not just as cameos framed by the circumstances of their demise. In this case some knowledge of Miles' job responsibility and lifestyle would be invaluable – I could ask the family, I know, but I don't want to bother them at such a terrible time...'

'I'm sorry I can't help but, as I told you, I never met him.'

'...There are rumours there might've been some financial irregularities. And here's where the second responsibility of a journalist comes in: to the relatives. If it's true then, should the case go to the Old Bailey for trial, there would be no way of stopping it coming out. So you see, if you could furnish me with any information now then I could both represent Miles in as true colours as possible, and, if forearmed, also warn the family – off the record – to save them the public humiliation of shock and embarrassment. I would consider that nothing less than my duty.'

Roger pushed his fringe back off his forehead and stared at Jack as if one of them had just trodden in a cowpat. May felt the thrill of superiority spike her blood – no wonder Jack enjoyed looking down on others so much. The ace investigative reporter had made a pig's ear of things by laying it on too thick. Roger might not be the sharpest chisel in the toolbox but he hadn't worked behind a bank counter for years without being able to spot a clumsy attempt at fraud. She coughed to break the awkwardness of the moment, then stepped over to join them.

'I'm afraid that Mr Cahill has been trying to spare my blushes. The truth is, Roger, that there's been a terrible mistake with some filing in the coroner's office and I'll lose my job if I can't clear

278

it up. Mr Elliott gave something to Colonel Tindal as evidence and it's gone missing. I don't know exactly what it was but I'm pretty sure it had something to do with money. But of course I can't possibly check with Mr Elliott, and if I were to go to your manager in my official capacity and ask what it could have been then I'll be bringing the coroner's reputation into disrepute. Do you see my problem? It would be a tremendous help if you could reassure me there's nothing untoward about Miles Elliott's affairs and then I can cross that possibility off my list.'

Roger turned to Jack. 'I don't know why you made me listen to all that guff. If you'd have told me the truth in the first place then Miss Keaps wouldn't have been forced into making such an embarrassing confession. I suppose it's a prime example of the sensation seeking everyone accuses you press people of.'

He stared at his hands for a moment as if mentally counting-up on his fingers.

'I told you we do the Elliott Shipping accounts and one of my jobs is to itemise the expenses. I'm not breaching any banking regulations if I tell you that Miles Elliott wasn't shown any favours and only received the going rate for the job – which wasn't very much. Although I didn't handle any of his personal transactions, he never wrote a cheque against the business account that couldn't be reconciled, and the books always balanced at the end of the month. I am certain there could be nothing there to concern your coroner because the branch manager has been over everything with a fine toothcomb; Elliott

Shipping has effectively ceased trading, you see. Without any creditors. Does that help?'

May smiled at him. 'Very much. I can't tell you how grateful I am, Roger; you've probably just saved my job.' She looped her arm through his. 'Now, shall we go and see if we can find any trace of that mystery settlement of yours? I'm sure you won't be interested in joining us, Mr Cahill, so I'll say goodbye now. I've no doubt circumstances will throw us each others' way some time in the future.'

Chapter Twenty-Nine

Monday found May sorting which of Colonel Tindal's old reports could be consigned to the storage Braxton Clarke had secured in the Town Hall. The papers were technically the property of the late coroner's estate but as he had no relatives and had left no instructions as to their disposal, she'd thought it best to box them up until the new incumbent made a decision about what to do with them. After responding to a couple of requests for information that came in the morning post, she was at last free to concentrate on just how far she'd got in her investigation into the death of Miles Elliott.

She opened her notebook. The first thing she came to was the list of witnesses supplied by Mr Elliott. She remembered Roger had said the shipping business had effectively ceased trading; had

Mrs Elliott taken a turn for the worse or had the poor man become incapacitated through grief himself? Perhaps he had simply lost heart. The tableau of Colonel Tindal and Mr Elliott sharing their lost hope for their lost sons flickered before her eyes: two old men with little left to live for. Colonel Tindal hadn't survived the night. She wondered if Albert's death had taken her father the same way once the numbness of the first few months had passed. But he'd still had his daughters. Not as special in a man's world perhaps, but surely important enough to rally for all the same.

She took her time sharpening her pencil, the leaves of wood curling down into the wastepaper basket like so many discarded memories. On the next clean page she wrote a summary of everything she'd found out to date. When she finished she realised it didn't amount to an awful lot. So far she knew only that Miles had been murdered, his body found outside Brilliant Chang's restaurant. Dr Swan thought his death might have occurred some time earlier, and that he died from an overdose not the beating which had been administered posthumously. Brilliant Chang had told her he was being framed by an enemy. She had yet to identify who that might be. If Brilliant Chang was a drug dealer – something he consistently denied – then the Tong leader was an obvious suspect because Chang's relocation to Limehouse would surely upset the established patterns of trade. Liza said there had been an escalation of violence amongst the street dope-runners. She had seen the witness, Richard Weatherby, cosying up to one on Three Colt Street. Someone killed Miles, and someone was supplying him with opium. The same person? Lastly, Roger had told her that Miles hadn't earned very much, and Jack had confirmed the opium dens charged middle-class white boys top whack.

May jumped as a commotion started up in the street outside the window; a horse was involved by the sound of it. The break in her concentration was what she needed to shift her thoughts sideways. What if Miles hadn't had to pay for his narcotics at all? What if he was getting them straight off the boat? Lots of sailors made a tidy living by what they picked up on their travels, and a man working in a shipping office would be perfectly placed to offer some sort of quid pro quo arrangement. Could it be someone other than a street dealer she was looking for?

She went through her routine of securing the office and notifying the public when she would be available. The Blakeney's Head wouldn't be busy yet. The landlord knew everything there was to know about the alternative sources of income in the docks and would be sure to tell her if there had been something going on at Elliott Shipping.

Her eyes adjusted to an interior deprived of sunlight by the grimy etched glass of the windows. There was a group of men – ship's stokers by the look of them – sitting at a table playing cards. They all tracked her progress as she walked up to the counter. Bert Ford was washing glasses at the end. He was an ex-prize-fighter with none of the muscle turned to fat. His nose had been broken in numerous places, his large ears were tattered, and the elbow of his right arm stuck out at an alarming angle. Not all of these injuries had been sustained in the ring; the Blakeney's Head was the haunt of sailors who wanted more than a drink to liven up their shore leave.

'May Keaps, as I live and breathe. Last time I clapped eyes on your pretty face was when you was delivering your old dad's flask of cocoa as he was on nights. Terrible what happened to him. I was meaning to give my condolences at the time but you know what it's like...'

This wasn't what she'd come to talk about. 'It's all right, I understand.'

'You sit yourself down and I'll bring you a drink on the house. What you having?'

'That's very kind; half a shandy, please. And I'd like a word if you've got a moment.'

'Official like?' He blinked his hooded eyes a number of times. 'I heard you was working for the Beaks.'

'The coroner. But it's just to satisfy my curiosity. It won't get repeated in court, I promise.'

'That's okay, then. Wouldn't like to have to turn a girl down but I've a reputation to keep and if it got out that I've been playing the snout then that'll be half my customers taking themselves off to the Crown and Dolphin.'

May chose the table tucked in the corner near the sooty fireplace. The smell prickled her nostrils. Bert served the stokers another round then came over to join her. She noticed how he stood with his broad back to the door, shielding her from sight. For her protection, or his own?

'Make it quick, love, there'll be a shift ending in

283

the engine works soon and I won't have time to fart then.'

'There's a business on Anchor Wharf. Elliott Shipping. Have you heard about anything that might have been going on there recently?'

'The boy who got himself topped at the Chink's place on the Causeway? So that's what you're here about.'

May wondered if she was the only one who thought Brilliant Chang innocent. She sipped her drink and waited. Bert tucked his thumbs into his waistcoat pockets.

'Can't say as I've had a sniff of anything that's not common knowledge. The likes of him didn't drink in here. Preferred the lounge at the Eastern Hotel I reckon. Better class of clientele they gets up there; not so ready with their fists or a broken bottle when they've had one-over-the-eight. But he'd always stop to pass the time of day when I was seeing to the deliveries of a morning. Seemed nice enough. Certainly not deserving of getting his head bashed in.'

He whipped a grubby cloth from his back pocket and bent to wipe the table.

'Except there has been talk of summat funny with regards to Anchor Wharf – a rumour only, mind, so don't go taking it as gospel. Lumper came in here the other day – wouldn't credit how a drop can loosen a tongue because, sure as eggs is eggs, I wouldn't have been spreading the same – but he'd heard whisper the Bow Kum are angling to take over Anchor Wharf lock, stock, and barrel. And if that's kosher it won't be for the unloading of tinned meat, you mark my words. That end of

284

the quay's out where the Basin ain't got enough in it for ships to berth, so discharged goods are brought ashore by lighter, and the customs men often as not can't be arsed – pardon my proverbial – to trek all that way. Makes the place worth a packet in the hands of those who know the un-official import/export business, if you get my drift. But I ain't as green as I'm cabbage looking so I won't be saying nothing more on the subject – not even for a pretty face like yours.' The door banged behind him. 'Back in a minute, love.'

May took another swallow of shandy. The wharves were privately owned and not patrolled by the Port of London Authority police so Elliott Shipping, isolated on the end of the quay, would be the perfect place for bringing drugs ashore. Had Miles been working for the Bow Kum Tong and there'd been some sort of falling out amongst thieves? Perhaps he'd become greedy – from the little she knew about habitual drug taking, more and more was needed over time to achieve the same result – and threatened to blow the whistle on them. So they killed him, taking the oppor-tunity to remove a rival in the rackets – Brilliant Chang – in the process. If that was true it would be impossible to gather enough evidence to prove: Bert hadn't said much but it was more than anyone else was ever likely to.

She finished her drink and took the glass up to the counter. The landlord broke away from his customers.

'Another?'

'No thank you. I need to be getting back. Just one more thing though ... what did you and

Miles Elliott talk about? Did he ever say anything concerning the business?'

'Not so you'd notice. Sometimes about a particular ship maybe. We had this joke running. Don't seem very funny now but he wore the key to the office around his neck and I'd always be saying that if he fell in the water it'd be that sank him to the bottom and drowned him.'

His mouth dropped open as if he'd been hit over the back of the head with a brick.

'No offence, May, love. I didn't mean nothing by it. For what it's worth none of us think your old dad topped himself. Reckon it was an accident. Even men like him who could walk a plank with a sack of sugar on his shoulder can go tripping over their own feet when full to the top with whisky. Except – and I remember remarking on it when we heard – I ain't never known him touch the stuff before. Always said as hops were the only thing should go into the drink of a true mudlark. Do you know the one time when he...'

May laid her hand on his. Bert hoisted himself up on the counter on his tree-trunk arms and bent over to give her a peck on the cheek.

'You down this way again, love, you come on in.'

She threw him a thin smile and left.

It took her to the corner of Chrisp Street to clarify her thoughts. It essentially came down to there being two ways she could go about getting to the bottom of what might have been going on out at Anchor Wharf – the Braxton Clarke way, or the East End way which, although unorthodox, would be sure to produce some sort of result. Bert had reminded her that she was a child of the docks, and that meant she had methods at her disposal that Mr Clarke with his posh accent and expensive suits could never so much as dream about. If this was to be the last case she would investigate as the Poplar Coroner's Officer then she'd see to it that the jury's verdict was at least a fully-informed one.

She doubled back along East India Dock Road to drop into the police station on the chance she could catch PC Collier.

The desk sergeant shook his head. 'You'll have to go to Bow Circus if it's him you want particular, he's on point duty up there.'

May's shoulders slumped. Once set on a course of action, she felt an almost physical need to see it through. Especially when she knew it to be questionable.

'Can I help? I'm only here covering all them what's in bed with the Spanish Lady but I know my way around the law.'

He didn't look like the sort who would demand forms in triplicate.

'I'm May Keaps, the coroner's officer.'

His thread-veined cheeks squashed up to his eyes as he grinned. 'I've heard a lot about you from the lad. Truth be told, I reckon he's a little sweet on you. And – old married man with three nippers though I am – I can see why.'

She flushed. Partly at the compliment, and partly at the white lie she was about to tell.

'The coroner asked me to check on the details of what was found on a body discovered three weeks

287

ago in Limehouse Causeway. Miles Elliott. He's been released for burial but the inquest hasn't been concluded and Mr Clarke thought there might be something amongst his effects that could help reach a verdict. He was called back to the City of London Coroner's Court before he had time to sign a warrant but I wondered, as I was passing, if I could...'

The sergeant tapped the side of his nose as he pulled a ledger from under the counter. He scanned it then disappeared into the back room. May almost crossed her fingers. He returned with a brown foolscap envelope sealed with string.

'I'll have to ask you to sign for it if there's anything you're wanting to fetch away with you.'

'That won't be necessary; I only need to take a look.'

With his fat fingers, it took him an age to unwind the string from around the cardboard disks. At last the contents were spread on the counter before her. A pigskin wallet, a ration card, some coins, a cigarette lighter, a folded piece of yellow paper, two wrapped mints ... but no key. Finally one of her hunches was paying off. Someone came in behind her and she took the opportunity to thank the sergeant and leave before she was forced to embroider her story even further.

Splashing out on a taxicab she could ill afford to take her into Millwall, May executed the next stage of her plan by paying a hasty visit to a man who'd helped her once or twice in past investigations. One she knew would be home in bed at this time of day.

Once back in the office she picked up the telephone receiver and put in a call to the switchboard of the *East End News*. Jack wasn't there so she pretended to be one of his informants and left a cryptic message for him to meet her outside the Ship Aground at midnight.

Chapter Thirty

The stage was deserted. Having opened on Easter Monday to catch the locals itching for entertainment after rattling around the house and pubs all weekend, the manager had followed custom by giving the performers a night off the following week. Horatio had opted not to capitalise on the empty theatre by shoeing-in an extra rehearsal; he was finally ready to perfect the finale of his act and hadn't wanted anyone present who might see how the sawing a lady in half trick was done and go around blabbing the secret. Vi, he'd asked to represent the viewpoint of the front row audience.

She was sitting there now waiting for him to come back from the dressing room with his assistant, Molly. Dressing room? That was a laugh. It was a closed-off backstage corridor smelling of gas and drains, partitioned with blankets strung over a rope to provide minimal privacy between the sexes. There were two rooms for the regular performers but, although now one of them by dint of slots on the regular bills, Vi had elected to share the rat hole with the amateurs in a misguided fit of solidarity. She'd already determined to move her make-up and costumes piece by piece into the better accommodation as the talent show got closer, and the turns didn't need her Mother Hen routine so much.

Horatio virtually flew onto the stage. 'Can you believe what the stupid bitch has done? Only gone and got herself pregnant. Caught her throwing up in the sink.'

Vi was seized with a spurt of alarm before she remembered Molly was engaged to the son of a wealthy stockbroker.

'If she doesn't *show* yet then it shouldn't be a problem.'

'Oh, but it is. Seems they're bringing the wedding forward to the end of the month and she's been trying to find a way to tell me she wants out. Didn't try very fucking hard, did she? All cheery chatter when I met her at the railway station this morning.'

Normally Horatio considered swearing the province of the working classes so he must be very angry indeed. Vi tried to think of what she could say – and what he needed to hear – to calm him down sufficiently for them to work out what could be done to retrieve the situation. She bought time by leaving her seat to join him on the stage. When she got there he was dismantling his equipment, flicking open the catches and flinging the sections of the coffin-shaped box into an untidy pile. She wanted to tell him to take care or he'd damage something except didn't dare.

But in the short walk she'd found the solution. She'd do it. Be his conjurer's assistant. She could learn the routine easily enough; there really wasn't anything to it: stand around showing a lot of leg, hand him the props on cue, escort a member of the audience up on stage if he chose to go that way; lay in a box and pretend to be sawn in half. She'd been a dancer – her father had insisted she learn ballet to broaden her repertoire – and she was still supple; could do the splits if required. She was second on the bill, and he was closing the show; plenty of time to change costume, apply fresh make-up, and come on with a centred poise that implied she'd been sitting in a darkened room waiting for her big moment. Kitty – the Cockney act with her Pearly Queen impersonation – had the perfect wig she could borrow.

She walked over and tried a sympathetic embrace. But Horatio was too buzzing with thwarted energy to endure it and she ended up merely patting the back of his shoulders.

'Molly was never right for you anyway. Oh, she could do the business well enough – should do after all the coaching you've given her. But she didn't have nearly enough stage presence for such a great illusion. It's the climax of the whole show–'

'Don't I bloody well know it? The half-witted cow has really left me in the lurch this time. It was bad enough when she decided in Brighton that the varnish brought her out in blisters. Thank Christ I never intended including her in the Glasgow engagement. Now I'll have to get the posters redone for here, and with only nine days to go they won't be worth the ink if I can't get them turned around virtually overnight. More buggering about I could do without; as if I haven't enough carrying this whole debacle single-handedly...'

His ranting was dissipating some of his anger, and the hurt and pain of his potential failure was beginning to grin through.

'Sorry, Vi, it's not your fault. I know I shouldn't take things out on you but you're the only one close enough to understand what this means to me.'

The warmth of his smile made up for everything. But she knew him too well to make her proposal outright: like all men, he had to believe it had been his idea.

'What you need is someone who knows how to draw attention to herself at the moment of distraction, and then blend in to make herself part of the trick itself. It's a tough act to pull off but something any good actress does naturally every time another player enters the stage. And the truly generous ones can take their energy and project it – a little like a vent does his voice – so the audience is left in no doubt who to focus on.'

'She'd have to be pretty as well. No point her having all that stagecraft if she hasn't got every man in the place wishing he was me bedding her down in her box, and every woman imagining what it would be like to have such power.'

'Agreed. Being supple is just as important though: remember her movement to curl up has to be slick if she's to avoid the saw. You don't want to be afflicted by cramp at a time like that.'

'You are marvellous.'

Horatio threw his arms around her waist and lifted her off the floor. It was so unexpected Vi let

292

out a little scream.

'You've given me such a brilliant idea.'

He whirled her around, laughing, and Vi's world was complete. Once her feet were back on the stage he let go and headed for the wings.

'Where are you going?'

'I've got a picture in my head and don't want to lose it. I want to imagine it on the publicity board...'

He was through the pass door and halfway down the auditorium. Vi had to run to catch up with him. They entered the foyer together.

'There'll have to be costume alterations of course – there may not be an awful lot to it but spangles and fishnet but it has to fit perfectly to not look tacky. Which, I must say, it had a tendency to do on Molly at times.'

'Don't you worry your lovely head about that, I'll ask around for the best seamstress in Poplar. Maybe get her to create a completely new look, something more glamorous and sophisticated.'

She'd got him thinking exactly along her lines They were standing in front of the publicity board at the bottom of the gallery steps, and he was staring, squint-eyed, at the photograph he'd had taken of himself mid-act. Only his assistant's hand was visible as she passed him a playing card. That would have to change. Vi waited for him to communicate this wonderful vision of his so she could think of which poses would present her in the best light. A clink of coins made them both turn. Alice was in the box office. Horatio bounded over to her.

'I thought everyone had the night off.'

293

'Not front of house, worst luck Money weren't right Saturday night and he had me come in – *when it's quiet so you can resist all those distractions interfering with your ability to count.* It ain't fair, him making out like I'm stupid or something. Turns out it was a bunch of tickets he'd tucked away for his pals. But it's taken me hours to work that out.'

'Cheer up.'

Horatio took a shilling from the pile, held it in his thumb and forefinger, shot his cuffs in the manner of the great Howard Thurston, and half a dozen sixpences dropped down with a rain of tinkles on the metal counter.

Alice laughed with such childlike delight that Vi felt a hundred years old in comparison.

'And that is only a fraction of the good fortune this evening has brought you... How would you like to be the assistant in my magic act?'

'Would I like it?... Crikey... Why pick me?'

'Because you'd be perfect. It was Vi's idea actually, she's always so good at reading my mind for exactly what it is I need. So, you'll take it on then?'

'Course I will. If you think I'm up to it.'

'Between us, Vi and I will make sure you jolly well are. We've the full dress on Sunday, and then another two rehearsals – bags of time. Can you stay behind after the theatre closes Saturday night, so I can show you the equipment and what you'll be expected to do? It'll be a late one though.'

'That's okay, I'm bunking around the corner with a mate and they keep a key on a string so I can come and go. Her ma says how she knows the theatrical life's not one of the regular variety and that...'

The wisdom of Mrs Gibson was swallowed by the swishing of the foyer door as Vi managed to make it into the auditorium before the sobs burst out and she knew that – like the rabbit in the hat trick – she would never be able to squash them back down.

Chapter Thirty-One

It was close to half past twelve when Jack turned up outside the Ship Aground. May had only been prepared to give him another ten minutes. With his hands in the pockets of that ridiculous jacket he sauntered up to her, the attempt at casualness ruined by the electricity of his excitement.

'So what adventure have you got in store for me this time, Miss Keaps?'

At least he had stopped calling her that ridiculous *Blossom of May*.

'I knew it would be you the minute I saw the message. A real agent provocateur doesn't talk like that, you know; you might as well have said "and come alone" it was so obvious.'

She kept her sharp retort to herself. He was a man full of words with every intention of saying them; better he get them out of his system now.

'You're lucky to get me. It's only because some pals of mine are over from Dublin that I'm not out chasing more leads for my exposé. What's the scoop? Are we off to taste the delights of another yen-shi establishment?'

He was smiling as he eyed May up and down. She was wearing her sailor's garb but with a jumper instead of the pea-jacket.

'You can go smoke more opium on your own time; this is something altogether different. I've asked you along because I wanted a witness but if you're to be a part of this, then you'll have to do what I say and not try to turn it around to your own advantage.'

'How can I agree to that when I don't even know what it is?'

She beckoned to the doorway behind her. 'This is Sid. He's a cracksman.'

'A safebreaker? You thinking of robbing the Crown Jewels?' Jack's grin grew wider.

'We're going to pay a visit to Elliott Shipping. Miles always kept the key on him but it's missing. And I think his murderer might have taken it because there's something incriminating in that office. And we're going to find out what it is.'

'Have you finally lost all your marbles?'

May noted with satisfaction that the patronising amusement had gone.

'Even if you're right, he's had weeks to retrieve it. And wouldn't Mr Elliott have noticed if there was something strange?'

'Why would he know? He said in his deposition he hadn't set foot on the premises after he handed the running of the business over to Miles, and I happen to know since his son's death he's winding it up. As for the killer, maybe he's waiting until the coroner's indicted someone else before he draws

296

attention to himself by going back there.'

'I've never heard a story based on anything like such half-baked notions.'

'That including your own?'

'Answer me this: do you, or do you not, know who has the key?'

'I've a pretty good idea.'

'Get them arrested then. Jesus, May, I don't see why you have to make everything so difficult.

'Maybe it's something I learned from you. Are you coming or not?'

'Do you have the faintest notion of what my uncle will do if I end up in a police cell again?'

'He'll cut off your sweetie money?'

'Don't be facetious. I'll be packed up and shipped off back to Ireland in disgrace.'

'Some Great Journalist you are.' His self-regard was jangling her nerves. 'There's much more at stake tonight than your job – or mine either for that matter, which, if it interests you, I will probably lose anyway. So you can shut up and come along, or go back and get drunk with your cronies – no doubt to weave this into some funny little tale with you at the centre of it all. It's entirely up to you. I couldn't care less. Come on, Sid, it's time we got going.'

She started to walk away and then turned back.

'You're nothing but a schoolboy playing in the East End because you think it's spicy to see how the other half lives. Well, some of us have no choice but to get our hands dirty because we've nowhere else to run to. Neither, in case you've forgotten, does Miles Elliott any more; he was another rich kid who thought he'd got the measure of what

297

goes on around here. Someone made him pay for that. And I'm going to find out why.'

They arrived in Narrow Street in a strung out zigzag – May in the lead, Sid a few yards behind and on the other side of the road, Jack as an adrift afterthought. The stumpy alleyway they wanted was formed by warehouse walls and ended in a high metal gate and railings. According to Sid – who knew a thing or two about concealment – the main entrance to the wharves on Limekiln Dock was exposed by the open ground in front and overlooked by the watchman's hut, but this gate was no longer in use since the grain ships had started using Millwall.

Sid made a sign to indicate that there should be no talking and then, grabbing hold of the fence, started to walk up the adjoining wall like a lop-sided crab. When his feet were above his head he twisted his body until he could wedge them between the railings and the first of the horizontal bars, then pulled himself up hand over hand into a crouch. He repeated the effort twice more then uncoiled the rope he had wrapped around his waist under his shirt, tied it to the top of the gatepost and threw the end down. May's stomach began to churn a little less. She'd thought she might be expected to replicate Sid's acrobatics, but the rope was dangling just above her head. Then Jack was beside her, making a cradle of his hands for her to step into. With Jack hoisting her up, and Sid reaching down, she laboured up to the top bar. From there she had to twist herself over, find the bar again on the other side with her feet, then clutch hold of it and lower her body until she had a drop which was reasonable enough not to end in broken ankles. She took a deep breath and let go. Her joints and spine juddered as she hit the ground but she'd made it. Sid had climbed down the rope and was giving Jack a bunk-up until he could pull himself up to the top and drop down beside her. Then Sid did his crab impersonation once more and joined them on the wharf.

With Sid leading the way they scurried around the bulk of the first building; a timber warehouse, its stored hardwoods releasing the exotic odours of jungles and spice islands. Ahead stretched the wide concrete of the quay and beyond that the sleek nothingness of the River Thames, the lights on the far bank glinting enticingly. A run across open space and then a square brick edifice with a flaking sign spanning the front: *Elliott Shipping Company.* It was the last building before a lamp glowing in the drifting river mist signalled the end of the quay.

Sid pulled a set of skeleton keys out of his pocket and got them inside before May had time to catch her breath. He closed the door and locked it again.

'Don't want no one trying it and falling in arse over elbow.' He produced a torch from inside a canvas waist belt and handed it to May. 'Keep it steady mind and don't go flashing it window way. You, keep your ear to the door. Watchman does his rounds about now. Hear anything, snap your fingers; he'll be tuned for what he's not expecting and that'll sound like rigging on a mast.'

Jack stayed where he was instructed while May

shuffled across the wooden floor as soundlessly as she could to stand beside Sid. The safe was a small one set at head-height into the brick wall.

'Reckon they couldn't be stashing no dosh here with only this to keep it company.' Sid ran his fingertips over the dull metal. 'Have this baby open in a blink.'

Three slow turns of the dial and he was as good as his word. He stood back for May to see inside. A red ledger. She lifted it out. Underneath was an envelope. She took them both over to the desk, the torchlight quivering in her hand. Jack left his post to join her.

'What you got, Sherlock?'

She wanted to slap him; he was almost dancing on the spot with excitement.

'Keep your voice down if you don't want to be back on the boat to Dublin.'

Sid sniggered. May gave Jack the torch and opened the envelope. Inside was a sheet of paper. Her legs began to shake as she read:

Just make sure you're fucking here when you're
 told to be.
One more slip like the last and that piece of
 yours will find
the sides of her face no longer match.

Jack was shining the light down over her shoulder and she heard him suck his breath in through his teeth.

'Charming, I must say. Spared the details, I notice. Acid? Razor? Broken bottle?'

'What the hell does it matter? Whoever wrote

this knew Miles and knew he had a fiancée.'

'Is this what we're looking for?'

She ignored the implied collusion. 'I don't know. Part of it perhaps.'

She debated for a moment whether to tell him anything else but decided that a second opinion might be useful.

'I'm pretty sure some illegal imports were coming in here. I thought maybe instigated by Miles, but I'm not so sure he was a willing participant after reading this. Perhaps he was at the beginning then changed his mind. But it explains why he wasn't bankrupted by his need for opium.'

'No need to thank me for my insightful direction in that regard.'

'Can't you two put a sock in it? Worse than my missus.'

'And I think the Tong are behind it. Trying to get Elliott Shipping for themselves.'

'Why would they bother threatening Miles? Kill him outright, yes, but blackmailing him first just isn't their style. He was being given an option here and the Tong don't give options. They bleed dry.' Jack opened the ledger. 'If you're right then perhaps this is a record of the transactions he handled. There's a chance he wasn't the pushover he appeared to be and was preparing his way out of the deal with a little arm-twisting of his own.'

'Against the Tong? And with his fiancée's well-being at stake? He'd have to be a fool to do that.'

'Or someone whose capacity to think rationally was impeded by opium. I've had a lot of practise at working with figures recently; perhaps I can find a pattern here against ships dropping stuff off–'

301

'It's called discharging. You'd obviously have never got through a proper interview for a docklands' newspaper.'

'Cut the rabbiting. One of you take my place. Must be something here for the lifting to make this worth my while.'

Sid slipped over to the desk beside Jack and started to go through the drawers. May didn't feel she was in any position to stop him and retreated to the door. Away from the weak beam of torchlight the room felt both small, and limitless. She was conscious of the damp smell of the river trapped in the air. Straining to focus on the outside world she could hear the deep boom of a siren – probably a P&O liner entering far away East India Dock – the ever-present background chorus of cranes and winches, and something else... She pressed her ear to the wood... Muffled voices... Coming closer. The watchman and a companion? She tried to snap her fingers but her skin was too sweaty and they slid apart with a soft rustle. She wiped them on her trousers and tried again. This time the crack cut through the air like a cap-gun. Sid stopped rifling immediately.

'I'm for a long stretch if I get nabbed. Out the back window for me. Don't reckon you two can talk your way out of this one neither, so you'd better get on my heels sharpish.'

May saw him vanish from the orbit of light. Then, seconds later, heard his feet slap on the stairs at the back of the room. She hurtled after him, banging her thigh heavily on the front corner of the desk. Holding in the cry of pain she flailed her arm out to catch hold of Jack. The torchlight

302

whirled around to illuminate the way ahead. She heard the screech of a sash window being jerked open. A billow of cold air reached down to meet her. They were on the narrow landing at the turn of the staircase when Jack stopped.

'I've got to go back.'

'The watchman will be here at any minute.'

'For the letter. I shut it inside the ledger. It's the only evidence you've got.'

'How could you be so...' But he had gone.

She held her breath as she heard a key being waggled in the lock. Jack wouldn't have the time to get back to the stairs. She hoped he'd had the sense to switch off the torch as she tried to remember if there was anywhere for him to hide. If they just looked in and didn't turn on the light then he might be able to press himself into one of the dark corners... Heavy footsteps crossing the room... The desk drawers being yanked open. Was the watchman doing a little light fingering of his own?... Or had the Tong sent someone to search for what they'd just found? Would he go to the safe next and notice it open? Her body began to shake as she heard objects hitting the floor. Her breathing was so shallow her head began to swim. She shoved her knuckles in her mouth and bit down on them to stop a sob from escaping. A low laugh, followed by: 'Got you'.

Not Chinese. Not the Tong.

Footsteps on the floor once more; the door opening and closing. Then words so clear she thought they were being whispered in her ear: 'Torch it.'

May's legs felt like rubber. She crouched down

with her back against the wall. The explosive shattering of glass. The searing reek of petroleum. The soft *whump* of liberated flame. A sinister crackling began to fill her shrinking world. A hand grabbed her and wrenched her up. She screamed and hit out with her fists.

'Cut it out. It's me. Move. Now!'

But everything in her body was disconnected. Except her lungs and her throat and her voice and the screaming. She felt the stinging slap of his hand across her face. Now every part of her wanted to move at once and she stumbled up the stairs on her hands and feet. She saw Jack silhouetted in the window in the brief moment before he jumped. She climbed up onto the ledge and looked down. It was a long way. Too far. Behind her, the fire's roar grew stronger with everything it devoured. A sudden whoosh and a flash of heat. It was coming up the stairs. The smoke was tearing at her throat and making it hard to swallow. Her body shuddered with one sob after another.

'Jump, for Christ's sake! I'll catch you.'

She wanted to make them but her fingers wouldn't let go of the frame.

'Jesus, May, isn't one suicide in the family enough?'

Alice. She took a deep breath and tumbled into space.

Chapter Thirty-Two

Her eyes stung as she opened them. At first they refused to focus through the tears. Then she saw the fuzzy shape of someone bending over her. The clang of a bell quivered through her muscles. She tried to sit up. The effort made her cough until she retched. A hand behind her head and the cold rim of a glass against her lips. Something spicy. She took a sip. The brandy set her coughing again, but less painfully this time. The muzziness subsided a little. She was indoors, lying on softness.

'Back room of the Ship Aground, love.'

It was Charlie.

'Me and a few of the others was mooring our lighters when we saw the smoke. Reckoned it might be the wharfinger playing fast and loose with the insurance – robbing us of bleeding work into the bargain. So we got ashore as quick as you like and set about bailing from the river to do our bit while they was getting the fire engine horses hitched. I was running to fetch more pails when I tripped over you. Out cold you were. You right as rain now? Nothing broke?'

'Is Jack here?'

Her voice was as raspy as a striking match.

'He a pal of yours? Dreaming of him?'

'He was there with me.'

'Not when I got to you he weren't.' He stared into her eyes. 'I reckon I should be fetching the quack. A bang on the noggin can get you in funny ways. And I should know because I've had enough of them in my time.'

May put all her energy into shaking her head. She didn't want to have to face any questions from an over-inquisitive local doctor about what she was doing in the middle of the night outside a blazing Elliott Shipping. Charlie, on the other hand, would never presume to ask any such thing.

'I'm fine, really. Just bruised. And a little woozy. What would do me more good than anything is to be in my own bed and sleep it off.'

'Reckon I'd be feeling the same way myself and a stroll in the fresh air might be just the thing to sort you out. So I'll take you back. But if we can't get no further than the Eastern Hotel without you looking set to peg-out then I'm hoisting you over me shoulder like a sack of grain and it's straight up to the hospital for you.'

She smiled. He handed her the glass and she drank the rest of the brandy in one long, slow, swallow. The warmth replaced the weariness in her limbs. Taking Charlie's hand she swung her legs off the couch, stood for a moment to get accustomed to her wavering balance, then looped her arm through his and walked as purposefully as she could towards the door.

The first thing she did was go upstairs to strip away the reek of smoke. She had to have both feet on each step before she could move onto the next and with her palms flat on the walls to steady her, she felt as though she was climbing a mountain. She'd started sweating and shaking when she'd first faced the stairs but had forced herself to remember that this was her house ... that she was safe in it ... that the arsonist couldn't have known she was in there ... that it hadn't been the Tong and a firebomb was not going to come hurtling though the window.

The journey back down to the kitchen was easier. Wincing as she bent her stiff back, she stoked up the range. Despite what she'd told Charlie, there was no point in her even trying to sleep. Not when Jack could still be in danger. She had got him into this. Where was he? She poured some milk into a saucepan and set it to heat. Why did he leave her? She should have made Charlie realise that she hadn't been imagining it, that she hadn't been alone; he could've got some men together to try and find Jack. Whoever had let themselves into Elliott Shipping wouldn't have wanted to confine themselves to shaking hands if they'd bumped into him. A dog barked in one of the yards. What if they'd knocked him out and thrown him back in the burning building? May felt her panic rising along with the bubbles in the milk. She had to stop imagining the worst. But when there was nothing other than that to go on, what else was there to do?

She sat at the kitchen table with her hands around the mug of cocoa, the heat on her skin bringing back her moments of terror. It was at times like these when she wished she smoked or that she could add to the brandy in her system and deaden her whirling brain with alcohol. But she never kept spirits in the house. Another legacy from her father, she knew she could take it or leave it but what if Alice developed the same thirst for spirits he obviously had? Except Bert said he hadn't. But then the landlord of a pub probably would say that in case she held it against him for not stopping her father drinking so much that night. Had he actually been in the Blakeney's Head? She couldn't remember, the reports she'd been given of the inquest had been filtered through a blur of grief and disbelief. Since then, all she'd felt was such bitterness and anger that she'd never stopped to ask the question. But recent events had left her with nothing but questions.

In the stillness, she could hear the Naylors in the basement going about their early morning routines; the poker clattering against the range grate, water gushing from the tap, a muffled voice calling for someone to get up. Soon she'd be able to smell the bacon frying ready to be put into the husband's lunchtime sandwiches. She'd never felt more alone. Not even when Alice had returned after the summer with Aunt Bella and she'd had to sit her down – the pain of it still vivid even now – and tell her that their father hadn't felt life was worth living. Now, of course, she knew the truth: that he hadn't felt them worth living for.

May laid her head on her arms and sobbed.

When she awoke she had a crick in her neck. Her eyes were sore, the lids swollen from crying. There was enough dawn light for her to extinguish the gas mantle. Her brief sleep had been punctuated by sweat-inducing nightmares of a Chinaman standing over her holding a cleaver so the biting edge looked like a ribbon of quicksilver. She walked stiffly across to the sink and splashed her face with cold water.

What she needed was someone who could help her think clearly again. She thought she knew just the person. He was notorious for his ability to unravel impossible situations such as three ships needing to berth on the same quayside at the same time, all with perishable cargo when every minute was money rotting in the hold. And most important of all: she trusted him. He'd sought her out when she'd got back from France and said he would arrange for her rent to remain at the dockers' rate and, although it was nothing really to do with him, he'd been as good as his word. He also started work as soon as it was light enough for the pilots to bring the ships down the river. If she hurried, she could get to him before he became embroiled in his first seemingly intractable problem of the day.

'So, how are you coping?'

Alexander Laker, the wharfinger, towered above her so much May felt as she had the first day she'd met him. Then she'd been holding her father's hand – he'd taken her along to ask for a job because he'd heard that the toughest of the wharf owners had a soft spot for children. It had nearly gone badly wrong when she'd started grizzling with the cold, but he'd bent down to fold her in his arms and said her father should do a double shift to buy enough coal to give her a blazing fire to go home to. This didn't happen of course because the wages were only sufficient for rent and food and she and her brother had to continue to run behind the coalman's cart to pick up any lumps dislodged by potholes.

'Can't complain. Alice has left George Green School for her first job. In the box office of the Gaiety. The manager jumped at the chance to take her on.'

'All the credit down to you, I'm sure. When you going to take up the offer of a post in my office? I meant it, you know.'

He'd asked her if she wanted to clerk for him immediately after saying he'd fix the rent. May had never been able to figure out why he'd been so kind, it wasn't as if he made a habit of it. Now she wondered if it was because he'd remembered the little girl with a runny nose wearing a pair of Albert's hand-me-down shorts. In winter.

'I'm very happy in my present job, thank you. But that is what I've come to talk to you about.'

'Well, take a seat as it's official business we're about to embark on. I reckon I've about...' he looked at his wristwatch, 'ten minutes until the next is due to berth. All hell will be let loose then as it's a tight turnaround so don't stand on ceremony, spit it out.'

May swallowed hard. It was difficult to know where to start; there was so much she couldn't divulge due to the nature of the investigation; however, Bert had told her enough to surmise what was common knowledge.

'Elliott Shipping. Is it on one of your wharves?'

'No. Wouldn't own Anchor if you paid me. Dog of a situation that is, last before the river so ships get unloaded by lighter. No profit in it.'

This made things a little easier, it meant he

310

wouldn't feel he had anything to protect. Although, she of course, still did.

'The son of the owner was found dead in the Causeway three weeks ago.'

'Heard about it. Shame when it gets taken out on the children.'

'What do you mean?'

May sat forward on her chair, a flick of energy bringing her numb brain to life. Had there been something even bigger than she'd guessed at going on? He waved his hand like a giant parting the sea as if it were a puddle.

'Only that boys should be given a chance to step into their father's shoes to see if they measure up. Last few years tells us that way of the world's long gone.'

He'd been referring to the Great War. May let go of the hope and tried to pick up the thread of where she'd been going.

'It's my job to investigate on behalf of the coroner so that the right people can be called to court to account for what happened to him. I think the death was connected with something underhand going on at Elliott Shipping but the only lead I had has gone up in smoke. I've no proof, and am not likely to come across any now.'

She looked at her shoes, suddenly ashamed at having to admit defeat in front of a man who probably ate the toughest of stevedores for breakfast.

'So, the truth is, I'm getting precisely nowhere.'

'And you know why that is, don't you?'

'Tell me. I need all the help I can get.'

'Because you wear a skirt.'

Of all the things she'd thought he might say, she

311

hadn't expected that. Alexander Laker's father had worked the docks – and his father before him – and although a man's domain, tradition demanded women be respected for their contribution. It was not those from the working classes who usually dismissed the female sex because anyone who'd witnessed women on the quayside at five in the morning gutting fish knew that to be a mistake born of ignorance.

'You can stop widening those cow-eyes at me, Maisie...'

She hadn't heard that nickname in a long while. Probably not since she'd outgrown Albert's old shorts.

'Whether you like it or not, you are to be up against those going to exploit the fact you will ask questions rather than stabbing a man in the back then bending to hear his dying confession. Look, I've only a couple of minutes left. Once the ship's siren signals she's about to tie up, I have to be on the quay or they'll be squirreling away what have you behind my back. Now, you know your father and I were at loggerheads over this Trades Union business – I won't deny I could cheerfully've strangled him at times – but he was a straight talker and I admire that in those I'm up against. We had our rows, we had our differences, but we stood toe to toe and said it like we saw it. So I'm going to do you the honour of treating you the same. But I warn you that you won't like it.'

May could feel her legs begin to shake. She told herself it was the damp of the river seeping up through the floor.

'I've heard word that the Poplar Coroner's Officer is as corruptible as a hold of fly-blown carcasses. You want me to go on?'

'Please.' She could hardly get the word out, her mouth was so dry.

'I don't believe none of it of course. Not least because you're George Keaps' daughter. But someone is set on tarring your name. And it's because of the company you've been keeping. Shoulder of Mutton Alley ring any bells?'

The yen-shi den. So had the Tong recognised her after all?

'Talk in the loading sheds amongst some as worked beside your father is that you're stepping out with a newspaperman who's partial to the black pearl.'

'I'm not... And he isn't.'

'Whether it's as straight up as a ship's mast or not, all the dope dealers in Limehouse now reckon they'll be spared the cat for some of their darker dealings as you'll be backing off so as to keep his antics battened down.'

May bit back a scream as a blast from the ship's siren nearly tore her eardrums. Alexander Laker stood and headed for the door.

'Pound to a penny there's a link between them taking the wind out of your sails and the young Elliott business. I'm a wharfinger and as such there are two things I'm certain of in this life: vessels have to be discharged, and cargo placed somewhere under lock and key until the owners are in a position to lay claim. I deal in commodities, not speculation, so I'm saying no more as to what might've been going on at Anchor Wharf except that tea's not the only thing to make its way over from China. There'll be submerged reefs on that particular trade route, Maisie, so watch yourself or you might find yourself grounded with no high tide on the horizon.'

Chapter Thirty-Three

It was past ten o'clock when she dragged herself into the office. She'd gone home after leaving Alexander Laker to have a quick strip wash at the sink and change her clothes. Her hair still smelled of smoke but she'd rammed her green hat on and hoped that nobody would get too close to notice. She'd checked that no bodies had arrived in the mortuary overnight, collected the post, and taken the cover off her typewriter when the telephone rang. It was the clerk from the City of London Coroner's Court.

'At last. I've been trying your number for hours.'

May wished she'd had time to make herself a cup of tea, her mouth felt claggy and she wasn't sure if any of her words would come out intelligibly.

'Mr Clarke asked me to give you a message. Unfortunately his wife has contracted influenza and has been rushed into hospital. He's beside himself – as you can imagine what with her being an invalid and not in good health at the best of times. But of course you already knew that.'

She hadn't.

'Here I am gassing on when you must have a mountain of paperwork to get through and are just wishing I'd let you get on with it. Mind you, as he won't be around then you'll be able to do what I do and just file away any non-urgent stuff. Ha. Ha. I'm sure you wouldn't get up to such tricks; Mr Clarke is always singing your praises and saying how efficient you are...'

May's wrist began to ache under the weight of the receiver. Would she never stop talking?

'...He gave me express permission to issue you with his home number in case of emergencies. Not his town flat, mind, but the family home so I'd be wary of calling him out for just any old death. As our patch is regarded a bit of a flagship by the Lord Chancellor's Office we will have a locum deputy in Mr Clarke's absence – a Mr Halliday from Liberty of Tower District – who will be available to attend to those. You only need pick up the telephone if anything of that nature crops up. Well, I think that's all for now. A pleasure talking to you. Good–'

'But you haven't given me his number.'

'Oh, sorry. Silly me. I expect I'd forget my head if it wasn't screwed on. Lewes 9350. Have you written it down? Remember, Miss Keaps, for emergencies only. Cheerio.'

May sat for a moment to recover from the onslaught and stared at the number on the pad. Did nearly meeting a horrible end in a place she had no right to be constitute the sort of emergency he'd want to hear about? Would he thank her for disturbing him at what must be a very difficult time? She remembered when Alice caught influ-

315

enza last year; she had been desperately worried for her life and Alice was a robust young girl, how much more dangerous must it be for an invalid? Should she go and tell the police what had happened last night? Not withstanding that if she did she could be charged with trespassing, she'd been schooled by Colonel Tindal to involve the police as little as possible – he'd thought them fit only for filling their cells with drunks. May doubted Braxton Clarke shared such views but she didn't know him well enough to tell. Although there was the possibility he'd draw the inference she'd gone to the police because she couldn't do her job properly. And then it was only a short step to concluding the coroner's officer role too dangerous for a woman; a twinge in her knee from the jump worked to tell her that he wouldn't be far wrong.

She'd spent much of the night wracked by self-doubt and knew she could put an end to this bout with a simple telephone call. She took a deep breath, wiped her sweaty palm on her skirt, and picked up the receiver. Her voice sounded as dry as crackling paper as she gave the operator the number. Nine, three, five, zero. A short pause and then she heard the phone at the other end begin to ring. She was counting the seconds when the street door banged. She dropped the receiver back in the cradle as if about to be caught in the act of something she should feel guilty about. It was PC Collier.

'Morning, Miss Keaps. Bright one, don't you think?'

May hadn't noticed.

'Can't stay – what with me back on the beat

316

over in Canning Town again. There must be some other body they can give them streets to but somehow it's always my name the desk sergeant says he's pulled out of the hat. I reckon he's got it in for me. I'm going to put in for a transfer soon as I've time to get a point on my pencil. Anyhow, a nipper gave me this in the street and asked me to pass it on. Which I'm duly doing.'

He handed her a folded piece of paper with her name written on the outside.

'I'll be seeing you soon, like as not. That's if they ain't got me down to run Scotland Yard single-handed.' He chuckled to himself as he walked out.

May opened the note. It was from Jack. She felt a rush of elation that he was safe. He wanted her to meet him after work this evening. At the same place they'd hooked up with Roger and the others when they'd gone rambling. The thought flashed through her mind it could be a trap and he'd written it under duress. But then she noticed the postscript: *It goes without saying that you're to be sure to take care you're not followed.* He'd been relaxed enough to make a little agent provocateur joke at her expense. But she would keep her wits about her nevertheless.

It seemed to be the most difficult thing in the world to wait for a bus and not look around to see who was joining the end of the queue. May had decided that one of the precautions she would adopt would be not to take the train where she would be in a carriage compartment with no hope of getting off if someone should jump in at the last minute, but to get the bus to the terminus

317

at Woodford and there pick up the one out to Loughton. The entire journey would take her the best part of two hours but Jack hadn't given her a time and, anyway, it would do him good to be kept waiting; plenty of solitude to think about how he could've spared her all that worry.

At last the bus came into view. She boarded and sat downstairs on one of the seats facing the platform. She wished she'd picked up a newspaper or brought a library book so she could pretend to be reading but instead she found herself scanning the faces of the passengers who got on at each stop – even after she was a long way from Poplar. She was on the second bus and well into Essex before she relaxed.

A wind was swaying the tree branches as she trudged to the signpost where the ramble had started. Had that really only been two days ago? She felt so wrung-out she couldn't imagine ever having had the energy to walk all the way to the ancient wood cresting the horizon. But the clean air felt good in her lungs and she took off her hat and increased her stride until her skin was slicked with sweat and her hair no longer tainted with smoke.

Jack was sitting on the stile at the beginning of the footpath. He waved, then sauntered over with his hands in his pockets. On the journey over she'd anticipated she'd be overjoyed to see him unharmed but now May could see that broad Irish face with its idiotic grin, all she felt was aggrieved.

'Where the hell did you go? What kind of a selfish bastard leaves a woman lying there unconscious for who bloody well knows what to happen?'

'Feel better now, Miss Keaps? Want to shout and swear a little more, or are you done? Indignation quite becomes you actually; you've a bloom in your cheeks.'

May wished there was a rock she could pick up to hit him with.

'Seriously, though, I can't tell you how glad I am to see you're okay. For the record, and so you don't hold it against me for the rest of our – what I hope will be – long association together, I thought the fire might be the work of the Tong so considered it best if I made myself scarce to remove the possibility of them making the connection between us. Me, we know they know. You, we're not sure about. So I showed a clean pair of heels for your sake; that big docker was arriving on the scene, so I knew you'd be in safe hands. I reckoned if anyone followed me I could easily throw them off the scent in this bleak nothingness you call countryside.'

She wasn't going to forgive him. Not yet.

'I've been whiling away the hours trying to piece together what might've been behind such dramatic events. I admit I got myself a little distracted from the important business of getting a message to you. But I'm sure you didn't come out all this way just to listen to me grovelling in apology – even though I can see how much pleasure you're getting from it.'

May capitulated a little. 'I take it you've reached some conclusions?'

'Not sure I'd go that far, but I have been

319

racking my – I'm sure you'll say not overly substantial – brains and I reckon I could have put my finger on what might've been behind that letter we found in the shipping office.'

He took a packet of cigarettes from his jacket pocket. Then proceeded to strike match after match in an effort to light one. If he tried to prolong the tension any longer, she was going to ram that casual *we* down his throat. At last he was puffing away and seemed ready to continue.

'I can tell by that steely look you're fighting to have any patience with me but it's a long story and I'm going to have to fill you in with all the background or it won't make any sense. It concerns my gambling investigation.'

'I might have known. Everything is always about you, isn't it?'

'That's not fair. It was you who involved me in this, remember? Now are you going to shut up for five minutes and listen?'

May put her hat back on and pulled it down. She'd give him until the wind threatened to give her earache and then she was leaving: however revelatory his scoop.

'After spending most of my nights in the gambling den, I finally got the man who works the bar to talk to me. Seems he bears a grudge towards the owner and was more than happy to spill some of the secrets of the operation. He doesn't know I'm a newspaperman of course. Anyway, every new punter is assessed to see how addicted they are – games thrown in their favour or the chance to stack the odds by using their own pack of marked cards a couple of times. Then, once the punter feels they are invincible, they provide only opportunities to bet on things that require no skill – cockroach races or which fly will reach the spilt rice wine first. All the alcohol is free and sometimes spiked with cocaine. So you can see that the poor dupes don't really stand a chance... Am I boring you?'

She'd yawned. Unintentionally, but her lack of sleep was catching up. May started pacing in an attempt to keep focused.

'Most of these new boys are rich and white – rather like me, in fact; no wonder I blend in so seamlessly...'

She snorted.

'...and they are encouraged to write promissory notes – usually with their fathers' business interests as collateral. These debts are allowed to build up until, one day, they are told it is time to pay up. After that, things start to get very nasty. First comes the intimidation. Then the violence. If none of that works there is a convenient fatal accident. Crooked lawyers then swing into action to enforce the debt through the courts and, with the son out of the way there is no one to deny that it hadn't been accrued through a foolhardy business venture. They have a number of dummy companies set up for the purpose.'

Jack paused to light a fresh cigarette from the stub of the old one.

'You have to admit that it's ingenious. You said the Tong wanted to take over Elliott Shipping, didn't you? Now can you see where I'm going with this?'

May kicked at a piece of flint with her toe.

Maybe she hadn't been paying enough attention but she wasn't seeing things illuminated in the way Jack obviously could – although she certainly wasn't going to admit it. Jack smoked for a little more in the silence.

'What if Miles was up to his neck in debt with them and had – or was about to – complete the process of signing over Elliott Shipping? If he'd tried to back out for some reason then that explains the blackmail, and maybe on his final evening they gave him enough opium to ensure he provided that last signature, and then the fatal cocaine to make the transaction watertight.'

May stopped pacing and looked up as a flock of crows returned noisily to their roost. Jack had something. But there wasn't any evidence Miles Elliott had been a gambler. She walked a little way down the hill in an effort to try to get everything straight in her mind. Perhaps he hadn't been and the Tong had simply used the same tried-and-trusted method to secure the business for themselves. Which, in turn, would give them exclusive use of Anchor Wharf. And Bert had heard that was what they wanted. Add to that Alexander Laker's strong hints that drug smuggling was involved. The two together meant that Miles Elliott's usefulness to the Tong was distinctly time-limited; once they had got him to test out how secure the place was for a base of operations then all they had to do was to cut him out of the picture and move in there themselves.

She strode back up to the signpost, her tiredness blown away on the wind.

'Are you coming back with me?'

'Thank you for your help, Jack... That's quite all right, Miss Keaps... In fact it was my very great pleasure to spend what was left of last night kipping under a hedge with a herd of bulls.'

'I think you'll find they were only cows. Do all newspapermen exaggerate so much or is it only you?'

'Uncle Paul's coming to pick me up. I'd say you'd be welcome to stay and hitch a ride but he's got some business out his way and I suspect we'll be going straight on to dine with Lady Dewberry at Monkams Hall.'

May shrugged and turned away. She was striding down the hill when his voice reached her on the wind.

'...And I think you'll find the female of the species is almost invariably more dangerous than the male. But I'd make an exception to the rule in your case and say, most definitely...'

Chapter Thirty-Four

Vi had just finished a slot in the Wednesday afternoon show and was taking off her greasepaint. In the proper dressing room; she'd moved out of the amateur one on Monday night, straight after Horatio had dealt that body blow about Alice. What was it the girl had said during her so-called acting in rehearsal? *Not going to allow you to make me feel I'm dirt.* Well, neither was she. The other turns had either all gone back to their digs or

323

were in the wings waiting to go on. There was a tentative knock on the door and the cause of her recent heartache came in.

'Alice, I'm busy right now, can't it wait?'

'I'm sorry, Vi, really I am, but I need to talk to you.'

The girl was so keyed-up she was making the air in the stuffy room shudder. Vi swiped the square of damp muslin over her forehead.

'Another time.'

'It has to be now.'

Vi looked at her in the mirror. She was a picture of perfect misery; it would take a monster not to feel a pang of pity.

'Spit it out then. But be quick because I've things to do.'

Alice let out a quivering breath. 'I know being his assistant could be my big break and I'm very grateful to you for thinking of me – truly – except ... except...'

'You're right; a thousand girls would give their right arm to be given such a chance.'

'But what if I mess things up? I've been going over and over it in my head – ain't slept a wink since he asked me...'

Her diction – which had been noticeably elevating over the past five weeks – had slipped back to Poplar's finest.

'...Those tricks he done, they were so clever...'

They were simple sleights-of-hand, performed in parlours for children.

'...I couldn't bear it if I let him down. I've never met anyone so wonderful. And he treats me like a proper grown-up – you both do. Singing's easy,

324

I've been doing that all my life, but being on stage like that with everyone thinking what he's going to do ain't natural, then if I do something stupid and show them they was right…'

Stage fright. Vi knew what that was like well enough But her compassion for a fellow performer's plight didn't stop her from wondering what would happen if she were to heap on a little more pressure so the girl would make a debacle of Saturday night's run-through. Whatever Alice thought of him in her hero-worship haze, Horatio wasn't a tolerant man; one slip of her attention and he'd send whatever self-belief Alice had left, crashing like a stage weight. Leaving him with no alternative but to ask Vi to be his assistant. It would be a bit like accepting cold seconds, but you didn't get anywhere in the theatre by being proud. The truth was that Horatio knew deep down she would be perfect for the role but, like every man, he'd allowed himself to be momentarily blinded by the dewy freshness of youth. And, as Vi remembered only too vividly, youth was easily spooked.

'Sit down, Alice. I know this feels like too much all at once – there you are working in the box office of one of the most popular Music Hall and variety theatres in the East End when you're thrust into the limelight by being offered your own slot on stage, and then to cap it all the impresario, producer and director of the show asks you to step in at the last minute to save the whole thing from being a humiliating disaster. Because you are aware he has everything riding on this, aren't you? It's his way of showing his father he can make it on the boards and that walking out of the family firm is an act of passion, not rebellion.'

Her speech was having the desired effect. Alice now looked like she'd been stung by a swarm of wasps.

'It takes a real pro to rise magnificently to all that. Every show is only as good as its last turn – it's what the audience remembers most as they leave the theatre – and the sawing the lady in half trick will only work if the assistant is up to it. Which I know you are or I wouldn't have insisted Horatio ask you in the first place. There are so many things that can go wrong and end up making the magician look a fool. And it's new over here; Horatio let slip he'd paid a fortune to a member of the Magicians of America for the secret.'

'I don't want to do it.'

Her voice was so quiet that Vi would've missed it if she hadn't been listening so intently.

'Will you explain to him for me? I couldn't face it.'

She didn't look so dewy now.

'Will he be very cross with me?'

'No performer likes someone to go back on their word. There's the matter of professional pride…'

'You could do it. You'd be so much better than me anyway.'

Her spirits were rallying a little but Vi wasn't about to let Alice give in to false hope.

'I have to say in all honesty that's true but there comes a time when every established performer has to stand in the wings and allow a newcomer their chance to shine. I know the responsibility feels overwhelming at the moment but being

326

thrown in at the deep end is the only way of testing if a person is up to the rigours of theatrical life. I'm doing you a favour here, Alice. Please don't let me down.'

Vi took the lid off her box of face powder and handed Alice one of the small packets tucked inside; her precious stocks were getting low, but this would be worth the sacrifice.

'Take some of this no more than half an hour before the run-through on Saturday; not in water, mind, just a dab on the end of your tongue.'

'What is it?'

Why tell the girl it was cocaine; and that the last thing it would do was calm her down?

'A little something even the West End actresses take to deaden the nerves and sharpen performance. Look on it as the first of many stage secrets you'll learn before the week is out.'

Chapter Thirty-Five

May stepped out of the taxicab. She'd had to raid her motorbike fund for the fare but she'd never have been able to walk to the Causeway in this dress. Besides, despite the dark green velvet cloak she'd also borrowed from Sally, the way the glass beads weighted the silk-georgette so it caressed the outline of her thighs made her feel almost naked.

The house didn't look any different from its neighbours – tall and mean – the only note of individuality a door knocker in the shape of an anchor. Her sharp rap was answered straight away by a tall figure in an embroidered kimono the colours of a peacock feather. It was when she glanced down at the blue and gold brocaded slippers that May realised it was a man. The light in the hallway was soft but sufficient to reveal he was wearing a rosebud of lipstick, and thick black eyeliner. She'd seen enough cross-dressing on stage to know he was extremely good at his art.

'Yes?' His voice was husky and of an indeterminate register.

'Sadie sent me.'

He turned on racehorse-delicate ankles and beckoned her to follow. Her lilac dance shoes sank up to the instep in carpet. Two flights of stairs with a doorway on the landing between – *the facilities* he told her – and they were at the main room. He pulled aside a beaded curtain and pressed her lightly on the back to go through.

Blood-red floor-length velvet curtains graced the windows, pierced brass lanterns hung from the ceiling; the walls were covered in paper decorated with dragons, herons, and goldfish so metallic they gleamed. A Japanese lacquered screen inlaid with birds of bright yellow and blue plumage; deeply dyed rugs of various oriental designs; armchairs and couches, and intricately carved rosewood knee-high tables. On one was an ivory figurine of a nude woman draping herself around a tree-trunk, an upraised arm pulling May's gaze towards the shape of her perfect breasts.

She sank into a deep wicker armchair. It creaked and settled. There was a knock on the front door and a handful of minutes later two women and a man drifted in through the bead curtain. May thought they must have come on from somewhere else, their loose-limbed gait suggesting they were already three sheets to the wind.

'Fix me a bone-dry martini, Algie, there's a lamb.'

'Oh, yes, another, another.'

'Chinks don't serve drinks; hey, I'm a poet and I don't know it. Teetotal, the lot of them.'

The man was not unlike Jack in height and build but he was wearing a double-breasted tailcoat with silk lapels. The bottle-blonde had on a chiffon dress trimmed with lace, and the slimmer, prettier woman, a lemon yellow crêpe de chine gown. May had given her cloak up at the door and felt as out of place as if she'd worn her beaded dress to a matinee at the pictures. At first the others pretended to ignore her, huddling together like children sharing a secret. But then the man walked over, flicked open a gold cigarette case, and held it out.

'Chandu. Direct from Buenos Aires.'

The cigarettes were impossibly slim, the paper a dusky pink. May declined with the faintest shake of her head. The man lit up.

'Not seen you here before, have I? Never forget a pretty face.'

The compliment had been thrown away in a puff of smoke.

'Sadie sent me.'

'Ah, lovely girl. Lovely, lovely girl...' His voice grew thick and dreamy. 'Sure you won't have one?' The case was proffered again although this

329

time his thumb was planted over the needle-thin retaining bar. He swept a glance towards the women who were seated on a couch, their shoes kicked off and their legs tucked under them.

May realised that this pantomime was all for their benefit. To make them jealous. But it wasn't his attentions he wanted them to crave. It was the opium-laced tobacco. A door latch clicked and the kimono-swathed man appeared from behind the lacquered screen. May looked at the size of his feet again and nearly giggled. Inhaling the sickly smoke was beginning to drug her as the frazzling of the opium pellet had in the yen-shi den.

'Do you wish to be together or separate? There is one apartment free will accommodate you all in comfort.'

'Together, together. Can't better a good time with three luscious ladies.'

May felt her stomach turn. Was he proposing some kind of sexual orgy? She stood, the wicker chair creaking once more as it released her.

'Separate, if you please.'

'Then as you were first to arrive, I will see you settled. Have you brought your own pipe or do you want to select from our range?'

This was all going too fast She didn't want to smoke any opium. What she wanted was to get a look at who it was secreted somewhere beyond the screen.

'I'm more than happy to wait until you see to these ladies and gentleman. Perhaps I could look at your pipes in the meantime?'

He sashayed across to a mother-of-pearl encrusted cabinet and pulled out a brass-banded domed casket which he placed on the low table in front of her before leading the others from the room.

In it were three opium pipes, in sections like fairies' fishing rods. The first had a bamboo stem so smooth the knuckles of the grass were merely slightly ridged discolorations, and a glowing amber mouthpiece. The brass bowl was not unlike a tiny upside-down ship's bell The second was smaller, slimmer, and May thought of such fine craftsmanship it should be in the window of the most expensive jewellers in London. A dark-wood stem peeped through an intricate lattice of silver filigree. She had to pick it up. The wires were finer than Sally's thread. It was only when she screwed it to the jade mouthpiece that an image of a dragonfly with lacy folded wings floated up at her. Its head was pointing towards the silver bowl, seemingly wanting to lick the contents. For the briefest of moments she wanted to feel the jade resting between her lips, to suck narcotic smoke from the dragonfly's belly and feel it come alive. She dismantled the pipe and replaced it in its cradle. The last was ivory. Plain and simple but mounted with gold at its joints. She had an image of Brilliant Chang cradling it in his manicured hands, curling his long fingers towards the bowl. May snapped the lid of the casket shut. The fumes of the man's Chandu cigarette had softened her mind.

She stood and turned her back on temptation. What was taking the man in the kimono so long? Deciding she would pretend she was trying to find him, May skirted the lacquered screen and went through the door that lay behind.

Soft voices, wordless murmurings, and the unmistakable sound of a woman weeping accompanied her as she walked down the corridor. Her footfalls were lost in the carpet. She reached the window at the end and then turned back. Six doorways. She supposed that behind each door men and women lay wrapped in their opium dreams. Was there an office on the floor above as there had been in Brilliant Chang's nightclub? Somewhere the owner sat and counted his profits as under his feet his patrons greedily burned through their entire wealth. But there weren't any stairs back here.

And then the door on her right opened. In the light leaking from a red-shaded lamp, she saw a woman reclining on a divan surrounded by jewel-coloured cushions. The smell of burning opium tickled May's nostrils and she almost wanted to go inside to fill her lungs with more. A man emerged from behind the door, closing it gently behind him. It was Richard Weatherby. He made to walk past her but she touched his sleeve.

'Yes, what do you want? If it's drugs you're after then go see the man in the dress.'

'We met in court.'

He looked at her as though it was a variation on a line he'd heard before.

'I appreciate you don't recognise me but I'm May Keaps, the coroner's officer. Miles Elliott…'

'I'd rather you didn't mention this to anyone.' He spoke out of the side of his mouth as if they were being watched. 'I wanted to talk to you anyway.'

332

'And I, you.'

They walked in silence back to the main room. They had seated themselves in opposite armchairs when the kimono man reappeared. May couldn't work out where he had come from; he hadn't been in the corridor and the bead curtain across the doorway was undisturbed. He nodded once, and exited behind the screen.

'Why did you lie under oath?'

'I had my reasons.'

'Were you Miles' dope-runner?' May didn't want to waste what was left of her wits on subtlety.

He laughed. A dry croaking sound that was painful to hear.

'If you knew how absurd such a suggestion is.'

'I saw you in Three Colt Street cosying up to one of the cocaine sellers, and now I find you coming out of a room in which a woman is smoking opium. It seems a perfectly logical assumption to me.'

'Do you have any idea who she is?'

'One of your customers worthy of individual attention?'

'My sister.'

'You said she was in Italy.'

'I lied about that as well. She was in Switzerland. At a clinic. To help her get off drugs.' He shrugged. 'And as you can see, it didn't work. Miles, the bastard, got her hooked. If he wasn't already dead I'd kill him for that. But he is, so I've been forced to settle for the next best thing which is to find out who supplied the shit and take my revenge on them.'

He glanced down at his hands. May could

333

imagine his thick wrists straining as he squeezed around a neck. When he looked up again he had tears in his eyes.

'And of course bringing Amelia here to get her fix – which she needs more and more often these days. I can't make her stop, and I can't let her smoke alone. She no longer knows how much her weakened body can tolerate. So I am like some sort of degenerate doctor dispensing a prescription I know will kill her. But I've no choice. And she's going to die soon anyway. At least this way she's spared much of the pain.'

May wanted to wrap the bear of a man in her arms. He was now openly weeping, the shame of emasculation nothing compared with the guilt of aiding and abetting suicide.

'I am so sorry. This must be terrible for you.'

He sniffed. 'Worse for her of course. She wakes most mornings vomiting – I have to sleep on a cot in her room to make sure she doesn't choke. Sometimes she is overcome with such tiredness she sleeps wherever she is and whatever she's doing, like a child. Then there are the nightmares. I wish she wouldn't but she has to tell me about them; the specialists said that if she can express the horrors then they might diminish in her mind. But I don't think they do. All about death of course. Decomposing bodies, worms writhing in empty eye sockets, bloated corpses dragged from the river and exploding under the pressure of her fingertip. Every sensation she describes in such great detail because that is how she experiences it in her sleep. Look at me...' he outlined the bulk of his body with his hands, 'I'm a man of action, not imagination. I couldn't make any of that up. It's what she lives every night and re-lives every day. Now do you understand why I bring her here? On the journey home tonight she will have this dreamy smile on her face and she'll tell me stories of wizards and magical creatures, unicorns and talking trees. And she will be happy. By God, this fucking poison is the only thing that can stop her suffering.'

May flicked a glance at the casket on the table and hoped that, at least once, his sister had experienced dancing with dragonflies. She pulled herself back. Richard Weatherby had nothing to do with Miles' death. She wanted to ask what he'd learned from the drug-runners but thought it too cruel in his current state.

He produced a handkerchief from his pocket and blew his nose. 'Will I be subpoenaed when the inquest resumes?'

'Yes.'

'Does this have to come out?'

May pictured his sister screaming out her nightmares to the walls of a prison cell and shook her head. 'Just tell the truth of what you know about Miles. Nobody else need know the rest.'

She couldn't bring herself to tell him that, if his prognosis was right, he'd shortly be having to reveal all of this – and more – at his sister's inquest.

'There is one other thing we can do for each other: if you go down and secure me a taxicab, I'll stand guard outside her door and make sure no one takes in another pipe.'

Richard Weatherby gave a weak smile. His knee joints clicked as he heaved himself up.

'I'll be back in a tick. And to save you the trouble, no, the depraved creature in the girly get-up isn't the one. I've been successful in finding out that much.'

It was a horse-drawn hansom he'd found her. Like the sailing ships with their masts touching the sky and their bowsprits protruding over the back yards of Millwall, it was a relic of the past that belonged to an age before men and boys were mown down in trenches, and women bled tears for their loss. May sat back on the cracked leather seat and dozed as they clopped through the streets. Occasionally a shout or gale of raucous laughter made her look blearily out of the window at the workers trudging to and from the docks, and the gaggles of Friday night drinkers listing from pub to pub.

She wished the journey could last forever but all too soon they were at the fried fish shop on the corner of Ellerthorp Street. The carman wanted to continue up to the stables beside Limehouse Cut, so May climbed out to walk the last hundred yards. Gliding down the road in dance shoes and a dress and cape added to her sense of unreality. She'd half expected to have travelled back in time but there was Mrs Toombs calling for her boy to come in off the street, and Mr Alano setting off for his evening ritual of walking the dog as far as the public bar of the Green Man.

May let herself in the front door and went straight upstairs to change into the comfort of her overalls. One disadvantage of Alice not being around was that she had to make every trip to the coal pile in the yard herself. She would stoke up the range and boil some water for a cup of coffee; the pleasantly dreamy effects of the Chandu cigarettes were fading into a cold sickness in the pit of her stomach. She wondered if it was this empty feeling that made people take more opium. The yearning must be irresistibly strong for those who indulged on a regular basis because she'd only inhaled fumes but, even so, she was gripped by a sensory hallucination that she could still smell a hint of cloying carnations.

She walked through into the kitchen and lit the mantle. The scent in her nostrils now felt so real she could taste it... And no wonder ... there on the draining board beside the empty kettle, was a smouldering opium pipe. Slim. Dark wood. Unadorned. How had they got in? The sash window was closed, the yard door bolted, and the front had shown no signs of being forced. The flickering gas flame spluttered, and then burned brighter. Out of the corner of her eye she thought she saw a shadow skip across the wall. She turned. Daubed in red on the whitewash were a series of Chinese characters and, on the table's oilcloth beneath, a rat's corpse lying in what was left of its blood. May's heartbeat reverberated as loudly in her ears as a ship's siren. Slug-trails of sweat stuck the coarse material of her overalls to her skin. The kitchen began to feel unbearably small. She lurched to the back door and threw the bolt. The chill air stung the back of her throat as she gulped breath after breath, waiting for her disorientation to subside.

Once she felt her as though her legs could hold her, she darted down the narrow passageway beside the house, and onto the street. She didn't care she'd left the place open – no sneak thief could possibly add to her sense of violation – but she had to get away from the whirling images of nameless threats by nameless people. The clock over the gateway to East India Dock chimed eleven. She'd go over to the newspaper office on the off-chance Jack was working late. Right now, the distraction of company was what she needed, and his was as good as any.

Chapter Thirty-Six

At first he didn't look up at her. And when he did, she could see why. A shiner the colour of a ripe plum was only partially obscured by his glasses.

'What on earth...?'

'I'm only going to tell you this once, and then we'll forget it ever happened. Okay?'

May's chest tightened. Had the Tong opted to deliver a more direct warning to Jack?

Although it was impossible not to consider a blood-drained rat on your kitchen table pretty personal.

'I was engaged in a little research at the fan-tan tables. Asking a question or two of the regulars when an old lady the size of a locomotive swiped me with her handbag. Said I'd ... now, how did she put it?... *Sodding well gone and caused her not to catch the last number with my bleeding rabbiting.*

338

Seems she was all set for the biggest win of her natural.'

The tension exploded out of May in a belly-laugh that she couldn't control. Even when her muscles were hurting so much she had to press her folded arms hard across her diaphragm. Then, when she was gasping for air, the laughter turned into gulped sobs that were equally impossible to stop. She was dimly aware of Jack taking her by the elbow and leading her out of the newsroom.

He didn't let go until he'd seated her at a table in the Resolute Tavern. The place stayed open through the night to pick up trade from the docks and newly-berthed ships but they'd hit it during a lull – only four groups of men who paid them no interest, and an emaciated woman crying softly into her gin. May felt quite at home with her overalls and tear-streaked face.

Jack returned with two brandies. The good stuff by the smell of it; nowhere near as expensive as Colonel Tindal's, of course, but the best Thomas Salter kept under the counter for emergencies and valued customers. May wondered which category she – or Jack – fell into. He offered her a cigarette, which she accepted. The entire evening had been one of firsts.

'I don't know what came over me back there. I wasn't laughing at you, honest.'

'Yes you were; don't lie to me now, Blossom of May.'

She sipped the spicy spirit, grateful he was giving her time to collect herself. He had replenished their glasses before she'd finished tumbling the whole story out – the opium den, Richard

Weatherby, the desecration of her home... She had to work hard to keep her voice steady. But under the table her knees were shaking so much she thought at any moment the movement would leach upwards and set her teeth chattering. Jack knew she was distressed: she wasn't going to let him know she was frightened.

'Are you going to report the break-in to the police?'

'Technically they didn't use any force but, yes, of course. First thing in the morning ... second thing ... after I've scrubbed the kitchen with carbolic.'

'I wouldn't do that if I were you.'

'What, for evidence? I doubt PC Collier can read Chinese.'

No. I meant go to the police at all. The Tong will know you're running scared.'

'They'd be right, then.'

May was pleased the words had come out with the double-bluff of bravado she'd intended. Jack would think it unnatural for her not to take the threat seriously but she wasn't going to let on how much she believed it wasn't an idle one. The only way she could get them off her back was if she dropped the investigation into what had been going on out at Anchor Wharf with Elliott Shipping. And she couldn't – wouldn't – do that.

'I can't take on the Bow Kum Tong alone, Jack. The police aren't able to do anything about their activities but perhaps they could offer me some protection the next time I'm in Limehouse.'

Except as soon as she said it she knew waltzing around with a boy in blue would make any remaining sources of information clam up tighter than a sailor's knot. So the investigation would be dead anyway.

Jack tipped her one of his mock-salutes. 'Except you're not alone, Blossom of May. Partners, remember?'

Was he doing one of his muscling-in-on-the-story manoeuvres?

'I'm not sure what good you think you'll be when you can't even take on a harmless old lady without getting beaten up in the process.'

A flush was on his cheeks as he made the slow and careful movement of buttoning up his lips. May smiled at both the childish gesture, and his discomfort.

'I'll be the first to admit my talents don't extend to the strong-arm stuff, right enough. But I am a newspaperman and, as such, no slouch when it comes to getting to the heart of the matter. Brains, not brawn, May Keaps, is what you need right now. For a start I can help you work out why they chose to deliver the warning to you at this precise moment. Can you pinpoint exactly what it is you might have blundered across recently?'

'If that's an example of your insightful questioning then no wonder you got whacked at the fan-tan tables – if I'd been there you'd be lucky to be able to see clearly out of either eye. And the timing isn't particularly relevant anyway; surely you can't have forgotten they firebombed Mrs Loader's?'

'No, no. It was me they were after on that occasion. Because I'd been stepping too hard on their heels in the gambling dens.'

'How secure it must make you feel to be so much the centre of your own little world. Far be it from me to disabuse you but the Tong have been tracking my every move. Do you really think it was a coincidence they chose the night I was in there to torch Elliott Shipping–'

'I seem to recall being present on that occasion as well.'

'–and they knew I was out tonight. Probably had me followed to the Causeway. Maybe even sent that little party of dope smokers to keep me there.'

'All I can say is thank the Virgin Mary they did or if you'd have got home earlier it could've been much worse.'

Much to her annoyance, May realised that Jack was helping. Not with his fatuous theory that she had unwittingly discovered something worth killing her for, but because she began to appreciate exactly why they wouldn't.

'I don't think so. They wanted to warn me ... threaten however you want to put it, but they did ... so because they thought it'd be enough to scare me off.'

'I never had the Tong down as being stupid.'

She refused to bite. 'They're careful. Disposing of someone actively involved in the drugs racket – and it's beginning to look as if that included Miles Elliott – is one thing. Trying to get a rival, Brilliant Chang, indicted and hanged for murder, another. But they'd never risk killing an Officer of the Crown. The full force of the law would come down on their heads for that and put paid to every one of their little sidelines. You saw how quickly the Palm Court Club had to close

342

once the police surveillance started.'

'Pardon me for pointing this out, but don't you think your attendance at an opium party might be interpreted by some as having a foot in both camps?'

May slammed her glass on the table. The buzz-saw of drunken exchanges died around them. Thomas Salter wandered out from behind the counter.

'You all right there, miss? He bothering you? I can fix it for a couple of the lads to chuck him out arse over elbow if you see fit.'

'Yes, he is bothering me, but that won't be necessary. Thanks all the same.'

The landlord returned to his station leaving May irritated further by every man's assumption that she couldn't handle things herself and needed rescuing. Across the table, Jack was grinning at her. She could kick herself for being so weak as to need to seek him out in the first place. And for the tears. Especially for the tears. Her self-loathing spiked into viciousness.

'You reporters have a habit of casting out information to reel people in, don't you? I wouldn't be surprised to learn it was you dropping hints to the Tong about where to find me; after all, everyone's fair game in the search for a story, isn't that right, Jack?'

'Jesus, May. You really do have a low opinion of me, don't you? I didn't even know where you were tonight – in fact, I can't say I spend much time thinking about you or your activities at all. Besides, I was nearly trapped in the fire at Elliott Shipping, too, remember? And if I am really such

343

a hard-nosed callous bastard of a newspaperman as you take me for then it would be completely out of character to flirt with the possibility of the story dying with me, now wouldn't it?' He stood. 'I'm having another brandy. To soothe my hurt feelings and quiet the temptation to forget you're under duress and punch you in the jaw. In my professional opinion as a low-down bum, you've had more than enough of the hard stuff.'

He stalked up to the counter leaving May with the sour taste of an apology on her lips. She wasn't sad to see him begin a conversation with the landlord. No doubt about her. Well, she deserved that. She'd never really considered Jack a snitch. But someone must've made it easy for the Tong to keep tabs on her. Brilliant Chang's words in the courtroom came back to her: *A carefree future often rests in the hands of those with the means and inclination to destroy it; do not put yourself in the position of having to learn that firsthand.* She hadn't listened closely enough then, but now she was hearing every word with ringing clarity. Being wise after the event was the easiest thing in the world: she had to start wising up to events. So who had known she was going to the opium party? Sally. But that was absurd. Liza? She'd been terrified when she'd seen Richard Weatherby outside the café and might've set May up to protect herself – or her son. And if Liza had told Richard Weatherby, then that would've given him plenty of time to perfect his story about Amelia. Except she found it hard to believe anyone could fake such emotional despair. But there had been other men on Three Colt Street who could've see them

344

together and threatened Liza afterwards: the dope-runners.

And that was where her thinking stopped. The combination of opium smoke, the shock of what she found when she got home, and the brandy had finally caught up with her. She'd go home, use the last of her energy to dispose of that disgusting corpse, and go to bed. With any luck she might wake up in the morning with a bright idea of what to do next.

May staggered a little as she walked up to stand beside Jack.

'I'm sorry for the things I said. You are a friend ... a good friend. Thank you for being there when I needed you.' It hadn't been so hard to say it after all.

'It was all my pleasure, Blossom of May. Well, not all, truth be told, but I'm not so dim not to know that even only having a part-time partnership with you entails taking the rough with the smooth. Give me a second to down this and I'll escort you home.'

She laid her hand on his arm. 'I'll be fine, thanks. I've taken up too much of your time already; Andy Taylor will have your guts for garters if you don't finish whatever it was you were working on in the newsroom.' On impulse, she raised herself on tiptoe and gave him a peck on the cheek.

The warmth of his smile would be more than enough company back to Ellerthorp Street.

Chapter Thirty-Seven

It was Sunday, and the long awaited – and much needed – dress rehearsal. Vi was as jumpy as a lodging house mattress, she so desperately wanted everything to go well. And then there was that other plan she was hoping had all miraculously fallen into place: that of arranging for Alice to have made a pig's ear of her run-through with Horatio last night. Except it appeared she was to be disappointed in that regard because she was over in the OP corner with him now, her hand on his sleeve, and a beaming smile putting the spotlight to shame. Perhaps she'd read the girl all wrong and she was used to the effects of cocaine – that little talk they'd had would've guaranteed she'd have taken some – so had still been capable of following his instructions to the letter. Although ... she looked to be high on something now. Even from here Vi could see the tell-tale signs of too-bright eyes, and glowing red cheeks like a penny ragdoll. She was jabbering nineteen to the dozen; tossing her hair back to command Horatio's attention every time it strayed. It was an object lesson in distraction; Vi reluctantly admitted that if Alice could keep her mouth shut on the night she would make the perfect magician's assistant.

But then she realized that was exactly what she couldn't do right now. The cocaine was doing the talking for her. Maybe the rehearsal was going to be even better than she'd hoped, because with the combination of lowered inhibitions and inexperience, Alice might well not be able to control her performance. Horatio hated nothing more than displays of public humiliation. Particularly if he was shown up in their wake. All she had to do was bide her time and let Alice do the rest. He was already beginning to look a little hunted as he twisted away from the girl to signal to the band director.

'I believe we're ready to begin now. If you'll get your boys to take their places...'

'Can't you get them to jump a little higher? I'm sure they were better than that at the try-out; the gallery will be hard pushed to believe they're not nailed to their podiums.'

Mr Dansi threw a despairing look at Vi but Horatio was directing the thing and, as far as she was concerned, if he wanted the poodles to pirouette on one leg, then that's what they had to do. They finished their routine with a little more spark, the tabs closed, and she strolled on pushing her coster barrow – they'd gone back to the original plan of her working front of curtain. The band struck up and she poured everything she had into her song. In the pause she allowed for the audience's reaction she felt waves of admiration reach her from the wings. A little business with an imaginary bunch of daisies, then her monologue. She knew she'd pitched the tone perfectly: a measure of haughty dignity mixed with pathos to leave the audience not knowing whether to laugh or cry. When she bobbed her ironic little curtsey she was rewarded with an outbreak of spontaneous applause. She dropped her gaze to Horatio sitting in the front row. He blew her a kiss.

'We'll take a short break. I want that lighting sorted out before we go any further.' He looked up at the gantry. 'How about if you dim that main spot a little and bring up the sides to compensate? It's atmosphere I'm after, not the effect of a bull's-eye lamp in a fog. And on the first opening of the tabs, make sure you pick out the poodles and not Dansi; he's not the one they've paid to see.'

A loud guffaw issued from the wings. Followed by a high-pitched snort. Vi looked across to see the comedy duo bent-over with mirth, Alice in the throes of finishing off the punch line. With any luck she was giving them some fresh material. But there was a chance it might prove doubly rewarding because Horatio had swung around to glare at the stage.

'Shut up, back there. A break isn't permission for you to start screeching like deranged monkeys. This isn't a school playground. Rehearsals are a serious business. It's not as if any of you have the luxury of perfect routines.'

Alice stuck her head around the flat. The silly girl.

'It was my fault, Horatio. I thought a laugh would do us good.'

'Well, you thought wrong, didn't you?... Now, move that spot a little more ... that's it ... keep it there for the next turn and we'll see how we go. Okay, the vent's up next. And from now on we'll be fixing timings so I want you all ready to come on as if we're doing this for real. There'll be no

348

introductions in the performance, just the running order in the programmes, so pay attention to who's on the bill before you. When it comes to the show proper, you're to wait for the applause – please God let there be some – to lull, but not die, then step into your places. I don't want Vi having to push you on.'

She wished he'd tone it down a little. Horatio was always uptight when confronted by time pressures (which today took the form of any overrun costing his father a fortune in stagehands' time) and although she had enjoyed his snubbing of Alice she didn't want the rest of the turns to be battered into falling to pieces. She made a point of going up to each of them and uttering a few consoling, and encouraging, phrases. All except Alice, of course.

The end of the first half was drawing to a close. The band and Ethel, the male impersonator, seemed to be locked in a race to finish the number. Vi made a note of it. After this rehearsal, Horatio would be so wrapped up in getting technical matters sorted that he'd expect her to pick up any issues with the actual performances.

Alice was on next. But when she came onto the stage she didn't stand in the centre in front of the drop, but walked up to the footlights.

'What are you doing?'

'I reckoned I'd come across better from here.'

Vi heard Horatio's tip-up seat spring to attention.

'Please just do it as we rehearsed; it's a little late now to make any changes.'

349

'But last night you said the audience would want to get a good look at me.'

'That was as my assistant. Because it's a necessary part of the illusion. Rest assured you look delectable whatever part of the stage you're on. And, anyway, this isn't all about you: the lighting boys have their instruction too, you know. Now, be a good girl, and go back to your position.'

'The gallery won't hardly know who I am from there.'

'They can read in Poplar, can't they?'

'We ain't stupid.'

'I never said you were.'

His voice was dangerously low. Vi almost wanted to go on stage and drag Alice towards the backdrop herself. Almost...

'If that Ethel can do hers front of tabs then I don't see why I shouldn't; I work here and they'll be loads come to see me.'

It was as if the cocaine wasn't only making her voluble and argumentative; it was bringing out her childish petulance as well.

'I will give you one more chance, Miss Keaps. Go to the back of the stage and do your number without another word, or I'll scrap your slot.'

'You can't–'

'Right! That's it! Consider yourself no longer doing the song.'

Alice looked bemused for a moment as if she hadn't expected him to go through with it. Then she stomped off, hurling, 'You can sodding well stuff your stupid rotten show,' over her shoulder.

Vi looked over the footlights at Horatio; his expression was a delayed echo of Alice's disbelief.

350

The rehearsal staggered on. Terrified at putting a foot wrong and suffering the consequences, the turns delivered shambolic performances. Alice's defection had also upset the stagehands who had become decidedly uncooperative, making every changeover take twice as long as it should. When it was all over, Horatio called the performers together and announced that the entrances and exits needed to be crisper; there would be no taking a call however enthusiastic the audience's reaction; and that those who hadn't got their costumes finalised had until tomorrow's rehearsal to do so. He hadn't needed to follow up that last point with a threat – every one of the guilty parties was giving a pantomime performance of imagining their names sliding off the bill.

He went into a huddle with the ASM, and Vi began the long task of going through the notes she'd made on each performer. She felt curiously flat about Alice; the satisfaction she'd expected would follow the victory of experience over stage-struck youth had eluded her. Instead, she was left with a hollow sadness that it should have been necessary in the first place.

Chapter Thirty-Eight

May spent the majority of the weekend cleaning. She had intended only to scrub everything in the kitchen with carbolic, but once she'd started she couldn't bring herself to stop. Housework depressed her whereas pulling out furniture, dismantling the range, and throwing out everything she'd allowed to accumulate in cupboards was altogether more satisfying. As if she was putting her life in order.

The opium pipe was the last thing for her to deal with. She'd considered keeping it in case it could prove useful at the inquest but then remembered Alexander Laker's warnings of rumours concerning her personal connections to the drugs world – via Jack – and decided it would only serve to mire everything in silt. So she'd re-lit the range, and thrown it into the fire.

Jack had also proved influential in the matter of whether or not she should report the incident to the police. After spending the best part of Saturday mulling it over, she'd concluded that little would be gained – the Tong had made their point. However, aware of the dangers of drowning in the shallow waters of complacency, she had gone around to Mr Krantz's hardware shop on Chrisp Street and asked him to change the lock. Afterwards, she'd popped into the Gaiety and given Alice her new key; her sister's beaming face as she'd shared the news of her elevation to magician's assistant had been the only joyful sight for days.

All the physical activity hadn't resulted in the nightmare-free sleep she'd been longing for and May was up and dressed for work by seven o'clock on Monday morning. As she walked down the street she wished she'd skipped breakfast and set out earlier. It must've been a spectacular sunrise to judge from the ribbons of lilac, pink, and apricot floating across the sky – the one blessing to come out of all the smoke from the industries and steamships. The scent from the silver wattle tree that Mr Dewar, the cooper, grew in a barrel wafted over the wall as she turned the corner of Ellerthorp Street. He'd planted a seed brought back from Australia and it flourished in the sheltered back yard, making every spring a foretaste of long hot summers to come. This year she would get out for as many walks as possible, perhaps even go with Roger on that jaunt into Sussex.

She became aware of footsteps behind her. Measured. Unhurried. Not a docker on his way to the morning call-on. She increased her stride slightly and heard a corresponding change of pace. Her skin prickled. Had the Tong not had an informant at all and had simply taken to watching the house? Her pursuer was gaining on her. Fumbling in her messenger-boy satchel for something she could use as a weapon – the ring of courtroom keys could do some damage if thrust in the face or groin hard enough – she whirled around. The man raised a finger to the peak of his cap as he continued past, tugging a little on the lead for his dog to keep up. May let out the breath she'd been holding. No wonder she hadn't heard the animal, it was a slip of a greyhound seemingly run to exhaustion on the canal towpath.

Her frayed nerves served to tell her that she had to start getting some answers before she did the Tong's work for them by scaring herself witless. She decided she would leave Alf Dent to open up the public areas of the court and pay another visit to the Black Cat Café on Three Colt Street. There was a chance that Liza might be up and about early if her mother was still looking after her little boy. Liza was one of life's survivors, but she wasn't a liar: she'd answer a direct question about whether she'd been double-dealing with the Tong.

The place was full. Traders from Dolphin Street market tucking into bacon sandwiches after the gruelling work of setting up their stalls; a handful of woman eager to steal a march on the bargains; casual dockworkers – *the lump* – who'd been unable to secure a day's work at the call-on; a scattering of children looking to earn a copper running errands. But no Liza.

May took the one spare chair, at the table of a fat woman who was in the middle of an argument with her blind husband. He made up in volume what he lacked in sight. A young girl – probably fresh from leaving school – with acne and greasy hair came over to take her order. May didn't want anything but couldn't really take up space when they were so busy. She asked for a coffee and, when it was brought to her, tipped the girl a ha'penny.

'You have a waitress here – stooped, rather heavy around the waist,' she realised that could describe most middle-aged women in Poplar with hard work and babies taking their toll, 'rather badly-dyed orange-ish hair.'

The girl blushed. 'That's my ma.'

May regretted her bluntness.

'I told her not to do it as it would make her look stupid. But no one ever listens to me. She's out back. I'll fetch her, shall I?' She hurried off without waiting for an answer.

After a long wait in which May's companions had explored and discarded the topic of how they never would have taken up together if it hadn't been for 'poor, dear Fred, God bless him' dying of *the chest* (the only way East Enders ever referred to consumption), the older waitress emerged from the kitchen. Her broken-backed shoes slapped on the floor as she dodged between the tables.

'Daisy says as you want a word. Make it quick, dearie, I ain't paid to stand around looking beautiful.' She laughed and May was engulfed in a cloud of halitosis.

'Do you remember me? I was here at the end of last week with Liza. She's one of your regulars. I'm looking for her.'

'She in trouble? If so, then I'll tell you straight you won't get nothing out of me.'

'We used to work together in the tobacco factory–'

'Come up a bit in the world since then, ain't you, dearie?'

355

'–her little boy, Cyril, is sick and I wanted to help pay for the medicine if I can.'

The woman's wary look softened into something like compassion 'They're a sore trial, kids. Wouldn't have my brood if I had my time again. But what's to do, eh? You gets married, then you gets knocked-up before you can see your way to getting new lino. I suppose it's only nature but it's we who has to suffer for it.'

May looked down and played with her spoon. She fervently believed women should have the right to choose the direction of their lives but to say so could be construed as advocating abortion and a coroner's officer had to be seen to be upholding the law in word and deed. She felt a flush spread up from her neck as all the illegal activities she'd been involved in recently taunted her hypocrisy.

'Has she been in?'

'Not so as I've noticed. I know who you mean though; sort of worn out, but pretty looking. Not that a nice face will mean she'll get trade much longer, not when there's always fresh meat to be had on the streets.'

May flinched at the hard edge in her voice. But she didn't blame the woman for it, there must be many days and nights when, given the chance, she'd opt for selling sex instead of earning little more than she took in tips waiting tables. And there'd be precious few of those given the Black Cat Café's clientele. Then it came to May that maybe the waitress had secured herself another source of income from those more willing to part with their money. Jack had told her about ordinary

356

working women being part of a network to draw others into the circle of cocaine and desperation. If this waitress was already working for the Tong perhaps she'd been the one who'd told them about her invitation to attend the opium party. Had she been near the table when Liza had mentioned Sadie? May couldn't remember. And she wouldn't ask. Her conscience was heavy enough with the thought she might've brought some retribution from the dope-runners down on Liza.

She finished her coffee and slipped the waitress a threepenny bit. Tom's workshop opened out onto a view of Limehouse Causeway and she'd be able to watch the prostitutes walking their regular circuits from there. The first sign of Liza and she'd ask Tom to go and fetch her so they could talk unobserved – he'd complain but he'd do it.

He didn't turn around at her greeting. With a spanner in one hand and an oilcan in the other he was hunched over his workbench, no doubt adjusting and readjusting a screw or nut in that obsessive way of his. The space smelt of coffee and paraffin. May threw a glance at the hulk of canvas at the back. The morning sun coming in through the open double-doors was kissing the bottom edge with a promise to reveal the glory beneath, but she didn't want to walk up to inspect his progress on the Norton without his permission. He was so obviously in one of his moods that he'd probably throw the oilcan at her if she invaded his sanctuary any further. She'd place the money she'd brought with her – even without the threepence it should be enough for a spark plug – on the bench and leave him to come around to her company while she stood by the entrance and kept a lookout for Liza.

Tom paused in his tinkering to sweep the coins onto the floor with the side of his hand. 'Might as well chuck it away with the rest, missy; there ain't no point anymore.'

Belatedly, May remembered his ailing brother. 'I'm so sorry, Tom. Is it bad news?'

'Worst as can be.'

She bent down to gather up the coins to give him time to recover from what, to him, would've been a soul-baring display of emotion. When she thought the time was right, she straightened up again.

'Is there anything I can do?'

'Like what? Find another put out for the totter. Know the chances of that happening? I reckon less than me winning on the dogs which is as likely as buggery seeing as I don't go.'

May was as shocked by his swearing as she was by his callousness over the loss of his brother. But then she reminded herself that Tom didn't re-spond to the vagaries of life remotely like other people.

'Did you stay for the funeral?'

'You ain't no more brains than this spanner. I weren't talking flesh and blood. Wish I had been. You don't know how much I wish I had been.' And his voice cracked.

She watched a fat tear track down his cheek and settle in the crease around his mouth. He wiped his nose on the sleeve of his overalls then, in a lightning movement that rocked her back on her heels, shot out his withered arm and grabbed her wrist. His grip belied the wastage in his muscles.

'Ain't never known heartbreak like this, and ain't never likely to neither.'

May tried not to struggle and allow herself to be dragged to the back of the workshop. Once there, Tom whipped the tarpaulin off the Norton. She gasped. The gleaming chrome she'd so recently polished reflected the soft sunlight. Unevenly. In contorted shapes, not smooth lines. The forks of the Brooklands' Special had been flattened and bent back on themselves. The front wheel was buckled and minus almost a third of its spokes. She wanted to cry. But hers wouldn't have been a silent weeping like Tom's. She would've sobbed and screamed and battered her fists on the selfish old man who'd taken it upon himself to shatter her promise to Albert because of something he'd got into his deep, dark head. Other than the woodwork tools and a handful of his old clothes, the shared dream of getting the motorbike on the road again was the only thing she had left of her brother. Tom was speaking:

'...day before yesterday it must've happened. Friday. Left the place open. Didn't take a gander under the canvas 'til this morning.'

That'd been Saturday: the stupid cretin didn't have a normal person's concept of time, along with everything else. And then she realised he hadn't done something in a funk only to discover it when in his right mind again. Someone had come in and attacked the motorbike. Her motorbike. It'd been vandalised because it was her motorbike. They'd known. The Tong. Horrible though it had been she could understand why they would want to warn her off by threatening her, but to destroy such a beautiful – and rare – machine looked like an act of spite.

'I'll do what I can, missy. But I ain't no Saviour to set about raising Lazarus...' He stroked the leather seat. '...Excepting I ain't let no assemblage of metal and rubber, wire and doodads, get the better of me yet. We'll show 'em what I'm made of, won't we?'

May thought for a moment he was talking to her but the soft smile on his wrinkled face and the crooning lilt of his voice made it clear he was addressing the Norton. She apologised over and over again to him in her head – for her suspicions, and for the fact that his space had been violated for no other reason than he was doing her a kindness – and slipped out into the shadow of the dock wall. Someone was going to be made to pay the consequences of this mindless viciousness. It wouldn't be Tom, and it wouldn't be Albert. And she was damned if she was going to let it be her.

Chapter Thirty-Nine

May's anger turned into a hard and brittle lump in her chest when she saw the dope-runner – the one who'd been talking to Richard Weatherby – strolling along the road, exuding an arrogance as if he owned the place. His hat was tipped back, a smug smile broken intermittently by the matchstick he was lazily flipping between his lips with his tongue. She knew the Tong had to have policemen and local politicians – probably magistrates, too – in their pockets to get away with conducting their despicable activities so brazenly, but was it bribes or fear put them there? Her nerve endings fizzed at the thought they now assumed she'd been successfully added to the list.

She strode over to stand in front of him, refusing to have her presence hidden from the street by skulking around the corner; if they had someone watching her then she'd give him something to report.

'What can I do you for?'

'Do you know who I am?'

'Should I?'

He smirked and she longed for him to swallow the matchstick whole.

'Reckon I've seen you around but you ain't availed yourself of my services before. Know that for a fact. Need a good memory for faces in this game. Got the notion to shop around a little? A wise decision if I may say so. Pure stuff I've got. Straight off the boat.'

He held open his jacket to reveal an inner pocket stuffed to the brim. The suit's cheap lining was streaked with white powder.

'My name is May Keaps and I'm the Poplar Coroner's Officer.'

'Well, well, ain't I the honoured one? I heard you was indulging.'

'Really? Who from exactly?'

'Oh, here and there. Sadie, I think might've mentioned it in passing. Quite a mine of information is our Sadie.'

May wondered if the girl existed at all or if her name was a sort of code word. If so, by Liza giving it to her and her repeating it to the man in the kimono, she might've unwittingly announced herself at the opium party. Come to think of it, the she-man had spirited himself away for quite a time during the evening; had he been the one who had told the Tong her house was available for entry? The growing conviction she'd been played for a fool drowned out the tiny voice of caution in her head, and sharpened her intention to take the upper hand.

'Do you work for the Bow Kum Tong?'

'Now, that would be telling, wouldn't it?'

'I want you to deliver a message. Tell them I know about their interest in Anchor Wharf. And while you're at it you can add that they murdered Miles for nothing as the coroner will be impounding Elliott Shipping until someone is indicted and arrested.'

That course of action hadn't occurred to her before and she'd only said it now to show she wasn't going to be intimidated off the case, but it wasn't such a bad idea. It was well within Braxton Clarke's powers to do such a thing and it might just force the Tong's hand into taking one risk too many. Except perhaps she'd got there first by allowing her fury over the mangled Norton to rule her head; issuing a threat to the Tong wasn't the response of an unemotional and rational servant of the Crown. But they were the ones who'd moved to make this personal. Deeply and bitingly personal. There would be consequences – May was sure of that – but she hadn't survived this long in the dog-eat-dog world of the docks, let alone the mud and blood of France, by being the sort to roll over and accept a kick in the guts just because those delivering it were bigger and stronger than she was. Besides, she had the law to call on to back her up. She'd head for the office where she'd put in a telephone call to the coroner. As well as recommending he issue that warrant for seizure, she'd ask him to arrange police protection: if they tried to silence her with another warning then it'd be within the confines of a trap. She stalked off savouring the satisfaction that, although the dope-runner hadn't stopped smiling, he had bitten the matchstick in half.

May was taking a shortcut down one of the alleyways off the Causeway when she heard footsteps racing up behind her. She turned just as the man drew level. She recognised the hat and suit. A glint. A flash. The dope-runner didn't break stride as she felt a sting in the side of her neck. She'd been slashed. She sank to the ground, her whole body trembling, her hand pressed over the wound. The warm stickiness of blood seeped between her fingers, not enough for him to have cut an artery, but enough. She began to pant, unable to keep any air in her lungs. Her eyes rapidly lost focus, the bricks of the wall opposite merging together into a pulsating black mass. Would she faint? If she moved, how far would she get before loss of blood made her too weak to continue? The memory of Miles Elliott's body lying undiscovered in an alley made her waste what little energy she had in whimpering out convulsive sobs.

She couldn't stay here. Heaving herself up on shaky legs, she took a step forward. Then another, the hand not clasped to her neck flailing for the support of the wall. She made contact with the cold, damp, bricks but leaned too hard into them and lost her balance. Her feet stuttered as she pitched forward, her arms a cushion against smashing her head on the roadway. The ring of confident heels from the far end of the alley. He had come back to finish her off. The bubble of a scream rose in her throat. It squeezed past her lips, no louder than a kitten's mew. Her worst fear was coming true: that of being a woman too terrified to defend herself. She had nothing. No weapon. No courage. No life force. The alleyway turned into a deep dark river, the waters closing over her head until she wasn't sure if she was even breathing anymore. The current buoyed her up – no, it was hands under her armpits. But he wasn't rescuing her from drowning. She had to try to swim away. Her feet kicked weakly against the muddy bottom. The silt swallowed her ankles. The tide had turned.

Chapter Forty

'Miss Keaps... May... Open your eyes... Thank God... Thank God...'

The words reached her from the other side of an ocean. The hardness at her back and the pressure on her shoulders told her she was being propped up against the wall. The sharp bite of her sliced neck was the only other thing she could feel. He hadn't added another. She reached up to renew the pressure of her fingers against it. His grip relaxed a little and she slithered down into a ball at his feet. She was aware of the shininess of his shoes before her stomach cramped and she twisted her head sideways to spew the bitterness of her earlier coffee onto the un-named slime coating the stone sets. Tears and blood soaked into the collar of her blouse. It was her best one. No amount of scrubbing with bleach would ever get it white again. Why was she worrying about that now? Because the alternative was too terrifying to contemplate: that he was going to take slow, painful, revenge on her for singling him out to the Tong – ending in a grisly demonstration of proof he wasn't a nark.

Her lips were moving, but no sound coming out. She wanted to plead for her life. Then, when her throat was finally loose enough to let some words past, she began retching again. The wound was opening – she could feel the prickle of air on raw flesh. She had to stop vomiting. There was nothing left to bring up. Except she knew it was really the fear her body was trying to expel. And that wasn't going to go away. Not when a man with a razor in his hand was standing over her. Not ever. She was aware of the gloom growing in density as he moved to block out the light from the end of the alley. Would he listen if she begged him to spare Alice? Did murderers ever respect their victim's dying wish? Had Miles uttered one? If so, had it come from the depths of an opium dream – or nightmare? He was bending over her now. She could smell mint and tobacco on his breath. And a spicy warmth clinging to his clothes. His hand was on her forehead trying to inch it back. His touch, gentle. She'd lost her hat. That silly green moth-eaten hat.

'May ... can you hear me?... It's Horatio Barley-Freeman...'

Alice's hero. Now her knight in shining armour.

'...I saw a man running out of the alley and knew he must've been up to something ... but I never imagined ... never thought it could be this... Here, sit up a little if you can...'

A glowing patch of white appeared.

'...Use this. My handkerchief... No, not for your face, your neck... Cover the wound until I can get you more comfortable and take a look at it.'

It seemed to take forever but at last she was upright, her back once more against the wall, her legs straight out in front of her. She felt a ridiculous urge to pull her skirt hem over her knees. Her mouth was dry and tasted of sick. She chewed on her bottom lip to generate enough spit to talk.

'What ... what are you doing here? Did they tell

you where to find me? Are they watching the Gaiety as well?'

'You're not making much sense but then an attack like that is bound to have shaken you up. Did he take anything?'

May looked around for her satchel. The only thing she couldn't bear to lose was her notebook; it contained all her thoughts and summations on the Miles Elliott case. Except it was almost a relief to believe that had been what he was after. Could he have snatched it off her shoulder? It had happened so fast she couldn't remember exactly what he'd done. But he'd cut her. She knew that much. Barley-Freeman got up off his haunches and walked down the alleyway a little.

'Don't leave me ... please don't leave me...'

Her voice was distressingly like that of a petrified child.

'I'm only going this far... Here, I've found it. Your bag. Was there any money in it?'

'What I'd saved for Tom.'

Horatio returned and set the satchel on the ground beside her before crouching where May wouldn't have to move her head to see him.

'It's lucky I came along when I did. I wish I could've been a few minutes earlier though and then I might've been able to intervene.'

'It'd only have postponed things; except I wasn't expecting it quite yet. I thought... I thought it'd be someone else... Why are you here?'

'My father's business. Barley-Freeman Cough Linctus; you know, the sponsors of the show. I was checking the warehouse inventory. We used Elliott Shipping but now it's ceased operating we have to find another carrier but don't know who to contract until we can quantify what spices we have left in store.'

That explained the comforting smell of cinnamon and cloves; she'd thought for a moment she'd conjured it up from long-lost memories of sickrooms. 'Do you work for him? How do you find the time to fit in all the rehearsals?'

May welcomed her brain's ability to think of facile questions when the one burning to be answered was: *did he intend for me to live?*

'He wants me as a full partner but that's my idea of hell to be honest. If this enterprise of mine's a hit, then I'll be making a career on the boards. Come on, let me take a look at what he did to you.'

He held her hair aside with one hand, and peeled her fingers from her neck with the other. His touch was warm. She shivered.

'Can you tilt your head? Just a little to catch the light.'

He removed the protective handkerchief.

'It's stopped bleeding. Doesn't look too deep, but I'm no expert. The hospital's not far from here, isn't it? I think we need a doctor's opinion. Sit quietly and I'll go and fetch a taxicab.'

'No.' She grabbed his arm. 'Don't leave me.'

He placed his hand on hers. 'I have to. I won't be long, promise.'

'You won't find one in Pennyfields. Help me up and we'll walk over to West India Dock Road.'

'I'm not sure it's a good idea for you to move right now. What with the shock and everything.'

May felt a surge of anger. He was trying to help

368

– she knew that – but she didn't want to be treated like a helpless little girl. Even if she did feel like one.

'I'll go on my own then.'

Her defiance was undermined by wobbly legs and she had to lean on his shoulders in order to stand.

'He certainly didn't damage your spirit, did he? Okay, if you insist. But we'll take it at a snail's pace.'

He hadn't been joking, and she couldn't have managed anything faster anyway. A violent trembling had seized her. It rattled her teeth and sounded in her head like a train on the London and Blackwall Railway going over the roof of Tom's garage. If she hadn't heard him. Hadn't turned when she did. Would he have got a clear swipe at her throat? The nightmare she'd had of her father after Sally had come to supper now seemed like a premonition. Heel to toe ... heel to toe... Keep walking. A little more of her strength returned as they stepped into the light at the end of the alley. May was absurdly conscious of her tear-stained face as they turned the corner and passed two women gossiping outside the pawn shop. Who cared what she looked like? She remembered how she'd arranged Clarice Gem's hair so she'd look neat and tidy in death. But she wasn't on a mortuary slab. Not now. And not in the near future. Think of something – anything – to stop dwelling on what might've happened. To feel that life still existed even if she didn't quite fit the part herself.

'How's Alice shaping up? We're trying a little

369

experiment in her independence and I haven't seen a lot of her recently – although I did drop by the theatre on Saturday and she was very full of herself.'

'Ah ... I'm afraid I may have just put the kibosh on that, I confess that at the rehearsal yesterday I raised my voice a tad to her. Or, to be more accurate, an impartial observer would probably say *bellowed*.'

'I doubt it'll do her any lasting harm.'

'On reflection, I might have gone a little far; it was in front of everyone and she left the stage in high dudgeon.'

'That's Alice all over, I'm afraid, she can dish it out but can't take it. I love my sister very much but I think it's about time someone cut her illusions of being the greatest talent to ever grace the boards down to size. Will you think me heartless if, on behalf of us all, I thank you in advance?'

'It's very good of you to take it that way.'

'Look, I'm really almost myself again now, and I doubt there's anything they can do with this,' she reached up and pressed her fingertips at the base of her neck, 'at Poplar General except stick some iodine on it and I can do that perfectly well myself. I'd much prefer to go home.'

'If you're sure you know best...'

'I do. Let's just say I've some experience in these matters.'

'Then how about we swing by the theatre first? Vi will have started the rehearsal but I'll square it with her to spare Alice. Is she working the box office tonight?'

'When I saw her on Saturday she said she'd

fixed the week off.'

'Perfect. She can travel back with you, then tuck you up in bed and feed you soup or whatever. I really do think you shouldn't be on your own after what's just happened.'

They found a taxicab for hire on West India Dock Road just at the moment when May didn't think she could walk another step. All the strength had drained from her muscles and it was as much as she could do to slump back in the seat, inspecting the handkerchief from time to time for signs that the wound had reopened. The sharpness of the razor had done her favours: the skin was holding together. Barley-Freeman had started smoking a small cigar. It reminded her of Christmas.

'Thank you, Horatio.'

'Think nothing of it. Anyone would've done the same.'

He smiled out a smoke ring. No wonder Alice had a crush on him. May tried to say something more but couldn't find the words.

The rest of the journey passed in a haze of shattered images. She wanted to sleep but knew enough about shock from her work in the field hospital to realise that she had to keep conscious for a little while yet – at least until she was sure she wasn't going to be taken unawares by another bout of vomiting. They arrived outside the Gaiety and Barley-Freeman patted May on the hand, told the taxi-driver to wait, and hopped out.

It could only have been ten minutes before he returned.

'Alice hasn't turned up for rehearsal. The poor

371

kid must be feeling terrible to give it a miss. Me and my big mouth, eh? I'll tell you what, let me prove to you I'm really not such a beast by playing the role of ministering angel in her place.'

The thought of Horatio Barley-Freeman stepping over the threshold into her gloomy hall made May hot with embarrassment. It was enough to rally her.

'It's a very kind offer, but I'm fine now, honestly. And please don't feel badly about Alice; this isn't the first – and it won't be the last – time she's gone off in a huff expecting everyone to come running after her with apologies. She'll be in bed faking a headache, I suspect. But Mrs Gibson's not as green as she's cabbage looking and will soon have her up and about again. I guarantee she'll be back in the theatre tomorrow acting as if nothing has happened. And don't worry about me, either. I promise I'll call on Mrs Naylor in the basement if I need anything.'

'You're not just saying that, are you?'

'No, I'm not, where I come from neighbours are always there to help each other out.'

'If you're sure you no longer need me, then I really should be getting in or I'll have Vi joining Alice in cursing me behind my back. Goodbye, Miss Keaps and do take good care of yourself, won't you?'

His thoughtful formality after her exposing herself so thoroughly was oddly moving. May reached out of the taxi-cab window and allowed herself a soft stroke of his sleeve before he turned and walked away.

Chapter Forty-One

The atmosphere rolling off the stage was thick with anxiety. It was as if a collective realisation had suddenly dawned that there was no stopping Wednesday's arrival and, with it, the *Barley-Freeman Cough Linctus Talent Show*. The performers were locked in their own little worlds as they ran through their routines – all except the comedy duo who had indulged in a spectacular row and weren't speaking to each other. Vi was attempting to bring some order to the proceedings when Horatio re-entered the auditorium, flung his coat at the first row of tip-ups, and called her to the footlights.

'What did you mean just now when you said Alice hasn't turned up?'

'Exactly that.'

'She does know there's a rehearsal, doesn't she?'

'I suspect it's something she's acutely aware of. Surely you can't be surprised she'd want to avoid further humiliation after what happened yesterday?'

'The silly girl: I was irritated with her, that's all. Heat of the moment stuff, just as easily forgotten.'

'I don't imagine it felt like that to her.'

'She'll come back to be part of our merry band when she's got over the sulks ... won't she?'

'I doubt it, not after betraying herself as such a

rank amateur.'

'Then what the hell are we going to do now?'

That *we* was the opening Vi needed.

'All I can say is that it's a good job this show can boast one professional on the bill; Alice's slot wasn't until after the interval, so it'll be no trouble for me to change costume and do her number. I'll speak to the wardrobe mistress when we've finished up.' She crouched down and, hidden from those on stage, tipped his chin up with her fingers. 'And, if you're a very good boy – and only because it's you – I might even see my way to acting as your assistant.'

He twisted away. 'Do you really think things could possibly be that easy? Think, woman. Molly... Alice ... what did they both have in common? That box was built for someone skinny and you're ... you're...' He threw his hands in the air. 'No amount of clever costuming can turn you into that.'

Vi wanted to hurl herself over the footlights and strangle him. But instead she walked back over to where the turns were queuing up for her attention.

The rehearsal muddled through – hindered rather than helped for the most part by Horatio's absentminded interference – and then it was curtain up on the second half. Vi had a quick word with the band director before positioning herself in front of the pub-scene drop. He'd wanted the *broken doll* routine performed with heartbreak laced with a glimpse of latent sexuality. She could do that standing on her head; after all, it was no more or less than the story of their life together.

By allowing herself to imagine the worst – that he hadn't simply been playing along with Alice's schoolgirl crush as an innocent dalliance – Vi's tears weren't stagecraft as she spoke, rather than sang, the line: *Don't tell me you were fooling after all.* Then she whipped her head up to stare defiantly at the gallery. Fired with the belief that need trumped flirtation and the man of her dreams – and the song – would come back to her, his love stronger than ever, her voice soared: *For, if you turn away, you'll be sorry some day...* She held the final note until the plaintive cry of the violin had died into a memory.

So lost had she become in the performance that the ASM had to come on stage and gently escort her off.

The rest of the turns passed her by. Vi was leaning on the wall by the curtain pulls when Horatio came to find her.

'You were fabulous. Wonderful. Breathtaking. The rest were just okay but you were ... magnificent. When you pulled yourself up for that last line I felt as though I was being slapped around the face by that easily quoted but much misunderstood adage: *the show must go on.* It's been unspeakably selfish of me to be so preoccupied with what Alice's vanishing trick means for my act. However, no longer...'

He grabbed a passing stagehand. 'Are there any bits of scenery and a black curtain I can fashion into an upright cabinet with a false back?'

He returned his attention to Vi. 'I'll rely on that old standby of making a child disappear. Less dramatic but the audience will still leave with an air of mystery. And if we select cleverly and find a little poppet who'll look suitably terrified, then they'll get a touch of the sinister into the bargain.'

The stagehand was scratching his head. 'Dunno, mate. I reckon as there's a couple of small flats in the basement storage somewhere. But it's a rabbit warren down there full of junk left over from every show's ever been seen at the Gaiety and I ain't got time to go looking, not if you want that backdrop change done smoother. Someone's gotta give the flyman a kick up the arse.'

'Vi, do me a favour and get everyone together will you? I'm off to have a root around.'

'I'll go. I know exactly what you need and it's more important you drill the acrobats to face front when they break into their juggling routine while they can still remember they didn't.'

He gave her a rib-crushing hug. 'I don't know what I'd do without you.'

His breath was hot in her ear.

'I'm sorry for what I said earlier; my only excuse is that my brain was temporarily addled by the spectre of the whole house of cards collapsing. Although the fact remains my words were thoughtless, insensitive, and patently untrue. You've got a beautiful figure and once we pack up shop here, I'll take you back to mine to show you just how much I appreciate it. Then after that – if we've still got the energy – we can work out how to stage the sawing a lady in half trick to best effect in Glasgow. There's a brilliant props builder lives local who I've put on standby to make me a new box; I'll telegram him in the morning once I've

376

reacquainted myself with your vital statistics.'

He planted a wet-lipped kiss on her cheek before disengaging himself to chivvy the next turn into leaving the safety of the wings.

Vi was dizzy with rapture. The fact he'd planned all along for her to appear as his assistant in Glasgow was all the confirmation she needed that he was secretly plotting an elopement. Professional stage magicians – and he was being paid to perform at the Britannia Theatre – only ever worked with their wives, the bond of trust and secrecy required was too all-encompassing for it to be otherwise.

She was walking on air as she left backstage through the pass door and headed into the band pit to plunge into the murky world below stage.

Chapter Forty-Two

May sat at her desk. She'd woken with few signs of the drama of the day before; the skin around the fully-closed cut pulled when she bent her head forward to wash and her hip was bruised from where she'd fallen to the ground but, other than that, she felt remarkably like her old self. Except for the fact that she would now have to wear that ridiculously bright scarf Sally had bought her to hide the results of her folly.

She opened her notebook and wrote a brief summary of the events of the past few days before settling down to re-examine the break-in. She'd assumed – because of the pipe – that it had been a warning not to attend another opium party, but what if the timing had been co-incidental and it hadn't been about that at all? What if it had been the work of one of the rival drug gangs hoping to achieve ascendency by fingering the Tong? Could those Chinese characters have been a name or some detail to incriminate Miles' killer? She could remember the shapes clearly – who wouldn't when they had been written in rat's blood? – and she flipped to a fresh sheet of paper and drew them. But who to ask what they meant? No one legitimate, obviously, because if the message was a reference to the opium party then she'd have to come clean to Braxton Clarke or risk finding herself arrested under suspicion of illegal drug taking. Perhaps Jack could show it to one of his informants in the gambling rackets? Much as it went against the grain to go cap-in-hand to the already insufferably arrogant Mr Cahill, she had to admit that, on this occasion, she was stymied without his help.

The office of the *East End News* was alive with reporters, copy-boys, runners, and members of the public placing advertisements and announcements. May paused to wave at Andy Taylor through his corridor window and then dodged her way down to the cubbyhole Jack had claimed as his domain. She wondered who else would find it incongruous for the nephew of a newspaper magnate to be sitting in what amounted to a broom cupboard with his shirt-sleeves rolled up, chewing the end of a pencil. However irritating he could be at times she had to give it to him that he did have character. May took a moment to adopt a bright and breezy façade and then sauntered up to perch on the edge of his desk.

'Not on that. I've two minutes to deadline.'

She lifted herself off again as he snatched a piece of paper from under her bottom.

'Stand over by the window if you're staying, and don't say a word.'

May swallowed a sharp retort and did as she was told. Jack had a surprisingly good view – if he ever raised his head long enough to appreciate the outside world – of the bottom of Wade Place with its fine white houses. The poshest address in Poplar; home to customs officers, and retired sea captains who'd probably made their money in the lucrative ivory trade. She fancied her lilac dance shoes might once have sat in one of the vast mahogany wardrobes up there waiting to be worn.

'Finished. Boy!'

Jack waved his copy in the air like a flag of victory. A lad of about fourteen with oiled-down hair ran into the room and took it.

'Wait while Mr Taylor looks it over, then down to the print room with you. Look lively.'

He leant back in the chair, his hands clasped behind his head. 'Miss Keaps. What a delight. And there was me certain I was in your bad books...'

May had to search her memory for what had happened when she'd last seen him. Oh yes, the altercation in the Resolute Tavern; did he really think she'd be so petty as to hold a grudge? Then she had to smile because, under other circumstances, she undoubtedly would've done. But the constancy of their relationship wasn't what she was interested in right now. There was a bigger fish needed frying.

'I've been wondering if it was someone other than the Tong in my house the other day.'

'Are you telling me you've done something to warrant death threats from another quarter?'

'We don't know it was that.'

'It's a pretty educated guess.'

'But it could have meant something else; maybe trying to point me in another direction. You see, I had a bit of a clash with one of the dope-runners in Three Colt Street yesterday.' She tried to keep her voice light. 'He took exception to my presence.' Good, just the right tone: professional ... and detached.

'I take it you gave him as good as you got? I'd have liked to have had a ticket; I'll stake my wages on it being better than a bare-knuckle prize-fight.'

May couldn't bring herself to re-live the details – her tiger was caged somewhere deep inside and she didn't want it roaring out and taking them both by surprise. On the other hand she wasn't going to let Jack get away with making a joke of it. She whisked the scarf from her neck aware that, with the light behind her, he wouldn't be able to make out the full extent of the damage.

'I didn't return one of these, if that's what you mean.' She felt a warm surge of satisfaction as he winced. 'I need to know exactly what it was they wrote on my wall.'

She outlined her theory that a clue about Miles

Elliott's murder could be buried somewhere in the message. Jack sat forward, took off his glasses and set about cleaning them with a crumpled scrap of material.

'If you're asking for my help–'

'That's why I'm here.'

'–then the answer's no.' He put his glasses back on and stared at her. 'I'm not prepared to run around and find more rope for you to hang yourself with. I can't believe you care for yourself so little. And care even less for the feelings of those of us who, for some reason that is beyond me right now, harbour a vestige of affection for you. What did you do, go up to the dope-runner and demand a sample of his handwriting?'

May gently re-tied the scarf before walking over to lean straight-armed on the vacant patch of his desk.

'I might well have done if I'd thought about it at the time. As it was I merely asked him to relay a message to his lords and masters.'

'Now I've heard everything. You're so out of your depth playing games with them; next time they won't be content with a little light disfiguring. Don't you see that it hardly matters whether the message was a death threat or not when it's your own foolhardy and reckless nature that will do the job for them?'

Andy Taylor stuck his head through the doorway. 'Cahill, my office. Now. Hello, May. That piece is going to be spiked. I need another couple of hundred words. Decent ones this time.'

'Shit.' Jack got up to follow him. 'Please don't make me ever regret falling for your charms,

Blossom of May, because I couldn't bear it if you let anything happen to bring our all-too-brief liaison to an abrupt and irrevocable close.'

Chapter Forty-Three

First thing in the morning, May was walking past the tobacconist in the High Street when Jack stepped out onto the pavement.

'I thought you'd like to know that I found someone else to do my translating for me.'

'Good morning, Miss Keaps. Yes, thank you, I slept very well.'

'I do wish you'd give up on your sarky comments about my lack of social graces, it's becoming very tedious.'

'Who?'

'Never you mind. Suffice to say that it was designed to scare me off the investigation.'

'I forbear to mention the fact that my educated guesswork was spot-on. Oh dear, that just slipped out. I suppose me saying *I told you so* all the time must be a tad wearing, too.'

May narrowed her eyes and shot him a dagger look. 'You can only call it *educated* when you know what you're talking about; I highly doubt that, even given the loose accuracy of your self-publicity, you can boast reading Chinese amongst your many talents.'

'What is it that makes you unable to resist having a go at me? I seem to be gifted enough when you want my help with something.'

'Stop whining. The point is that I rattled their cage by going to the opium party which proves I must be getting close to something.'

'Did the cut on your neck vanish overnight along with your high opinion of me?'

She couldn't help reaching up to check the scarf was still covering the scar. 'I've been thinking that maybe it wasn't such a bad thing I showed them my cards – isn't that what you gamblers say?'

'I'm not a gambler. I'm an investigative reporter working on a gambling story – there is a difference. Are you going to swallow your pride and get the police involved now?'

Is that why he thought she'd kept silent? And he had the nerve to accuse her of misjudging him. She was almost tempted to march him off to the police station right now so he could witness how little she cared about losing face. Except any assistance she might seek from that quarter had to wait until she had a foolproof plan in place to spring a trap, and not before.

'No. What happened is over and done with and no one will talk to me if word gets out I've been running to PC Collier and his ilk.'

'I hesitate to point out that precious few are talking to you now.'

'Well, clever clogs, that's probably because I've not been asking the right questions of the right people. Horatio Barley-Freeman gave me an idea–'

'Ah, he must be Einstein's brother then.'

'–he'd been over checking the spices in his

father's warehouse and that got me thinking that Elliott Shipping must've had someone doing the same thing. Miles couldn't possibly have kept tabs on everything they discharged and stored until the owners could pick it up. Especially if he was distracted by keeping illegal consignments under wraps. Even if it had been casual labour, someone on the quay might remember. That's where I'm off to now.'

Before she could stop him, Jack had reached out and pulled the scarf from where she'd tucked it into the collar of her blouse. He whistled.

'Jesus, I didn't know he'd cut you that badly. Let me remind you that you got it for opening your mouth and saying something stupid. You've done it before, and I know you'll do it again. Except the next time you won't be so lucky... Don't you realise the Tong only use razors as a weapon when they're playing nice?'

'How many times have I got to tell you that this is my job? I have to gather evidence to put before a jury and of course some of those with reason to hide the truth don't take kindly to me doing so. But I'd be useless at it if I allowed that to stop me ... and if you so much as think that I'm more vulnerable because I'm a woman ... it goes with the territory, that's all.'

She took the scarf from him and tied a knot this time.

'Besides, this is the only assault I've received in two years as coroner's officer whereas you were clouted by an old lady's handbag two months off the boat, so you're hardly one to talk.' Her point made, she relented a little. 'But you're right. I let

384

my anger get the better of me when I confronted the dope-runner – it doesn't matter why now – and I shouldn't have done.' She held her hand to her neck. 'This was a tough lesson but I've learned it now: the scar will be my reminder.'

Jack nodded. Just once. She knew he was remembering the firebombing of Mrs Loader's house and how it hadn't stopped him in his tracks. The look he gave her was one of professional respect.

'Okay then. If you're still alive tonight then would you care to accompany me to the beast's lair – the Tong's gambling den? I think it could be time for us to reprise the *sailors fresh on shore leave* act; if you're determined to scurry about under their noses then you might as well bluff them by turning up in the place they'd least expect.'

May wasn't fooled by his pretence that they'd be doing it for her benefit.

'I seem to recall you needed me as cover in Brilliant Chang's nightclub as well. All right, but only if it's on the understanding that neither of us interferes in each other's lines of inquiry. Leave a note on my office door with the place and time and I'll meet you there. And Jack...'

He had started to step off the kerb and he paused with his foot hovering in mid-air.

'...Thanks.'

'What for?'

'You know, caring about me.'

'Partners, remember? It's what they do.'

She watched as the back of that hideous jacket disappeared behind a parked delivery van.

385

May headed for Limekiln Basin. Not the river end where Elliott Shipping sat but the main gate where Fore Street met Three Colt Street. The roadway was as busy as Chrisp Street market on a Saturday night. A line of carts filled most of the available space as they waited for their turn to reach the dock gates and be loaded. The shire horses – the only ones strong enough for the job – had rendered the stone sets slippery with their urine, the spicy smell of their manure fresh and pungent by turns. The last few carmen had abandoned their charges to their nosebags and were presumably in the Fish and Ring watching through the windows for when it would be worth leaving their beer to move further up the queue. Recently disembarked sailors were rolling with their unsteady gait towards their lodging houses, sometimes stopping one of the sherbet sellers or muffin men for something to sustain them on the way. Boys with trays of steaming meat pies balanced on their heads were waylaid by those dockers and stevedores without wives or daughters to cut them lunch at home. Stragglers from one of the passenger steamers that called in on its way to the world beyond Tilbury were threading their way through the chaos.

May felt overwhelmed and disorientated. Her passage down the road was accompanied by the assault of the horses' snorting and stamping, and the rumble of iron-shod cart wheels; conversations in many languages and accents conducted in engine-room shouts; the heavy whump of ships' ropes as they hit the unseen quayside; the whirr and lumber of the hydraulic luffer cranes; and the constant clank and grating of chain links. Her eardrums reverberated in time to the thudding of a screw propeller in the distance: a large vessel making her way down Limehouse Reach.

She steadied herself against a cart side as she dodged a pair of boys being chased by a Chinaman screaming oaths. She took a moment to breathe in the scents she'd been wrapped in all her life. There was the smell of the sea – the muscular steam tramps with their hot oil, smoke, coal dust and metal, and the more romantic tang of hemp rope and oaky tar from the sailing ships. All intensified by the spice of salt. And the cargoes they'd brought with them from far-flung places. If she was blind to the spring sunshine and deaf to the house sparrows fighting over fallen grain from the horses' nosebags, she'd still be able to tell it was April. The oily animal-reek of the last of the wool bales; the nose-prickling sharpness of consignments of cut softwood; and the sugar. The sickly, comforting, luxurious taste of sweetness on the back of her throat that would hang in the air for the rest of the month, returning when the West India runs docked again in September.

May had almost reached her destination when she was caught up in a crowd of girls tumbling out of the bottling factory adjacent to the dock. Their screaming chatter reminded her of gulls in a feeding frenzy. She threaded her way through to reach the wide metal gates thrown open to the ebb and flow of the quayside and its six wharves. The watchman's hut was just inside. She waited while he checked off a list of discharged goods.

387

Two berthed ships were blocking her view of the water but beyond their hulks she could see the majestic masts of a sailing ship in Dundee Wharf waiting to go into the Graving Dock for repair. Everywhere men were dodging and weaving with loads she knew would be crippling their backs and producing calluses the size of oranges on their shoulders. The lucky ones were supervising the swinging down of crane-hoisted sacks, crates, and bales. She took advantage of a lull in the watchman's activity and walked over.

'Excuse me. I'm the Poplar Coroner's Officer.'

'Know who you are well enough, love. What are you wanting down this neck of the woods?'

But his face was new to her. Was everyone on the payroll of keeping tabs? May pulled her notebook from her satchel in an effort to appear distracted by professional matters.

'I'm making enquiries about someone who worked at Elliott Shipping on Anchor Wharf.'

'Young Miles, you mean? Poor bugger. Dope fiend, yes. Deserved to die for it? No.'

May was tempted to ask him what he knew about Miles' opium taking but she had now secured better sources for that information – Richard Weatherby, for example.

'A warehouse manager. There must've been one.'

'Can't help you, love. Get all sorts coming and going here as you can see. Hang on a mo.'

He lifted a red flag she hadn't noticed leaning against his thigh, and began to wave it frantically.

'You, yes you! Don't go leaving that there or I'll have your guts for garters! Stop being such a lazy git and get it where it should be going else I'll report you for malingering!'

He rested the flag against his leg once more.

'Now, where was I? Been on duty over Millwall 'til recent, ain't I? Tell you what...' He took a step past May's shoulder. 'Here, Ern!'

So close to her ear he sounded like a foghorn.

'Bring yourself over here and give this young lady the benefit...'

May turned to see a group of men leaving the nearest transit shed wheeling empty hand trucks. She watched as the stockiest detached himself and trundled towards them.

'You got a fag, miss?' The watchman tapped the side of his nose. 'It's no smoking on the quays and Ern's freer in his talk with a gasper between his lips.'

She should've thought of that. It would've been no trouble to pop into the Greek tobacconist's on her way over. She'd been away so long from the commercial end of the docks that she'd forgotten the way things worked: a little something, for a little something in exchange.

'Tell him I won't be a minute.'

She hurried up to the last of the girls leaving the factory and bought three Woodbines for the same price she could've purchased a packet of twenty. But it was too little too late because when she returned to the hut she had the feeling that the watchman had already filled Ern in on the background for her visit. She would've given all that remained of her motorbike fund to have heard it. May offered the docker a cigarette. And then belatedly, the watchman.

'Don't mind if I do, love. Ta very much.'

The two men stood and smoked – the watchman scrawling his signature on every piece of paper thrust under his nose – sharing a story that involved a stevedore who had unearthed a rats' nest in the number four transit shed and been bitten so badly he'd had to go off to Poplar Hospital. It seems it was the funniest thing they'd heard for a long while. Ern had his arm draped over the top rung of his hand truck as if around a lover's shoulders.

'Got to be getting back.'

But he didn't seem to be in any hurry to leave. May gave him the last of the cigarettes. He tucked it behind his ear.

'Never knew his name. Didn't have much to do with us – lightermen do the discharging for Anchor and the other wharves down that end. Some dealporters work the timber warehouses on Old Sun but it was only ever casuals got stints at Elliott Shipping. Reckon he was picking them off the street and paying the monkeys peanuts. Bleeding scandal if you ask me. Heard said the latest had a crib in Oak Lane. One of my mates got into a bit of a do with him once down the Vine Tavern. Made it up, after like, and got invited back to his place to bury the hatchet over a bottle of rum had found its way into his back pocket. Might still be lying on the floor there dead drunk for all I know.'

Then he turned and, pulling his hand truck behind him, set off across the apron to the catcalls of his gang.

Chapter Forty-Four

Oak Lane looked unpromising. There was a paint factory down one end and an engineering works at the other. In-between were buildings that seemed to have been long disused – those not with their windows bricked in had all the glass broken. None appeared habitable, but would serve the purposes of a man intending to make himself difficult to find. Why else wouldn't he have come forward when he'd heard about Miles' death? Perhaps because he knew more than was good for him about drug smuggling.

Conscious that she was wearing her second-best skirt and a pair of un-darned stockings, May picked her way through the debris filling the doorway of the only premises not to have planks nailed across the entrance. The smashed windows let in sufficient light to reveal a cavernous space with iron pillars propping up a ceiling that had shed enough laths in places to reveal the joists above. It had been a warehouse or home of one of the lighter industries serving the docks – perhaps sack making or oakum manufacturing; the walls smelled musty enough for either – before it had been stripped of anything and everything useful.

There was one thing remaining. A hump of what looked to be blankets in the left-hand corner. Keeping half an eye on the doorway, May skirted along the wall until she could get a better look.

Beside it were the unmistakable signs of a make-shift fireplace; a brick hearth on a heat-buckled sheet of tin, a scattering of ash and bent nails nestling in the centre. It couldn't have offered much heat but any larger and it would've risked setting the timbers alight. Goosebumps raised the hairs on her forearms as she thought of Elliott Shipping. That, in turn, reminded her of the story of the rats' nest in the transit shed. Glad that she was rarely without gloves, May returned to the doorway to rummage through the old sacks and broken crates until she found a length of lath to act as a poker.

She slid her reluctant feet towards the evidence of habitation. What if the warehouse manager was still here as the docker had intimated ... not dead drunk ... but just dead? There was no stench of rotting flesh though. Just a thin veil of urine – rodent and human. Turning sideways so she could run to the door if necessary, May stopped when she judged she was at the outer limit of the lath's reach then stretched her arm out and prodded the nearest end of the bundle. She was sure something was under the covering but knew she'd have to get closer to establish what. Her throat was tight, her stomach fluttering. Another two steps and she poked again. Three large furry bodies bolted. Her scream echoed. Two of the rats made for holes in the wainscot but one – the biggest and blackest – headed straight for her. Her reactions sharper than she would've thought possible, she whacked it on the back before it shot past her feet.

Her heart was racing as she edged towards the bundle. There was something else she could smell now. Without a name as yet, it was metallic – clean and cold. May reached down and pulled at the corner of the top blanket. Underneath was a filthy bolster, a rip at the seam spewing feathers. She poked at it with her stick in case it was the nest. Nothing. Bolder now, she levered it from the pile and tugged the second blanket clear. Three boxes. Oblong and all the size of a baby's coffin. She squatted beside them. They had sliding tops. She inched the first lid aside to reveal the contents. Packed head to toe like sardines were sticks of dynamite

The air left May's lungs and she had to struggle to refill them. Had she got it all wrong and this is what Elliott Shipping had been bringing onshore from the deepest recesses of ships' holds? It was probably the one consignment that would command a higher price than drugs. Or had it been hidden by those intent on a conspiracy of a far more sinister and catastrophic nature: Sinn Féin's bid to bring down the British Government. She replaced the coverings and picked her way out onto the street.

It was mid-afternoon by the time May had finished reporting her find to the police. The detective at the Limehouse Station had made her wait for someone to arrive from Scotland Yard. In her deposition she'd come up with a perfectly acceptable reason for being in the disused building that satisfied both sets of officers. It was the truth anyway; she had been trying to trace a witness. Given the power and autonomy of a coroner's court she wasn't obliged to say for whose inquest.

By the end of her session with them she was convinced her find had nothing to do with Miles Elliott anyway.

Jack's note with the details of their evening assignation was waiting for her when she got to the office. She made a cup of tea and took it back to her desk where she sat and studied the contents of her notebook. The facts – as opposed to ideas and speculation – she'd gleaned about Miles Elliott's death could all be condensed into one page. She felt she was letting him down; he may not have been the most upright of citizens but that didn't mean his killer deserved to get away with it. Twiddling a pencil between her fingers, she started to go through everything she had written from the beginning to see if there was anything she'd missed.

She was digesting the final few paragraphs when she heard it. A shuffling just outside her door as if someone was gathering themselves together to enter. She called out but there was no response. Anyone with a legitimate reason for being in the building would have answered. May's hand involuntarily went up to hr neck. What if the news had already got back about the questions she'd been asking at the docks? She'd told the dope-runner who she was; what if the elusive warehouse-man – and not the Tong – was his supplier? Could one or other of them have come to teach her another lesson in keeping her mouth shut? There was no way out. Unless she could run down to the coroner's chambers, unlock that door and the one to the courtroom, then out into the vestibule and head for the side exit to the mortuary complex.

Except she was frozen. Couldn't move. Could hardly think. The handle turned and her mouth went dry.

A giggle escaped her as Alf Dent, the caretaker, stood in all his shabby glory in the doorway.

'Thought my ears was playing tricks when I didn't see no light. Why ain't you put it on? Damage your peepers you will.' He flicked the switch. 'Couple of stiffs been delivered. The undertaker brought them in at sparrow's fart. Don't know why people have to go dying in the middle of the night; no one ever thinks of my beauty sleep – let alone the gout what with me going up and down them stairs. They're all tucked up waiting. Husband and wife, he said. Gas, he reckons. Well, just so as you know. I'm back off up to my pit. If you hear a clattering it'll be the pins giving way and tumbling me down the stairs. End up with a busted neck, I'll be bound.'

He scratched his unshaven chin. May could almost feel the bristles prickling his skin.

'Not a bad way to go though. Good job we've got plenty of drawers going begging. See I'm given a decent send-off, like. Black horses with plumes if the collection will stretch.' He laughed exposing almost toothless gums and backed out, chuckling.

May wobbled on rubber legs into the kitchenette. She held her wrists under the coldwater tap until her heart slowed, and her hands stopped shaking enough to feel useful again.

Back in the office she walked to the window. Standing to one side and with her palm pressed against the frame, she looked out. Okay, so she'd been wrong about the caretaker but that didn't mean she wasn't having her movements stalked. Going over everything that had happened since Miles Elliott's body had been found had confirmed her suspicions that someone was always one step behind. Or ahead. She had to do something to put them off the scent, thereby allowing her enough freedom to work on setting a trap.

As she watched the smoke from the factory chimneys settle into smudgy grey clouds, her thoughts coalesced into a plan. After she'd finished up here she'd go to the newspaper office and get Andy Taylor to write up a piece for tomorrow's early edition; carefully worded it would hint at the suspicion of a link between the dynamite she'd uncovered, Sinn Féin, and a young man's body recently found in Limehouse Causeway. The Tong would know it was a fabrication and make the assumption she'd heeded their warnings and was delivering a blind alley for Braxton Clarke to conclude the inquest with. She wanted to cheer with the beauty of it. Instead she returned to her desk and picked up the telephone receiver: Miles Elliott's wasn't the only death demanding attention.

Once put through, May waited until the garrulous woman at City of London Coroner's Court had finished telling her that they were about to close up early because of an official function, before giving her name. The voice turned gossipy as she was told that Braxton Clarke's wife was no longer in hospital but still needed his constant care and attention. May interrupted her description of the house and grounds in Sussex she'd once visited for a charity tea to announce she needed to make arrangements for the new arrivals in the mortuary. Did May want to speak to the coroner's officer? No, she did not (he might be the one to take over her job and she didn't fancy swapping professional niceties with him). In that case, as the locum deputy Mr Halliday was at Southwark Court, it would have to be the coroner himself. May felt she was being granted an audience with Royalty. The thud of the receiver on the desktop. It was a few minutes before it was picked up again.

'Atkins here. I take it you have the facilities to conduct a postmortem in Poplar?' He made it sound like an outpost of the Empire in Darkest Africa.

'Yes, there's no problem there. It's simply a case of the formal viewing.'

'How many corpses do you have for me? I do hope it's not another of those explosions you seem so fond of in your armaments' factories down there.'

'That's Woolwich. We're on the other side of the river. The Thames,' she added just in case he thought she meant the Limpopo.

'You'll have to organise for them to come here. I don't have the time. In fact, we might as well do the PM.'

May thought of Dr Swan's loss of fees. 'If you don't mind me saying so, I'm not sure that would be acceptable to our juries; they are...' how could she describe men schooled in Colonel Tindal's distrust of medical men? '...rather set in their ways.'

Mr Atkins' harrumph rumbled in her ear.

397

'Get your undertaker to be waiting at the back entrance to my court at five o'clock sharp. There'll be no need for him to unload. Include the paperwork and I'll sign confirmation of viewing. But the inquests will have to wait for at least...' His voice trailed away from the mouthpiece: 'Miss Parry, when is my next vacant slot?'

As the seconds stretched into minutes, May wanted to scream with frustration. No wonder Braxton Clarke appeared to think her efficient. Mr Atkins breathed again into the mouthpiece.

'A week. I suspect these interim arrangements will be over by then anyway.'

Did he know something she didn't? Were plans in place for the new coroner – and coroner's officer – to be in post at the beginning of next month?

'I think that concludes the business in hand, does it not?'

May agreed that it did and said goodbye before putting the receiver down as if it were the carrier of an infectious disease. She'd pop into the undertaker's on the way to the newspaper office but first she had to tell the caretaker to expect Mr Chivers' van, and get the forms ready to accompany the bodies. With any luck she could get it all done and still have time to fit in a nap before getting ready to babysit Jack.

Chapter Forty-Five

She met him at the appointed time outside the gates of the Paperboard Mills alongside the locks between Regent's Canal Dock and the river. They had to wait for a bridger – the opening of the swing bridge to let a large coal barge through – before continuing down the Ratcliffe stretch of Narrow Street. They passed a series of ship's chandlers, their open doorways passages for the warm smells of tarred ropes, varnish, lamp oil, and freshly-sanded wooden blocks. To their left the incoming tide lapped against the wharves – Duke Shore, Chinnock's, Broadway, Victoria – and moored lighters bumped against creaking jetties. Grey-boarded warehouses loomed like substantial ghosts, their wooden balconies beckoning fingers to the night.

They turned into Horseferry Road to meet with what seemed like every soul inhabiting this area of Limehouse. Laughter and singing accompanied by pianos, tuned by the fog and damp, from the full pubs – the White Swan, King's Arms, Angel and Trumpet – formed a backdrop against which men leaned on walls, and women with a bag or basket full of shopping from the evening Butchers Row market hooked over sturdy arms latchkeys dangling from forefingers. The thin light from the gas jets played with their shapes and shadows. They passed a fried fish bar, its steamy windows covered with Scandinavian phrases, then a Japanese tattoo parlour. On the corner with Medland Street stood a boarding house for Norwegian sailors, a stuffed sea-parrot in one of its big square windows, an arrangement of shells, seaweed, and dried fish half-filling the other. The gambling den was next door, the buff rendering of the boxy building giving false expectations of a Quaker Meeting House or Baptist Mission.

'What are you hoping to learn from tonight?'

'Not much. I really only wanted to put in an appearance to see if the Tong leader does. This isn't the den I normally stake out – that one's higher class and caters for rich whites like I said – but I've never been altogether sure how this one fits in. I reckon it could be simply that it's more legitimate, as in straightforward gambling instead of games designed to end in losing an inheritance, and the Tong leader's presence would confirm that he's never in attendance at the other sort. I suspect it's so as his tricksy lawyers won't have to lie too much if the legitimacy of any of his newly-acquired holdings is challenged in court.'

'So we just blend in and wait for the great man to arrive?'

'Or spot any evidence he's here already. Failing that, any connection will do. If, when I go back to the other place I see any of the same closed faces dealing cards at the ends of the tables, then I'll have established a link. It might help, I don't know, but it'll certainly give credibility to my line that these gambling dens are part of a sophisticated network and not just lone enterprises.'

Jack twisted the handle and they went in. The

hallway was flanked by two open doors and finished by a tight dog-leg staircase. May allowed herself to be led into the left-hand room. It was full of men – she assumed the segregated women were playing pak-a-poo in the other. The oblong dark-wood tables were topped with bone dice and matching shaking cups; discarded hands of cards; and blue, green, and red inscribed ivory mahjong tiles. Glasses slicked with oily spirits and bottles of beer sat close to the elbows of the focused gamblers. A Chinaman in a bowler hat swept them into two empty places before asking 'what is your delight?' May deferred to Jack in this also.

'Beer.' As the man walked away, Jack turned to May. 'Less easy to adulterate.'

None of the gamblers at the table seemed to have noticed their arrival but when the next hand of grubby pasteboards was dealt they were included in the round. May had never played cards in her life. A dense layer of blue-grey smoke – by the now familiar smell some of it opium-laced – hovered at table height like a strata of seawater in a river mouth and made it hard for her to distinguish the suits. There were no numbers. And no one was placing any bets.

'Abacus,' Jack said under the cover of a cough.

The dealer clicked four red beads to the right of an intricately carved ebony frame.

'Tallies losses.'

Now she understood: by the expediency of not demanding money up-front on the table, the gamblers were lured into underestimating the amount of debt they were accruing. The alcohol – drug-spiked or not – would eventually make them forget

401

it completely. She lowered her hand a little so Jack could see her cards. He banged his knee against hers. Then again. She laid the two.

'Will I win?' She'd spoken down into her lap – their companions looked to be foreign sailors so fresh-in they didn't understand English, but she couldn't be sure.

Jack didn't respond until a flurry of curses from the next table provided him with cover.

'No, you'll lose, but someone else will lose more at the end of the game; they're out to catch them, not the table decoration.'

May was about to bite until she remembered her disguise: Jack hadn't been commenting on her gender. The hand concluded and the dealer clicked over his abacus. Then he slid another round onto the table. The other players grabbed the cards like drowning men. May was reluctant to look at what luck – or sleight of hand – had given her in case she stood a chance of winning; she didn't want to be fingered as the next recipient of red beads.

They played a further four hands, and drank another bottle of beer each. The smoke was stinging May's eyes. She removed her scarf (which she'd dirtied with soot from the range to fit more into character) to wipe away the tears. Sly glances noted the scar. The man to the right of her shifted his chair an inch or two away. The sense of power she felt from his assumption about her propensity for violence was thrilling. A movement at the back of the room caught her attention. Someone had slipped out from behind the bamboo curtain. Someone who looked to be as out of place here as she and Jack would've been in civilian clothes. May thought it could've been Richard Weatherby although it could equally have been a thinner man in a bulky overcoat. A hat brim shielding his face, he was almost in as much disguise as they were. He hugged the walls on his way to exiting through the door.

May leant in towards Jack. 'Follow him.'

'Who?'

'The man who just left.'

Jack continued dithering over which card to select. May suspected the bug was biting and he was beginning to hate the thought of being branded a perpetual loser.

'It could've been the Tong leader for all you know.' May doubted it but she had to get Jack out of his chair somehow. 'Come on.' She virtually dragged him up by his sleeve.

The man was loitering in the light from the windows of the Norwegian boarding house, seemingly searching his pockets for matches to light the cigarette nestling in his pursed lips.

'Go on. Speak to him. I obviously can't in case I blow my cover.'

'What about mine?'

'For God's sake, Jack, I'd make a better reporter than you with one hand tied behind my back. Stick to the sailor routine and make out you lost big in there or something. Ask him if he thinks the tables are rigged... I don't know, use what passes for your wits.'

Jack lurched forward at her push. May nipped around the corner back into Horseferry Road. Things were quieter here now. An exchange ... the sound of a match rasping on brickwork … a faint whiff of sulphur, and cigarette smoke from refined tobacco … more words bandied. The voices moved out of range. Should she go back into Medland Street and follow in case Jack was on to something and wanted to keep his quarry company to wherever he was going? Opting for the safety of concealment, May paced in front of the Japanese tattoo parlour in a steady rhythm. She had no idea how long they'd been in the gambling den but drunks were reeling out of pub doors to the accompaniment of *haven't you got a missus to go home to?* by the time Jack came sauntering up. He was laughing.

'Gave me a ticket, of all things,' he held up a thin strip of card. 'Obviously there's more to him than just good looks because he was concluding his business of lining the Tong leader's pockets – although of course, he didn't actually say that in so many words…'

May's frustration reached such a crescendo that she started to pound her fists against his chest. He took her wrists in his hands, still with that simpleton's grin on his face.

'Protection racket, ever heard of it? According to this, your man there is putting on a show at the Gaiety tomorrow.'

Horatio Barley-Freeman. May hadn't been expecting that at all.

'Well, from my own vast store of knowledge I can tell you that the Tong regard all forms of entertainment as their exclusive preserve and demand a little inducement not to have an impromptu Chinese riot or some such to scare the queues away.'

404

'Why didn't you tell me they didn't limit themselves to drugs and gambling earlier?'

'You didn't ask. Anyway, I thought it was common knowledge. If you'd wanted to be let in on it then you only need ask the stage doorman or the scenery shifters or even the manager. Hell May, I bet even your little Alice knows how things are organised by now.'

A shudder rattled May's shoulder joints at the thought Alice might've been approached in the box office by a member of the Tong. But the connection with the Gaiety wasn't the thing she was most interested in. The protection rackets. If Miles was smuggling drugs onto Anchor Wharf and the Tong hadn't been the paymasters at all but shielding the operation in return for a cut from both sides ... and Miles for some good reason decided to stop paying... Here was a solid motive even the most obtuse member of one of Colonel Tindal's juries could understand. Because the docks were run on interlocking waves of protection: the gangers who selected which of *the lump* would be offered a few hours casual work; the old soaks in the pubs who let slip the word of a job going for a little consideration in their back pockets; the ship owners who paid for the privilege of tying their ships on the open water side of another in order to have their cargo discharged through already customs-cleared holds. According to wharfingers like Alexander Laker, the Trades Unions themselves were nothing more than heavyweight protection mobs. Jack had let her arms fall and was scuffing a toe against the bottom of the wall.

'Come on, there'll be no more action tonight.

405

At least you got something out of it, so let's seal your good fortune with a drink. One of the hostelries along here suit you? In that get-up you'll look perfectly at home in any of them.'

May shook her head. 'Feel free to indulge on my behalf but I think it's time I headed back. Work in the morning. You can buy me one another time for smoothing your way in and playing my part so deftly. See you around.'

Chapter Forty-Six

Vi wanted to pull her hair out – or someone else's. The show was in six hours' time, and there were more last minute hitches than it would take the England cricket team to field. The flyman had gone down with influenza and his replacement couldn't seem to distinguish one backcloth from another, despite the fact that was all he had to do; the small bridge they'd decided at yesterday's rehearsal the comedy duo could do their patter atop had collapsed the moment the fatter had stepped on it; the mother of one of the acrobats was lecturing the rest of the troupe in Japanese that he had a sore foot and mustn't somersault – Vi had heard the English version. Twice. And, as if the onstage problems weren't enough, Mr Dansi's poodles had all acquired upset stomachs and befouled the entire dressing room.

The only bright thing about the morning so far was that Horatio was on sparkling form, conducting the lighting boys on their changeovers by using a rolled-up newspaper as a baton.

'Right, I shall now leave all in your capable hands and go and make sure the old crone in the box office knows to get the stalls sold before offering tickets to the gallery. They cost more but we're going to be throwing in a small bottle of linctus as an inducement. Not that I think we'll have any problems filling both after the last-minute build-up I've given us.'

He poked Vi in the ribs with the newspaper.

'Take a look when you've got a moment. Hot off the press. Collected it myself. Page eight. Have you heard anything from Alice, by the way?'

'Why should I have done? She's not been due to work the box office this week, and if she's not in the theatre then I wouldn't know where she was.'

'I still feel badly about what happened.'

'Well, don't. If she hasn't got over it by now then it's her look out. Such a childish girl isn't worth worrying about.' Vi took the newspaper and laid it on the tip-up beside her. 'Go and do your promotion and leave me in peace to iron this lot out.'

It took half an hour to dispel the chaos on stage sufficiently to be able to get on with sorting Ethel. She was a good little male impersonator – although, of course, no Vesta Tilley – with the right amount of swagger, and she looked cutely convincing in her dapper suit. But she just couldn't seem to get the hang of not rushing the last chorus. After they'd been through the song for the third time, Vi made the decision on Horatio's

407

behalf to ask the band director to provide the minimum of accompaniment and hoped that would do the trick.

Vi told everyone onstage to take a ten minute break and collapsed gratefully into the front row of the stalls. She picked up a copy of the *East End News* and flicked to the entertainment section. It was a full-page splash, laid out like a theatre bill but with no names to go with the description of each act. Except when it came to who was appearing as the magician. She smiled at the man's blatant vanity but couldn't help being a little miffed that as the only professional – and understudy director to boot – she hadn't warranted a mention. When they did the publicity for Glasgow she'd make sure her name was just underneath his. Or maybe, even better: *Barley-Freeman and his lovely wife, Violet Mary.*

Ethel very sweetly came over and asked if she'd like some coffee from the shop across the road. Vi could've kissed her. Deciding to wait until she'd been suitably restored before attempting to hammer the importance of the mystical art of timing into the not-so-comic duo, Vi glanced at the front page of the newspaper in the hope of a little light relief. The headline wasn't exactly what she'd been hoping for: *Explosives Cache Found in Abandoned Dockside Warehouse.* She wondered uncharitably if she could ask for the loan of some to blow up the vent's dummy. She idly scanned the columns that stretched below a photograph of Lloyd George. It was a something and nothing story full of speculation about a possible Sinn Féin bombing campaign and making references to the recent disturbances in Liverpool and Manchester, followed by a précis of the debates during the Second Reading of the Government of Ireland Bill. It was pretty dry stuff. Until she came to the last paragraph:

The Poplar Coroner's Officer, Miss May Keaps, has let this paper know she is regarding this find as connected to an ongoing inquest. In her opinion it will be instrumental in the jury being able to reach a verdict as to the cause and manner of Miles Elliott's death, whose body was found in Limehouse Causeway almost exactly four weeks ago.

Vi had liked May very much when she'd met her but was at a loss to understand how she could do such an unfeminine and distasteful job. It wasn't surprising that she hadn't got herself a man. With the hindsight of her new-found security, she smiled at how foolish she'd been to imagine Horatio could find a woman who acted like a man in a skirt attractive.

The object of her thoughts arrived carrying a mug of coffee, Ethel following on juggling her own and a tray of buns. Vi made a point of thanking the woman – she wouldn't put it past Horatio to have taken the credit for himself otherwise. The two of them sat side by side companionably sharing their elevenses.

'So what did you think of my effort?'

'Well, you certainly didn't sell yourself short. No, I'm teasing; it had just the right flavour: it'll ginger up those who are already intending to come so they'll be busting with excitement the minute they join the queue, and convince anyone who was in two minds about shelling out for a ticket. I take it you saw this?' She put her mug on the floor and unfolded the newspaper. 'No wonder you're full of the joys of spring.'

'What do you mean?'

'You must be pleased the Miles Elliott inquest is going to be brought to a close.'

'Why should I be? It's got nothing to do with me. Right, let's crack on. Which rough diamonds have you left to polish?'

'Laughing boys over there – obviously; the vent; and the acrobats need tightening up.'

'See if Mr Dansi's around as well, will you? The manager's chewed my ear once too often about the stink backstage. And, Vi, thanks for all this, I really appreciate it.'

He stroked her cheek with his fingertip before vaulting over the rail into the band pit.

'Where will you be?'

'Down in the bowels seeing if I can't find some embellishments for the front of my cabinet. The scenery boys managed to knock up something pretty good from the stuff you unearthed, but I've a fancy it would look less like a last-minute replacement if it had some cut-out lightning flashes on the sides.'

Vi leapt up, kicking over the dregs of her coffee.

'Horatio, you'll be missing for hours if you go down there. The show's at four o'clock, remember?'

'It's okay...' his voice was muffled by the stage above his head '...won't be long.'

'I'll come with you; I know where to look.'

But just as her foot was on the top flight of the steep stairs, the anxious Japanese mother grabbed her arm in a shark-like grip and refused to be shaken off.

Chapter Forty-Seven

May finished cutting out the piece from the morning's *East End News*. Every time she reread it she felt the same degree of satisfaction: Andy Taylor had performed a miracle of misdirection. There had been a telephone call from Braxton Clarke shortly after she'd got in but she'd decided to wait until he was back in the office (which he thought would be any time soon; his wife just needed a few more days' convalescence) to tell him about what she'd done. He might not see things quite the way she did. And, anyway, she hadn't wanted to dampen his mood because he'd sounded bright as a button, fulsomely apologetic for *leaving her in the lurch to stem the tide of the bereaved* as he put it. It had made her laugh.

The street door banged and PC Collier strode in. She gave him a cheery smile but the young man's face remained serious. He made no attempt to remove his helmet.

'I thought I should be telling you there's a body been found. Young woman. Mother, too. I'm to go fetch her boy and take him to the Institution. No father, see. Makes your heart bleed at times, this job.'

411

She reached out and touched his sleeve. 'When will she be brought here? I'll need to get in touch with the City of London Coroner's clerk to arrange the inquest.'

'Oh, no, no. She weren't found in Poplar. Just lived here. Had her ration card on her. Washed up on Greenwich Strand she was. Could have fallen in off a bridge or jumped ... either way, there's nothing but the boy we have to be dealing with this side of the river.'

May felt a bleak dismay for the poor child's future. George Lansbury and the other Poplar Poor Law Guardians didn't run the workhouse in the accepted way of making life for the inmates miserable in order that the seeking of poor relief was a last resort. However there wasn't an enlightened approach in the world could make growing up in the place bearable for a young orphan.

'I'll take her name for the records and in case someone comes to me to make enquiries.'

PC Collier took out his notebook and flicked to the last page. 'One Elizabeth Trow.' He replaced it in his top pocket. 'Best be on my way. Unpleasant duties don't get no better by the putting off.'

Left alone, May sat staring at nothing. Liza hadn't jumped or tumbled off anything: she'd been fingered by the drug dealers as an informer and dealt with accordingly. She hadn't asked what state the body had been in. Please let her not have been beaten. A film reel played in her head of Liza frantically struggling to fill her lungs with something other than water. She should have gone to the police and asked them to keep an eye on her.

When exactly had they picked her up – shortly after she'd left the Black Cat Café, or had the pimp who'd once sliced her stalked her to the river? May listened to the chatter and clatter of the High Street snaking through the gaps in the sash window. Sounds Liza would never hear again.

Anxious to have something to do before guilt incapacitated her completely, she walked through to the vestibule and fished the afternoon post from the letter-cage. On opening, the first missives failed to provide her with the distraction she needed: an invoice for his recent services from Dr Swan; a cheque from the LCC reimbursing her expenses; a copy of the forms confirming the date for the inquest on the gas explosion couple. But halfway down the pile was an envelope delivered by hand and marked *personal*. May slid her finger under the flap. Nestled inside the single sheet of paper was a key. She took it out and laid it on the desk.

Dear Miss Keaps,

I hope this finds you as well as it leaves me. Although I am sure you will feel some distress after reading this. Apologies for not delivering this news in more personal a manner but I cannot leave the theatre as the show will be starting shortly. Without Alice, I am sorry to say. She has just this minute left after telling me that although she felt awful about letting everyone down, she couldn't face setting foot on the stage. Then she went on to ask if I'd fetch some of her clothes and take them to her at the gates of Limekiln Basin just before nine o'clock tonight. I am unacquainted with the docks but could there be a chance of her boarding a steam packet from there? Putting two and two together I'm concerned she might feel unable to remain living and working where she must now only taste failure.

Far be it for me to tell you what to do but can I suggest that instead of going to your house, I wait for you here (I'll be free of all post-show commitments by eight-thirty) in order we go to the rendezvous together? I'm sure whatever state she's in will be no match for the two of us, and we'll be able to talk her out of anything stupid. She is a talented little performer and, if only she could master her stage fright, could look forward to doing very well for herself on the boards.

Yours with very sincere consolation,
Violet Tremins.

May didn't know whether to laugh or cry. She had no doubt her sister didn't intend bolting permanently to anywhere – she'd never have let anyone else choose her clothes if that was the case – catching the last steamer up to Aunt Bella's in Southend was probably the most she had in mind. But, even so, she must've got herself worked up into a pretty bad state to miss her beloved show. Vi had described how incapacitating the terrors of stage fright could be when she'd been over for tea and if you topped them with the humiliation of being shouted at by the man you thought yourself to be in love with, then perhaps it was no wonder Alice had turned tail. She'd go to pick her up and, once the dust had settled, maybe the girl could be made to accept that she didn't have the temperament for the theatrical life and should quit the

Gaiety for an office job and night school.

Conscious she was trying to avert potential disaster in an equally immature way, May picked up the telephone receiver and put in a call to Braxton Clarke. A soft Sussex burr at the other end announced herself to be the maid followed by the fact that the Clarkes had left a half an hour ago for the seaside to set the seal on madam's recovery. May declined to leave a message, the only thing she wanted to utter was a scream of frustration and she didn't think that appropriate for the coroner to receive on his return.

She filled the last hour of the working day with paperwork. On the dot of five o'clock she packed up, and left for Chrisp Street market to get some food in for Alice's return As she walked away from the court building she thought it'd be a nice gesture to include in her purchases some of the almond cakes she knew her sister loved

The Turkish baker's was opposite the *East End News'* offices. On her way out of the shop, May realised that Braxton Clarke wasn't the only one she owed an explanation concerning this morning's article – if only to forestall Jack from saying something stupid and giving the game away. She'd pop in and see him before continuing on to the market.

'...so I reckon there's a fair chance that now they think they've got me off their backs, they'll push ahead with their plans to acquire Elliott Shipping. One slip up in their haste to get it secured is all I need to tie them in to Miles

Elliott's murder.'

She was standing by the window in Jack's cubby-hole looking out at the early evening sun turning the white stucco of the houses in Wade Place a soft apricot, the bag of freshly-baked cakes in her satchel pressing warmly into her side.

'Don't go getting ahead of yourself. You'll only have bought a little time, that's all.'

May felt a stab of childish peevishness that Jack hadn't acknowledged her cleverness, before putting it down to the fact that it was something he'd never have thought of himself.

'Tell you what, why don't we have that drink tonight? I need to give the dens a wide berth for a while, and we could celebrate your temporary release from the jaws of death.'

That wasn't funny in the light of what had happened to Liza but, to be fair, she hadn't told him about that.

'Can't,' she turned and smiled at him to show she wasn't being offish, 'but we could make it the Spotted Dog tomorrow at around eight; I expect I'll need a break from exhibiting endless patience by then. But, of course, you don't know. Alice was to be in that talent show on at the Gaiety until her nerves got the better of her – so much so it seems there are suspicions she might do a flit. I'm pretty confident it's another of her dramatic gestures for attention but, knowing her, there's always the chance she won't know when to stop and carry it too far. My sister's not one to back away gracefully when she's manoeuvred herself into a corner–'

'Like peas in a pod, you two.'

May shot him a look. 'So tonight I'll be making a trip out to Limekiln Basin; I checked the tables and the steamer from Gallions is due to dock at Old Sun Wharf at quarter past nine. It'll be a quick turnaround to catch the high tide, so I shouldn't have to hang around – just scoop her up and head for home. Do you know what irritates me most about this ridiculous plan of hers? That she must've saved up money when she should've been giving every spare penny to Mrs Gibson for putting her up. But that's Alice's selfishness for you: a ticket in her hand will always be more important than food in someone else's mouth.'

'Hey, why don't you try easing up on her a little? The poor girl must've learnt some very hard lessons recently and, from what you tell me, she's not exactly equipped to find a rational solution to crippling stage fright – not to mention her entire theatrical career being over before it's begun... I'm sure she's not leading you a merry dance on purpose.'

For once May wasn't tempted to ask him what he knew about it. His open face was full of nothing but the desire for there to be a happy ending to it all. A sentiment she shared so strongly that she walked behind his desk and gave him a peck on the cheek before seeing herself out.

Chapter Forty-Eight

May headed down the alley to the Stage Door. Once inside the theatre she could hear the muffled sounds of an audience in the throes of hysteria – the evening show must be well under way. The doorman looked up from his newspaper.

'Reckon you've gone and taken one turn too many, love. Entrance is 'round the front. But I'd save the shoe-leather if I was you. Best acts 'ave wiped off the greasepaint; nothing but second-rate bill fare after the tabs are pulled on the *Monoped Dancer* – and, if I'm not mistaken, Peg-Leg Bates is bopping the boards now with 'is comic closing.'

'I'm to meet someone here; Violet Tremins.'

'Ah.' He swiped a pile of cigarette ash from the counter. 'Shame she ain't booked for tonight. Classy artiste, she is: good in the footlights at the same time as being not too la-di-dah to pass the time of day with the likes of me. But you're out of luck. Came through some time back – not long after that amateur whatsit finished. Tell you what; she's thick with that posh fella what put it on and if I put a call through to the manager's office perhaps 'e'll come down and tell you where she's at.'

May smiled her thanks. She listened to the doorman fulfilling his request, then passed the time waiting for Horatio to arrive by reading a call for auditions from *The Stage* someone had tacked to

418

the notice board. It seemed odd Vi had left the theatre seeing as she was the one who'd suggested they meet up. If she'd simply popped out for something after the talent show had finished then she'd have been back by now. And she couldn't have gone to pick up the clothes Alice had asked for because she'd slipped the house key in with the note. May's musings ended abruptly as the backstage door swung open and Horatio Barley-Freeman almost bounded to her side.

'Miss Keaps. Vi told me to expect you. Many apologies for not being on hand but my father couldn't resist making a full-scale production out of toasting our success in champagne. I think I have clinked glasses with every dignitary he saw fit to invite, and not a few I'm sure didn't even attend the performance. Their loss.'

'It went well, then?'

'Like a dream. I'd almost go so far as to say it made all the shenanigans over the past few weeks worthwhile. Although, of course, I still have deep regrets about that little contretemps with Alice; however Vi was a real trooper and filled in perfectly... Sorry ... that was unspeakably thoughtless of me; your sister's whereabouts is why you're here, after all. I suspect Vi underplayed her concern in her note – she's always been one to restrict her emotions to performances – but when I heard about Alice's apparent plans, I must admit to being pretty worried – not to mention guilty about the part I might've played in bringing us all to this...'

He waved away May's protest before she could properly articulate it.

419

'...I sent Vi down to the rendezvous early in case Alice got it into her head not to wait but get someone to row her over to East India Dock Pier instead. If she boarded one of the Blue Funnel Line steamers then it'd be a hell of a job tracking her down – they're bound for places more exotic than Southend or Margate – and the authorities checking ships' manifests would be the order of the day. I felt sure that, in your position, you wouldn't want such a public fuss made, and be happy to forgive my, no doubt, over-reactive caution.'

For the second time since she'd made his acquaintance, May felt awash with gratitude; as if saving her from any further retaliation from the dope-seller wasn't enough, his solicitude had now extended to embrace protecting her reputation. She turned her face away as her cheeks grew hot. A handful of missed beats hung in the air before he stepped into the silence.

'My intention was to take Vi's place and accompany you to Limehouse but my father is insisting on my presence at the supper he is hosting. And he's in such a rare good mood that this could be the perfect time to broach the subject of my change of career path.'

'Of course, you must.'

'I knew you'd understand. There's the added bonus that some of his business cronies have been so impressed about the publicity the show's bought for Barley-Freeman Cough Linctus they might see their way into being sweet-talked into sponsoring one of their own.'

It was Horatio's turn to flush.

'I must admit to quite having caught the bug

for this directing lark.'

May laughed at his school-boy embarrassment at being caught blowing his own trumpet.

'Allow me ... say ... an hour or so... I gave Vi the key to our spice warehouse on Dunbar Wharf and told her to get Alice into the warm – I know to my cost how the wind coming off the river can cut through your bones, and I'm guessing your sister will be feeling miserable enough as it is. If you don't catch up with them on the wharf then that's where they'll be. When I arrive I can let us all off the quay via the side gate and we can head to a nearby eatery. I'm acquainted with. My treat, of course. I suspect Alice will be famished, and somehow I feel a little neutral company might be called for until you both get used to the fact that nothing awful happened tonight – apart from your sister losing a little face, that is. And with Vi in the party she'll be chivvied out of that in no time.'

Chapter Forty-Nine

The area around the gates to Limekiln Basin was as busy as a dockers' call-on when a tea clipper was due in. The passengers had been unceremoniously herded off the steamer and were blocking the way of those needing to board in the few minutes before the mooring ropes were loosed and the ship ploughed out to the river again to catch the tide. May was bumped and barged as she tried

421

to fight her way through to find Alice. At one point she thought she recognised Vi's shapely figure but it turned out to be a pock-face woman who hurled curses at being accosted on her way to the gangplank.

In too short a time there was no one left on the quayside but the gatekeeper and sailors scurrying fore and aft to release the ship. The thudding propellers were churning the water as May slunk into the shadow caused by the overhanging roof of the nearest transit shed. The night watchman had arrived to assume his shift and was rattling the gate bolts into place. She waited until he was safely ensconced in his cabin – no doubt with his flask of cocoa and the evening dog results – then skirted the front of the remaining sheds until she was clear of the glow from the gas light at the dock entrance and could walk to Horatio's warehouse on Dunbar Wharf without risk of detection.

Keeping to the centre of the quay to avoid the hazards of tying-up rings, coiled ropes, and bollards, May walked on through the chill mist that always gathered over dockside concrete. As she moved further towards the river the usual night-time noises were distorted and flattened by the widening expanse of water. She could make out the whooshing of coal into half-full holds way over to the east and some cranes operating on the wharves fringing Limehouse Cut, but the rhythmic slapping of rigging on masts beyond the Millwall side of the Basin and tide-agitated wavelets lapping the hull of the moored ship she had passed were the only sounds close to hand.

Her ears were beginning to sting with the cold

before the massive edifice of one of the timber sheds for which Dunbar Wharf was renowned hove into view. These didn't house planks of the common-or-garden woods such as pine, spruce or larch but cradled intact de-branched tree trunks from all around the world. On the rare occasions her father had been available – and inclined – to indulge her and Albert in a bedtime story, he'd recite their origins and uses as if they were a docker's poem:

Rosewood for pianos comes from Honduras,
Greenheart from British Guiana for fishing rods,
North American Maple Root for veneer;
West Indian Locust and Mangrove to be made
into furniture.
The dyeing trade uses Bar Wood from West Africa,
Nicaragua Wood
from Central America or Jamaican Logwood;
but the best is Red Sanders from the East Indies.
Ask me my favourite and I'll tell you it's the pink,
like a skinned rabbit,
Peroba Wood from Bahia in the forests of Brazil.

And when they did ask him, he'd pretend to be weighing up chips or sawdust in either hand, but would give them the same answer every time. Passing the huge doorway, open to allow the wood to season slowly in the foggy dampness, May felt sure she could smell the earth and leaves and sunshine that had once caused the trees to grow so big they were worth chopping down. Dead forever now, she hoped whoever was sitting in a chair that had once breathed in a forest thought it was worth the sacrifice.

The spice warehouse was set a little way back. A sign spanning the brick frontage read: *The Barley-Freeman Cough Linctus Company.* A small door sat off to the right of the large loading ones. It was ajar. The glow from the lamp at the end of Anchor Wharf barely stretched this far but May could smell the acrid tang from the burnt-out Elliott Shipping office. She stepped into the relative warmth, and perfumed gloom, of the building. She called out but received no response. Could Alice have evaded her to board the steamer after all, or was she at this moment sailing away from the distant East India Dock Pier? But, if she had done either of those things, Vi would still be here waiting for Horatio – someone must've opened up and she had the key. Perhaps they had given way to tiredness and fallen asleep; the air was heavy with enough soporific smells to cure the most hardened of insomniacs. May took a couple of steps further inside.

The wedge of lightness from behind narrowed to a sliver. Then, that too, vanished. Someone had shut her in. She hadn't heard them approach. But the clank of a metal bar being dropped into brackets was like a clap of thunder. The ring of a heavyweight padlock rattled in its hasp. May lurched at the door. She shouted and banged her fists on the wood until her voice was croaky and the sides of her hands pierced with splinters. Panic started tears coursing down her cheeks. She took baby steps backwards until she could press herself against the comfort of one of the large chests. All she knew now that she was alone: if Alice or Vi were in the warehouse then they'd have come rushing to her side the minute she'd started raising enough noise to wake the dead.

Breathe. In ... count to three ... out ... count to four ... again ... in ... out... May tried the squash the writhing in her stomach. Think. Nothing was going to happen to her now. They'd had the chance to stab her in the back but hadn't taken it. They wanted her alive. Clinging on to that as a sailor would to driftwood in a shipwreck, May lowered herself to the ground, curled into as tight a ball as her trembling limbs would permit, and allowed the warm scents of exotic lands to soothe her nerves. Any moment now Horatio would arrive. One sound from the other side of the door and she'd scream until even a steamship's stoker deafened by engines would hear her.

By the time the West India Dock clock chimed eleven, she knew he wasn't coming. Perhaps he never even left his father's celebration party, after all, promises were glibly given, and just as easily forgotten, in a champagne haze – it wasn't as if Alice was his problem to worry away at the top of his mind. With the morning would come a way of getting herself out of this. She was May Louise Keaps, Poplar's resourceful coroner's officer, ex Great War ambulance driver, daughter of a man who braved Alexander Laker nose-to-nose and had stood up to and overcome every challenge thrown at him. All except the final one. She shivered and whimpered until she'd shaken away the last of her energy.

Sleep was a long time coming but eventually, thankfully, it stole up and granted her peace.

May opened her eyes. The lids were swollen and gummed together with dried tears. The concrete at her feet was patterned with stripes of watery sunlight. She craned her stiff neck. Barred windows ran under the roof line as far around as she could see. They were too high – and the bars too close together – to afford any means of escape but they let in a little of the outside world and that was consoling in itself. Her spine clacked and grated as she stood, and a sharp pain shot down her left leg: the mercy of physical discomfort. It was something she knew how to deal with. She limped over to the corner to empty her aching bladder then paced in front of the double doors to loosen the kinks in her muscles. By the time her strides were long and brisk and she could stretch her arms above her head her mind had begun to focus on what she needed to do to cope with incarceration. Activity. In the field hospital the worst times had been the waiting, the loading and unloading of half-dead soldiers had been nothing compared to that. So she would explore her surroundings, formulate plans, devise schemes to evade her captors when they came for her, and not give the snakes of fear anything to feed on.

The warehouse was large – but not nearly as big as the timber shed next door. Stacked crates covered the floor with shoulder-width passages between them. May chose to plunge down the one immediately in front. The crates towered above her and she hoped they'd been positioned firmly on top of each other and wouldn't come crashing down. Words were stencilled in black on their

426

rough planking: the names of the Barley-Freeman and Elliott Shipping companies, the contents, and origin. The ones on her left contained Lotus Root, Jujubes, and Apricot Kernels – all from China. On the right, crates of Liquorice Root from Russia were topped by a row containing Black Haw Bark from America. She walked on, trailing her fingertips on each crate she passed until she reached a branching aisle that seemed to stretch to the back wall. Barrels were ranged along this one. She reached the end. The stencils were less easy to read, even though the light was better, and she guessed they had either been here for some time or had suffered from being rolled across the concrete quayside on their way into storage. She could make out Fenugreek from the Lebanon; Black Pepper from Singapore; Cinnamon Flowers all the way from the East Indies. In different circumstances – very different circumstances – this would come close to her idea of heaven as film pictures played in her head of natives with hoppers on their backs picking spices in the hot sun. Another twist and turn and she arrived at barrels marked Aniseed Bold, Spain.

The muffled sound of the clock over the East India Dock gateway chiming the hour reached in through the windows high above. May held her breath between each bong. It was ten o'clock already. She found her way back to the doors and shouted and pounded on them in the hope of attracting the attention of any of the lightermen who might be down this end. But it was for form's sake really because with Elliott Shipping closed, and fresh cargoes of timber not due until the

427

winter months, they would be seeking work on the riverside wharves. It had been a stupid thing to do anyway as now her throat was scratchy and raw and she needed a drink. A bubble of laughter escaped from between her lips at the irony of being surrounded by all the ingredients to make cough linctus, but not a drop of water to dissolve them in.

But the lack of response had served to remind her that she was shut up in this warehouse against her will – however many games she might play to distract herself from the fact. No escape plans had come whilst she'd been conducting her own amateur inventory. Her breath fluttered in her lungs like a ship's gaff-flown ensign in a cat's paw breeze. She mustn't give way to panic again like she did last night or she would be next to useless if an idea did surface of how to get herself out of this. Not to mention when the door was finally opened and she had only a handful of seconds to take them by surprise by springing through it. This last thought made her opt for sticking to this end of the warehouse so she could hear the moment someone started to grate the key in the padlock. She walked over to the far long wall. The air was thicker as if it had never been disturbed or replenished by new forcing its way through the doors. Hessian sacks stuffed so full as to resemble boulders were propped side by side, their stencils eaten into ragged shapes by the coarse weave. Zanzibar Cloves, Wild Cardamoms from the East Indies. Once she'd passed these, the aromas waiting to be identified were softer and had an edge of mustiness about them. This must be where the dried herbs were kept.

May decided to allow herself the luxury of one more flight of fancy before she settled down to rational thought. She would walk down the line with her eyes closed and see if she could guess what the sacks contained; she was no expert in botany but her countryside rambles – and Roger's obsessive need to categorise every plant and flower – had given her a better than average knowledge to marry with her naturally keen nose. She put her hands up to her face so she wouldn't be tempted to cheat, and took enough steps to leave behind the cloying scents of the exotic spices. The first pillow of fragrance was peppermint. The next, thyme. Another half a dozen paces before the tone of the air changed again This one was more difficult. A flower of some sort. She'd smelt it growing. Could conjure up an image of pressing her nose into sprays and inhaling deeply, soft, ethereal, white. But the name wouldn't come ... and then it did. Elder blossom. She allowed herself a little smile of congratulation.

The astringency of sage. Then citrus lemon balm. Her first defeat came as a blow to her pride. Try as she might she couldn't recognise it. Forced to peek in order that she could move on, she read Horehound North America, on the front of the sack. That had hardly been fair; she couldn't possibly have been expected to know that one. She closed her eyes again and resumed the game... Nutmeg was easy, as was valerian – there was a stall in Chrisp Street market sold sachets of it as a sedative... Then a smell she couldn't place; even though it was somehow familiar with its metallic

429

tinge. She tried to picture a scene where she might've come across it before. Except her poor nose was growing confused. She took a step forward to bend in closer. The soles of her shoes met something tacky. Was it, in fact, a barrel of some sort of oil that had begun leaking around the bung? She was leaning so far over it now she feared she might topple forward and hit her head. There was nothing for it, she'd have to look.

May dropped her hands to her sides, and opened her eyes. Then she screamed. She screamed so loud and long she grew dizzy and thought her lungs would burst. There, slumped amongst the sacks and looking so like one she hadn't at first been sure ... was Vi Tremins. The *East End Smile* of her cut throat grinning with victory at May's expense.

Chapter Fifty

May thought the retching would never stop. The pungency of the spices had combined with the shock to make her guts want to get rid of even the memory of anything that had ever been inside her. Her legs had refused to function and she was kneeling in blood at the corpse's feet.

She scrabbled in a crawl along the aisle, her wrists jarring on the concrete floor, her shoulders bumping into crates as she flailed to get distance between her and the appalling apparition. Sounds came out of her, a caught sob, the high-pitched keening of a starved and thrashed dog. The scar on her neck throbbed as if threatening to prise apart like a badly-stitched sole. Her body convulsed every now and then with another urge to vomit but her mind refused to let her: she had to get to the door. Only she'd forgotten the way. Following the line of herb sacks would lead her there but that meant turning around and going past the thing... No ... she had to stop that... It wasn't a thing ... it was Vi Tremins ... one time actress and Music Hall turn; a person ... a body ... a corpse... Perhaps it was better to remind herself of who she was, rather than who Vi had been. She was a coroner's officer. It was her job to deal with death. Now the horror of the find was passing, she had to inhabit that role again and switch off her emotions

May hauled herself upright with the aid of the protruding corner of a crate. Nothing had changed in the sense that she still had to conserve her energy for when they came. Except everything had changed, of course, because now she knew they intended to kill her. Grateful for the childish distractions she'd indulged in earlier – how she wished for a return to that innocence – she traced her way back to the crates of Liquorice Root via the barrels of Fenugreek, and Cinnamon Flowers. The light from the windows above the double doors was growing brighter; was she actually any closer or was it the sun shifting in the sky?

And then a thought that was so terrible that at first it flitted across her mind too quickly to grasp. But she wasn't to be afforded such kindness and it resurfaced like a drowned sailor. If they had done that to Vi – would do it to her – why not Alice, too?

431

Was her sister lying gruesomely in wait for her to stumble across? Could she be down the aisle she'd just passed? Or that unexplored passageway off to her right? The words of the song her sister was to have performed in the show came to her complete with all Alice's sweet intonation: *For, if you turn away, you'll be sorry some day, you left behind a broken doll.*

Stripped down to nothing but animal responses, May clawed at the nearest crate. If she could prise off one of the metal bands then she would have something with which to attack the door hinges. She managed to hook her fingers under the soft tin, only for the sharp edge to slice her palm. But she didn't stop ... she couldn't ... if Alice was here then she wouldn't survive being the one to discover her.

Her hands were lacerated into uselessness before she came back to herself enough to recognise the futility of the effort. She was heaving out dry-eyed sobs. When had that started? She pulled off the scarf from around her neck and caught the rolled and stitched edge in her teeth. It wouldn't tear. By worrying it against the crate's now bent and proud metal band she managed to rip it in two. Wrapping each strip tightly around her bleeding palms and keeping them in place with her thumbs, she stumbled her way towards the light.

At last she was beyond the first line of crates. The warehouse doors were straight ahead. May lurched towards them, forgetting in her panic to stop so that she smacked herself against their solidity with an almost knock-out blow. She sunk to the ground. Now, for the first time since she'd

432

heard the padlock being fastened, she longed for the Tong to come for her. Because she knew that some of the inmates in lunatic asylums were there with less cause that having to share a gaol cell with a corpse. She clenched her fists tight in a search for the relief of mind-numbing pain.

Then she pressed her back against the sun-warmed wood and cried.

Chapter Fifty-One

It was night again when the small door creaked open. May had been twitching her way through a dreamless sleep punctuated by the West India Dock clock knelling the hours. Her eyes had flicked open immediately at the unfamiliar sound. A man was silhouetted in the orange fringe of the lamp's glow. Her calf muscles cramped as she leapt up and hurled herself at the figure. She was within a few yards – bloody fingers already curved into talons – when she recognised him. It was Horatio Barley-Freeman.

'Thank God ... thank God... I thought...' her lungs were finding it hard to refill. 'The Tong locked me in. They left me here ... all night ... with ... with...' She shuddered. 'Vi Tremins is dead. Her body's in here somewhere,' she swept her arm towards the crates, 'you have to fetch the police. They can work out where she is; I can't go back there, I can't...' the words were tearing her dry throat raw '...because ... because ... because

433

of what else I might find.'

She wanted him to step forward and take her in his arms. To comfort her like a parent would a distraught child. Instead he turned and left. He hadn't said anything, hadn't reacted, but perhaps he was like her and took refuge in action when confronted by situations impossible to comprehend. He could only have moved a little to the side because now he was back. And he was not alone.

'Is this who you're scared might've met the same fate as poor Vi? As you can see she hasn't–'

'Alice! Where were you? I was supposed to meet you here with ... with...'

But the relief was too much for May's weakened body and she crumpled to the ground. Alice seemed to be in a similar state of exhaustion because she was slumped like a ragdoll against Barley-Freeman, her head lolling forward and her face hidden by a tangle of curls.

'Is she ill? Where did you find her?'

May sat on the concrete floor until the cold threatened to numb her leg muscles beyond use. Summoning up every reserve of energy, she got to her feet.

'You can leave her with me while you go for the police.'

'I'm sorry to disappoint you but neither of those things is about to happen.'

He had curled his arm around Alice's shoulder and he twisted her slightly so that the light glanced off their profiles. He was holding something to her throat. The memory of Vi's false smile closed down all thought in May's head. Except it wasn't a knife. Cradled between his fingers – his thumb poised – was a hypodermic: Alice's peculiar stance was a result of being drugged.

'Miss Keaps, May – after all it's stupid to follow the conventions of formality at a time like this – what I have here is full of cocaine and water. Please believe I will empty it into your sister's pretty neck unless you co-operate.'

Too many unexpected things were happening for May to understand what was going on. Except for the fact that Horatio held the power of life and death over the most precious thing in the world to her. She wanted to rush him but knew that even if she could summon the energy he'd have the time to carry out his threat before she'd covered half the space between them.

'I'll do anything you want, just let her go.'

'It's a little late for bargaining and, as you can see, I hold all the cards. I'm truly repentant at having to play them like this but yours is not the only hand being forced by circumstance. Things have happened recently beyond my control and I have to put them right or, like you, I'll find myself locked out of the game. Now, you can start by telling me what you found in Elliott Shipping that night.'

May's breathing turned shallow. 'It was you set fire to the place. *Torch it!* I heard you.' She felt lightheaded; her throat, dry and scratchy. 'You knew we were inside...'

'Actually, no, not at the time. I only found out later when I overheard one of the lightermen on the wharf.'

And then suddenly the air in her lungs felt as heavy as river mud. He had let himself into the

435

building with the key. The key Bert said Miles always wore around his neck.

'You killed him.'

The words hung in the silence

'I know you won't regard this as any sort of defence, but I really had no alternative as far as the Tong were concerned, it was him or me. Their profits were being threatened by the increased activity of the other drug gangs and they set their sights on Anchor Wharf as a new base of operations. Well, I owed them–'

'Gambling debts. That's why you were in the den, not paying protection money at all.'

'It was as it happens, but, you're right, I did have a few other things to tie up. How did you know anyway? No matter. So, back to Miles ... they instructed me to get Elliott Shipping off the wharf. Well, I knew the only way the old man would give up his lease was if something so terrible happened out here that he couldn't bear to be reminded of the place.'

A little of her reasoning returned and May remembered the wood chips Dr Swan had found during the post-mortem. 'If you murdered him in the timber shed, then why was his body found in Limehouse Causeway?'

'None of my doing I'm afraid, the best laid plans and all that. But as a consequence it began to look as if my bright idea wouldn't get the desired result which, as you must by now be aware, was very, very important to me so I had to produce another business-closing trick from up my sleeve. Which brings us neatly back to your snooping. And I haven't got all night while you make up your mind to tell me a pack of lies, I've the sleeper to Glasgow to catch where another undoubted triumph awaits me. Did I tell you I brought the house down when I made the little girl disappear? It was shortly after that I had to perform another little disappearing trick on Vi.'

The bastard was smiling. But he was also pressing the needle of the hypodermic against Alice's neck; May could see the flesh dimple.

'We found a blackmail letter from the Tong in the safe.'

'Very good; now you're playing the game. And who was with you?'

'Jack. Jack Cahill. A newspaper reporter.'

She'd been hideously wrong about Barley-Freeman coming to rescue her, but there was always a chance that Jack might. He must be growing fretful by now at her not turning up for the loose arrangement they'd made for a drink at the Spotted Dog. Except, of course, he would be doing nothing of the sort; he'd simply think she'd gone back to being stand-offish with him. But Barley-Freeman didn't know their history...

'I told him I was coming here to pick up Alice. We were to meet at my house and when he realises we're not there, he'll come looking. I expect he's on his way even now.'

'Then maybe some things are beginning to go my way at last. When he turns up on his white charger he can keep poor Vi company.'

'You'll never get away with it.'

'Oh, but I shall because everyone, naturally, will think it the work of the Tong. How does this sound?... Mr Cahill came out here hot on the trail of the story of why the Bow Kum were so interested in Anchor Wharf. Except, unfortunately for him, it led to his stumbling into the midst of another terrible episode in the ongoing turf war between the drug barons and, having seen and heard too much he was dispatched and his body dumped in a nearby open warehouse... No coroner could prove that didn't happen. As for Vi, she had enough of a reputation for indulging in snow for everyone to believe she was after further supplies, thereby becoming an inconvenient witness – with the inevitable results.'

May was beginning to realise just how clever this man was, which meant that he must already have a plan for her and Alice. She clenched her fists and felt the reassurance of pain arcing through the cuts across her palms.

'What ... what...' she could hardly get the words to un-stick from her mouth '...about us?'

'I have to admit that I had been in two minds about your particular fate, that is, until I had that inspired misdirection concerning Alice possibly rowing out to East India Pier. Once your acceptance of the idea confirmed such a thing was possible, I secured the services of an obliging sailor and a rowboat now awaits you at the bottom of the wharf ladder. Indulge me for a moment...' He laughed. '...Not that you can refuse. Imagine if you will, that the two of you decided to go for a jaunt on the river to see the stars shimmy on the water – after all, stranger fancies have been known to come to the best of us in the thrall of cocaine. Which was such a thoroughly reckless thing to do because who knows where you might end up?

Most probably right in the path of one of the ships leaving the busiest docks in the world; now, what are the chances of a ocean-bound captain noticing a matchstick of a craft when there's a tide to catch?'

The snakes of fear in May's stomach started to uncoil. Any moment now and she would scream. Her eyes burned from staring at the hypodermic as she tried to see if he had loosened his grip enough for her to leap forward, knock it out of his hand, and grab Alice. Except what good would it do when there was nowhere to run except across the vast desolation of an empty quayside? She could hear herself panting like a rabid dog.

'Just me. Let Alice go. She knows nothing of the investigation. I doubt she's even heard a word of what we've been saying.'

'That's as may be on both counts. But I'm really not to blame here because it was Vi who made your sister's demise inevitable. When I found out what you did for a living, I wanted to keep Alice as close as possible – as a sort of gambling chip I could play if it became necessary. I was even prepared to go so far as to offer her the role as my assistant. Thank God that little ruse was never put to the test, such a cocky show-off would've been a disaster with her inclination to upstage me at every turn. However, all that aside, Vi became fixated in her over-imaginative mind that I wanted to have Alice by my side, and in my act, for entirely different reasons. A woman of her dramatic and possessive temperament was bound to do something to remove her rival for my affections sooner or later. Poor Vi–'

'For Christ's sake stop bloody well saying that.' It just slipped out; May didn't want to provoke him but his crocodile concern was twanging her already taut nerves.

'Yes, quite right, it is a tad hypocritical. Bad enough, I suppose, to lead her on in believing ours was more than a theatrical dalliance without insulting the truth further.'

He mimed a slice across his throat. Too late: it was the one moment the needle hadn't been pressed on Alice's flesh but his revelation that he'd had no compunction in cold-bloodedly murdering his lover had forced May to double over in a paroxysm of dry-retching.

'Oh, dear; the smell in here is a little over-powering, isn't it? I think it's time you were out in the fresh air anyway.'

He took a handful of steps backwards. The doorway was now clear, but Alice was out of reach.

'As I was saying … Vi took it upon herself to re-move temptation from me. During the two days I thought your sister was nursing her wounded pride as far away from the theatre as possible, she was, in fact, sedated and locked in a storeroom under the stage. I only found out yesterday morning quite by chance. I needed to reclaim Alice, and Vi didn't want to give her up; I'm afraid some of that over-heated exchange will be – despite the drugs – lodged in your sister's memory. Not least of which will be that I lied to you about not knowing Miles. My tongue must've run away with me on occasion because it seems I had shared with Vi some of the details of my arrangements with him. In vino veritas, eh?'

'The note setting all this up came from you, didn't it?'

'Every conjurer knows the planning of an illusion is every bit as important as the execution and, if you'll forgive me a moment's indulgence, I do seem to have pulled everything off to perfection. Vi didn't suspect a thing when I suggested a little private celebration here after the show. And a waiting taxicab meant I could watch you enter the warehouse, lock the place up, and be back in the theatre for yet another toast to my success before my absence became noteworthy. As ever, attention to detail – aided and abetted by slick timing – always pays dividends.'

He pulled something from his pocket. It was a small packet of white powder. He tossed it at her feet.

'And now for the grand finale: I want you to take some of this – not too much, mind – and rub it into your gums. Do it nice and slowly. Remember who it is I have in my arms. You can be out on the river sharing your last moments together or I can push the needle in and she will die in agony.'

As Clarice Gem had done. The thought of Alice suffering so horribly made May exaggerate her movements in pinching up some the cocaine so that he could see she had made her choice. She held it up for a moment and then bent her head as she moved her fingers to her mouth, contriving for a least half of it to blow away in the quickening breeze. He didn't appear to notice and, when she looked up at him again, seemed satisfied.

'Time to go; here, take your sister from me. I'll

441

be on the edge watching and won't leave until you're well on your way so there'll be no sneaking back up. You'll be better off conserving every bit of the empty energy that'll soon be firing through your muscles for keeping yourself out of trouble on the water.'

In the long walk towards the end of Anchor Wharf May could hear the river slapping against the quayside as the outgoing tide sucked at the depths and set up eddies; the wind trapped between the spars of the sailing ships in the far-off Graving Dock making the rigging cry ... and another sound from the distance that hadn't been there before. Was it the cocaine or the realisation that these could be the last moments her feet would ever touch land that made her senses so keen? The screech of metal as the dock gates down at Fore Street scraped stone. Someone was coming onto the wharves. Could it, after all, be Jack? Had he persuaded the watchman to let him through? Had he brought the police? If she could slow time then perhaps she stood a chance of finding out. Her movements were calculated as she sat Alice on the ground and pretended to be having difficulty untying the rowboat's mooring rope.

The soft purr of a coasting motorcar. Then the explosion of headlight beams being flicked on, the searing light stretched out over the water, thrusting a giant shadow of Barley-Freeman onto the rippling surface. He held up his arm to cover his eyes. May leapt into life and dragged Alice as far as she could towards her rescuer before her legs betrayed her and they both collapsed onto the cold concrete.

Chapter Fifty-Two

The vehicle pulled up a few yards away in front of the timber warehouse. A figure stepped out and walked with a smooth glide into the lamplight. It was Brilliant Chang. He didn't look surprised to see them.

'Good evening, Miss Keaps. I was expecting to receive a consignment tonight but to find you here instead gives me the more pleasure; I cannot tell you how relieved I am to see the threat you brought to me for translation was an empty one.' He slipped his coat off his shoulders and held it out. 'I think the young lady is in more need of this than I am.'

May snatched the garment from his hand, too agitated to worry about pleasantries. She bundled Alice up until everything but her feet was covered, and her nose poked out from the fur trim. Her sister wasn't safe yet but May knew she needed to wait until the quivering in her own muscles slackened before she could attempt to move her. With Alice's head in her lap she cradled her like a baby and waited for the silence to break. Brilliant Chang was sweeping his gaze beyond the end of the quay along the stretch of water May thought she'd now be rowing. She wondered why the only thing her mind could hold onto was how long the watchman had been in the Chinaman's employ.

'Mr Barley-Freeman, this is the happiest of

coincidences. I have been waiting to meet you for some time. Yours is a name I have heard often. A coroner's officer is not the only person with access to information and I have been receiving many answers to my questions. And so I come to the one I have been waiting to ask you. Can you tell me why you have taken it upon yourself to cause me so much trouble?'

'I haven't done any such thing. Do you think you could switch those lights off? I feel at a disadvantage being so blinded I can't see who I'm taking to.'

'I fail to appreciate why I should do that when you have endeavoured for so long to keep me in the dark. Do you not think it terrible, Miss Keaps, when an honest businessman is forced to close his nightclub for no reason at all? And then think how much worse it becomes when he is accused of something he is innocent of and could not have done because he was not even there. Do you think it a reasonable conclusion to draw that this man could be left with the impression that he is being persecuted? Do you now know who I am, Mr Barley-Freeman?'

'The Chink who started all this off in the first place.'

'The very same. Except I prefer you to observe the formality of calling me Mr Chan. It is so much more respectful, do you not think?'

May was swamped by the sensation that they were speaking in a language she couldn't understand. The cocaine had made her ears sharp, but her mind as skittish as a flea-bitten kitten.

'You! You're the one at the head of the Bow

Kum Tong.'

He surprised her by unveiling a smile of the most perfect symmetry. May could see his teeth glisten in the lamplight.

'I suspect someone of your capabilities does not often find herself in the wrong, Miss Keaps. However, on this occasion, and at the risk of wounding your pride, I am compelled to correct your erroneous assumption. I have not, and will never, lash my fortunes to the mast of a ship that requires a crew to sail her. There is always the risk of mutiny – as Mr Barley-Freeman here knows to his cost.'

'What are you implying? I did everything they asked of me. They'll be waiting on street corners with cleavers if you go spreading the word otherwise.'

Why was Horatio worrying about that when he was undoubtedly going to hang for the murders of Miles Elliott and Vi Tremins? The unreality was growing into such proportions that May began to hum one of Alice's favourite nursery rhymes under her breath.

'Is it not more treacherous to turn on your friend in preference to those you would not seek to make your enemies? A statement with which I am sure Miles Elliott would agree.'

At last her wits were together enough for something to penetrate.

'You knew all along who'd killed him.'

'No, Miss Keaps I did not. Do you think I would have kept such a thing from you and your handsome coroner when I had taken a solemn oath under peril of my eternal conscience? However, I was aware that Elliott Shipping was importing opium and cocaine on behalf of the Bow Kum Tong. This I would have revealed had the question been asked.'

But she hadn't known that at the time. Her bitter anger switched focus from her persecutor, to the rescuer who appeared to be taunting her with no less pleasure.

'If you hadn't been so bloody inscrutable when you delivered that warning to me in court then I might've made the smuggling connection sooner. Liza, at least, would still be alive.'

'What you fail to appreciate is that had you done such a thing, you, too, would be dead. You are a young woman of much passion but without the commensurate restraint and therefore would have been sure to try to approach the Tong directly, whereas what was needed was to wait until this shark masquerading as a fish with a hook in his mouth came to you.'

May's head felt as though it was going to explode. 'They blackmailed Miles Elliott. I read the letter. It was vicious and evil. They threatened to slash his fiancée's face...'

And then she saw behind Brilliant Chang's words. Miles Elliott had kept the note because it had been written by Horatio Barley-Freeman. A man May now knew would have no compunction in carrying out his threat She held onto Alice tightly.

'You self-serving bastard. First you run up gambling debts, then you make Miles pay for them with his life. And Vi. Gullible, heartsick, Vi who had her head turned by your easy charm and empty promises. You killed her not because her foolish kidnapping of Alice might have unravelled your arrangement with the Tong, but because she had the temerity to try to play you for a fool.'

She bent to kiss her sister who could so easily have become another victim of this man's ruthlessness. For a long moment she couldn't stop crying. Once she thought she had herself under control again she looked up at the Chinaman standing in front of her. His face was contorted with the same deep empathy she'd witnessed when he'd communicated his grief to Mrs Gem for her loss. He blinked, once, and his soul retreated.

'Life and death are your business, Miss Keaps, mine is the altogether more straightforward world of commerce. One in which the only currency of any value is reputation. As you can imagine I have been hard at work clearing my name from any association with this unfortunate affair brought about by the fact that the Tong leader – with whom I have a longstanding enmity – had the body beaten and placed outside my restaurant in the hope it would result in my swinging from the end of a rope.'

'No one would have thought it was anything other than a hop-head's death if those slit-eyed sons of monkeys hadn't decided to try to capitalise on it.'

'Although I do not approve of their ways, I am prepared for them. What I cannot, and will not, countenance is a man who knows nothing of honour thinking he can treat mine as a commodity without value.'

He walked back to the motorcar and flicked off the lights, and Barley-Freeman was no longer pinned to the night.

'This. This I wish for you to see.'

He reached around under the back of his jacket. May saw him pull something from the waistband of his trousers; the cut of his suit so perfect she wouldn't have known anything had been concealed there. She caught the gleam of metal as he revealed the object in his hand. Two short, fat, lengths of wood tethered together at one end by a chain. She'd heard talk of the Chinese nunchaku fighting sticks but never seen them.

Brilliant Chang let one of the sticks fall from his grasp. With a flick of the wrist he set it whirling softly from the end of the chain. A slight straightening of his arm and it increased in speed. Faster and faster until she could feel the displaced air slapping her cheek and hear a sound like a gale through rigging. She broke the spell to look at his face. There was a hard edge to his mouth.

'Tell me, Mr Barley-Freeman. Do you know what violence really is? It is not murdering someone in an alley or fighting with a knife over a spilt drink. It is not killing someone at all – which would be too easy – but to leave them at the mercy of a more lingering fate.'

Without shifting his gaze, he spoke down to May.

'The Bow Kum Tong are not so well versed in subtlety and failed to understand that with your father.'

May had felt she was beyond registering any more shocks. But this one electrified her nerve endings. Her spine tingled.

'This quayside should not be witness to any

more premature deaths, so I suggest that you take the young girl to safety and alert a policeman before I forget myself and give in to my desire to re-honour my standing in this community. You see, you have slurred me, Mr Barley-Freeman, by letting those who know no better think that I would allow a man to be forced to take cocaine on my premises. It is my philosophy that a drug should be treated with respect and taken with consent – like whisky, do you not think, Miss Keaps? The other way is the work of a thief of life. And I am not a thief. I am a businessman.'

Alice shuddered in May's arms and began coughing.

'Take her now. The watchman will be making his way along the quay in the belief that he is about to offer me assistance. Please be so good as to tell him that I would rather he do whatever it is you wish of him. I will see you again, Miss Keaps, in your elegant skirt and blouse, across the court-room. This man will see me every night in his dreams.'

He released his fingers and the sticks whirled straight up in the air like a top. They had touched the black above the lamplight before they re-turned. Brilliant Chang caught them gently as if they were a bird fallen from flight and slid them back into his waistband.

Chapter Fifty-Three

May trudged along the street from the railway station on her return from the week's holiday Braxton Clarke had insisted she take after the conclusion of the inquests on Miles Elliott and Vi Tremins. Alice had been kept in hospital under observation for three days. After she'd got home and they'd had a series of long and tearful heart-to-hearts May had taken her to stay with Aunt Bella and then continued on up the coast, sleeping in cheap guesthouses and walking every footpath she could find. But she hadn't once been able to outpace her worry over their future.

Jack Cahill was lounging on her front step. He was the last person May wanted to see. She didn't feel like engaging in idle chitchat and wanted nothing more than to dump her things and take herself off to the bathhouse for a long soak.

'All that fresh air under those wide skies has done you the power of good, Blossom of May.'

'I thought you'd finally outgrown calling me that.'

'Once a poet, always a poet. Or at least a man with a poet's soul. I wanted to be the first to tell you the news.'

She wished he'd move so she could get to the door. But he just sat smoking, an idiotic grin on his face.

'Your man Barley-Freeman's had the date set

for his trial at the Old Bailey. I expect you'll find your subpoenas waiting on the mat.'

She pushed him to one side with her thigh; did he really think she'd needed reminding they'd be required as witnesses? May knew it was going to be especially traumatic for Alice and wished her sister could be spared the ordeal. Damn. The key wasn't in the pocket of her windcheater; it must've fallen out in her knapsack. Now she'd have to put up with him for a while longer while she found it.

'His father has engaged a barrage of slick lawyers – Sir Ernest filled me in on them over dinner – but he'll still hang. And that's not the only good news...'

'What makes you think I want to hear any more?'

'Because we're two of a kind, naturally nosey, and deep down you hate the thought of me knowing something you don't.'

He'd forced a little smile from her with that one. 'I suppose the sooner you spit it out, the sooner you'll get off my doorstep and leave me alone.'

'Uncle Paul was so impressed with my part in the wrapping up of the Miles Elliott case that he's given me the job of roving crime correspondent for the whole of the East End.'

May couldn't be bothered to argue about how Jack had done little more than confirm some facts before she'd presented them to Braxton Clarke.

'It's a sop really because he's got a deal going with the Nationals and wants me to drop my investigation into the gambling dens shenanigans. Although I'm still a little narked at having

451

to hand over my passport to the big time – but rest assured that'll come in due course – I must say I'm relieved it means I won't have to look over my shoulder every five minutes for shadow-lurking Chinamen. Which is just as well as I've had it up to here.' Jack chopped the side of his hand on his forehead, 'with living in the rarefied atmosphere of Hampstead. Give me real people any day. Uncle Paul's offered an advance on my wages in order I can buy a house in Poplar.'

May wondered if he'd said that to spare her embarrassment over her own strained circumstances and was really about to be handed the mother of all gifts.

'So that's what I'll be up to this afternoon. I'd appreciate any tips you could give me on the best areas.'

She found the key at last. Should she warn him about the dangers of complacency? The Tong weren't likely to forget he'd been snooping around the yen-shi den. An image of Brilliant Chang's smooth smile when he'd acknowledged he was a drug trafficker came into her mind. Instead of being pleased her initial instincts about the suave Chinaman had been right she was unaccountably disappointed in him. She had so wanted to believe he was as noble as his countenance. Would she ever learn not to take people – especially men – at face value?

Jack finally finished his cigarette and stood up. 'And I know how badly you feel about what happened to Elizabeth Trow. I did some asking around over the water in Greenwich and it seems the coroner there has indicted a respectable

452

married man and father – one of her regulars – who confessed in court to losing his temper when he'd been unable to perform. So it was a trick gone wrong, May, and nothing to do with you. I had a word with Uncle Paul and he's arranged for the Poor Law Guardians to give her son a place at the Training School out in Essex.'

May felt a stab of gratitude that something good would come out of so much pain; the boy would escape the stigma of the Institution and be taught a trade. He need never return to Poplar which, after all, must hold nothing but bad memories for him now.

'I wrote a rather good article – even if I say so myself – about the whole Barley-Freeman business. Happened to mention in passing that you were the brightest and most diligent coroner's officer from here to Timbuktu; there's a copy of the edition on your desk. You might want to wave it under the nose of your new boss when you go into work tomorrow. The elections took place on Wednesday but the results haven't been made public yet. Hope he's a good one. Well, that's all I came to say. See you around.' He walked off.

As she turned the key in the lock, May suspected she'd find out an awful lot more than the name of the new coroner by the end of the day.

There was a note propped up against her typewriter asking her to go into the chambers as soon as she arrived. She hung up her hat and coat and put her shoulder bag by the side of the chair. This was it. The moment she'd been dreading ever since Dr Swan had given her the news of Colonel

Tindal's death. But the forthcoming prosecution of Horatio Barley-Freeman for murder had to count for something in her favour. Mr Clarke's report on the Miles Elliott inquest had made no reference to her somewhat unusual methods of investigation, and, reading between the lines, his replacement couldn't fail to see the presence of an efficient officer who had gleaned all the evidence they could to assist the jury in making an informed decision.

Nipping into the vestibule lavatory to wash her hands, she took the opportunity to check the collar of her blouse was sitting right, and her new peach scarf knotted securely. She'd made a particular effort getting ready this morning. Polishing her best black strap shoes until they shone, and putting on a pair of expensive silk stockings she'd been saving for a special occasion. Reaching into the pocket of her skirt she plucked out the lipstick Alice had donated for the betterment of her image. As she twisted the tube to reveal the confident red she felt a gulp of sadness for poor Vi who had once used it to paint that wonderfully mobile mouth of hers. Despite what Barley-Freeman had said Vi had done in her jealousy (and, given her sister's hazy recollections, they would probably never know the truth of that) May still thought of her as that vivacious, amusing, and open, woman who had sat at their kitchen table and held them enthralled with her wit and backstage wisdom. At that moment – whatever else happened afterwards – she had been a good friend to Alice. May tentatively slicked a thin layer of colour onto her lips. And then went over them again. It wouldn't do any harm; there was no way she could disguise being a woman so she might as well advertise the fact. One last check in the mirror and she was as ready as she'd ever be for her first – and she hoped not her last – day in the new coroner's employ.

May knocked on the door to the chambers with more determination than she felt. The response was bright and immediate. To smile or not to smile? She didn't want to look as if she didn't treat the job seriously but neither did she want to seem unfriendly. She opted for what she hoped was an expression of professional courtesy. It was the only time she wished she wore glasses; at least then she'd look intelligent.

She twisted the handle, pushed the door, and walked in. The half-smile became a gape. Braxton Clarke was sitting behind the desk, silver-framed photographs and a mahogany pen tray neatly arranged in front of him

'Welcome back, May. How are you? How's your sister – Alice isn't it? I trust you enjoyed your holiday and are invigorated and refreshed. You're certainly looking tip-top this morning.'

She could only nod and mumble in reply.

'Surprised to see me, eh? As the LCC decided to subsume the role of Poplar Coroner into the post responsible for the whole of the North-Eastern District, I decided it was about time I set myself a new challenge and applied. And, look, I was successful. I've you to thank for that really; I wouldn't have been able to present myself nearly so well at the hustings if I hadn't absorbed some of your insights into how things tick in this neck of the woods.'

May wondered if it would do any good to beg him to let her keep the clerk's job. After his outburst at her overstepping her authority that time, going back to typing and filing was the best she could expect.

'Don't stand on ceremony, you make me feel as if I am about to issue an indictment. Take a chair. I feel the need to clear the air concerning a few things before formally instituting the new regime.'

From the angle at the side of the desk, May could see the photographs were of two young boys hanging off the neck of a big black dog, and the second a wispily beautiful woman in an off-the-shoulder evening gown standing in a garden. She was laughing into the camera. Seeing them made her feel unaccountably worse.

'I paid a visit to the Town Hall the other day and read through some of the files you'd had stored there. A few I decided to review in detail but in general wanted to get a flavour of the major causes of death in the East End – you never can tell very much from the official statistics. And I came away with a real appreciation of what a thorough job you did compensating for Colonel Tindal's in-adequacies. Your subtle approach showed loyalty and integrity beyond what he had any right to expect. On behalf of the Lord Chancellor's Office, I'd like to sincerely thank you for that.'

Why couldn't he just tell her and get it over with? It was too humiliating to have to listen to an end of term report – no doubt consisting of every one of her misdemeanours.

'But to bring us more up to date. On the Miles Elliott inquest, you demonstrated great tenacity, dedication to the job, and bravery; without you following up on your intuition, I doubt Barley-Freeman would ever have been brought to justice. I received a letter from Mr and Mrs Elliott while you were away. They are immensely grateful that they no longer have to contemplate their son may have killed himself with a drugs overdose. However, I would be unforgivably negligent if I didn't temper any praise with carpeting you for putting yourself in extreme physical danger during the course of your investigations.'

He tapped his fingers on the edge of the desk and looked at her under lowered brows.

'Oh well, having laboured the point, I doubt you'll ever find yourself making the same mistake again.'

He dipped into his drawer and pulled out a file which he slid across the desk. Even upside down May could read the name George Arthur Keaps. She felt as chilled as if a secret shame had been exposed.

'I came across this. The name struck me of course so I included it in my pile to be studied in depth. True to form, Colonel Tindal appears to have been blinded by his distrust of expert medical opinion. Because, if he'd had the right questions asked, he would've discovered it was impossible for your father to have voluntarily drunk so much whisky without passing out with glass in hand. Not dissimilar, in fact, to the revelation that Miles Elliott wouldn't have mixed cocaine with the amount of opium he'd smoked. Your father was heavily involved in the Trades Unions wasn't he?'

May unstuck her tongue. 'Yes.'

'I was fortunate enough to be having dinner with the Minister of Labour the other evening and our discussion turned to the subject of the perennial state of unrest in the docks. His view was that much of it has been due to the wharf owners trying to prevent a repetition of the strikes of 1912 and to that end they've been orchestrating systematic retribution against those instrumental in leading them. And that got me thinking...' He leant forward. '...It is a possibility that what happened to your father was that he was targeted as a troublemaker and consequently forcibly filled with alcohol and frogmarched to the edge of the quayside. After that it doesn't much matter whether he fell of his own accord or was pushed. A decent coroner's jury would return a verdict of *an act endangering the life of another and ultimately occasioning his death* at the very least. Most likely *murder with malice aforethought.*'

May felt the blood drain from her face.

Braxton Clarke laid a snow-white pressed handkerchief on top of the file. 'If you will excuse me, May, I think there ought to be something I should be attending to in the courtroom.'

As he brushed by her she could smell the woody spice of his cologne.

She'd never felt so grateful for good breeding. Left alone she screwed the handkerchief around and around in her fingers in an effort to ward off the tears. His analysis had sparked off so many thoughts she didn't know where to start. There was the shock of knowing her father's death may have been deliberate, and the consequent relief

458

there was no inherited black dog of melancholy waiting to knock Alice off balance into despair. But the wharfinger who'd employed her father had been Alexander Laker. The man she'd gone to speak to and seek his advice. And it'd been he who had told her about the drugs syndicates' belief she was corruptible. What if they never had and he'd planted that idea in her head in the hope she'd slacken off the investigation? Because Old Sun, Dunbar, and Hubbock's wharves – all owned by Alexander Laker – shared Limekiln Basin with Anchor, and Charlie had said the Tong were beholden to a wharfinger who let out his premises for opium dens. Had Miles smoked his drug not ten minutes' walk from Elliott Shipping?

The side door opened and Braxton Clarke folded himself back into his chair.

'Now, we may not have worked very long together but I think I've got a pretty good inkling of what you're like, May Keaps, and I want you to promise that you'll do nothing to follow up on my dock owner conjecture–'

'Wharfinger. They're called wharfingers.'

'–Not without proof of evidence. And if you come across any, you're to bring it to me first.'

She wanted to do the *cross my heart and hope to die* gesture but settled for a simple nod.

'That's that then. I hope you understand that once I came across the records of your father's inquest I couldn't not delve a little into them. And sharing my conclusions with you was in some way a partial repayment on behalf of the Elliotts. I hope it'll change a few ways in which you see yourself; maybe lighten up a little on trying to get everything right all of the time. You've nothing to prove to anyone. Particularly to yourself.'

May did feel as though she might need the handkerchief now. She blew her nose as discreetly as she could. The cloth came away covered in lipstick. Damn. She'd forgotten about that. It was probably smeared all over her face now. She wondered if she could ask leave to go to the lavatory, but Braxton Clarke had replaced the file in his drawer and looked intent on embarking on something else. Well, the inevitable had to come sooner or later.

'I was under pressure at my appointment to seek the services of a deputy coroner. As Colonel Tindal's one-sided arrangement of keeping me on his books seems to have worked out so well for all concerned, I've agreed to take shares in the man who'll be taking over my old role as deputy for City of London and Southwark District. But with his consent of course. So that's sorted to everyone's satisfaction. As I'll be based for the most part at the court in Shoreditch, what I need here more than anything is a decent and efficient officer – one who is able to be my eyes and ears on the street but who also knows the appropriate time to seek the services of law enforcement.'

There was no point in her even trying to say anything, she knew the tears would stream the minute she opened her mouth. She was saved from the silence stretching into insurmountable embarrassment by a knock on the door.

'Come in.'

May turned to see PC Collier. He gave her one

of his sketchy half-salutes.

'Sorry to interrupt, sir, but there's a body been found in the old glue factory off Brunswick Road. I did a little asking around and they reckon she'd been living rough there. Dr Swan's looking at her now but he told me to tell you that he wants you to see her before she's wrapped up and carted off ... sorry, sir ... brought to the mortuary.'

Braxton Clarke stood up. 'No rest for the wicked, eh? I'm sorry that we weren't able to finish our discussion, May, but maybe we can pick it up later.'

She'd got the impression there wasn't much left to say.

'There's one thing I have to ask now before I head off with the good constable here: would you mind continuing as clerk for the time being until you can train somebody up?'

So this was it. Out of both jobs. She nodded.

'Splendid. Get your notebook then.' He plucked his coat and hat from the stand. 'And Constable Collier...'

'Yes, sir?'

'I've spoken to your station commander and he's agreed to release you to work more closely with my team here from now on. You can start by preparing a brief for my officer on the practice of evidence gathering according to *A Constable's Guide to his Daily Work*. She could do with a few pointers.'

May looked at him as he stretched out his hand. 'A new start, Miss Keaps?'

She bit her quivering lip, smiled, and pressed

461

her palm to his.

'A new start, Coroner Clarke. And I won't let you down.'

The publishers hope that this book has given you enjoyable reading. Large Print Books are especially designed to be as easy to see and hold as possible. If you wish a complete list of our books please ask at your local library or write directly to:

Magna Large Print Books
Magna House, Long Preston,
Skipton, North Yorkshire.
BD23 4ND

This Large Print Book for the partially sighted, who cannot read normal print, is published under the auspices of

THE ULVERSCROFT FOUNDATION